Also by Robert French

Passion of Shadows

The Diary of Nellie Mill

Josephine Littletree

Sigurdsen

Lynch

Robert French

Lynch

© 2019 Robert L. French

First Edition

978-0-9952671-9-0
978-1-9990223-0-3 (KDP MOBI)
978-1-9990223-1-0 (EPUB)

Cover design by Caligraphics.net

Formatting by Polgarus Studio

Wikimedia Commons, File: 500px photo (157583091).jpeg (archived version) modified. Photographer: Magdalena Roeseler (CC-BY-3.0)
Wikimedia Commons, File: 2013 Moore tornado damage, Raggedy Ann (130526-Z-TK779-017).jpg. Photographer: TSgt. Roberta A. Thompson (PD US Military)

Questions, comments, contact: afterwords@shaw.ca

Chapter 1

Lynch leaned into the hot wind, khaki trench coat dark with sweat stains and slick meat grease flapping loose against the forward curve of his spine, fraying jeans of knee knobs pumping stick legs to drag boots flopping after him. All of the close conspiracies were on him, taking a personal interest in worn-out bones. A vendetta, impersonal curses, muttered replies tossed anywhere. The scuffed soliloquy of pavement accompanied in a common grief at the last hot day of summer.

"Fuckin' heat. Dying a thirst. Get something to drink. Stomach. Hurts. Beer be good. If it ain't the heat, you're soaked to your skin or freezing your ass off."

It was sundown, horizon at his back a fading flame over indents of warehouses, flat molars between cavities rimming an edge of the downtown eastside. A block ahead and on the south side of the street was Pacific Packers, a squat red-brick slaughterhouse behind a wire mesh fence and electric sliding gates. On the north side and next to the curb, headlights on, a diesel idling, its cargo of pigs packed into multi-tiered stainless steel cages. On the sidewalk people with flashlights, cameras, smartphones and water bottles, the water for the pigs, inquisitive snouts protruding between cage openings. Bottles with nozzles attached were used to spray the pigs in the higher tiers. Some in the mostly quiet crowd were speaking to the pigs. "Here, Sweetie," a woman said as a thirsty pig guzzled water. A few minutes later the gates slid open and the truck, driver invisible in the dark cab, turned into the parking lot. "Bye, Sweetie, we love you," the woman said, tears in her eyes. Another woman leaned her head against the shoulder of a third, crying. Lynch stopped, feet sore, empty belly groaning.

"Why ya giving 'em water?"

"This is a pig vigil, we're bearing witness," a man in a white T-shirt said. "Go Vegan" was printed in green on it. On his unzipped jacket was a pinned badge. In the growing darkness all Lynch could see was "Save."

"Vegan? You one of them other space aileens?"

The man smiled, charitably.

"We're giving them succour in their last moments, letting them know that there are people who care. It's the only care and love they'll ever know."

"What's the difference? They're gonna be pork chops in a while."

"We're trying to stop that. We're against eating meat, or any other foods from animals."

"You want to stop people from eating meat?"

"We're trying to persuade them not to by showing that loving animals is better than killing them."

"It ain't better 'n eating 'em."

"You can get all the nutrition you require from a plant-based diet."

"How the fuck you figure that?"

"It's a fact. Doctors and health organizations say so."

"I'll make it simple for ya. Cows eat grass, people eat cows."

A woman with a water bottle approached. She was stocky and middle-aged, dyed hair but no make-up.

"Don't you have any pity for these poor creatures, or any of the others being murdered by the billions every year?"

"I'm hungry and thirsty. Got any pity for me?"

"You can find something to eat. You're not going to be murdered like these poor pigs."

"I could starve to death and you wouldn't give a shit. People sick and close to dying ery day down here and nobody's crying over 'em."

"There's charities to help you out. Don't compare yourself with helpless animals being caged and tortured and murdered."

"Been living in a cage my whole life. Nobody never fed me nuthin' 'cept garbage. They don't bother killin' me 'cause I ain't worth it. That's the only reason I'm still walking 'round. And now you people want to take away what meat I can rustle up."

"Didn't you listen to Brad? You can live on a plant-based diet."

"I ain't sayin' beans don't keep ya going if you're hard up. I had some good corn, too, when my teeth was better. But that stuff is for when you're desprate. That's why there's corn dogs and cans of pork and beans."

The woman and the man glanced at each other and he took a pamphlet out of his jacket pocket and held it out to Lynch.

"Read this. Find out the truth behind the meat and dairy industries."

"Don't want no toilet paper. Shove your bullshit."

Through the now dark evening another truck was arriving, headlights burning beside the glistening mouth of its grill, coloured lights across the top of the dark cab, the driver invisible, the air brakes grabbing and hissing as it slid to a stop alongside the gathering. The man and woman turned to the tiers of cages rising high above them. But others had been listening. Dressed in stonewashed jeans, sneakers and T-shirts with vegan slogans, two girls, one holding a smartphone and the other a water bottle, were talking. The one with the phone was tall and slender, had shoulder-length hair of a colour that used to be called flaxen. The girl with the water bottle was a little shorter, had green eyes and wavy dark hair down to her waist. Fourteen, they were there without their parents' knowledge.

"Wonder how old he is?" Madeline Dalrymple, the dark-haired girl, said.

"Old," the other said. Her name was Gwen Chalmers. "He looks like a scarecrow. It's almost September. Wouldn't take much for him to freeze this winter. Eating meat hasn't done him any good. Dr. Todd would call him a carnivore."

"Dr. Todd" was Dr. Todd Ghiselin, MD, ND, whose You Tube vlogs routinely drew upwards of 150,000 viewers. Called the "tofu guru," he was also head of the New Dawn Vegan Institute, author of several books on the vegan philosophy and diet and was a lecturer at health spas and a speaker at vegan and animal rights gatherings. The girls were subscribers to his channel. He was their go-to vegan luminary.

"A pamphlet wouldn't help him," Madeline said. "Probably sleeps in alleys and lives out of garbage cans."

She stared up into the cobalt sky at its forgotten stars.

"Hey."

She flung her arms wide, her water bottle thumping a woman in the back. The woman turned and glared, Madeline oblivious.

"Why don't we take him to your place and put him in the boiler room? At least he won't freeze this winter and we can give him some good food."

Gwen pursed her lips.

"What about Krappy?"

Krappy was their nickname for the caretaker at Glen Loughran Tower, where Gwen lived. Madeline was sleeping over for the weekend. Gwen was thinking about how to get the tramp into the building. Madeline read her mind.

"We'll sneak him in the back way. Get the boiler room key off Krappy. Tell him it's only for a while. Won't tell your parents. They're not coming back till tomorrow, anyway."

Gwen nodded.

"All right. Krappy is always trying to suck up to my father, so he's not going to say no."

Lynch was making his way through the gathering, stomach growling. The girls stepped in front of him. Close up he looked even older. What was left of his hair seemed pasted in grey strands to the sides of his head. His stained trench coat was too large for him, his jeans had faded to a grimy grey and his buff boots had worn soles, the toecaps swollen as if ready to explode, like the boots of a character in a cartoon.

"We'd like to help you," Madeline said. "Would you like a clean place to sleep and good food?"

Lynch's eyes narrowed.

"Beat it," he said in a low voice.

"We're serious. We have a place for you in an apartment building."

"What's the catch, you girls nymphos? I ain't much good at that kind of stuff no more."

"We heard you complaining that nobody cares about feeding you."

"We'll give you better food than what you're used to," Gwen said. "It's getting late. We've got to get back. Make up your mind."

"Ya better not be kidding me."

Lynch's stomach decided for him. Gwen phoned for a taxi. Madeline gave her water bottle to somebody. Lynch slouching along behind, they walked to the nearest corner and waited. When they reached Glen Loughran Tower, Gwen used her key to enter through the front door and went to the rear exit. The exit doubled as the service entrance, was on the first floor and opened onto the alley, where there were parking stalls for visitors. Not quite halfway back along the hallway leading to it were the fire escape stairs to the basement, where the boiler room and storeroom were. Below the basement were the underground parking stalls for tenants. Next to the first floor fire escape door was the caretaker's suite. Madeline and Lynch were waiting. Gwen's parents, out of town on a visit, would be returning the next day. The girls decided to take him to the apartment before going to see the caretaker.

"What's your name?" Madeline asked after introducing herself and Gwen as they rode up in the elevator.

"Lynch. Ya got good grub up there?"

"We'll make you a peanut butter sandwich," Gwen said, trying to ignore his smell, more intense in the confines of the elevator.

"I want meat. Ya got steak?"

Gwen and Madeline looked at each other. He couldn't be turned into a vegan overnight.

"I think we have some slices of roast beef left, and you can take a shower while we're getting your food ready."

"Don't need no shower."

"You'll take one if you want to eat."

When they entered the apartment, Gwen got towels and soap for Lynch. She took his trench coat and directed him to the bathroom. Wanting to subdue the smell of the coat, she stuffed it down into the foyer wastebasket before she and Madeline went to the kitchen. They got roast beef from the refrigerator and made two thick sandwiches with wholegrain bread they toasted, adding lettuce, mayonnaise and slices of tomato. Madeline poured a glass of apple juice as she listened to the shower. A couple of minutes later Lynch came out rubbing a towel behind his ear. Gwen inhaled his stink and coughed and touched the dry towel. The girls yelled and he went back into the bathroom, this time for the quickest shower ever taken in that building. When he came out the second time Lynch's reek was somewhat muted. In faded denim shirt and frayed jeans, he sat on the living room chesterfield, which had been quickly covered with a sheet. As he tore apart the sandwiches and took painful sips of apple juice, forced to accept it after the girls said they wouldn't listen to his demand for a beer because alcohol wasn't any good for his health, they sat on the floor, looking up at him.

"Why are you homeless?" Madeline said.

"Don't you have a family?" Gwen said.

"I was snatched when I was a kid, taken to Madgaskee, off the Africee coast, raised by a gang of thieves. Taught me to steal. Said they'd kill me if I didn't. 'Scaped when I was sixteen, helped by a beautiful native girl called Mawimbee that loved me and we run away to Tanganyikee, sailed a boat there, and I hunted zebree to feed us, but she got run over by a elephant and died and the natives thought I killed her and were going to boil me in a pot but a beautiful native girl that loved me name of Wappoonoonee saved me by cutting a hole in the tent I was prisner in and we got away and crossed desert in the Sudanee to Arabee where she died from falling off a camel but the Ayrabs blamed me and were going to cut my head off with one of them big curved swords but a harem girl name of Harinee seen me once through a screen in the Emiree's palace where I was in a dungeon and she loved me and wore that gauzee stuff over her face and them billowy pants and you could see her belly button and she saved me by dancing for the guards and I got out the back way and we stowed away on a boat to the Black Sea and travelled into Russee where she fell through the ice and drowned and the police 'cused me and were going to hang me but a Russee girl called Olgee that loved me dressed up like a cleaning woman and stole the key from the warden's office to get me out of prison and we skied through Siberee and over the Pole into this country where she choked on car pollution but the police said it was too

6

quick and come after me and I been hiding out since."

"You really had bad luck," Gwen said, looking sideways at Madeline.

"I met them beautiful girls. I have memries of what they done for me 'cause of love."

"That's a lot of love to remember," Madeline said, glancing at Gwen.

"You girls be lucky having memries like them."

"I don't think we'll be that lucky."

It was time to see the caretaker. They left Lynch in the apartment, telling him not to touch anything because Gwen's parents would notice. She draped a blanket over the sheet on the chesterfield and Lynch lay down, closed his eyes. The girls smiled at each other. Their plan was working. Gwen picked up the sandwich plate and glass of apple juice. She poured the rest of the juice down the kitchen sink and washed her hands. Charity had its costs and cautions.

"Did he think we believed that garbage?" Madeline said as they were riding down in the elevator.

"Guess so," Gwen said. "He needs to believe it."

In his late thirties, Alexios Kyriakopoulos had emigrated from Corinth, Greece, seven years ago. He had been caretaker for two and a half years. He was unmarried and had a girlfriend named Gina who spent weekends with him. He wore too much cologne and was especially attentive to the women and girls in the building. He was known to have made frequent visits to one old widow on weekdays. Her relatives found out and he had been warned to stay away. She had died and Kyriakopoulos was looking for willing sacrifices to the power of his charisma and cologne, Stampede, for the man who doesn't want to wait.

The last time they had seen him the girls were leaving the building by the service entrance. He was in the alley, spitting into a garbage bag. They hesitated, staring at him. A pendulous gob of spittle dangled and swung from his lips on an almost invisible string before it plopped into the bag. Blue coveralls spotted with paint, hair slicked back from his forehead, mustache shaved like an arrowhead down to pulpous lips, he smiled at them.

"Hi, geyurls."

They had nodded and passed, choking back laughter until they were out of the alley. "Puke on it." This was Madeline's latest expression for anything or anyone she found disgusting. "Call the zoo, we've found it." "Get me to the hospital, I'm terminal," Gwen had moaned. "Yuck. He's got more hair in his nose than my dad's got on his head."

Kyriakopoulos suspected the girls didn't take him seriously. But they were silly, immature. How could they appreciate the virile power of someone like him? Probably dreamt about rock stars and thought any guy under eighteen without pimples was a real man. Still their blithe disdain was irritating. Maybe in a couple of years they would come to him, when their bodies would draw them to a sexually mature male. He thought of Madeline's long hair and lashes and green eyes and creamy skin and Gwen's blondeness, intense blue eyes and slender white neck. When they were young women they would be enticingly beautiful. Too bad about Ruth Catterall. She had been fun and her body not decayed, like those of some older women. Gina would never be enough for a man like him. She was always talking about marriage, had big teeth and there was that shadow of a mustache. He was certain his next conquest would be Cathy Painter, a middle-aged divorcée on the third floor. They had chatted about Greece. She had toured the Acropolis several years ago and had her picture taken standing beside one of the columns of the Parthenon. She had shown him the snapshot in the hallway but had not invited him inside. That would come. He would lend her a recording of bouzouki music and give her some of his sister-in-law's filo pastry, so sweet and flaky. Eventually he would invite her to his apartment for an authentic Greek meal, which his sister-in-law would obligingly help him prepare. He saw Cathy, fingers sticky with pastry, undressing in his kitchen and the two of them grappling as plates of partially consumed moussaka smashed onto the floor. He would rerun that video as he vacuumed the lobby carpet.

Gwen knocked on the caretaker's door. When he opened it and saw them, his eyes widened. He was wearing an undershirt, an old pair of black pants and leather slippers with much of the stitching gone or loose. He smelled of beer. The little bitches had come sooner than expected. Could he handle two? Sure, but they were still young. He had to be careful.

"Mr. Kyriakopoulos, would you help us?" they asked in unison.

"What do you geyurls want?" he said, grinning, imagining for a moment something delightfully sensual and forbidden.

"We have a problem you could handle so easily," Madeline said.

"What problem?" Kyriakopoulos said with a wider grin.

"There's this old man in Gwen's parents' apartment and he has nowhere to stay for the next few days until we can find him a permanent place. We've fed him and now he needs somewhere to sleep. We'll keep feeding him. You don't have to worry about that."

"Worry?" The grin was gone.

"We'll take care of him."

"I would like to help you geyurls but I cannot. Regoulations. I lose my job. Sorry."

Gwen smiled, conscious of trying to appear polite instead of friendly.

"It'll only be for a few days. We'll take the blame if anything goes wrong. My father owns a couple of buildings. And if I told him I'm sure he'd get you a job in one of them if you ever needed it. We'd be so grateful for your help. This is a poor old man who won't cause any trouble. Isn't there someplace he could go, like the boiler room?"

"You don't have to be afraid," Madeline said.

"I am not afraid. I want to keep my job."

"But Gwen said you don't have to worry. Why don't you get a place ready and we'll bring him down in half an hour."

The girls smiled at the same time without looking at each other, and Kyriakopoulos, staring at the unblemished beauty of their faces and their young bodies, allowed himself to imagine how grateful they would be, hesitating long enough for them to assume his assent, turn and hurry away.

"Geyurls," he said after them, but they were already out of sight.

When Gwen unlocked the apartment door and walked into the living room, Lynch was sitting on the floor, legs stretched out in front of him. His back was against the chesterfield and he was taking swigs from a whisky bottle. She looked at the liquor cabinet and saw the open doors. She hadn't thought of that.

"Ya know," he said, taking another gulp before letting the bottle slide along his chest onto the floor but still gripping it, "I got so miserable thinking 'bout them women that died after saving me I had to have a drink. Memries last inside after somebody's died, like a terrible ache. I lost so many women I got so many aches. There was Katrinee in Helsinkee."

"We're trying to help you," Gwen said, heaving a rather large sigh of impatience. She went over and pulled the bottle from his grasp. He belched, shut his eyes. Gwen found the bottle cap on the carpet, screwed it back on and put the now almost empty bottle back into the liquor cabinet. She hoped her father wouldn't notice the difference.

"We're going to see the caretaker," Madeline said. "He's getting a place ready for you."

"Ya stupid little bitches," Lynch murmured inaudibly.

Gwen and Madeline helped him up and put his trench coat on him, one skinny shaking arm into an armhole and then the other. The coat stank. With each holding him by an elbow, he staggered out of the apartment and into the elevator. On the first floor they dragged him to the caretaker's suite. Wearing his coveralls, Kyriakopoulos opened the door, smacking a hand against his forehead when he saw Lynch. But he said he would put him in the boiler room. The elevator too risky for this move, he led the way to the fire escape stairs and held the door open. They pushed Lynch's frame through the doorway, grabbed him again and directed his wobbly legs down the one flight to the basement. He stumbled a few times but didn't fall. More hauling along a concrete corridor to the boiler room. Kyriakopoulos unlocked and opened the door, reached in and switched on the light, a bleary forty watt bulb in a wall bracket beside the door. Much of the interior was taken up by the steam plant, its gauges, pipes and boiler all painted in glossy grey enamel. The concrete floor was clean and bare. The air was stuffy warm and the boiler looked as if it would be hot to touch. Lynch collapsed onto a one-piece plastic chair in the only free corner.

"He'll need blankets," Madeline said.

"There is heat," Kyriakopoulos said.

"We'll bring him some blankets and a pillow with his next meal," Gwen said, pointedly ignoring the caretaker's attempt at sarcasm.

"I hope you geyurls are not going to forget he is here."

"You think were children?" Gwen said.

The caretaker threw up his hands and left. The girls went over and looked at Lynch. He was snoring, so they tiptoed out and closed the door. At the apartment they prepared more roast beef sandwiches and talked about his future.

"Maybe your father could hire him to be a caretaker or watchman or something in one of his buildings," Madeline said. "He couldn't be worse than Krappy."

"I'll ask, not mentioning of course who's in the boiler room."

"If he's too old for that, maybe he could be your butler."

"We don't need one. Can you imagine that guy cleaning up? Serving drinks? Wouldn't be much left in the glasses. Or the bottles."

When they returned an hour later to the boiler room, Lynch was still asleep and snoring loudly. After putting some woollen blankets and a pillow nearby on the floor, together with a tray of food, they tiptoed out with exaggerated steps.

Early Saturday morning Gwen's parents returned. Roger Chalmers was a tall beefy man in his early fifties and bald except for a sparse fringe of greying hair. He looked busy and usually walked briskly regardless of where he was. Thin and ash blonde, Carol Chalmers had a small nose and finely shaped lips, in contrast to her husband's stolidly blunt features. Gwen was denied nothing, even though her mother demurred mildly sometimes. Even-tempered, emotionally cool, Gwen had never been unreasonable. They gave her much of their free time, always in short supply. He was an important real estate developer and she had become one of the most prominent civil attorneys in the city.

"You girls keeping busy?" Roger said, hanging his and Carol's coats in the foyer closet after the four had exchanged greetings.

"Yes, Dad."

"Doing what?"

"This and that."

"Don't care to tell us, I guess. Very hush hush."

He went to the kitchen and opened the refrigerator door.

"What happened to the roast beef? I thought you guys were vegans."

"We had a cheat meal. Sorry."

"I'm not," Carol said. "The sooner you get back to a balanced diet, the better for your health."

"Mom."

"God knows what you're doing to those young bodies of yours."

"A plant-based diet is the best."

"Why are you taking supplements?"

"No diet is perfect, even a carnivore's."

"I'm a carnivore because I eat meat occasionally?"

"We're thinking of the animals."

"This may come as a shock to you, Gwen, but you're an animal too."

"I'm not being gassed and chopped up and sold in supermarkets."

"I blame the Internet. All those frauds. Convincing the gullible to go vegan so they can sell their books and T-shirts with stupid slogans. And get you to go to vegfests and buy overpriced junk food."

"It's not like that."

"You're fourteen. You'll find out, hopefully before you do too much damage to your body and your brain."

"There are plenty of healthy vegans."

"How do you know they don't cheat?"

"Dr. Todd wouldn't."

"That guy. There's a limit to being an understanding parent. Don't push me too far. We're going day by day with this. Don't you forget that."

"We promised you and her mom we'd quit if we noticed anything."

"You must have been starving," Roger said as he picked up a plate from the kitchen counter, only a crumpled piece of plastic wrap in the centre.

"Sorry, Dad," Gwen shouted from the hallway as the girls headed for her bedroom. "I know it's your favourite."

"Never mind," he said.

"I'll make us an omelette," Carol said. "Try to make do with second best."

In Gwen's bedroom, which Gwen and Madeline had dubbed their "consultation chamber," they shared an organic granola bar and a bag of organic baked chips, Gwen going to the kitchen afterwards for a couple of bottles of preservative-free cream soda. She put on her computer, checked the social media and clicked on favourite sites on You Tube, Dr. Todd catching her interest.

"He's posted a new video. He's interviewing Vegan Slut."

Vegan Slut was a pop music star who had become vegan a year ago. Her band had recently recorded her latest songs, "Slaughterhouse Cemetery" and "Rack of Lamb." She was skinny and went braless, with breasts like partially melted artillery shells, and they were always exposed to her nipples. Her dyed black hair stuck out in spikes at the sides, and there was a curl in the middle of her forehead. Everything was pierced: ears, nose, lips, tongue, nipples and down under. What wasn't pierced was tattooed: a jaguar, a python, orchids and lianas and a heart with a dagger through it and the slogan, "She Rocks." Her line of cruelty-free vegan products featured Shades of Black lipsticks, Deathpallor face powder, Bloodstone nail polish, Keelhaul facial cleanser and Crypt Musk deodorant. Her jewellery line included Rattler and Cobrafang necklaces and Monster Hag earrings. Her You Tube channel had more subscribers than Dr. Todd's, and her book, *Life of a Meat Whore*, was a NY Times runaway bestseller. Her fans adored her and when she went vegan many followed. A critic once described her as "a role model for terminal narcissists."

Dr. Todd was one of the more popular self-appointed vegan authorities on You Tube. He wore a physician's white coat and was prone to make blanket statements based on cherry-picked studies to support the vegan agenda. On nutrition panels and at the lectern he was chatty and friendly. He liked interviewing guests on his channel. His style was more talk show host than medical authority. He always interviewed in his office, using Skype. He began this interview by asking his guest (real name Tara Weinus), the obvious question.

"What made you go vegan?"

"One of my boyfriends a couple of years ago was a raw vegan and he convinced me to give up eating animals. He made me aware I was contributing to a holocaust. What is going on daily is the same as went on in the concentration camps. It's unnecessary because we can get all the nutrition we need from plant foods."

"What's your response to those who say you're selling yourself and your products, don't care about animals?"

"You mean shithead snobs like Decidedly Vegan? Criticizing me for not going to pig vigils or marching in animal rights parades. And those hints about me being a crackhead and using meth. Lying scumbag. That bitch eats cheese. I dare her to deny it. I'm an artist spreading the vegan message through my songs. I never had things easy. Everything came to me the hard way. I was molested by a blind man. Had to help him out."

"You want to talk about your line of vegan foods that will be coming out this month?"

"Our newest ventures at Vegan Slut include pine-scented granola bars for that woodsy mountain atmosphere, firecracker-scented chips for party times and rock concert chips with that special smell. More soaps are coming, including Black Passion, Citrus Kiss and Cherry Rub, and our first striped toothpaste, Zebra Savannah, licorice flavoured."

"She sounds like a corporation," Gwen said, reaching for her mouse.

"Dollar signs everywhere," Madeline said, "but no animals."

At ten o'clock they went to bed hungry, Madeline satisfied she was suffering in a good cause. Gwen promised herself she would plan better in the future. They would have to buy extra vegan food and share it with the old man. Gwen dreamt of tearing the wrappers off granola bars and finding nothing as Lynch laughed at her.

Chapter 2

Lynch woke up a little after eight o'clock Sunday morning, his head aching and his tongue numb. After taking a while to remember where he was, he got to his feet groaning and lurched to the boiler room door. He grabbed the knob and turned it but the door wouldn't open. "Bitches locked me in," he mumbled, turning away. Stumbling over the blankets and tray of sandwiches, he knocked over a paper cup of juice, but Gwen had put on a lid and it rolled away. He flopped onto the blankets, propped himself up on his elbow and pulled slices of meat from the sandwiches and dropped them into his mouth. He threw the slices of toast away. "Take a leak," he muttered and used the corner behind the chair. When he returned he slumped onto the pillow like a parachutist leaving a plane.

Kyriakopoulos lay beside Gina in bed, her head on his shoulder. She had noticed Saturday evening that he was behaving differently. Usually he would begin playing with her clothes and fondling her when she entered his suite but this time he left the door partially open. Coveralls on and staring at the ceiling, he was lying on his living room couch. She asked him if he felt sick and he said no, he was tired. They watched television for a couple of hours, something they had never done before on a Saturday night, usually being busy in the bedroom. Later he had gone into the bedroom and undressed, gotten into bed and fallen asleep. She had followed and done the same.

"What's wrong, Alexios?" she asked when they woke up, rubbing her cheek against his shoulder.

"I am hiding someone in the boiler room."

"Why?" She was curious but not alarmed, knowing he was a careful man most times.

"Two stupid geyurls got me to do it. They wanted to hide, they said, a poor old man, and I said suppose I am caught and they said I would not be, and the one that lives in the building said her father owns some buildings and I would get a better job."

"How long are you supposed to hide him?"

"I don't know. Few days, maybe."

"What are they going to do with him?"

"I don't know."

"Talk to her parents."

"What would I say? I do what two stupid geyurls tell me to do?"

"Is he crazy? Could he hurt someone?"

"I told you, he is an old man."

"Why don't you see the girls tomorrow morning and tell them he has to leave?"

"They will be angry and tell that geyurl's father I put the old man in the room. I lose my job."

"So wait and see what the girls do with him."

"I must wait for two stupid geyurls to do something. If they forget him, what do I do?"

"If they forget about him, you can get rid of him and they won't care."

"You are right, my Gina." He reached over and pulled at her panties.

At nine o'clock Gwen and Madeline went down to the boiler room, found the door locked and went to the caretaker's suite. Gwen kept knocking until Kyriakopoulos opened his door. He was wearing only boxer shorts and was rubbing his eyes. He scowled.

"Would you please unlock the boiler room door?" Gwen said.

The caretaker turned abruptly and went back into his bedroom and returned wearing a bathrobe with the black terrycloth worn down to a slick shine. A silent ride in the elevator to the basement and he unlocked the door and headed back to the elevator without looking at them.

"Really grumpy, isn't he?" Madeline said.

Gwen opened the door.

"It's us. Did you sleep well?"

Peering into the dimly lit room, they saw him sprawled on the rumpled blankets. The air smelled of pee and sleep sweat. His body odour was as strong as before his shower. They took shallow breaths.

"Guess we should wake him," Madeline said. "He might be sick. He's been in here a long time. This place stinks."

Gwen nodded.

"Didn't think of that," Gwen said. "We'll bring him something and he can empty it himself."

Madeline stood over him. "Get up, it's morning."

"Ha?"

"Wake up."

"Go 'way."

"What's that on my shoe?" Madeline said.

She stamped her feet, stepping on the blankets and Lynch. He yelled and sat up.

"It's on mine," Gwen said and they hurried into the corridor, scraping their shoes on the concrete. When they looked down they saw the squashed remains of wet toast and tomato. They looked at each other and grinned. Lynch was rubbing his ankles and swearing in a low voice when they returned.

"My goddam foot's hurt bad. I dunno if I can walk."

"You'll have to try," Madeline said. "You've got to walk for exercise. You can't stay in here all the time. It's not healthy for your circulation."

"We're going to bring you some breakfast in a while," Gwen said, "and we'll show you some exercises you can do."

"I'm getting out of here right now. I was crazy for coming."

"We'll have pancakes for you, with maple syrup and sausages."

Gwen felt guilty offering this final inducement—the roast beef had been bad enough—but someone like him wasn't going to be an easy convert.

"We'll be back in an hour."

They left and Lynch tried to get up but his feet hurt and his head ached from the whisky and he collapsed onto the blankets. He lay there groaning, lapsed into torpor, a lassitude of not caring what happened. He began to think about the sausages. He remembered the liquor cabinet upstairs.

Gwen's parents slept in late on Sundays as one of their few concessions to time, so Gwen and Madeline didn't have to cope with any questions as they got together the pancake mix, buttermilk, butter and sausages for the meal. Madeline held the handle of the cast-iron skillet, tilting the pan over the hot electric element so the pat of butter slipped and disappeared in foamy swirls. "Ready." "I know I shouldn't but I love the smell of melting butter," Gwen said, dipping the ladle into an earthenware bowl and pouring batter into the skillet. Following the sizzle the aroma of batter and butter together. Taught by her mother, Madeline waited for the edges to bubble. They bubbled and she took a spatula and flipped the pancake, exposing the rich golden yellow and brown mottling of its underside. A little while longer and the first one was done. They made three more and Madeline fried four pork sausages. "We'd better hurry down. Pancakes taste best when they're right out of the pan."

Madeline carried the plate of pancakes and sausages, Gwen following with a syrup bottle and a cup of her parents' best coffee. They tried not to inhale the aromas. The hallway and elevator were empty, so the procession had no onlookers. Lynch was sleeping when Gwen opened the door.

"Here we are. Your breakfast will get cold if you don't eat it right away."

Awakened more by smells than sounds, Lynch sat up and snatched the plate from Madeline. Ignoring the knife and fork, he picked up a sausage and began chomping on it. Doglike chews, guttural swallows, and the others went as noisily. As he chewed they could see he had four front teeth left, worn down to blackened stumps. Gwen held up the maple syrup in front of him. He grabbed it, soaked the pancakes in syrup and tore them apart. He crammed the dripping pieces into his mouth. When he finished he wiped his mouth with the cuff of his trench coat. Rummaging inside the coat, he took out a crumpled package of cigarette and cigar butts. He straightened a stubbed out cigarette end and looked at them.

"Get me a light."

"You can't smoke in here," Gwen said. "You could start a fire."

"I want a goddam light."

"You didn't even thank us for the food. The least you can do is keep from burning the building down."

"Don't tell me what to do. Ya locked me in here last night. Like in jail. That's false 'prisinmint. I could go to the cops. I won't if ya get me a light. And a drink."

"We're trying to help you. But you've got to cooperate."

"Listen, ya little bitches. I got to do nuthin'. I could get up and walk right out of here. So cut the bullshit."

"Calling us names is stupid. Leave if you want to, but you're not going to get room service where you've been living."

"We know it's hard for you to show gratitude," Madeline said, "but don't take advantage."

Lynch grinned. "I didn't tell ya 'bout Desiree from Eiree."

Madeline yawned. Gwen bent down and picked up the plate, utensils, cup and bottle.

"We haven't decided yet where you should go. You'll be all right here until we do. Don't worry about the caretaker. He's not very bright but he won't bother you much. Later today we'll bring your dinner and something for when you pee. For the other there's a toilet next door, beside the storeroom. Please use it because the caretaker may lock you in later on. He doesn't have much nerve. We'll begin your exercise program after you've had your dinner. We're going. If you want to go back and live on the streets, that's your right. You'll disappoint us but we're young. We'll get over it."

Lynch sat stupefied after they left. The butt hung from his lower lip, glued there with saliva. After a while he groaned to his feet and used the toilet next door. When he returned, gravity claimed another victim and his snoring filled the boiler room.

"You were good, Gwenner," Madeline said as they were riding up in the elevator.

"What are we going to do, Maddy?"

"Something will come to us. It's going to be a bit impossible getting his dinner past your mom and dad."

"You eating sausages now too?" Roger said. He had found the open package of pork sausages in the refrigerator.

"Another cheat meal," Gwen said.

Carol grinned.

"You used to say you felt like throwing up if you smelled them cooking."

"We had a couple of bites with our pancakes and threw the rest away. Hope you don't mind."

"Classic combo, flapjacks and sausages," Roger said as he headed for his easy chair in the living room with some office papers.

They couldn't think of a way of smuggling food past Gwen's parents that afternoon. They decided to buy something for Lynch but at the local health food store passed up the boxed organic breakfast cereals, cookies and chips.

"That's not what he needs," Gwen said.

"He smells mouldy," Madeline said. "A dumpster diver. Won't eat peanut butter. Maybe we should get him some tofu wieners, a loaf of organic sprouted wholegrain bread and a jar of organic stoneground mustard. He could make sandwiches. Think he'd catch on?"

Gwen shrugged.

"Probably used to the smell and taste of wieners and bologna, with the leftover parts of the steer, like lips, ears, tail skin and hooves. They're full of pesticides, herbicides, growth hormones and antibiotics, a white soup with all that stuff melted into it and dyed red and cooled to a paste and shot into plastic bags and allowed to congeal so you can slice it. Better make it a soy burger. They make one with beet juice that bleeds like blood."

"Got it," Madeline said. "He's not ready for an all-vegan diet because he's like a germ used to living on garbage. Let's get him that vegan burger and something that won't poison him too much but is rotten enough to keep him happy. Chips made with rancid fast-food oil."

They bought a Super Double Veggie Cheeseburger and went to Binkey's, famous for its extra wide fries. They removed the cheeseburger from its wrapping and put it into the box of fries. With grease soaking into the burger, they returned to the boiler room. Lynch was dozing, sprawled across the blankets, boots off and eyes closed. He squinted when he heard the door open.

"We've brought your dinner," Gwen said. "Do you want to exercise now or after you eat?"

Lynch stretched out a hand. "Gimme that."

"Answer first."

"After. Let me eat in peace."

"We'll be back in two hours."

"Think he'll ever appreciate what we're doing for him?" Gwen said as they waited for the elevator.

"Probably not. We shouldn't expect too much. He doesn't understand what we're doing. We've got to accept that."

"Yeah. I didn't even care when he called us little bitches. He is so pathetic. If he knew what we're trying to do for him, he wouldn't need our help."

"Exactly."

After finishing his meal Lynch put on his boots, went to the door and listened for any noises in the corridor. He heard none and opened the door. The corridor was empty. He stepped out and saw the elevator doors. The elevator was too risky, so he climbed the stairs to the first floor and pushed the heavy red fire escape door open a bit. He peeked out, didn't see anybody and crept past the caretaker's suite. Kyriakopoulos and Gina were sleeping. Stepping cautiously along a hallway of ash grey floor tiles and cream walls, he reached the lobby, saw the glass entrance door with its glass side panels, the steel doors of the elevator, and in each corner an umbrella tree in a large ceramic pot. Another pot, much smaller and on a stand beside the entrance, contained a cactus. It was twenty after four on the kind of sunny day in late August that seems to have a leftover warmth. He was getting thirsty. He had drunk the breakfast coffee but the urge for something stronger was growing. Where was that 'partmint? They gone out? Find it, pick the lock. He fingered the wire ring with keys strung on it he kept around his neck. He hurried back along the hallway to the fire escape door and climbed two flights, coming out on the third floor. Behind the first four keyholes he put his ear to he heard music, a television or conversation. Behind the fifth, 305, nothing. He knocked and waited but no one came. He slipped the wire ring over his head and selected a key. The door opened and Lynch, squatting to see better, fell onto the shoes of a woman in her early forties, plump and wearing glasses.

Lynch gasped and began writhing at her feet. "Can't breathe, need a drink."

Dressed in a white, frilly blouse and tan jacket and skirt, the woman stepped back, asked in a timid voice, "What's wrong?"

"I thought them pushers was going to get me," Lynch wheezed. He shoved the wire ring into a pocket of his trench coat. "Somebody was coming in the building, so I come in and run up the stairs. In bad shape. Need a drink."

"You can crawl in here. I'll get you a drink. Would you like some tea? Coffee?"

"I need something strong," Lynch moaned as he scrambled across the living room carpet and propped himself against a couch leg.

"Would gin be all right?"

"Yeah, but it's got to be lots."

She went into her kitchen and Lynch heard the sound of glass clinking against glass. He took the wire ring out of his coat pocket, slipped it over his head. No chance of losing them. She returned with a large tumbler half full. Taking it in an upturned palm, he lifted it with both hands and made himself drink slowly. When he finished, he coughed and looked up at her.

"I'd be fine if I could have a bit more."

This time she returned with much less and Lynch gulped it down, felt a surge of relaxed confidence flowing through him and closed his eyes.

"You're a kind lady. I'm feeling better now."

"Why don't you rest here for a while? How did you become involved with drug pushers?"

"I like helping people. Been volunteering with this bunch of poor kids that's got no toys. Sunshine Kiddies. Probly never heard of it. Down in the dumps 'cause I got laid off as a 'pliance 'pairman, so I figured I'd give 'em a hand. Erything was fine till them pushers showed up wanting to sell stuff. I wouldn't let 'em. They said, 'We're going to get ya when ya don't 'spect nuthin'.' They come after me today. But I snuck off."

Lynch opened his eyes and looked around. The buffet and side tables were crowded with framed photographs. One showed the woman standing in front of a classical temple. He pointed at the photograph.

"That's one of them real old buildings, ain't it?"

"That was taken a few years ago, on a wonderful afternoon on the Acropolis. I'm standing in front of the Parthenon."

"I seen all that stuff once, and lots more of it even worse off."

"What were you doing there?" She couldn't hide her incredulity.

"I went there from Italee with a beautiful girl named Renatee. She was the daughter of a big cheesemaker who didn't want her to marry me. But she loved me, so we run away to Greecee. It was full of fallen down old stone buildings, hardly no roofs, lots of stone poles sticking up in the air. Cold at night when ya slept on them bare foundations. Anaways, one of them poles fell on her. The cops blamed me but a beautiful Greecee girl name of Alice Atheenee, she always put on silk nightgowns, blew up the jail and saved me and we run away to Germanee where she died from having a allergee to beer."

"You seem to have had some bad luck."

"I have. But some beautiful women loved me. And died beside me. I got my memries."

She sat on a walnut rocking chair, across from the couch.

"Those are wonderful to have, aren't they? I've got mine too. I was married once but my husband left me, four years ago this month. Still, I hold onto memories of our good times together."

"Don't take this the wrong way, but any guy drop you got to be cuckoo."

"We were happy, but he met someone else and told me he loved her. And no longer loved me. It took me a long time to accept that, and I don't think I have, not completely. At least I'm not crying every day now. And I've lost some of the weight I gained after the divorce. I was two hundred and fifty pounds. It's hard for me to believe I was that heavy."

"Ya don't look heavy to me, not heavy at all. Your figure is perfect, if ya don't mind me saying that."

"I think I've coped rather well. There were only two suicide attempts, not really serious, though. There weren't near enough pills the first time. And the razor in a bathtub full of hot water was something I read about. I couldn't have actually gone through with it. The water was so hot it burnt me quite badly. I was treated in the burn therapy unit at the hospital."

"We're kind of the same. Ya got a shitty guy and I had bad luck."

"You don't understand. Bonwit couldn't help himself. Love took him from me. He was helpless. He cried on my shoulder when we parted."

"Seems to me the guy wanted a bit of fresh stuff. But she must have been a beauty for him to leave ya. You're not bad at all. If you'll let me say that."

"How could you understand what Bonwit went through? You're ordinary. He was special. I was fortunate to share almost seventeen years of marriage with him. Friend and husband."

"Forget that asshole. There's lots of guys would like to tickle your button."

"I'm a fat woman, an ugly woman, and no man wants me or ever will."

"I been out of that business for a bit, but it wouldn't take much for me to have a go at ya. Get me another shot and pour one for yourself and come over and touch elbows and we'll see what we can do. I'm not making promises but I'm feeling a bit peppy right now. Get the gin 'fore I lose my edge."

She sighed, prim elation and stoic regret laced with breath mint, and pointed to a framed photograph.

"That's Bonwit over there. You can see how special he is, with those eyes, eyes of a rare soul."

Lynch focused on a group of framed photographs on a buffet across the room from where he sat against the couch. Most of them were of a round-faced man with curly hair. He wore the same simpering grin in all of them and his blue eyes were as vacant as a clear sky. The photographs had been taken over a number of years, the latest in his forties. They showed an aging choirboy relying on drink and self-pity to handle the rot. In one picture the couple are standing apart from others on the lawn at a summer garden party, she all in white and he in a white suit and she gazing up at him, her pudgy face transfixed with adoration. Smirking into the camera and oblivious of her, he exuded the general air of one who feels too good for the planet.

She had that same worshipful look as she gazed at the photographs. She had a pleasant face and her toffee-coloured hair fell in waves to her shoulders. But the extra weight on hips, legs, shoulders and arms was confessed weakness and punishment for it. Her heaviness gave her the appearance of permanent self-exhaustion, a burden to bear as suffering for love.

All that meant to Lynch was the little likelihood of having sex with her. His joints were stiff and pleasure now came more from bottles and on plates, in warm places out of a cold wind. But there was passing regret her soft body wouldn't be in one of those places with him. Eats a lot a cakes.

"He's too good for any woman," Cathy Painter said, sighing again. "I knew that when we first met, at Saint Paul's. He looked like one of those angels in an early Renaissance fresco, with downysmooth folded wings and shiny golden hair and bright blue eyes. I remember when he first looked at me, turned in his pew and I caught my breath. I thought I was having a vision."

"Jesus Christ."

"Yes, almost Christlike in his appearance, and certainly in the effect he had on me. He's the only person I'll ever meet who has that natural spirituality that pours out of him."

"Speaking of pouring, I'll need another drink if ya want me to listen to this."

"I suppose you need artificial stimulants to achieve any sort of happiness. Bonwit would've pitied you, and so do I."

"Pity me all ya want but get me a drink."

She went into the kitchen, returning this time with the bottle, put it on her coffee table and sat in the rocking chair, leaning back, watching Lynch. He slurped down half a glass of gin, tilted his head back and moaned in lazy pleasure.

"I like Scotch and don't refuse rum or rye, but this gin's all right, 'specially to a man who's on the run."

"I'm sorry. I was talking so much about my problems that I forgot yours."

"Had a dog once that was spirtual, if ya want to know. Name of Regal, black lab. Smartest dog I ever seen. Friend of mine give him to me when he left town. That dog and me used to panhandle in front of pubs and stores. Walk with his head up by the doors. Like he was marching. And people give me lots of money 'cause of that. Shared my food with that dog. Even when I got steak. We made a pair. Had this way of holding hisself sitting alongside of me. Like he knowed what was in the heads of people passing by. He knowed what I was thinking when he looked at me. But I couldn't never have no bad thoughts 'bout him."

"Where is your dog?"

"Some punk run over him with a van and broke his back. Never wanted another dog after that."

"You must get lonely, without even a pet to keep you company."

"No more 'n most, 'cluding lots I seen that's got wives and kids."

"I'm lonely. I cope by doing church work and travelling."

"Don't take this wrong, but don't ya never get so's ya need a man?"

"I know what you mean, but after Bonwit no other man could ever satisfy me."

Prick wouldn't be no good at filling a pencil sharpener.

"Thanks for the gin. I better be going, find a place to flop. Can't go to my place. They'll be waiting for me. See where I can get some money. If I'm lucky. Got to keep from starving."

Lynch coughed and groaned as he got to his feet, then sat on the coffee table, next to the bottle of gin.

"I can give you enough to keep you safe for a while."

"I don't like taking money from a woman. Funny that way."

"Don't be silly. If you're in danger, you've got to forget your pride. It would be charity work. I'd feel better about myself."

"It ain't right."

"It's little enough to give, and it's my duty as a Christian to help you."

"Seeing it that way, guess you're right, but only a few dollars. I can get by on practicly nuthin'."

Cathy walked briskly into her bedroom, shoulders slanted forward and hands close together, as if she was anticipating opening her purse. Lynch heard a bureau drawer slide open and a purse catch click, muffled sounds of a leather wallet on wood and the riffling of bills. He stood up, glanced around the living room. There was a ring in a crystal bowl on the buffet. It was made of gold and four claws held a solitaire, which shot lasers of white light as he picked it up. He shoved it into his pants pocket. He hurried back to the coffee table, knocking over the bottle when he sat down. It made a loud thud hitting the wood and sounded like a drumroll moving across the table. Lynch swore and grabbed it as Cathy returned. Holding a folded wad of bills, she walked over to him.

"This should help you."

He let go of the bottle and she handed him the money. He put the bills into his shirt pocket.

"I feel bad 'bout this."

"You shouldn't. I think I should phone the police."

"Them pushers be waiting outside the station or anawheres else to get me, like I told ya. Best thing is to stay out of sight. This'll make it easier. Better get going now, 'fore they come back."

As Lynch moved towards the door, Cathy held out her hand.

"I'll have to phone the police if you don't give me the ring you took."

"I got no ring."

"It was over there, on the buffet. Keep the money, even though you're not running away from anybody. But you are a homeless person and you need charity. Give me the ring."

"I got no goddam ring."

"Do you want me to call the police? They'd be here in a few minutes and they'd have no trouble catching you. You'd be charged with theft and vagrancy. Better give me the ring."

Lynch reached inside his pants pocket, took out the ring and threw it at her. He yanked open the door and ran out into the empty hallway and down the fire stairs. When he reached the basement, he stopped and stood in the corridor. He walked to the boiler room. The door was unlocked. He went inside, shut the door and counted the money. She had given him thirty dollars, smelling faintly of perfumed handkerchiefs. He jammed the bills into his pants pocket, collapsed onto the blankets and fell asleep.

Chapter 3

An hour later Gwen and Madeline went up to the snoring heap of blankets and trench coat and looked at each other. Gin and pee smells had mixed with stale chip oil. And permeating everything was Lynch's sleep sweat. The boiler room heat turned it all into a stinkfog. Madeline wondered how long she could hold her breath without passing out. Gwen was holding a large glass jar she had brought as a chamber pot. She put down the jar, opened the door, took a deep breath and returned.

"We're here for your exercises. You can't sleep away the whole day."

"Don't need no exercise," Lynch mumbled, his face into the pillow. "I'm tired."

"You'll have more energy once you've worked out."

"What'd ya think I am, your pet dog?"

"If you were a dog, we'd take him to a vet," Madeline said and took a shallow breath.

"Get me a steak and a bottle."

"Meat isn't good for you and you drink too much."

Lynch rolled over onto his back and looked up at them in the dim light. He wanted to get up and leave. Smart-mouth bitches. Never been hungry. Never slept outside in freezing weather. Too young to know how to piss right. Telling people what to do. If ya got money, do as ya please. Warm in the building. Steady grub too. Empty 'partmints. Get in 'em. Pick up jewry, cash. Plenty to get through the winter.

"What kind of pissass shit ya going to put me through?"

29

"When you talk like that, it makes us think less of you."

"Don't care."

"We've brought you something to use if you're locked in."

Gwen pointed to the jar. It was in front of the boiler. The lid was on top but unscrewed. Lynch stared at the ceiling.

"We'll begin your exercises now. We'll start with stretching exercises and do the rest somewhere else. Get up and I'll show you how to do them. They get you ready. They're easy."

Lynch got to his feet slowly, grimacing.

"Raise your arms above your head."

Lynch raised his arms as if he were surrendering to the police. He yawned, still groggy.

"No, stretch them like this." Gwen raised hers as high as she could.

"Think it's easy for a man of my age to do this? Not no teenager, ya know. Been through a lot. Desert and jungle, mountains and deep seas. Nearly got drownded off Javee. 'Bout died a thirst in the Saharee. Nuthin' much left."

After several arm raises, Lynch was told to bend over, his back straight and hands on hips. Next came extending one leg and then the other to stretch the calf muscles. Then arms up to chest, fingers touching, before turning his torso from side to side. After a dozen, done as unenthusiastically as the rest, the preliminary session was over.

"Where do we go?" Madeline said.

"Krappy's apartment."

"Think he'll let us?"

"He'll have to."

Kyriakopoulos responded quickly to Gwen's light, insistent knocking. He felt pleasantly tired. Gina was in the shower and would be leaving in a while. His relaxed look disappeared when he saw the girls and Lynch. Gwen didn't give him a chance to order them away.

"We're going to need your apartment for half an hour for him to do exercises."

"You are keeding.'

"We're trying to get him into shape and your suite is the safest place to do it."

"Look, geyurls, I am keeping quiet about him being here, which I should not. But you cannot use my apartment for him. This is my place. There is somebody here now. A woman."

He smirked. Gwen pursed her lips and stared straight into his eyes.

"My father said this morning that the carpets in the building should be much cleaner and that those plants in the lobby are all dying. I said you had been very busy lately and told him not to complain to the owner of the building, a personal friend of his."

"This is blackermail."

"It's probably the only time that we'll need your place."

Kyriakopoulos swung the door open wide to let them in, turned abruptly and went into the bathroom. He shut the door and muffled shouts came from behind it. The girls glanced around the living room, saw the black vinyl sofa, the laminated coffee table with plastic veneer and screw-on legs and the violent red carpet. A television sat on a small table with a glass top. A clock radio was on the floor next to the table. On the yellow walls were four black velvet paintings of matadors in various stages of dispatching a bull and one of a naked woman lying on a tiger skin rug, her breasts pale balloons and a glass ruby in her navel.

"We're in the zoo man's cage," Madeline said, "where he feeds and where he meets his mate."

Lynch didn't see a liquor cabinet or a random bottle and figured his best chance for a drink was a beer in the refrigerator. The bathroom door opened and Gina came out with a large white bag slung against her hip by a shoulder strap. She wore a fluffy white sweater, a short black leather skirt and shoes with four inch heels. Tomato red lipstick was smeared at one corner of her mouth and some strands of dark hair fell over her left eye. On her way out of the apartment she stopped and glared at Gwen and Madeline.

"You girls are pests. Why don't you leave this poor man alone and stop bothering Alexios? You must have other things to do. Don't you have boyfriends?"

Gwen looked at Madeline, as if to say, will you allow me?

"We're trying to help him. He's homeless and needs good food and a place to stay. We're doing our best. We'd appreciate any suggestions?"

"I'll give you one. Stop interfering in other people's lives."

"You're not interfering when you're trying to help someone," Madeline said. "But selfish people don't want to be bothered."

Gina left, slamming the apartment door. Kyriakopoulos came out of the bathroom and glanced at the door as he went into the kitchen. Gwen lay down on the carpet, on her back and face down, and jogged around the room a couple of times. Satisfied, she began Lynch's workout.

"Lie on the carpet on your stomach, so we can begin with pushups."

"I'm not doing those. They're hard."

"You can cheat a bit. Don't lift your whole body. Only your head and chest. That's what we do at school in exercise period when we're tired."

Madeline went to see Kyriakopoulos. He was leaning against the kitchen counter and taking swigs from a bottle of beer.

"We need something for him to drink when he's finished. Do you have fruit juice or bottled water?"

"I drink the water that comes from the tap, and I have beer, but you have to pay me for that."

"Tap water? We're trying to help him, not poison him."

The caretaker put his bottle down and picked up a glass. He turned on the cold water tap. When the glass was almost full, he held it up in front of Madeline. She could see his distorted face through it. A swollen smirk.

"What is wrong? It is clear."

"You don't understand. You can't see the bacteria, the herbicides and heavy metals."

"I cannot see them because they are in your head."

He put the glass on the counter and stared at the ceiling. Madeline returned to the living room. Lynch was on his stomach and lifting his upper body a couple of inches off the carpet. Boots off and skinny arms extended from rolled-up sleeves, he looked as if he was trying to get up after a fall.

"A few more," Gwen said.

"Nothing but tap water and beer for him after the workout, and Krappy wants to be paid for the beer," Madeline said.

"Assuming they use filtered water, I suppose beer is better," Gwen said.

"Goddam right beer is better."

"You're not getting any until after your exercises. You're not finished yet. Try running on the spot next. Get up, please."

Lynch stood up, adding groans to his effort. His running on the spot was more of a slow motion jog than a run.

"Don't step on that nail," Gwen shouted and Lynch froze and lurched backward a few steps with a burst of energy. She stooped and pretended to pick up something and put it in her pocket.

"Why didn't ya tell me? I could've hurt myself."

"I didn't see it before."

"You brats going to kill me."

"Why don't you try touching your toes?"

Frowning, Lynch raised his arms and bent over. He appeared to be bowing to a deity in a shrine. Ten bows and he stopped. Arching his back, he groaned.

"I'm getting real thirsty."

"One more exercise," Gwen said.

That was simply walking around the living room as fast as he could, which was not fast. Madeline sighed and sat down.

"Pretend it's a hot day and you're walking to get a beer," Gwen said. "We're not going to pay for one unless we're convinced you're doing your best."

"Two, I walk faster."

"All right."

"Three, I walk real fast."

"All right."

"Four, I run."

"Four is too many but we can keep one for later."

Lynch raced around the living room, bumping into furniture and swearing. He stumbled over the clock radio and limped away dragging a foot. Tripping over a footstool he fell, the side of his head glancing off a corner of the coffee table before he slumped onto the carpet. Hearing Lynch's fall and the girls' cries, Kyriakopoulos hurried from the kitchen and saw the crumpled form. Gwen and Madeline were on their knees beside their workout dropout.

"What did you do?" Kyriakopoulos yelled. "He is dead."

"No, he isn't," Gwen said. "He tripped and fell. He's temporarily unconscious. I felt his pulse."

Madeline tugged tentatively at Lynch's shirtsleeve.

"Can you hear us?"

There was a low hum, wavering in intensity before dying out. Lynch opened his eyes.

"Beer."

"I am only going to charge five dollars a bottle," Kyriakopoulos said, grinning at Gwen.

She stood up and reached inside her jacket for her wallet. She took out a five dollar bill and handed it to him. He went into the kitchen and returned with a bottle of beer from the refrigerator. The bottle felt cold and slippery when she took it from him, by the long neck so she wouldn't touch his fingers.

"You want another one?"

"No, thank you," she said with polite acidity as she twisted off the cap and kneeled down.

The blow had been slight and all Lynch felt was the throbbing of the bruised area, swollen to a red knob. He sat up, grabbed the bottle and drank in gulps, choking once and letting foamy beer dribble from his lips and chin. It soaked into his shirt. When he finished he tossed the bottle onto the sofa. The caretaker picked it up and returned to the kitchen.

"Ya said four," Lynch reminded Gwen. He leaned back against the sofa.

"He's charging too much. I paid for one to get you on your feet. I'll get some more from my father. Somebody gave him a case. He doesn't drink beer, anyway."

"You brats be helpless without your people giving ya stuff. I wasn't never lucky. Kicked out of the house at ten. 'Go make your own living,' my pa said. Met a little girl, name of Jenny. Short red hair like a bush. We stole from stores to live. Jenny got sick from some kind of fever and died and I was alone again, but I couldn't stop to feel sorry for myself. Had to keep going to keep from starving. The cops was after me for Jenny's death. Chasing a kid, figure that out. I got away easy. Went up the Amazonee with a beautiful girl named Doloree. But she was squished by one of them boas constrictees. Them headhunters blamed me, was going to shrink my head, but a beautiful shrinkee name of Popocanee snuck me out of this hole they stuck me in and we rode on llamees high up into the Andees, heading into Chilee. She froze solid there. That's why it's called Chilee."

Gwen looked at her watch.

"Let's go if you're feeling better. It's almost seven o'clock. You're overdue for a meal. If I ask this guy to give you one, he'll probably want the building."

Madeline had to return home by nine. Roger Chalmers promised to drive her. She was only supposed to stay the weekend and Mary Dalrymple wanted her daughter back. Since her divorce five years ago, she needed to be seen as a good parent. She must never appear to be palming her daughter off on anybody.

Gwen was thinking about Madeline having to leave. She knew she could phone, text or email her for advice. But she felt uneasy about dealing with Kyriakopoulos without Madeline beside her. The way he stared made her uncomfortable. To continue their plan they needed the caretaker. But she would never allow herself to be alone with him. She would make sure Lynch was with her. The irony of finding support in his presence wasn't lost on her.

"We're leaving," she said in a loud voice. "Better lock your door. Never know. Someone might steal your velvet paintings."

There was no answer from the kitchen. Groaning, Lynch got to his feet. Gwen shut the door when they left and noted in her backward glance a plaster statuette of a naked woman lying on the carpet. It had been knocked off the table by Lynch's fall. The woman was bending over and washing her legs, exposing most of her body. It was anatomically clumsy and some of the gold-coloured paint meant for her hair was on the back of her neck. Gwen hadn't noticed the statuette when it was on the table. Now the upset figure seemed somehow violated, the accident having revealed a poignant vulnerability in this crude depiction of female beauty.

"What are ya up to now?" Lynch said in the basement corridor, tacitly accepting their authority.

"Go to the boiler room," Gwen said. "Sleep there tonight and tomorrow we'll decide what to do. The caretaker won't bother you. He's afraid of my father. I'll bring you your dinner as soon as I can."

"I guess your mom won't let you stay a few more nights," Gwen said in the elevator.

"You know her, playing Super Mom with spotlights on her. I've got to be there tonight. Maybe she'll let me come back in a couple of days. What are you going to feed him?"

"I've got granola bars in my bedroom and I think I can get a piece of steak from the fridge and some leftover vegetables."

"Don't forget the beer." Madeline smiled.

"I'll tell my dad I dropped a bottle and it broke. Why don't you leave right away so he won't be there. My mom is usually so busy I can take anything I want. We've got to move that guy. Maybe there's an empty apartment we can hide him in until there's something better."

"We'll need Krappy's help and I don't think he wants to help us any more."

"We'll tell him it's the last time. That my dad is going to do something."

They got out of the elevator and stood in the hallway, thinking the same thoughts. Had they started something they didn't know how to finish? But the project had its own momentum now, as if someone had given them a problem they must solve no matter how difficult it was. It was easier to talk about details.

"Gwenner, can you handle Krappy without me? He's creepiest, worst of the world's zoo men."

"Our guy will be with me."

"You going to move him tomorrow?"

"I'll try."

"I'll phone."

An hour later Madeline was driven home, an apartment ten blocks away. It was dark, street lights passing like a cordon of robot police keeping back an imaginary crowd from a parade of cars. She looked at the empty streets and wondered how many people were homeless, forced to sleep outside. Because she was leaving early, she hadn't eaten dinner yet. She hoped there was something good in the refrigerator, maybe one of her mother's pies. She leaned back against the seat and inhaled. She could smell crust.

"How's your mother?" Roger Chalmers asked.

"Fine."

Why do grown-ups ask the same dumb questions? She's got the rarest disease in the world, Mr. Chalmers, mindyourownbusinessitis. Makes you blind, deaf and dumb, except when you eat or have to go to the bathroom. You get so you don't know what's happening in other people's lives and go crazy. She giggled.

"Something funny?"

"I was thinking about a movie I saw last week."

Lynch snatched the plate from Gwen, tore off the aluminum foil and with unwashed fingers ripped apart the steak and began gnawing on the chunks. Gwen left the knife and fork she brought in her blazer pocket and looked at the ceiling. Steak gone, Lynch tilted the plate to gobble the carrots and peas before shoving the granola bars into his trench coat pocket. He drained the bottle of beer, his Adam's apple bobbing like a fish going down a heron's gullet. Looking at Gwen's upturned face brought on Lynch's deepest belch.

"Ya said four. You're two short."

"We've got to move you first. Tomorrow I'm going to see about a new place in the building. You won't have to stay here. It's too cramped."

"I stayed in worse, but a better one be good. Keep the grub coming. Want to get some sleep. That guy ain't going to lock me in? I'm used to open spaces, can't stand being locked up."

"You going to stay here all night?"

"Ain't going nowheres."

"I'll see him."

Kyriakopoulos took two minutes to answer the door. He was in a bad mood and had been drinking, and the five dollars he got from Gwen hadn't made him feel much better. Gina had asked him again to marry her after they had made love for the second time. He said no and she had cried. Hair done up in braids, her hands in the pockets of her dark green blazer with yellow piping, Gwen stood in front of him. He wanted to slam the door but looked at her eyes, blue water in a polar sea, and that slight ruddiness now in her cheeks. Lust picked open the lock of its cage.

"He doesn't like being shut in. He's claustrophobic because of the way he's lived. Sleeping outside most of the time. Would you leave the door unlocked?"

"Yeah. I leave it."

"While I'm here I may as well ask you about getting him a different place in the building. We can't leave him there. There must be a couple of empty suites. Could we put him in one of them for a while? Until Madeline and I decide what to do, which won't take long."

"Yeah, empty suite."

"Are you all right, Mr. Kyriakopoulos?"

"I take you now."

"I could have a peek tonight. Look in for a second."

"You peek."

He went into the kitchen and took a key from a board of them hanging on hooks. The key was to an empty suite on the ninth floor at the end of the hallway. As they walked to the elevator, Gwen could smell beer on him. They rode up in silence. She told herself she would glance in and leave, not even step inside the apartment. The doors opened onto a silent, empty hallway. Kyriakopoulos led the way to suite 901. Keeping his hand steady, he aimed the key at the lock. He opened the door, stepped inside and switched on the foyer and living room lights. Gwen could see furniture draped in white sheets. Kyriakopoulos moved so she could see more and she instinctively leaned forward. He put his hand on her shoulder and drew her inside the doorway before she could react. He kept it there, with enough pressure to hold her. His hand felt like an animal with many legs gripping her, but still she could not react, almost fascinated by what he was doing. He shifted around so he was between her and the open door. A push of his foot and it closed with the loudest click she ever heard.

"You are a nice geyurl. I always think so."

He moved a little closer. He had not taken a shower after having sex with

Gina. He reeked of stale secretions and nervous sweat. His breath stank of beer. Her nausea made Gwen react.

"I was only going to have a peek."

She knew she had to keep from panicking. He was short, below her height. But he was compact and quick. And his hand was beginning to hurt her.

"My little peek," he murmured, moving still nearer. His rancid cologne gave his body odour a musky stench that close and Gwen felt she was going to be sick.

"Mr. Kyriakopoulos."

He wasn't listening. Suddenly pulling her to him, he pinned her arms to her sides and kissed her, smearing his lips over her face. Gwen winced from the rasp of his mustache and unshaven face. She squirmed and this excited him more. Rubbing against her, he put a hand on her rump, cupping and squeezing it hard and almost pulling off her skirt. Gwen gasped. The hand lifted her skirt and slid between rump cheeks and under the hem of her panties. Callused fingers like sandpaper tried to get inside her, nearly lifting her off the floor. The hand came around to the front and Kyriakopoulos shoved a knee between her legs. He lifted her skirt again and pulled down her panties. Gwen felt a rush of cool air. She began to scream and he slammed her head against his chest, stifling her with his stink. She kicked him in the shins. He slapped her hard twice. To Gwen they were like punches. She felt she was passing out and her head went slack. Kyriakopoulos tore away her jacket, blouse and skirt and pulled off her panties and let go and she slumped to the floor. Lying there naked except for her undershirt and sneakers, she felt the cold carpet on her legs. He yanked his pants and boxer shorts down and she could see his partial erection. She knew from sex education class what he wanted to do and she reached for her jacket. One chance and the knife was better but she got the fork. Two steps and he fell on top of her, stiff now. With both hands Gwen jabbed upwards as he fell, sticking the fork into his belly. He yelled and got up, pulling at his shirt to see what had happened. The fork stuck out of him like a second erection, bobbing as it oozed blood.

Gwen crawled to the door and pulled herself up by the doorknob and kept turning. She twisted the knob hard and the door finally opened. But

Kyriakopoulos had pulled out the fork and thrown it aside. He rushed towards her, holding his belly with his hand. She ran to her jacket and snatched the dinner knife.

"Stay away from me." The knife shook in her hand.

The door was ajar. Kyriakopoulos shut it, again with his foot. Gwen started to whine. Kyriakopoulos stepped free of his crumpled pants and kicked them away. They were both half-naked. Still holding his belly, he advanced in a crouch towards her. Gwen moved away but he forced her into a corner, waving his free arm and coming closer. His stink smothering her, she could sense his hatred of her easy presumption of superiority. Erect again. Gwen stopped whining, waited for him to move close enough for the one stab she would have. Grimacing with pain, he lunged and grabbed her by an armpit, squeezing so tightly Gwen thought the flesh would rip, but she pulled to get low and swung her free arm up like a hook, driving the knife into his scrotum, slitting the penis shaft and sliding deep into underbelly. The knife was from Carol Chalmers' best set. The blade disappeared into the caretaker as if he were a pudding. He howled and fell over, hands clutching at the handle. Gwen ran to the door and it opened easily this time. She raced up the fire stairs to her apartment and pounded on the door. When Carol opened it, her half-naked daughter fell fainting into her arms.

Five minutes later a patrol car and five minutes after that an ambulance, its siren wailing, came to the front entrance. About to check suites on the fourth floor, Lynch put the ring of keys back around his neck and crept across the hallway to the fire stairs. He scurried down to the basement and, seeing no police, ran for the boiler room. Later some tenants talked as they waited for the elevator. He put his ear to the door.

"Hear about the caretaker? Tried to rape one of the girls in the building. I heard the cops talking. She practically cut his thing off with a steak knife. Ambulance took him to the emergency ward. The doctors are going to be busy. Sewing up his guts and his junk."

Chapter 4

Madeline and her mother came to see Gwen the next afternoon. She was in bed. Madeline sat on the bed and looked at Gwen's bruised armpit. Left alone afterwards, they didn't say anything for a while. Madeline's sigh broke the silence.

"I should have stayed. Told my mom something."

"It wasn't your fault, Maddy. I shouldn't have gone alone with him to that suite."

"What's going to happen to that slime?"

"Mom says he'll be charged with the attempted rape of a juvenile and also assault and battery. He'll probably plead guilty because there's so much evidence against him, and so there'll be no trial. She says his defence counsel will tell him to plead extenuating circumstances and throw himself on the mercy of the court. Say he'd been drinking. The police took my statement and that's all they need from me."

"Your mom told us about you carrying the knife and fork. How come you had them with you?"

"I took them with the dinner. He eats with his fingers. I was planning to improve his table manners. I had everything wrapped in foil and he tore it off and shovelled everything down before I could take them out of my pocket. I thought, this is the last time I try teaching you any table manners, you old bastard."

Her smile twitched into fragments. Madeline gave her a hug.

"I can't go near the caretaker's suite or the boiler room," Gwen said after another long silence. "You'll have to take him his meals and to his new place. We can't wait. There'll be a new caretaker right away."

"Don't worry, Gwenner. Mom says I can stay."

That afternoon they watched Dr. Todd's latest video. He was Skyping with Earthworm Bart, who explained the idea behind Bug Save, his animal rights organization. A chaos of hair and a full beard covered his head and face, except for his eyes. His beard parted when he spoke.

"All living creatures are sentient beings and shouldn't be killed. That includes insects and what I call 'creatures of the soil.' I remember I went fishing when I was a kid and some of the boys put worms on their fish hooks. I never forgot the sight of those worms wriggling on the hooks. It changed my life. Without worms no soil, no grass, no animals, no people. It's as simple as that. It's not only cruelty-free, it's essential for life."

He outlined the aims of Bug Save.

"Ban insecticides, including domestic bug sprays. Ban the importation of dried bugs from Thailand. Put pressure on the Chinese government to stop the sale of bugs in open-air markets. Centipedes, millipedes, water bugs, locusts. Begin a campaign in Cambodia and Laos to stop the disgusting practice of breaking open termite mounds and swallowing the queens. Their bodies are swollen, rippling with eggs."

Dr. Todd had questions.

"What about mosquitoes? They carry diseases."

"Use window screens, netting over beds. Coils outside."

"What about the bacteria that live in and on our bodies?"

"I respect them by not washing and by not combing my hair."

"And what does your girlfriend or wife think about that?"

"My girlfriend left me."

"I've noticed there's lots of room around you at animal rights parades and conferences, and I don't think it's your signs and T-shirt slogans. 'Don't Bug the Bugs.' 'Sentience Flies, Digs and Crawls.' 'Soap Kills.' 'Life Stinks.'"

"They don't want me around because I'm not campaigning for cute faces with big round eyes, the kind of stuff that looks good on posters."

"Would you kill a wasp if it was going to sting you?"

"No."

"And if you faced an attack by a whole nest?"

"I'd find cover somewhere."

"Suppose there wasn't any?"

"I'd sacrifice my life so they could live. If I had made them angry, I'd deserve to be stung."

"What's your view of agricultural spraying? Even organic farmers have to kill pests."

"I don't like that word. You can't outsmart bugs. Enough will survive any spray. You get into a downward spiral of using stronger and stronger chemicals. We're poisoning the earth. I'm a fruitarian, travel the world and eat ripe fruits in season. We have to plant orchards everywhere. Along with their vitamins and minerals, the fat and protein in fruit provides you with all you need to be healthy."

Gwen reached for the mouse.

"Enough of his crazy grin and staring eyes. Fat and protein in fruit? He's a skeleton, looks ready to fall over. Why is Dr. Todd interviewing the walking dead?"

Madeline shook her head.

"He's after subscribers, it's a business. Notice he mentioned his new book again?"

Late in the afternoon Madeline took a bag down to Lynch. He had been waiting, knowing she would come, that they wouldn't abandon him. The other one come with grub, 'cluding meat and that bottle of good beer. Two more coming. Keeps her word. Lots of money and pull. Nuthin' hammer them flat. Always get up singing.

"Don't sprise me," Lynch said after Madeline told him what had happened. "Dangerous looking. Reminds me of a Turk name of Mustaphee I come across in Tripolee in the Sixties. Good with a knife. Sliced me up a bit. But I was too fast for him and got away. Jealous 'cause a harem girl called Serenee was in love with me."

"What did she die of after she ran away with you?" Madeline said, grinning.

Lynch stared at her before groping inside a trench coat pocket and taking out a granola bar. The crumpled remains of his late lunch were strewn between them. He was sitting on his pile of blankets and Madeline was sitting a few feet away on an old coat Gwen had given her. It seemed nobody wanted to use the one-piece plastic chair. Madeline noticed Lynch needed a shave as well as another shower. She had left the door ajar. He stank like rotten fish. Did he smell it? Must be used to it. How long had he been like this? All his life? Did he ever do anything else?

"How long have you been homeless?"

"More years 'n you had hot dinners."

"What did you do before?"

"Worked at different jobs. Longest was couple of years as a gandy dancer, fixing track on the railway."

"Why did you quit?"

"Got tired making it easy for people to go places and me going nowheres."

"Have you ever been on welfare or received unemployment benefits?"

"Tried to get some govmint money years ago. Went to a 'ploymint office. The smartyass bitch says I got to have docmints, like a certifeycat that shows I was born. Ya can see I was, can't ya? I says to her. She says I got to get a birth certifeycat saying I'm a citizen, ain't snuck in like them 'llegal miggrants or refuges. I ain't the right colour to be one of them, I says. Asks where was I born? Back East somewheres, I says, but I left 'fore I found out the 'xact spot. Wants to know my birthday. Told her don't know 'cause nobody never give me one. She asks how I know my name. One time a guy yells at my pa, 'You dirty bastard, Lynch.' I figured the only part belonged to me was 'Lynch.' Pa called me a 'little bastard' a few times 'fore he throwed me out, but like the other time I reckoned 'little bastard' weren't mine. Smartyass tells me I got to have records of 'ploymint. Told her jobs I worked don't keep no records, 'cept for the railway, and that was more 'n forty years ago. Probly forgot me by now. She wants my phone number so the govmint can reach me. Got none, I says. Ask 'round the missions and the waterfront, you'll find me. Wants my address, but I told her I don't stay long enough in one place. Tells me she's a case worker and she's passing me on up to her supervisor and I should get busy and rustle up some docmints. Told her I ain't got money to go searching and don't know where to start. She says best thing is to get a job so I can have a 'ploymint record. Never went back, figured govmint money weren't comin' my way 'cause of too many politicians divvying it up 'tween theirselfs like they own it aready."

"It must be hard living your way."

"I get meals at the missions and a bed there. If it's real cold and erywheres is full up, I get a bunch a newspapers and sleep in a dumpster, out of that wind. Summers is all right for sleeping outside. Liquor costs a lot. But I always been good at bumming money."

Lynch peeled the wrapper off the granola bar and bit off half the bar and began chewing with his sparse stumpy teeth. As his jaw worked down and sideways, hesitating occasionally on the gummy wad, Madeline could see that eating was difficult for him sometimes. The exaggerated stretch and contraction of cheek and jaw muscles covered with dirty stubble gave him the look of an old dog. He noticed her watching him.

"What's in these things?"

"Oats, nuts, dried fruit. Good for you."

"Don't taste so hot."

"You need protein. And carbohydrates for energy. They've got both. Next time I'll bring peanut butter sandwiches."

"Peanuts is for squirrels. Don't bring me none of that junk. I won't eat it. I want meat."

"Meat hasn't done you much good."

"Don't get enough of it, that's why. Lot you know. People been eating meat for thousands of years. 'Cause it's 'portant. Why'd ya think meat costs so much and all them fancy restrants serves it? It's so 'portant, guess what? There's even a day reminding ya to be sure and fry some."

"Friday's named after the Germanic goddess Frigga," Madeline told Lynch politely.

"Ya. 'Cause frying's named after her, that's why. She's handy with a skillet. Ya got to go back to the beginnings."

"I think I'm getting a headache."

"Come up 'gainst me, ya got to have aminition. I know more 'n you'll ever know. I know some men make more money 'n your father. Stockbrokers. Used to kick in joints. Corner stores. Shoe stores. Took safes right out of buildings. Go through travellers' stuff in hotels when they was out. Fixed it up with the desk clerk. They're big shots now. Pretens they don't know me."

"Why aren't you a big shot?" Madeline felt she was being unfair but had to teach him to see things differently.

"Never had the luck. But I got time. Got plans that'll get me that luck. Get in anawheres I want."

"How?"

"Pick keys." He opened his shirt to show her his ring of keys.

"Where did you get them?"

"Biggest fence in the city. Guys buy 'em off him for jobs. Fences what they get. He had 'em made by a reglar locksmith. He don't know I know."

"Are they expensive?"

"I didn't pay."

"Does he know you've got them?"

"What'd ya think?"

"You shouldn't steal."

Madeline thought about the morality of one thief stealing from another. And about wealthy men who had been thieves. This wasn't like school. It was a kind of school, though.

Lynch grinned, his jaw dropped. The gaps in his front teeth made him look like a shrunken Halloween pumpkin.

"Ya haven't lived my kind of life. Don't know what tough is. You girls are babies. You're spoilt too. I hung around with other guys, that wore 'spensive suits and drove fancy cars. They ended up doing time or dying of a overdose. No more easy women. No luck."

"Do you know anyone who isn't dead or ignores you?"

"Sure. But ya wouldn't like 'em 'cause ya don't like me. Don't gimme that look. I know what you and your friend thinks of me."

"Why do you stay?"

"I stay where there's grub and a place to flop."

"And maybe we can't resist helping a dirty bum who thinks we're spoiled bitches."

Lynch slapped his knee.

"Tell ya what. Want to meet some friends of mine?"

"Now? All right. I have to tell my mom I'll be away for the afternoon. She's upstairs."

Madeline returned in less than fifteen minutes, told her mother she was going to visit a girlfriend for a few hours. To Gwen a few whispered words. She decided to change her clothes. From her overnight bag she picked out her sweatshirt, poplin jacket and an old pair of jeans. She gathered her hair in a ponytail. They left through the rear exit and walked to a bus stop, Madeline with their bus fare. Lynch waited for a bus that would take them to the downtown eastside, the oldest part of the city, long ago abandoned by pioneers. Working class families had succeeded them, living in or replacing the old houses and businesses. But now the business core, with its stores, hotels and pubs, was skid row, a place for drug addicts, winos, hookers, the homeless and a few pensioners. They got off at a stop across from the Western Hotel. One of the oldest in the area, it had a reputation. Many of the rooms were used by hookers for their tricks. In the pub downstairs drug deals went on openly without any interference from the police. Stabbings were common, ambulances routinely picking up the wounded and dead. Backs to the wall, veteran Western customers watched for flying beer bottles.

Lynch led the way across the street, passing the corner on which the hotel stood. They walked three blocks north towards the waterfront and four blocks east. Madeline saw hookers almost as young as she was talking with gaudy pimps or being picked up by customers in cars. She saw a man suddenly run over and for no apparent reason push a mailbox and a newspaper box into the road. Another man continually waved his arms at buildings and swore. A woman carrying a bag of groceries close to her chest turned around every few seconds and shouted at the empty air, "Get away, ya fucking bastard." Lynch would look up every so often and Madeline wondered why until he pushed her towards the wall of a hotel as a beer bottle casually tossed out of a window a few storeys above smashed nearby on the sidewalk. Occasionally, someone would step towards them, asking in a low voice if they needed anything. She knew this meant drugs. They passed two policemen talking to a barely conscious wino sitting on the sidewalk, his shoulders propped against a wall, head on his chest. Up the block a middle-aged woman sat in a puddle of her own pee, staring ahead stupefied as a long finger of it ran into the gutter. Across the street two other policemen were talking to a dazed man bleeding from a slashed arm and his right ear. It was hanging by a flap of skin. She heard a siren and looked as an ungainly ambulance was swung against the flow of traffic. It parked on the wrong side of the street and two white-uniformed paramedics jumped out with first aid kits and a stretcher.

Lynch's destination was an old two-storey wood frame house near the waterfront. It stood on a block of similar homes. Across the street were warehouses, machine shops and the offices of shipping and stevedoring companies. Some front yards were overgrown with weeds and the fences leaned over. A clutter of car parts, sprung mattresses and boxes of junk filled many porches. Lynch stopped at a grey house with peeling white trim. He lifted the latch on a rusted gate made of pipe and wire mesh. A broken sidewalk led to sagging porch steps. On the porch wooden crates once used for glass pop bottles were full of gears and other machine parts and stacked beside a rusty hot water tank. A rough square of pale blue sheet metal was nailed next to the house number. Painted on it in broad brushstrokes of navy blue, "Al's Splendid." Inside the glass panel in the door hung lace curtains brown from dust and smoke. With two knuckles Lynch rapped on the panel. A minute later the curtains parted slightly.

"It's me, Al."

"Ah kee." The voice sounded thin, nervous.

"I'm with somebody. She come in?"

"A wimman?"

"She's a girl."

"Ah kee."

The door opened slowly and they stepped into a dim hallway. Madeline saw a small, pale man, almost bald. He tilted forward on tiptoe, seemed to be bowing, his hands clasping and unclasping continually. He looked at her as if she were going to hit him.

"This here's Madeline. Who ya got floppin'?"

"Farmer."

"How's he doing?"

"Ah kee." The little man kept glancing at Madeline.

"She's all right, Al. Let's go see Farmer."

"Ah kee, beeb, wee're un ur wee."

The man swivelled half a turn on the balls of his feet. He ran towards the back of the house, hands clasping and unclasping. He was quickly out of sight. A screen door creaked open.

"Al's 'fraid of women," Lynch said. "I brung ya 'cause you're a girl. He'd never let a grown woman in. Thinks they're going to hurt him. Was raised up by his aunt. She beat him all the time, starved him. Used to lock him in the cellar. Had a girlfriend long time ago. A lady truck driver. She beat him up real bad once 'cause he's late for a dance. Had some bad luck with women."

Madeline could see through a glass door a small dining room to the left of the hallway. To the right through a broad archway was the front parlour. Everything in shades of brown, a musty smell came from it. The buffet and coffee table were heavy and dark, the sofa and padded armchairs worn, stuffing spilling out of backs and cushions. The floor rug, pile gone, had a tear running almost the entire length of it. Both ashtrays on the coffee table overflowed with cigarette butts. They walked along the hallway, old studio photographs in oval frames hanging on the walls. At the back, the large kitchen gave off a sour stink. The door under the sink was open and Madeline could see bloated plastic shopping bags piled there seeping a fermenting decay. Noisy flies crawled over them or swarmed above, making the most of late August.

Lynch opened the screen door and they stepped out onto the porch. A wooden lawn chair with a leg missing leaned against the railing. The stairs led down to a cracked walkway and a scrap of lawn full of tall dandelions, late summer breezes thinning their fuzzy seedtops. Inside the back fence two rows of cedar stakes for tomato plants still stood but the plants had vanished years ago. Surrounded by thistle, horsetail, buttercups and vagrant daisies, the weathered stakes tilted at odd angles. Beside them was a garage, the siding

49

grey from age and rain. The little man had gone inside and the door was open. As they walked towards it, he came out with a tall, rawboned man who looked about fifty. He had a square face with thin lips and the most vacant eyes Madeline had ever seen. She thought of eyes in a puppet.

"Hi, Farmer," Lynch shouted. He went over and shook the man's hand.

"Hullo." The man's voice was dull, without inflexion.

"How ya doin'?"

"Ahm doon fyhn." He looked at Madeline but didn't seem to see her.

"This here's Madeline."

"Hullo."

"Hi." Madeline nodded as she answered, a little afraid of him.

"You know 'bout Balvoline? I use nuthin' 'cept Balvoline."

"That's his engine oil," Lynch told her.

"Everything uses Balvoline. The car 'specially. The train. The ship. Plane. Combine harvester. You need some, girl."

"She's got plenty for now, Farmer. Give her some later."

"Girl, you'll take some. Ahm working on the car. Every part needs Balvoline. The pistons, 'specially. And the bearings, chain, cams."

"Ah kee, Farmer, wee know. Wee'll be un ur wee."

Farmer turned, walked stiffly back into the garage and shut the door.

"Put that nut case back into his crankcase," a woman said from the next backyard. A high wooden fence blocked their view. The little man ran into the house, his hands clenched in front of him. The screen door squeaked open and shut.

"Scurry, little spider," the woman said.

"Hi, Sylvia," Lynch shouted.

"Thought I heard you, Lynch. Haven't seen you in a while."

"Meet ya by the side gate, Sylvia."

A concrete walkway ran between the houses. Parallel with the front of the house was a gate similar to the one at the street. The wooden fence ended there and a low wire one replaced it. The woman was standing where the fences met. Big but not fat, she had a round face with hazel eyes and full lips and grey hair dyed light cinnamon. She seemed to have been born with a challenging grin. Her housedress was blue with a pattern of scarlet roses, a white apron was tied around her waist and gumboots came up to her knees. She handed some tomatoes in her apron over the fence to Lynch.

"You're still skin and bones. Why don't you eat better?"

"'Cause I don't have a beauty like you growing stuff for me."

"You drink too much. Who's your friend?"

"Name's Madeline."

"How are you, dear?" Sylvia smiled, dimples in her cheeks.

"Fine, thanks."

"You're a pretty girl. Such fine white skin. I had skin like that once. Leonard, my husband, he's dead, used to say it was like silk. But you get older and fatter."

"You're still a beauty, Sylvia. I'd show ya if ya'd let me."

"Sure you would, you old bastard."

Sylvia shook her head as she looked at Madeline's jeans.

"You're dressed too tight, dear. Like most young people."

"I feel comfortable."

"Because you're young. You'll feel all scrunched up when you're older. Stomach and everything else. Tight's no good for your circulation."

"I'd get your circlation going, Sylvia, wherever it's slowed up."

"Look after your own, Lynch. Eat a tomato and shut up. Loose clothes are better, dear. I bet you wear panties. I wear shorts."

She lifted her dress, showing a large pair of chocolate boxer shorts encircling her hips and belly. Her dimpled thighs were mottled pink and white. Madeline saw that Sylvia's legs were covered in pale hair. Wolf woman.

"When you want to pee, pull them aside and squat. Lots of room, see?"

Sylvia pulled at the legs of her shorts. Madeline nodded, trying hard not to grin.

"Growing anything 'sides tomatoes?" Lynch asked. And hair, Madeline thought.

Sylvia let go of her shorts and her dress fell over them.

"Green beans, cucumbers, squash. garlic. Why'd you take a girl to that house of loose screws?"

"Meet my friends."

"That'll make her think a lot of you."

"Wants to know 'bout homeless people."

"She won't find out from that place. That little guy isn't homeless, he's gutless. A picture of a naked woman is enough to make him dive under the bed. And you know what the one in the garage does all day. Sits in an old car. Pretends he's fixing it. He wanted to give me some of his Balvoline once. Came to the backyard gate. I put the hose on him. Never bothered me again."

"Al's a good guy. Gives ya a place to flop. Free grub, too. Left the house and money by some relations. Cousin, I 'member."

"If she wants to see how the homeless live, take her to the packing crates under the viaduct and the dumpsters along the alleys in skid row. Find Slouch Annie, who wheels her belongings in a shopping cart and sleeps in doorways."

"I ain't hiding nuthin'. But no place is like Al's."

"You're right about that. She met any of the others?"

"Not yet. We better go. It's getting on. Got to get her back 'fore dark."

"Next time, Madeline, I'll give you some of my cucumber pie. Not like it sounds. Or maybe a blueberry sandwich. The secret is to melt your butter on wholewheat toast. But with strawberries you want white untoasted bread and cold butter."

"Butter your bread any way ya want, Sylvia, and I'll slip some meat in."

"Bet you would, you tricky little sneak. Bye, Madeline."

Madeline said goodbye, ambivalent about Sylvia. Boxer shorts and hairy legs. And that glimpse of armpit hair, like tiny beards sticking out. But honest, warm. Not a phony. Called her pretty. She knew that. Perhaps beautiful?

They entered by the front door again. In the parlour this time were two men, both in their mid-thirties. One was thin, of medium height, his hair in a ponytail. Over a white shirt he wore a green sweater with several holes in it. His jeans had shredded into strings at the knees and cuffs. He was sitting in one of the armchairs. The other man was shorter and pudgy and wispy tufts were retreating in a series of messy campaigns across the top of his head. What was left was uncombed. He wore a baggy beige corduroy jacket, a checked shirt and badly worn rust brown corduroy pants shiny smooth at the knees.

He was sprawled on the sofa and drinking coffee from a mug. When Madeline and Lynch walked in, the man with the ponytail was speaking.

"You can't reform society until you reform people's minds, and no one can do that. That's why utopias are doomed. People won't conform to what they can't be. Every reformer's plans go awry because they depend on perfect people to work, and that's the problem. No reformer ever factors into his equations that the human species loves its imperfections. Technology serves them, always has. Bigger bombs, more freeways, moronic television, video games, the narcissistic social media, government surveillance, junk food, fast food, all presided over by the editorial illiterati. Which makes the *Republic*, More, Owen, Kropotkin, Proudhon, Ruskin, Morris and all the misguided others ultimately irrelevant."

The other man sneered.

"What can you expect from retards who buy lotto tickets and watch the endless meaningless seasons called professional sports and bet the line or the point spread, have the aesthetic appreciation of road gravel, are spiritually inert and proud of it and worship technology. Because it gives them a digital thrill, making them the ape gods they've always wanted to be."

"You're looking too low," the man with the ponytail said. "The real failure is higher up, with the elaborately educated who peddle themselves because they don't want to dig ditches for a living. The advertising and public relations prostitutes, the bleating professors, the hired scientists who lie, all dedicated to the good cause of their own employment. It isn't called propaganda any more, it's called education and information. The emperor hasn't only got new clothes, he's got a whole new way of life. Anyone who would dare say it's naked self-serving opportunism would get smacked down by all the believers. Nothing like having your victims on your side. The problem for humans has always been that most can't think and most of the few who can are for sale. If any thinkers who can't be bought cause trouble, they're rounded up and put away. At the top are the buyers of brains, protecting their own interest by selling everybody else out and feeling good while they're doing it. And the current version of the public has been taught to want more and more things. Buy and sell, buy and sell, like a tolling bell. Don't ask why and spend like hell. It's the earth as one big shopping mall, it's the new religion."

"You sound like a defender of the great unwashed," the other man said, raising his eyebrows slightly.

"You prove my point," the other said. "Nobody wants to be equal. People have an inherent need to believe they're better or worse than others, most opting for better. Those who can take advantage of this need get their money or vote or life. I've known lots like you, you'll be sorry to hear. Educationally indoctrinated snobs who get a cheap high out of smirking at anyone without the correct set of authorized intellectual passwords. What's most pathetic is that each of you, with your knapsack of borrowed ideas making up the latest version of those battered eternal truths, secretly thinks and quite truthfully believes in your intellectual heart of hearts you're superior to all the rest of your type."

"Reform, to use your outdated word, will happen in its own time," the other said, face stiffening along with his voice. "It's an incremental blind force subconsciously evolving to a higher level. It's evident as a latent revelation first to the more perceptive. It inevitably reaches upwards for fulfilment to the ultimate state, oneness with the universe."

"I 'member reaching for 'filmint once 'fore she slapped me," Lynch said. He and Madeline had remained near the doorway and the men hadn't noticed them.

"Lynch," the man with the ponytail said and got up and shook Lynch's hand.

"Hi, Speaker. When'd ya get back?"

"A couple of days ago. Came here and have been talking ever since."

The three walked the few steps from the hallway to the parlour archway. The man lying on the sofa looked Madeline over with lazy eyes as he spoke to Lynch.

"We were discussing the lower orders. The intellectually deficient."

"I heard Speaker all right," Lynch said, happy to return the favour. A look at Madeline. "Better at arguing than anybody, 'cluding that Kevin over there."

"This here's Madeline," he said to Speaker. "She's visiting today. Got to get back pretty soon. To Lockin Tower."

Speaker smiled. His eyes looked kind to Madeline, as if he knew something nice about her.

"This must seem a strange place."

"I'm getting used to it."

"Don't get too used to it. Could be a bad influence. Keep you from believing everything you see on television or the Internet. Nothing is true here. It's all in your mind. You're seeing, hearing and judging with your experience. Less to do with us than you."

"Stop trying to impress her," Kevin said and yawned, stretched out and closed his eyes.

"I'm giving her an elementary lesson in perception."

"Sounds like elementary school."

Speaker grinned at Madeline and returned to his chair, picked up a book and began to read. The little man had come silently from the kitchen and was hovering in the archway, motionless except for his agitated hands.

"What's the talking about, Lynch? What'd Speaker say?"

"I dunno. Stuff 'bout Crackpot and Roughskin."

"Ah kee. Come to ask if you'll have something, and the wimman."

"Guess we got time. What ya got?"

"Oxtail soup."

"Catch me turning down a piece of meat."

"Ah kee, beeb, wee're un ur wee."

He skittered down the hallway, followed by Lynch, Madeline and a few minutes later by the others.

Madeline saw the same bags of garbage under the kitchen sink but smelled less stink and decided the smell of the soup was masking it. As she entered she saw a pantry to her right. The sink was against the east wall of the north-facing house and had a window over it, and the back wall had windows along the length of it, making the room bright even in the declining light of the early part of an August evening. Almost against the back wall was the table, long and narrow and made of maple. Knife cuts and cigarette burns scarred the edges. Farmer was already seated at one end, near the sink. He was staring straight ahead, an empty plate in front of him. Madeline and Lynch sat near the other end. Speaker and Kevin sat in the middle, one on each side of the table. The little man was at his stove, against the opposite wall. He was on tiptoe, stirring a wooden spoon into a large pot.

"A minute and wee're ready."

"Al's known for his soup and biscuits," Lynch told her. "He could make soup from a dead rat and the sewer scum it was floating on and ya'd swear it was from the best restrant in town."

"That's what the best restaurants serve," Kevin said.

"Too obvious," Speaker said.

The little man took the spoon out of the pot and sipped some broth. Nodded. "Ready." Speaker went over, and with each using a kitchen towel to hold onto a handle, they carried the pot to an evenly scorched circle on the table. Speaker got a ladle, spoons and knives, and a plate for everyone but Farmer. From the oven Speaker brought a platter heaped with biscuits, and from the refrigerator a butter dish. He handed out plates, spoons and knives, Madeline noting that he touched only the edges of the dishes and the handles of the utensils. Speaker brought the platter of biscuits to her and she took one. It felt warm and smelled of baked wheat flour and crust and slightly of soda. She picked up her knife and sliced the crunch of crust. She put both halves on her plate. Everybody had sat down, the cook and host at the opposite end to Farmer after he had ladled out soup to everybody.

She bit her lip. Better tell them.

"I'm a vegan. I only eat plant foods."

"I respect your choice," Speaker said, "but I think you're misguided."

"We don't need to eat animals. We can live on plants."

"You want to save the animals. Fair enough. But we don't thrive long-term on plants. Vegan authorities make that a corollary to the moral proposition because they know most people, if asked to sacrifice their health to save animals, wouldn't do it."

"I feel fine."

"How long have you been a vegan?"

"For almost a year."

"You're young. You could compromise your health."

"How?"

"Deprive yourself of animal foods and your body will get them from the only animal it can. You'll cannibalize yourself. Spirulina, chlorella, wheatgrass, tofu and other vegan miracles don't give you what animal foods do. We don't know more than nature and if we deny ours, we suffer. The fact is, we're omnivores, opportunistic eaters, and always have been. It's the world we live in. I didn't make it, you didn't. We're stuck with it."

He studied her for a moment.

"You remember the miracle of the loaves and fishes, when Christ fed a multitude?"

Madeline nodded. Why was he bringing in religion?

"When you can work miracles, you don't go halfway, you do the very best. I can hear the vegan take on that. The beans and rice combo wasn't handy. Couldn't fly in papayas and pineapples. Grapes and olives were available. And yet it was fish to go with the bread. Nutritionally it was the best combination. Still is."

"What about the Eucharist, the bread and wine? There's no animal protein."

"You're talking transubstantiation, ritual and symbol, not nutrition. Each in its place, Madeline."

"I hear some of the plant profiteers cheat," Kevin said. "Guzzle fish oil on the side. Been known to enjoy spare ribs. A fleshly pleasure hidden from the faithful. All the while preaching their message of turning the world into a petting zoo. Political correctness has moved on from declaring equality between races, minorities, ethnic groups and genders to warring against speciesism, now declaring equality between us and other animals. Where does it stop? Is a termite a sentient being? Doesn't have big round eyes or suck tits? The animal rights groups wouldn't get far with one of them on their posters. Mustn't confuse bugs with the real thing. People might catch on and see the fingers going for their wallets. Girls and soyboys go for the vegan bullshit, not letting facts get in their way. We routinely abuse and kill our own species and engage in organized slaughters called wars. But let's save the piggies.

"We're all here, I suppose. Joke, anyone? It's wasted on this air. Why bother? But that's the point of it all.

"Is nobody going to bless the meal? Bless me Father for I will binge. May we be grateful for this stuff we stuff into us. Oxtail soup. Tale of the ox, for those of us who need a story. Vertebrae for the peasants because they haven't the backbone to challenge the owners of this crummy society. I be not one of the gang at the trough who swill the swill with a will. I'm smart enough to work for them and stupid not to. But stupidities come in awful sizes, and mine is one of the lesser ones. There's nothing wrong with being broke, destitution is a state of mind. Under their very noses a rebel but a tame one after all. Nobody would hire me, anyway. I'm too much of a truth teller. One of the bastards who won't take the money and shut up about it. Don't worry, you human gods to whom the masses owe their souls, you will always be winners. No one else wants to be or can. Man is a ruthless animal and must be governed ruthlessly. And you dreamers of wet political dreams. Stop what you're doing unless it pleases you by hooking the voters, those animals. No politician loves those who vote for him. The con artist can never love the conned. They're the prey, raw meat on the hoof.

"Which brings me back to this soup lingering on my plate. Shall I eat it or fertilize the grass? Which brings up starvation. So the necessities bore us with their promptings. I know what the rest of you are thinking as I prate. Eat the shit—pardon me, mine good and kind host—and do shut up, for Christ's sake. And so I shall, and proceed with spoon. May we have silence, please, for one who gave up on others many years ago because he can't give up on himself.

"We all have excuses for what put us among the trash. I've given you mine. It's a lie, like all the others. We're liars, every one us, and we prove it by staying down here. Addicts, winos, alkies, whores, crazies of greater and lesser breeds. All we do is give the government one more excuse for the money it steals from the rest of society's pockets. And we mustn't forget the social workers, those so-caring folk that go home at five. We give them a pay cheque and a reason for living. What do they give us? Excuses for being what we were born to be: society's scum. You've got to have scum or you can't pretend you're better. Tour the asylum, visit the monkey house. And I'm one for cages, as long as I can open mine and leave when I want. I don't choose to now, but that doesn't mean I never will. So unlike the rest of you, I keep my options open. I won't give up on a mentally sick society that sees us as its crazies. That means there's hope for me to break out and get with the truly sick. I may do that for a laugh. But that means paying taxes and voting and living in a suburban idyll where people pick up their dog's shit and put it in the appropriate bin. You have to be taught about the trash so you know what to keep and what to throw away, or else how would you know? When it comes to us it's simple. We're trash, every one of us, and we know it. We don't have to be told about bins because we live in the biggest one of all. And when another piece of garbage lands among us, we know by the smell it belongs here. So, my fellow refuse, have a good sniff at life. It's the only one we're allowed, and it's not the worst. Beyond our borders lies the real asylum, where you have to be the kind of crazy that can't see the bars."

"So you're one of them," Kevin said, looking at Madeline. "Ruined my last Christmas. I'm expecting turkey and the sister-in-law brings this thing to the table, looks like a giant bologna, and sets it down in front of the assembled guests. We're having a vegan turkey, the dumb cunt says. Made with sweet potatoes, with nuts and seeds and bread crumbs added. That's stuffing, I said. You need a fucking bird to stuff that thing into. We're not having a bird, we've gone vegan, she says. You've gone fucking crazy, I told the bitch. My brother says he forgot to tell me. A cuck, that one. Always kissing her ass. One of those dumbfucks with his nose between a woman's ass cheeks. They have this monster. They call it their son. A vicious whiny little bastard. Starts in on me. You're not getting any turkey, you're not getting any turkey. I said, shut up, you little prick, or we'll shove you into the oven and cook you. He starts screaming and the sister-in-law goes into her act. You've frightened poor whatever-the-fuck-the-monster's-name is. I'm a meat eater, I said, and I don't really care where it comes from. You have any meat for a traditionally-minded atheist? Didn't have a fucking thing. She's quieted the monster by now and it throws a spoon at me. She slices the shit, puts a slab of it on my plate. Like a cross section of a vegan brain. My cuck brother says you've got to pretend it's real turkey. Am I the only sane one here? I said to him. Tubers don't have wings. I could've gotten a real turkey dinner at the Harbour Light or Union Gospel mission. Why the hell don't you get out and go get one? the sister-in-law says. The birds have all been served and eaten, I tell her. I came here in good faith expecting a Christmas dinner. Am offered something nobody in skid row would go near blind drunk. Meanwhile the monster's crawled over and is gnawing on my shin. I kicked it away. Go chew on your mother, get some good nutrition, I told it, before she's a vegan skeleton. I shall wander out into the snow. It wasn't snowing, but what the fuck? Took a bottle of the local Bordeaux—they make their own wine, in plastic tubs, but they use real corks—and had to celebrate a barren Yuletide. Thanks be to the gods booze doesn't have to be blessed vegan. Yet. A turkeyless repast is a bitter memory."

He waved a fork.

"The vegans will shame the missions into no longer serving turkey at Thanksgiving and Christmas. Make us tramps more miserable, but maybe that won't bother them. They're out to reform us, not make us feel better. They'll serve some fake meat shit in an amorphous shape. Don't want to offend the turkeys by having fake meat look like a bird. No gravy. No backsliding meat grease. The plum pudding and the mince pie won't have any suet. Plenty of mashed potatoes, sprouts and yams. Cranberries, anyone?"

"Why not let the animals live?" Madeline said. "You can find something else to eat. We can finally let the turkeys have their own Thanksgiving. And Christmas is about Christ, not turkey."

"A little punk like you knows everything."

Speaker looked at Kevin. He didn't raise his voice.

"Don't ever speak to her that way again."

Kevin froze. He knew Speaker was ready to pounce, was looking for an excuse. The room was silent. He shrugged, went back to his soup. Speaker kept staring at Kevin. Make him squirm, Madeline thought. But she suspected there was more to Speaker's reaction to Kevin's crude comment than a need to come to her defence. His quiet intensity stemmed from something else.

"I met some vegans," Lynch said as Speaker began eating again. "I 'spect they're other space aileens."

"Did they recognize you?" Kevin mumbled. He was staring into his soup.

"They's too busy saving pigs. I told 'em they're wasting their time feeding 'em water. Ya butcher hogs, ya don't water 'em. They's pork chops, not petunias. I 'spect they're on to something else, more like using 'em to put thoughts in people's heads. So when ya eat bacon ya get something ya didn't bargain for, like your brain's controlled by vegan thoughts telling ya what to do. Like not eat bacon. Whole thing's to get people off meat so's ya can weaken 'em, tell 'em what to do. And they're starting with hogs 'cause they're sposed to be having bodies like us and be smart. Don't see it myself. Snouting 'round in mud all the time and eating any old kind of garbage."

"Isn't that what you do?"

"Can't hear ya 'cause ya got your nose buried in your soup. 'Fraid of something? Some peoples got big mouths. Catches up with 'em."

Lynch paused to slurp soup from the edge of his plate, for Kevin's benefit.

"Like I was saying, them vegans is up to something, and it ain't good. I'd watch 'em. They get their way, be 'gainst the law to eat meat. I ain't kidding. Have to smuggle your pork chops and beefsteak like drugs. Means high prices. And jail time if you're caught at it. Way I figure it, there's something going on out there in other space, and aileens come here to make us slaves. Taking meat away is the beginning. Your brain goes dead. They can do what they want to ya. Anathing. 'Spermint on ya. Make ya part pig, so you'll start oinking and have a big snout and be thinking pig thoughts and all like that."

"You're almost there now."

Kevin was back in form.

"I'm speclating, that's all."

"Expectorating, rather, the bizarre contents of your brain."

"I'm considering things. Thinking."

"Is that what you call it?"

"Better 'n what you're doing sitting on your fat ass and mouthing off as if nobody in the world's got a brain like yours. Think you're smart telling the rest of the world its business. How it's gone wrong. As if you can see into erybody else's brain, what they're thinking. I heard loads of bullshit in my time but what comes out of your mouth beats all. Don't have to tell people what they are. They know. Now why is another question. Figure that one out and you'd be smart. That's something no one has. And you pretens like your bullshit is better 'n anabody else's. It ain't no better. What're ya doing down here with all us lowlifes? You're like some salesman selling shit 'cause he's got nuthin' else. Only the shit is you. You can't smell it but erybody else can. Ain't sprised any more by what I find in garbage cans."

"Ah kee. Anybody want more soup?"

Hesitating, a glance at Madeline.

"Biscuits?"

"I'm fine." Madeline shook her head, wanting to be certain she was understood. She didn't know why but felt that she was talking to someone who would never understand her. The words would always have different meanings.

Lynch picked up his plate and drank the rest of his soup, the rim against his lips. Another plate would be fine, with meat.

Speaker went to the fridge and returned with a jar and handed it to Madeline. It was a jar of peanut butter.

"I do eat nuts and seeds and legumes and vegetables. I'm not a carnivore. I don't chew raw liver while quaffing a flagon of ox blood. Brought this the last time I stayed here."

Madeline looked at the label.

"It's organic."

"Buy the best when I can afford it."

Madeline thanked him and he sat down and resumed eating. She unscrewed the top of the jar and the nutty smell helped her forget the greasy sweet odour of bone marrow and fatty beef permeating the kitchen. Her queasiness left as her knife spread the peanut butter on the bottom half of the biscuit. She put on the top half and bit into her sandwich and the comforting taste and chewy texture filled her mouth. This was much better. She heard the small sound of metal clinking against dishes as the others ate. After refilling Lynch's plate, the host carried the pot, lighter and cooler now, back to the stove.

"Girl, have you got your Balvoline?"

Madeline choked on her biscuit.

"She's got enough, Farmer," Lynch said.

"Never."

Madeline took another bite as the screen door opened behind her. Turning to look, she saw a large man, almost as wide as he was tall, wearing a black slicker over a grey undershirt and baggy black pants. His floppy hat and big shoes were black. His face was round, beef red, and he needed a shave. Teeth like a truncated grove of burnt trees, he grinned at Lynch. He was carrying a black plastic garbage bag in his thick-fingered hand. The crammed bag was stretched to the breaking point by a jumbled geometry of carton and tetrapack edges and appeared heavy. His massive hand held it easily.

"Hi, Waste," Lynch said. "Ain't seen ya in a bit. How ya doing? I see ya got lots of stuff."

"This is the man that gets what others don't want."

Waste had a heavy voice, as if his tongue were stirring molasses. He put the bag down and took off his hat and slicker and dropped them on the bag and sat down next to Lynch, across from Speaker. The hat left a ring around his enormous bald head. The little man took a plate to the stove, filled it and set it down in front of him, together with a spoon and knife. Waste took a biscuit and put it all into his mouth and chewed, making his cheeks explode for a few seconds. Two neck-stretching swallows and he took another biscuit and did the same. He lifted up and tilted the plate, and with his spoon shovelled the soup into his mouth. Slicing some butter, soft now, he spread it over the two bones on his plate. Using his fingers he scraped the meat off, then sucked on the bones and the marrow, digging the last bits out with his knife. His plate was smeared with finger marks.

"Takes up the time," he said to Lynch. "Trash is the diggings and I'm the prospector. Every day something. Not the big strike yet, but I look. Cans. Bags. Boxes."

"What'd ya find today?"

"Today is the usual. The broken watch. The two cigars. The pens. The box of salt."

"Not like when ya found the hundreds. Get to the city dump?"

"That takes up the money and the time. Month ago."

"This here's Madeline."

"You'd make more as a garbage man." As soon as she had spoken, Madeline realized her mistake. Waste's eyes, like dirty puddles, turned on her. He didn't answer but appeared to grow larger as he stared, his mouth opening. His belch, the roaring of a dyspeptic walrus, made her laugh nervously.

"What's been your most interesting find?" Speaker said to draw attention away from her. Waste turned to look at him.

"That is the hard question. The curved dagger with the blood on it. The head of the monkey. The skinned dog. The hand. The woman's part. . . ."

"Anything old or rare?"

Waste dragged his slab of a hand across his nose.

"That is hard too."

Madeline remembered he didn't wash his hands before he ate. The rest didn't either. But their hands weren't in garbage. She looked at Speaker. What was he doing there? He was the only one who wasn't crazy. But he was wearing that sweater with all those holes in it. His jeans were so ragged they looked as if they were about to fall off. He sounded as if he had spent a long time in school. Probably had gone to university. Maybe there was something wrong with him she couldn't see. He could be crazier than the others. The kind that looked all right and was friendly with women, then murdered them and cut their bodies into little pieces. She had to get out of there. It was almost dark outside. Her mother was probably getting tragic. Why had she come?

"That is the sack with the baby in it," Waste said.

"I've got to call my mother to let her know where I am," Madeline shouted.

Everybody looked at her. The little man grabbed his empty plate and held it in front of him. Already standing, her knees weak, she hurried to the front parlour. Her fingers trembled as she took her phone out of the pocket of her jacket and called the Chalmers' apartment and waited. Her mother answered.

"Mom."

"Where are you, Madeline? We were getting worried about you."

"I'm at a friend's place. I'll be leaving soon."

"Has the girl got her Balvoline?" boomed Farmer's voice from the kitchen, followed by a lower one in an urgent tone.

"Who was that? That was a man's voice."

"It's nothing, Mom."

"You told me you were going to see one of your girlfriends."

"They're some people I met today."

"You don't even know them?"

"I'll be leaving soon. Don't worry."

"I'll drive over and pick you up. What, Roger? Roger says he'll drive over. Where are you?"

"I'm all right, Mom."

"After what happened to Gwen, I don't think you telling me you're all right is good enough. I'm calling the police."

"I'm leaving right now."

"I don't know. Don't you let anyone drive you. Phone for a taxi. I'll pay for it when you get here. Will you do that?"

"Ah kee."

"What did you say? Madeline, have they drugged you?"

"I said something I—I don't know why I said it."

"It sounded strange. You never talked that way before."

"Don't make a big thing of it, Mom. Hang up and I'll phone for a taxi."

"If your father had been more of a father, things like this wouldn't happen."

"What's he got to do with this, Mother? Why bring Dad into it? You're always bringing him into things so you can criticize him. Don't think I don't know that."

"I'm worried sick about you and he's off somewhere carefree but I'm the one you're upset with. Well, I'm here, so I guess I've got to accept. . . ."

"Don't say it, Mother."

"It's true, though. I'll hang up now and you phone for that taxi right away."

"Didn't I say I was?"

When Madeline returned to the kitchen, the little man was washing dishes. Speaker was reading a book. Crouched on the floor, Waste was searching through his bag. To her relief, Farmer wasn't there. He had gone back to the garage. Kevin was upstairs asleep. Lynch went up for a shave, using the communal mug, brush and razor in the second-floor bathroom. A few quick strokes before he hid the thirty dollars. He tore a piece of plastic off a half-empty package of toilet rolls beside the closed door and wrapped the scrunched-up bills in it. He squatted beside the toilet and reached behind it, wedging the wad between a loose baseboard and the moisture-slick paint peeling off the rotten plaster. Never know when you're going to get mugged by some punks. Why spend yours, anaways? There's others throwing theirs away. Madeline was looking for him when he returned, bits of dried lather on his chin.

"I phoned for a taxi. Are you coming?"

"What for?"

"I don't know. I asked, that's all. Are you coming? I'm getting tired."

"Ya want me to come back. Be a 'spermint for ya. You two brats think ya know erything. And I'm only a bum. But I showed ya I got friends. And they treated ya nice and gave ya something to eat. Ya didn't even say thanks. And you're trying to learn me."

"I was going to before leaving." Madeline spoke to her host's back. "I want to thank you for your biscuit. It was delicious." She didn't like observing social niceties that were a convenient form of lying, but the biscuit was tasty with the peanut butter.

He turned from the sink and looked at the floor.

"Ah kee, food's free, yur welcome," he murmured before going back to washing dishes.

"So if I come back with ya, are ya going to get me a better place than that crummy dump I'm in?"

"We talked about that before we came."

"I think he wants to go back with you," Speaker said, piecing together the situation from what he heard, "but doesn't want to appear eager. He's doing what everybody does, bargain for the best deal."

"I want to be treated right."

"You're after as much as you can get off them."

"What'd I do to ya, Speaker, for you to talk 'bout me like that?"

"Cut it. The more I say, the more she's going to know. Keep your mouth shut and go with her. And whatever happens, Madeline, you and whoever is in this with you will regret it."

"We only want to help."

"You don't know what help means."

"It doesn't mean being sour about everything."

"You're not old enough to say that."

"You don't know me and my girlfriend."

"I know what usually happens when people help. Most times they'd be better off not bothering."

"Now I know why you're wearing a sweater with so many holes in it."

"Maybe holes don't bother me."

"Maybe they should."

"You're wasting your time with me. I'll never accept your charity. Take him. He's perfect. Greedy enough to be reformed. You don't even have to preach to him. Feed him and give him a warm place to sleep. He'll make you feel better about yourself."

"I don't need to feel better about myself."

Madeline heard knocking at the front door. More than ever she wanted Lynch to go with her. She was irritated with Speaker. He had been four different people. The poorly dressed intellectual saying things she never heard before, the man who treated her nicely at the dinner table, a possible homicidal maniac who hid his lust for female blood behind a smile and now the skeptic questioning the basis of her compassion and integrity. She wouldn't make any promises. Speaker was waiting too, grinning. Her determination made her rigid. She willed Lynch to return. She hoped she wasn't blushing. She didn't blush easily.

"The taxi's here. Are you coming?"

"Ya got to treat me better."

Triumph glowed from Madeline. The tramp was irrelevant. She had won. She wouldn't look at Speaker.

"See ya Waste, Speaker. Thanks for the grub, Al. Ya can keep them tomatoes Sylvia give me. I put 'em in the fridge."

Lynch stuffed some biscuits into the pockets of his trench coat. Drying his hands with a kitchen towel, the little man turned from the sink.

"Ah kee, beeb, yur un yur wee."

"That was the meal that was good, and the talk," Waste said on his knees.

"See you, Lynch. Goodbye, Madeline." Speaker's smile was for her. Madeline wasn't looking.

"Goodbye," she said to everyone.

As they were leaving, Madeline saw a new arrival on the parlour sofa, a ragged man stretched out and snoring loudly. Walking down the front steps, she felt sad. Maybe she would return. In case anybody was looking, she sat in the back of the taxi with Lynch to show that she was democratic.

Madeline had the driver stop half a block from the front entrance of the building and made Lynch go to the rear. Muttering, he got out and the driver parked in front. She pressed the suite button and her mother's anxious voice came over the intercom. Once inside, Madeline ran to the exit and let Lynch in and installed him in the boiler room, its door still unlocked. On her way up from the basement, she got out of the elevator and knocked on the door of the caretaker's suite. There was no answer. Kyriakopoulos' replacement hadn't been hired or hadn't moved in yet. The boiler room was safe for another night.

Chapter 5

Madeline stood and absorbed the assault of her mother's hugs and kisses. Average looking, Mary Dalrymple resembled her daughter only in having dark hair. It was a shade lighter than Madeline's midnight shadow and without those moonlit waves. An earring dug into Madeline's cheek. She was embarrassed to be the object of such emotion in front of Gwen's parents. Gwen had deserved the hugs she got. She had survived real danger. But these embraces and repeated kisses were like forgiveness for being naughty. Madeline broke free and mentioned that the driver had to be paid. She headed for the safety of Gwen's bedroom. Roger left immediately to pay, despite Mary's protests. When he returned, she was seated on the chesterfield with Carol.

"Thanks, Roger," Mary said.

"Forget it."

He sat in his easy chair, wishing the woman would leave. Tiresome. Opinionated. But some people had to be endured, and her daughter was Gwen's best friend.

"I was telling Carol how worried I was about Madeline being kidnapped by a pervert. They seem to be all over the place these days."

"No more than before."

"You hear so much about them."

"It's newspapers and television. Great money makers, perverts."

"What do you mean?"

"You've heard of Cobbie Kind, Mr. Windy Opinions."

"Of course. I don't think he's windy. He owns the newspaper and one of the television stations. Got his own network."

Roger grinned.

"He's got a media empire. Buys up newspapers and magazines cheap, when they're losing money. Turns papers into tabloids full of 'Mom Seeks Justice,' 'Mom Mad' headlines. Boosts circulation right away. Turns every one around in a few months. His radio stations are mostly talk shows about murder, molestation, capital punishment and abortion. Market share way up. The same with television. Newscasts cover nothing but murder, rape, child molestation. Unless there's a serial killer around or a psycho uses an assault rifle in a kindergarten, molesters are their favourite targets. Follow every trial day by day. Affiliates echo his station's editorial line to castrate molesters, execute those who've committed more than one offence. Station managers and owners love those high ratings. Look at the rest of the lineup. Left versus right political debates. Talking heads with the same old rants about who's screwing society. Journalism full of gotcha headlines about scandals: drugs, sex and wild parties. Rah-rah sports. Sitcoms. Reality TV about stupid boring people. Talent shows with singing four-year-olds. Movies about families who rediscover love when the dog dies. Or hubby forgets the wedding anniversary and wifey sheds a few. All for couch potatoes who want something to go with their popcorn."

"You're talking about mainstream television," Carol said. "Kind is adding his own to the mix, that's all."

"These perverts are out there," Mary said. "He's alerting people to that. Perverts are born that way and should be castrated and the worst ones executed. I have no mercy for anybody who preys on children. Sorry, Roger, but I can't be dispassionate about child molesters."

"Cobbie Kind knows that. And he's making money out of it."

"You think I'm being used?"

"I don't think making money out of this serves any good purpose."

"If you kill one of these monsters, he won't ever harm a child again."

"The next one will. Cobbie Kind wants you to wash them off like dirt. He's selling you his brand of soap. Everybody has fantasies. Some have bad ones. Act them out. I don't know why. I don't think he knows either."

"Some of us could never be monsters, no matter what," Carol said. "We can carry a disease and be immune to it. By the way, Rog, pedophiles are now calling for the age of consent to be lowered to almost infancy, believing prepubescent children can have orgasms. They've been waiting a long time to climb onto the sexual freedom bandwagon so they can indulge their perversion and call it another choice. Amazing how self-centred and selfish some people are when it comes to serving their sickness."

Mary stood up, red-faced.

"I'm not stupid and gullible and I'm not a pervert and I know that and I don't need to hear any more, Roger, thank you. I happen to know that the Kinds are doing very good work with children. I'm leaving, Carol. Madeline can stay until Gwen doesn't need her. I'll phone her every day, as usual. I hope you don't mind. I'm an old-fashioned mother and love my daughter."

Mary was blinking back tears. Carol got up and put a hand on her shoulder.

"Of course you can call her, any time you like. Don't mind Rog. He likes to think he can spout off about anything. He'd never knowingly upset you. Would you, Roger?"

A glance at him, dark meaning in it.

"Of course not."

Carol rode down in the elevator with Mary and walked with her to the visitor's parking lot. Roger usually accompanied her as a safety measure but tonight Carol had to mollify her longtime friend. She had known Mary since school, and though emotionally cooler and more intelligent, had remained friends as a link with the past. The friendship had been tentative at times and survived now mostly because of their daughters. Carol still enjoyed the reminiscences, albeit in smaller and smaller doses. Mary's chattiness seemed to have increased over the years, and especially since her divorce. Holding one of the exit doors open, Carol watched Mary's car edge out of its stall, though the neighbouring ones were empty. She waved and saw an answering wave. Her few words of sisterly comfort appeared to have worked. Later, Carol stood in the bathroom doorway watching Roger brushing his teeth.

"Did you have to be so bloody doctrinaire tonight, Rog? You know why she gets upset when she talks about molestation."

"Sorry," Roger garbled, mouth full of toothpaste. "Guess I screwed up."

"You damn well did. She accused Dave of molesting Madeline. Madeline denied anything happened. Mary was out of her head, trying to get revenge after Dave told her he'd found someone else and wanted a divorce. She was on nerve pills for a year. Took two years losing all the weight she'd put on. How could you forget that?"

"Sorry again," Roger said and came out of the bathroom. "Got carried away."

"I tried to make her feel better on the way down. I told her Cobbie Kind's paper came out against some downtown development scheme you had planned and that helped kill it."

"What?"

"I had to make poor Mary feel better."

"By making the whole thing a grudge?"

"Keep your mouth shut next time. Do respect our friends."

"That woman is your friend."

"Then respect my friends."

Carol's voice had risen to a level Roger knew meant that his next remark would lead to a fight, a prolonged silence or a good night's sleep.

"I'll use glue and duct tape."

Carol put her reading lamp on after she got into bed, which Roger knew meant she was simmering but would recover.

"Night, darling," he said as he got in beside her.

"Night."

"Wish I'd gone," Gwen said to Madeline later that night. They were sitting on the floor. Neither had been able to fall asleep. "What a bunch of free samples. Were you scared only that one time at the table?"

"Yeah. The rest of the time it was like a dream or being in a play and all those guys weren't real. I knew they were, of course. If I hadn't gone there I'd have missed a whole chunk of life that's right in front of us but sort of hidden away. Speaking of hiding, what are we going to do with him?"

"We have to move him quick. My father talked about the owner having a hard time renting a first-floor suite—101, I think. It's at the back. We have to find a way of getting him in."

"Easy. He showed me a whole bunch of keys he's got around his neck to get into places."

"A little of the old helps the new. Take him tomorrow."

That night legs kicked against Madeline in bed. Gwen's whimpers turned into a scream. "Mmmmm. Mmmmm. Keep away. Eeeee." In their pyjamas Carol and Roger ran in and he flicked on the ceiling light. Carol rocked Gwen in her arms. Roger shook his head. Make damned certain she sees a therapist tomorrow. Madeline hugged herself.

Fifteen minutes later they were alone, the night table lamp on.

"You'll be all right, Gwenner."

"I guess I'm experiencing delayed shock, or trauma."

"Whatever it is, it'll go."

"It was horrible, Maddy. He was trying to hurt me. We were like animals, circling each other. I knew he was creepy but never thought he could be dangerous. The worst was how fast it happened. He grabbed me, pulled me into the room and everything was automatic. I never knew I could hurt a person. I hate him for making me do that."

"You turned out to be a pretty good animal in saving yourself."

"Let's talk about something else. That tramp isn't like us. He must have gone through a lot of stuff. None of it's made him better."

"We're basically different from him. He's never had any ideas about right and wrong, only thought about what he wanted, and that's why he needs help."

"Noblesse oblige."

"*Mais oui.*"

"Pick it," Madeline told Lynch the next morning. He looked at her, took the wire from around his neck and crouched close to the lock. Three seconds and he turned the doorknob. They stepped into the musty interior of a small, unfurnished one-bedroom suite with a rectangular carpeted space of eleven feet by ten feet in front of them. This was meant to be the living room, with a railing to the left of it demarcating a tiny dining area. Through an archway to the right of the dining area and beyond the railing was the kitchen. On the right side of the living room were two doors, one to the bedroom and the other to the bathroom. There was a window near the archway to the kitchen. It was the only one in the suite. On the other side of the drapes was the back of an orange dumpster.

"Ya think this is better 'n that other place?" Lynch said as they stood on the sand grey living room carpet and stared at the blank white walls.

"Of course it is. There's lots of room here. You'll have your own bathroom. I'll bring some blankets. And food every day."

"How 'bout a TV?"

"I'll bring books and magazines."

"I don't read nuthin'."

What a surprise, no, wrong. She was supposed to be helping him, not making fun of him.

"Ya said at Al's I was going to have a easy time. And ya bring me to this dump."

"Besides you having more room, this place is cleaner and quieter."

"Like a goddam jail. I like the wide open."

"So you can starve and be dirty and cold and lonely and even get mugged?"

"You and your pal are such goddam know-it-alls. But Speaker told ya some things, didn't he?"

Madeline scuffed the carpet with her sneaker.

"Try to be a little grateful, it's free."

"Like to bring in my friends."

"We don't want the suite damaged. We'd be in trouble if anything happened."

"Wouldn't hurt nuthin'. Don't want me to be lonely, do ya?"

"I'll talk to Gwen. Why don't you look around while I get blankets and stuff?"

"Bitches," Lynch mumbled after Madeline had gone. He went to the window. "Take anathing out of here. Set myself up in no time."

"He wants to bring friends there," Madeline told Gwen after she had taken

Lynch his lunch, blankets and an old battery-powered clock radio of Roger's. As usual, lunch was made up of portions of everybody else's food, and Lynch complained once more about not getting enough meat. She explained again that sneaking it was difficult because Gwen's parents were meat eaters. "The girls have been eating more lately," Roger had said to Carol the day before. "Much better appetites. To be expected. Growing bodies. Good to see them eating beef."

"Tell him no," Gwen said. "We can't take a chance. They could break up the suite. Have a noisy party."

"I said no to a TV. Told him I'd bring him books and magazines and he said he didn't read."

"Try comics."

"Two soft knocks on the door. "Ready, Gwen?"

"In a minute, Mom. Therapy time," she whispered.

"Shock talk," Madeline said.

Gwen had an eleven o'clock appointment at the rape crisis centre downtown. Carol had phoned and explained that though Gwen had been assaulted, not actually raped, she needed counselling. The centre was in a two-storey grey stone building on a corner in the downtown eastside, on the edge of skid row. Once the city's main library and museum, the old structure had been converted into suites of offices for social organizations supported by public funds. They climbed marble stairs through semi-darkness to the second floor. Five doors lined the narrow hallway, four with frosted glass panels with black lettering. On the fifth door, furthest away, "Rape Crisis" had faded in green ballpoint capitals on a piece of brown cardboard glued to the panel. Carol knocked on the panel, waited before opening the door. A metal desk and three padded metal chairs filled the outer office. On the desk were a plastic coffee mug, a turquoise ceramic frog with its mouth open and crammed with pens and pencils, a telephone, a battered IBM Selectric typewriter, a notebook computer and a precipitously teetering stack of manila folders spilling crammed papers. More folders were jammed in an open drawer in one of the grey filing cabinets lining two sides of the office. Two doors faced the office. Between them hung a poster of a kitten. Claws clinging to drapes, its body dangled in mid-air below the words, "Hang in There."

Carol went over and tapped on the doors. One of them opened and a woman of about forty stepped out. She was stocky, had straight shoulder-length hair and wore blue jeans and a pink sweatshirt with "Loving=Caring" printed on it. Marianne Vandervelde had been a counsellor for almost three years. Formerly a primary schoolteacher, she had quit and taken a degree in psychology and training in counselling. "Burnt out by brats" was the reason she gave friends. But those who knew her well believed that the change was motivated by an acrimonious breakup with her longtime live-in companion. "Sorry, but our secretary couldn't come in today," she said after everybody had been introduced. She had a voice that wanted to convey excitement but she continually had to fight the impulse, believing that above all counselling required composure. After some preliminaries, Carol took a seat and Gwen went into the counsellor's office. It was small, with a metal desk and two padded metal chairs, a small bookcase filled mostly with pamphlets, and an ivy-draped filing cabinet. The desk was empty except for a writing pad and pen. There was a loose wood frame window with a sill latch. Overlooking a back alley, the window faced the rear wall of an importer's warehouse.

"Are you comfortable talking about what happened?" Marianne Vandervelde asked, smiling.

"I think so," Gwen said, seated across the desk from her. "This person, the caretaker where I live, invited me to look at an empty suite. We went up there and he opened the door and pulled me in and grabbed me and started kissing me and tearing off my clothes. I tried to get away but he hit me and I fell on the floor. He took his pants down, fell on me and I stuck a fork into him."

"A fork?"

"I was carrying it in my blazer pocket."

"All right."

"I ran to the door but he came after me and grabbed me again. He knocked me down. When he came for me I stabbed him with a knife. And got away."

"You were carrying a knife as well?"

"Yes."

"When you agreed to look at the empty suite, what were your feelings about him?"

"I was a bit scared."

"Why did you go?"

"I had to see this apartment. I was going to peek in and leave."

"You were afraid of this man. Looking at that suite must have been very important to you."

"It doesn't have anything to do with what happened to me."

"Wasn't there somebody who could have gone along with you?"

"I was there for a friend. She was busy."

"I think there's something you're not telling me. I'm saying this not to upset you but to tell you that in future you're going to have to weigh your priorities more carefully. Your safety must come first. Don't go anywhere with a man you don't completely trust. Never put yourself at risk. You gave this man an opportunity to attack you by ignoring your feelings about him. You were lucky. Do you often carry knives and forks in your pockets?"

"I happened to have them. They saved me. I gave him nothing. I won't go around scared for the rest of my life because of one man."

"Anger is a natural response after what you've been through. What are your feelings about the opposite sex in general now?"

"Don't worry. I'm not going to hate men. I was stupid. I won't be stupid again."

"That's commendable. You're a level-headed girl."

"Not level-headed enough not to have a nightmare like the one I had last night."

"Nightmares are a natural consequence after a stressful situation like the one you've been through. You'll have more but they'll eventually go away. The one you had last night. Would you like to tell me about it?"

"We were naked and he came after me and I cut his thing off with my knife and it came alive on the floor and slithered after me like a snake covered in blood and went up my leg and between and that's when I woke up."

She shivered and noticed the counsellor glancing at her legs. Gwen was wearing a scarlet and blue tartan wool jacket and skirt. She was sitting low in her chair. Marianne Vandervelde had looked that fraction of a second longer than notice requires but attraction will demand. Gwen sat up straighter and drew her legs closer to her. The counsellor wrote something on her pad. Gwen was a little frightened, as with Kyriakopoulos before they went up in the elevator. A tingling of apprehension mingled with an odour like distaste, and she shook her head. First the caretaker and now the caregiver, one trying to take and this one giving herself away. Macabre, Gwen thought, and wondered if she had chosen the right word. Who cared? It was macabre to her.

"I have nice legs, haven't I?"

The counsellor looked up. "What?"

"Not bad for a girl."

"I don't understand, Gwen. Are you all right?"

"Fine. Thanks for the support."

She got up and left, closing the door behind her as Marianne Vandervelde tried to say something.

"Let's go, Mom," Gwen said as she walked through the outer office. "Brief you in the car."

"I'm getting tired of adults," Gwen said, lowering her head and closing her eyes as Carol drove back to the apartment. She had mentioned everything but the legs.

"I'm an adult."

"No, you're not. You're my mom."

The new caretaker arrived that day. A small man of fifty-three, he was losing his hair. What was left clung to the sides of his head and the very top, in a tuft sticking up four inches above his skull. Ian MacDiarmid had emigrated from Dunfermline, Scotland, six years ago and this would be his third job since and his second as a caretaker. He and his wife Maggie were unpacking in Kyriakopoulos' old suite as Madeline passed by their open door on her way to see Lynch.

"Careful o' that, will ye?" Ian MacDiarmid said. "Ye'll break it."

"It's only a stupid trophy," Maggie MacDiarmid said. Big-boned and taller than her husband, she had a curly mass of fiery hair and her round face could redden easily.

"It's for ma golfing. Ye know that and yet ye seem to always want to break it and the others, drop them or throw them out of a window."

"There're always in ma way when I'm cleaning. Stupid things."

"They're important to me. I won them."

"Everyone ye play with is ninety years old and drunk. Talk aboot a handicap."

"You're jealous. Ye hae never won a thing."

"I won you and that's a booby prize."

Listening off to one side, Madeline realized that the new caretaker might want to check suite 101. She and Lynch had to have a contingency plan ready. She hurried to the suite and knocked on the door. "It's me," she whispered as loudly as if she were using her normal voice, thinking a strained hoarseness couldn't be overheard. A minute passed and she had knocked twice more before Lynch opened the door slightly. He had been dreaming. He and Sylvia were taking a bath together. Dressed in a nurse's uniform, Madeline had strutted in, ordering him out of the tub.

"What ya want?" he mumbled.

"The new caretaker's here. He might want to inspect the suite, so we have to have a plan."

"That all? Anybody comes in, I'm out the window."

"What if you're sleeping?"

"I'm like a cat. Nobody sneaks up on me."

"It took more than a minute to wake you."

"I was in the bathroom. I heard ya when ya first knocked."

"I hope you're telling me the truth. If you're caught, we're in trouble."

On her way back to the foyer, Madeline was thinking instead of looking and she bumped into MacDiarmid as he was coming out of his suite. He stepped back and bowed.

"Pardon me."

"He looks like an elf and he's crazy about golf," she told Gwen later. "I didn't see his wife but she sounds really witchy."

"He was snoring away when you knocked," Gwen said, thinking about Lynch. "We'll get him out of there for a while and we'll see the suite with the caretaker. Pretend we're interested in it for friends. He won't look at it again."

In the early morning Madeline knocked on the caretaker's door. Gwen wouldn't come, too nervous yet to go near the suite. But 101 wouldn't be a problem, she told Madeline. When Maggie MacDiarmid opened the door, her lips moved to one side of her face.

"Is the caretaker in?"

"Aye."

"May I speak with him, please?"

"Aye."

MacDiarmid came to the door and smiled.

"I saw you yesterday, didn't I? Somewhere in the building, if I'm not mistaken."

"I was returning to the lobby. I'm staying with my girlfriend in her parents' apartment here. I want to ask you about a suite on this floor, 101. I understand it's vacant. My girlfriend and I would like to see it for some friends. See if it would be right for them. They're older than we are."

"Ye want a showing? Think I could manage that. Ma schedule tomorrow isna full. At three?"

"Fine. We'll meet you there."

"Did ye see the way that young tart was dressed? Tight jeans and blouse. No wonder they get molested. Her arse stuck out like a whoore's."

Maggie MacDiarmid was speaking to her husband at dinner and he was trying to ignore her as he read a golfing story in the newspaper.

"They want to see a suite, do they? Probably to set up business, if ye catch ma meaning. Ye better turn them down if they're interested. And stay away from them. They could try to seduce ye, not that they'd have a hard time, especially if they put golf balls in their blouses. What's more, it's none of your business, anywee. The owner's got a real estate agent for such things."

"She's a kid and so is her friend probably and there's no harm in showing them," MacDiarmid said from behind his newspaper. "If they're interested, I'll give them the agent's name and number and that's the end of it."

"Kids dinna have arses like that," Maggie MacDiarmid said.

Madeline warned Lynch that night about the showing. He said he would put his stuff in the dumpster outside the window and stay there until they were gone.

"It's full of garbage," Madeline said.

"I been in lots worse places."

The next afternoon MacDiarmid unlocked the door to 101.

"Small, isn't it?" Madeline said to Gwen.

"Yeah, too small for them."

"A wee bit stinky in here," MacDiarmid said and went over and opened the window. They heard the sound of heavy metal blaring from the dumpster. "That sounds right outside the window."

"It's probably some poor homeless person trying to survive," Gwen said. "He'll move on."

"Sounds as if he's moved in. That's too near the building. I'll have to call the police. If you'll leave, I'll get to ma phone."

MacDiarmid shut the window. He locked the door, hurried to his suite.

They ran out through the rear exit and over to the dumpster. Gwen banged on it with her fist. "You've got to get out. He's phoning the police." She banged on it again. There was no response. They lifted the heavy steel lid. A soundburst detonated from the depth. The dumpster was two thirds full, mostly with crumpled cardboard boxes and bulging garbage bags. Lynch lay slumped on some bags in the corner nearest the building and was holding a half empty bottle of wine. A drained bottle lay nearby, a bent saucer shape of dark stain coating the bottom and side. The key ring had come in handy yet once more. He was face up, his eyes closed and his mouth open. He had drunk himself into a stupor. The smell of refuse mixed with the stench of pee-stained clothes.

"Peehew," Madeline said.

"Wake up, the police are coming," Gwen shouted. "He's not moving. We'll have to carry him over and push him out." With both hands she held onto the side of the dumpster and climbed over, manoeuvred among squishy bags and slippery box flaps to Lynch. The blare was coming from under an armpit. She lifted his shoulder, picked up the radio and shut it off. As she dropped it, she felt something brush against her back and heard the dull crack of bone meeting steel plate. Madeline had slipped on a box flap and careened sideways, her head colliding with a dumpster edge. Her head began to throb. Her knees felt weak and she collapsed onto some bags. Gwen wallowed across to her.

"You all right, Maddy?"

"My head hurts. I can help."

She extended an arm for Gwen to pull her up and put the other against a dumpster wall to steady herself. They wobbled over to Lynch. Each took a shoulder of trench coat and pulled, Lynch snuffling, dropping the wine bottle. It glanced off Madeline's sneaker and she kicked it away. They dragged their damp cargo over to the side facing the alley and lifted him by his torso onto the edge. Grabbing his wet pant legs, they pushed him over and into the alley, in too much of a hurry to care how he landed. They put their pee-soaked hands on the edge to hoist themselves out.

The fall stirred Lynch. His fingers scraped at the silt and oily grit on the asphalt. He remembered lifting the bottle and feeling the tide of wine, its chemical taste blunted by repeated swallows, gurgling down his throat. He had drifted into those paradisiacal lands of forget and don't care. The dumpster had been cosy. Punk bitches. What did they know about him? What did they know about anybody? Never had to fight for a goddam thing. Drunken father half-kicking, half-shoving him out of the way with the side of his shoe. Mother drunk and collapsed in a chair as steaks burnt in a blue haze on the stove. Bottle? Had it. The girls looking down.

"The police are coming, you've got to hide," Gwen shouted.

"Gimme drink, ya punk bitches."

"We'll have to hide him," Madeline said.

"That one over there," Gwen said, pointing to a blue dumpster across and further down the alley.

Four hands on his trench coat, they dragged him to the dumpster. He grumbled fragments of curses. They lifted the lid, inhaled the sharp stink of rotten produce. They hoisted him by his shoulders, clutched his wet pant legs and shoved him over onto slimy lettuce pulp and mouldy oranges. They dropped the lid, a bomb exploding in his head. The noise died away, he lapsed into dreaming. Pulling aside her boxer shorts, Sylvia was showing him how she peed. She gave him a glass of golden wine. When he took a sip, it tasted salty. He spat it out.

As Gwen and Madeline were walking away, a patrol car drove by. It stopped alongside the orange dumpster and two officers got out. They looked in and at each other, exchanging a few words. One of them leaned in and picked up the radio. They returned to their car and left.

"Too bad about your dad's radio," Madeline said, carefully touching with a couple of fingers a swollen bruise on her left temple.

"It was old," Gwen said. "Phew, do we stink."

After showering and a change of clothes, that evening they took a groggy Lynch through the rear exit to suite 101.

"Where did you get the wine?" Gwen said.

"None of your damn business. What did ya 'spect me to do, die a thirst?"

"That's not likely. Don't use those keys again. We could get into trouble. We'll clean your clothes and bring them tomorrow. We've brought you blankets and food."

"What am I going to sleep in?"

"The blankets. They'll keep you warm. Please get into the shower. Not that we don't trust you to take one after we've left."

"'Nuther damn washing and I'll catch my death of cold." Lynch stripped until he stood in his yellowed riddled long johns. "Ain't ya going to turn 'round? Or ain't ya decent enough to be shocked?"

"I don't believe any of this," Madeline said as she and Gwen turned around.

Lynch slouched into the shower and Gwen gathered up his clothes. She put them into a garbage bag.

"Should burn these, but I guess we can clean them. He needs new clothes."

As they rode up in the elevator to the laundry room, down the hallway from the Chalmers' apartment, the other passengers, a middle-aged couple and an obese man in a business suit, began to sniff surreptitiously and glance at everybody else.

"A good catch today," Madeline said.

"Aye," Gwen said.

"What happened to you, Madeline?" Carol asked at dinner later that evening.

"I fell. It's better now."

"Poor dear. Can I get you something? Salve? An ice bag?"

"No, thanks. Please don't tell my mom or she'll go intensely crazy."

"You girls don't seem to be putting on any weight after what you've eaten in the past few days," Roger said during a lull in the conversation. He passed a bowl of mashed potatoes to Madeline.

"We're getting a lot of exercise to build muscle and stamina for sports next term," Gwen said.

"Didn't know you were interested."

"Mind and body go together, as you've said many times, Dad. Neglect either and the other will suffer. Your words. I'm trying to live up to your expectations."

"A lawyer's answer."

"She had to get something good from one of us," Carol said.

"What are we going to do?" Madeline said afterwards in Gwen's bedroom. "We can't keep hiding him. If the caretaker doesn't find him, your parents will catch on sooner or later. Your father mentioned the food. Besides, we're going back to school."

"I've been thinking," Gwen said. "Guys his age are retired. He wouldn't want a job, anyway. Except taster of jug wines. We can't change him. He got drunk the first time we asked him to cooperate. He needs something big to happen to him. My mom and dad were talking a while ago about some waterfront apartments for pensioners. They're only a couple of years old. My dad knows the builders and people at city hall. He could get him into one of them. I'll say we're trying to help this deserving homeless person who's looking for a place. I won't say where he is. With their help, he can jump the queue. Be in there quick. Mom knows a lot of government and social workers and stuff. She can make sure he gets money to pay the rent and for food, enough for him to buy some clothes, too."

"He told me he tried to get government money once and they wanted documentation. He doesn't even have a birth certificate or a record of employment."

"My mom can handle that. Trace his name back where he comes from and get him what he needs."

"Suppose he doesn't want to go into one of those apartments?"

"He should. He'd be off the streets. After seeing how much his life has changed, he might stop drinking. I'll talk to my parents tomorrow."

The caretaker lay sweating on top of his wife, making love to her for the first time in over three months. As he thrust between her heavy thighs and rumpled nightgown he saw Madeline's naked rump, spotlessly white and perfect, with a delicate pink slit in her underbelly. So tight, she would be making little pleading noises for him to be gentle, not hurt her, not the grunts his wife was making like a sow lying in mud and half-dozing and he shoving into the impassable bulk of her. His wife's intense dislike of any woman who wasn't woefully ugly, her reading of sexual innuendo into almost everything, her fleshy body, the endless stretch of panties over her buttocks, her bottomless appetite for sticky candies, all disgusted him and yet he had been faithful. No guts and no opportunities. Except for that strange woman in church two years ago. She touched him on the knee while talking about God's grace.

"He can touch you like I'm doing, in a spiritual way," she had said with eyes staring and skinny body rigid. Gripping his knee, her spidery fingers had begun creeping up his thigh, kneading the tense muscles slowly. He had felt his own rigidity growing in that pew at the back, his wife off somewhere talking with the minister. The skinny woman had withdrawn her hand at his wife's approach, left hurriedly after dropping a bunch of pamphlets in his lap. His first instinct was to hide them but he didn't have time, so he picked them up.

"What did the tart want? She'd have your buckle undone before you'd finished your first cup of her tea."

"You're daft," he had said. "She gave me some pamphlets. Look." His wife hadn't bothered to glance at them. He did that night as he was throwing them out and found her name, Joan, and her telephone number written underneath it. Did she mean for him to phone? Nervous, he waited two weeks. A man with a high squeaky voice answered. Her husband, perhaps her father? He hung up, never phoned again.

Now as he came it was Madeline gripping him, pulsing around his thrusts and against the pounding he gave her swollen lips and small rump. Her young legs tried to embrace him, clasped high on his back. He collapsed onto his wife and rolled away, not wanting to speak to her or breathe the decay from her cavity-riddled mouth. "Ian," she whispered. She hadn't called him by name for years during or after sex. Despite himself, he thought of their early days. That made him feel worse and the soft white body faded from his arms, the girl's legs vanished from around his cold, sweaty back.

Maggie MacDiarmid, responding to her husband's most frenetically eager sexual outburst in years, reached over and touched his shoulder with her fingertips. He winced, shrugged them off. As they left, a memory flooded over him of a picnic in the Highlands when he and Maggie first began courting. She had baked scones and sliced and filled them with strawberry jam. They were delicious and there was hot tea in a thermos bottle to drink with them and he remembered how Maggie's red mouth glistened with the slickness of the jam and the wetness of the tea and how much he wanted to kiss her mouth, to tighten his arms around the sweet weight of her. But he hadn't the nerve, sat and watched on that spring hill above the loch as a breeze came up and ruffled her mass of curls, catching the sun and drawing it into spun filaments of scarlet blaze and brassy scroll. He picked at heather at the edge of the woollen blanket on which the picnic things were spread, fingers crushing the tiny white flowers, beautiful and useless. Falling asleep he saw an ooze of milky droplets between Madeline's thighs and wanted to lick them, kiss her there, smother his face in her. He wanted to cry. He must be sick.

The next morning MacDiarmid went to take another look at suite 101. The dumpster was too close to the window and the tramp might come back, perhaps bring friends and break into the apartment. The dumpster had to be moved away. The police had recommended that when he had spoken with them after they looked for the tramp. The owner would appreciate the suggestion, for safety and to improve the chances of renting the suite. Who would put up with garbage disposal outside the only window in an apartment? He unlocked the door and stepped inside. The drapes had been drawn since yesterday and no morning light filtered through them. Only at the edges were there hints of the day outside. No reason to waste electricity when all that needs doing is opening the drapes. On his way he stumbled over a dark mass on the floor. He fell, banging his head against the railing separating the living and dining rooms. Stunned, he lay there and watched as a grey lump rose from the floor. The grey slid off and a dead whiteness appeared, small and crooked.

"What the fuck?" Lynch yelled. One of the caretaker's shoes had kicked him in the head, the other stepped on his foot. The caretaker moaned, tried to get up but couldn't, slumping back onto the floor. Lynch whirled around, trying to find something in the dimness. He picked up one of the blankets and wrapped it around himself and headed for the window. As he stepped past the end of the railing, a hand reached out and grabbed his ankle. He tried to pull away, kicking out with his other foot. It hit something dark on the carpet. He kept kicking until the hand let go. He ran to the window and let himself out, dragging the blanket behind him.

Lynch walked as fast as he could down the alley. There were bottle caps, nails, sharp stones and other detritus hazardous to a naked sole. He ran across streets from alley to alley, receiving a few stares, but no police saw him. A barking dog ran after him and lunged for the blanket. He pulled it higher and kicked at the dog, which gave up after one alley. Two blocks from Al's he sliced a big toe on a jagged piece of bottle glass and had to hop the rest of the distance. He hammered on the front door with a balled fist.

When Speaker arrived a few hours later, Lynch was lying on the sofa and wrapped in one of Al's old bathrobe's, his foot bandaged. "Them bitches took my clothes and told me I'd be safe in this 'partmint. Caretaker come in this morning and falls over me in the dark. I got away and come here wearing only a blanket. Stepped on glass."

"Sure it was glass?"

A half hour after Lynch left by the window, Madeline knocked on the door of suite 101. She was carrying Lynch's breakfast in a brown paper bag and was returning his laundered clothes in a new garbage bag. She tapped with the knuckles of the hand holding the food. "It's me," she whispered. There was no answer. "I brought your clothes." There was still no answer. She put both bags on the hallway carpet and began banging with her fists on the door. "Wake up, will you?"

"Who's that? Will ye help me?"

The voice was weak but Madeline recognized it. She froze, undecided for a few moments before taking the bags to the foyer and hiding them behind one of the large potted plants. She ran back and tried the door. It opened and she pushed it into an intermittent darkness, light bursting from occasional flappings of the drapes at the open window. In one of those bursts she saw the caretaker, back against the railing. He was trying without success to stand up. Madeline went to him. He stopped trying and looked up at her.

"Who are ye?"

"I was here yesterday, looking at the suite. You all right?"

"Think so. I've got a headache. Couple of ma teeth are loose. When I came in, there was someone sleeping on the floor. That tramp, probably. I couldna see and tripped over him in the dark. Hit ma head on the railing. He ran for the window. I caught hold of a foot but he kept kicking me with the other. Knocked me out. I came to a while ago but I've been too weak to stand up."

"He left with no clothes on?"

"I didna say he had nae clothes."

"I meant he must have been in a hurry and didn't have time to put them on."

"Dinna they sleep in their clothes?"

"I forgot."

"Anywee, think I saw him holding a blanket. Why did you knock here?"

"I wanted to tell you our friends found another suite somewhere else."

"How did ye know I'd be here? I didna even tell ma wife."

"I was passing and saw the door was open a little."

"I shut it when I came in. I'm sure I did. Weell, perhaps I didn't. Will ye help me up?"

The caretaker held out his hand. Madeline took it in both of hers. Holding onto a banister with his other hand, he pushed as Madeline braced herself and pulled him. He was light and two inches shorter and came up easily. Unsteady on his feet, he shook his head and the ache increased. Her hands slipped out of his and he touched the side of his jaw. Two teeth were loose and hurt sharply when he pushed at them. He looked at Madeline in the flames of light made by the waving drapes. Her softness had come to him through her hands and now he saw a flickering whiteness of face as the drapes flared. Her dark hair glimmered in these strange uncertainties, her arms still towards him, lips in slippery shadow or pink welts pouting semblances of words. A vague weakness overcame him, became a plunging fear, and finally concern for his teeth. His tame self once more. She was only a girl. A white blur jumped into his consciousness again, feet kicking at him, sole and heel stale cheese rind crashing against his cheekbone and jaw.

"How did he get in? Yesterday I made certain the window was locked. The door was locked. Where are his clothes? I dinna see any."

MacDiarmid walked carefully to the window and opened the drapes. The sudden glare hurt his eyes and made his headache worse. He lifted a hand to shield them and turned to look around. He saw only two grey blankets and a pillow on the living room carpet. As quickly as he could, he checked the rest of the suite. Madeline felt a strong urge to pee, which happened whenever she was in trouble, late or didn't study for an exam. "I canna find a thing," the caretaker said when he returned. "I'll phone the owner and let him know what's been going on."

Madeline's urge to pee lessened. Stupid guy. Didn't see any link between her and Lynch. "I've got to go." She almost giggled. Clearing her throat stopped that. "Sorry you were hurt."

"That's nae worry. I'll recover. Thanks for rousing me. I'll lock that window."

"He ran through the streets with only a blanket around him," Madeline told Gwen a few minutes later in her bedroom. They were lying on the floor, elbows resting on the carpet, hands cupping their chins.

"I know where he went," Gwen said.

"Yeah."

"So much for helping him."

"Yeah."

"He didn't want to be helped, anyway."

"Yeah."

"You know we can't quit."

"Yeah."

"Dinna ye see it?" Maggie MacDiarmid said to her husband at lunch that day. "The tarts are involved. The tramp is their pimp. They were going to bring their customers there. That would've been something."

"You're daft. They're girls. They were looking at that suite for friends. They've nothing to do with him."

"How did he get in? Ye locked the window and the door. The locks weren't broken. The glass wasn't smashed. They let him into the building and got him in there. Perhaps used wax to make an impression for a key. I saw that in a film once. And he had no clothes. Or perhaps he was a customer. Ye said he sounded like an old man. Disgusting. Ye've got to let the owner know aboot those little whoores. They should be kicked out o' the building and the police told aboot them. I wouldna be a bit surprised if those aren't their parents in that apartment up there."

"I won't do it. I'd be making a fool o' myself. I could get fired too. They might be important people."

"You're a fool if ye don't."

Chapter 6

With Gwen carrying Lynch's clothes in a shopping bag, she and Madeline took a bus to the Western early Sunday morning. Skid row streets were almost empty, the only time they could have risked them. They brought money for a taxi in case they saw anything threatening after getting off the bus. They had already decided to take a taxi back to the apartment. All was quiet now to their steps in the sun. Like a cheap hooker, Saturday night had gone through the usual phallic puncturings, and those symbolic penetrations of gunshots and stabbings and injections, self-administered or obligingly provided at cost price, and lay spilled bruised skin of gasoline floating in morning gutters. The homeless trudged or sat or slept Sunday away, exuding the ancient smell of nomads, but compounded with city stench and dirt that made all clothing dust grey, and they were called vagrants and loiterers by custodial police who got out of patrol cars and slowly approached with shaved grins and whose crisp concern was clean streets.

Wearing pullovers and hoodies against the cool air of a late August morning, Gwen and Madeline walked quickly past the Western. Madeline took the wrong street twice before she saw the house. Nothing had changed, except on the front porch now was a television and on top of it tangled wire clothes hangers. A tawny cat on the fence edged away from them as they approached the gate. As Madeline opened the gate, the cat stopped and licked a front paw and blinked. They climbed the steps and Madeline knocked on the door. She waited, had to knock again before the curtains parted.

"It's me. We want to see him."

The curtains fell together. Nothing happened for five minutes. Madeline walked down and as she was about to go around to the back, the door opened. Lynch stepped onto the porch and Madeline climbed back up. Gwen put the bag down.

"Here are your clothes."

"You're sure nervy coming 'round here. I had to run through all them streets. Nuthin' 'cept a blanket. Cut my toe on some glass."

Still wearing Al's bathrobe, he raised one of the open-toed slippers Al had given him, showing the girls his bandaged foot.

"We're sorry the caretaker checked the suite again," Gwen said. "We've got a plan that'll help you."

"Not intrested."

"It means money for you."

"How much?"

"My father knows the people at city hall who look after those waterfront apartments for pensioners, and if I asked him he could get you into one."

"How 'bout the money?"

"My mother's a lawyer. You would get money from the government to pay the rent. And for food and clothes. I'm sure you qualify for a pension and lots of supplements."

"Don't need no 'partmint."

"They're almost brand new, and you'd have money. Once you get used to a good place, you wouldn't want to come back here. My parents are going away for the Labour Day weekend next week. You could stay with us while they're gone. That would show you what you'd be missing."

"Stay there while they're out?"

"With us."

Long weekend. There was the parents' 'partmint. Lots of good stuff there. Jewry and watches. Good liquor. Bunch of other places. Need help carrying out the stuff. Them computers, phones. Get a truck. Get rid of them punk bitches.

"Might want to. Like to stay by myself. Get the feel of the place. Get some friends in."

"You could sleep there alone," Gwen said. "We'll phone and come over every day. No visitors the first night."

She phoned for a taxi. After promising to be at the apartment Friday night by at least seven, Lynch took the bag up to his attic room. He put on his clothes. They smelled faintly of laundry detergent and felt newer and much softer, as if they weren't his. Gwen and Madeline had polished his boots and added a couple of plaid shirts to his wardrobe. He thought there had been a mistake and came up with excuses if they asked for them. When he realized the shirts were a gift, he decided to wear one on Friday. That would show appreciation, have them think he was going along with them on the pensioners' apartments. Sitting on his bed, he thought of candidates to help him. He decided on Doughnuts and Zimmo, auto mechanics who were small-time racketeers. They were close by and wouldn't cheat him out of his share.

Doughnuts was Johnny Donato and Zimmo was Andy Zimchuk, mechanics at Mott's Service and Repairs, a corner waterfront garage on Alexander Street. A white stucco leftover from the 1920s, it had two service bays with flame-red doors and trim facing one street. Diagonally facing the corner and next to a machine shop on the other street was the office, two pumps out front under an arch from the office. Mott had died years ago, leaving the garage to his wife. She had lapsed into senile dementia and didn't know where it was any more. There was a nephew lurking in the background, trying to get her declared mentally incompetent so as her nearest living relative he could take over her affairs. Doughnuts and Zimmo knew that the day he took control was their last day at the garage and were trying to make extra money. For years they had supported their declining business by fencing auto parts from Japan and Germany brought to them by forgetful longshoremen who occasionally mislaid a box. The white Mott's van would make deliveries without arousing any suspicion. Stolen goods from warehouses in the area were distributed by the van or picked up by customers. And they also had in their repertoire, charging for repairs not done, overestimating the time required on a job, overcharging on parts and replacing a good one.

Lynch knew Doughnuts and Zimmo through Waste, who took them

usable car parts he found. At the garage Lynch unloaded what he stole, from wallets to watches, and was paid in cash. From them he expected a smooth operation and a quick turnover. He decided to visit on Monday at noon, when they would be having lunch in the office. He wore one of the plaid shirts to convey an air of newly found prosperity. As he approached he saw between bottles of oil and jugs of anti-freeze stacked behind the plate glass window that the mechanics were seated on their high stools behind the counter, bare except for their lunch pails beside an antique cash register with inlaid arabesque on the back. Dating from the 1920s and still in working condition, it was an obvious target for thieves and never contained any money after hours. The office door had a loose brass knob and a full-length glass panel covered with faded decals.

"How you guys doing?" Lynch said as he stepped inside. He gave the door a backhanded push to shut it.

"How's it going?" Doughnuts said. He was eating a fried egg sandwich and drinking coffee from a thermos cup. Swarthy, with an aquiline nose, he had deep-set eyes that never seemed to look directly at anything. Zimmo raised a hand, fingers etched in black. His hair was thinning, his once muscular frame beginning to sag. He was eating a fat dill pickle with his fingers. The rest of his lunch was in his lunch pail, the black paint worn away at the edges and exposing some of the silver-coloured metal. Like Doughnuts, he was wearing coveralls washed too many times and freshly smeared and smudged from dingy collar to frayed cuffs. The odour of a lanolin hand cleaner drifted through the office. It didn't quite cover a residual smell compounded of decades of oxyacetylene cutting torches, welding rods, burnt metal, warm radiator hoses, and black crankcase oil. Through the open side door into the bays Lynch saw a car up on a hoist, wheels off, another sitting with its doors open, a third outside and behind with its hood up and a fourth near the street, parked next to the white van.

"Ya busy?"

"The usual," Doughnuts said. "Enough to keep ya going, not enough to make ya rich."

"How'd ya like to be rich?"

"How many watches ya got?

"This is big. I'll be staying in a 'partmint next weekend with two girls. Parents be out. There's lots of stuff there."

"Do we get a crack at the girls?" Zimmo said.

"They're kids."

"You after kids now? Shame on you, Lynch."

"Ya don't understand. They kind of 'dopted me, trying to get me off the streets into a 'partmint. So I'm staying there so I'll get to like it. It's all bullshit 'cept for what I can take out of there."

"What ya want us to do?" Doughnuts said.

"I need somebody with wheels. Show up when I tell ya. Park at the back. I'll let ya in."

"One suite's no good," Zimmo said.

"Labour Day weekend's coming up. Lots of people be taking off. I'm going to pick locks Friday and Saturday. Go through them fifteen floors, see who's gone. Ya can walk in, take the stuff."

"What about the caretaker?" Doughnuts said.

"Won't catch on if you're wearing your working clothes, like you're movers doing reglar business. Probly not going to see us 'cause we'll be too fast. He's small as me, anaways. I kicked the shit out of him without half trying."

"So he knows you."

"I was sleeping in this empty 'partmint they put me in and he come nosing 'round and I scram out of there. Was dark."

"What about the girls? Where they going to be?"

"Told 'em I want to be by myself, see if I'd like my own 'partmint. They're going to show up when I tell 'em to."

"We have time to do everything?"

"You guys know me. Fast when I got to be."

The mechanics glanced at each other.

"What's the best day?" Doughnuts said.

"Sunday. Eryone be back Monday. Anaways, I won't be able to keep putting 'em off. Parents be coming back."

Doughnuts put down his thermos cup and reached into a box under the counter and took out a business card, pulled a pen from the top pocket of his coveralls and jotted down a telephone number on the back of the card and handed it to Lynch. "Phone Sunday morning by nine. Let us know you're ready." He reached inside his coveralls into his shirt pocket and took out an empty envelope. "Mott's Service and Repairs" was printed above the address, and in the upper left-hand corner above the sender's address was the logo of a bank, which meant another visit to Mrs. Mott, to renew the lease this time, besides getting authorization for another draft upon her bank account. He turned the envelope over to write on the back. "Better gimme the name and street number of this place."

Seated at the edge of a parking lot later Lynch, propped against the eroding brick wall of an apartment building shared jug wine, anticipating success.

"Tell ya 'bout Maddee and Gwenee? Rich girls, want to 'dopt me. I been in them big 'partmints of theirs. Ya know why they call 'em 'partmints? 'Cause erybody's apart. While they're all stuck together. Figure that one. Not for me. I need room. Them buildins—skyrise, whatever the fuck they call 'em—are like fancy chicken coops. Only the chickens go up and down in elyvators and don't even squawk 'bout it. They got the liquor, though. Smooth. Like a woman's skin. Gimme that jug, will ya? I 'preciate anathing people do for me. But them girls aren't helping me. They're playing at it. Not going to listen if I tell 'em nuthin', anaways. Got their own ideas. Was telling myself the other day, don't trust nobody 'cept your pals, and watch them bastards too. Comes down to grabbing what ya can and being lucky enough they don't catch ya at it. Don't tell me them big boys don't do it that way. And there's lots of hired hands cleaning up their shit. Making 'scuses for 'em. Erybody wants in on the same stuff. And there's only so much to split up. So there'll always be a fight 'bout who gets what. And lots of bullshit flying 'bout who's got a right to it. I don't believe in nuthin' 'cept what makes me feel good. And I don't pick on myself for not having this or that. Life's a shithole. Trick is, don't get flushed down the toilet. I got my memries. All them beautiful women. They never believed it. Couldn't make 'em see. It ain't a simple thing. Ya hold onto something. Not 'portant how it got to be yours. Things get mixed up, anahow. The truth ain't easy. Don't matter how it got together. And from what I seen, none of 'em got nuthin' better. Let's have that jug back.

"There's this woman I'm going to see tomorrow, if tomorrow's Sunday. She cooks up tasty grub ya can sink your teeth into. Some is mysterious. I'll give ya that. But it's all hot and nurishin'. And she don't skimp on the meat. I'll root 'round in some garbage cans and come up with something for her dog. She'll 'preciate it. That dog, too. Animals got sense. Grub gets better when ya let it sit. Leave a stew go for a week and there's real taste. A fly knows. Flies go for ripe stuff. The high smell gets 'em. That's why they're after garbage. Wipe her off, trim her up and ya got damn good eats.

"Lemme tell ya something. Ya know your lettuce chewers? There was this woman raised her daughters on no meat. 'Magin' that? Nuthin' from a animal. Not even a hunk of cheese. Fed 'em nuts. Looking for 'em to grow up healthy on squirrel food. What ya eat is what ya turn into. They went nuts. When they got big enough they fried her up and ate her. Turned her own daughters into cannybulls. Serves her right. One of them crazy head doctors said they weren't 'sponsible for what they done. 'Cause their brains was 'fected. I heard they opened up a butcher shop. There's talk ya got to be careful of what ya buy there. Know who's spreading that? Your cud chewers. I got nuthin' 'gainst a good spud. 'Specially them fries. But without a steak next to 'em, they ain't a meal. All ya got's splinters. Put 'em together, ya got something.

"After I sober up tomorrow, if tomorrow's Sunday, I'll get spruced up in that washroom over at the Fountain, use some of that flowersmellin' runny soap nailed to the wall, whip out my razor blade and start working on my face. The weather's pretty good. She'll be out pottering in the garden. I'll come along, sling her a line and we're in business. Know what gives people misery? Spending time doing stuff they're no good at. Or being with somebody they can't stand or can't stand 'em. Now I never did. Spent my time pleasing myself. There's no better way. And all your busy ones hurrying by getting stuff done. It's a lot of nuthin'. But somebody's telling 'em this or that's 'portant. Know what's 'portant? Wakin' up and gettin' up. Take a leak, take a shit, get some newspaper and wipe your ass with some politician's face.

Gives ya 'spective. Where's that jug? Get comfortable with your smell. They're peddling high-priced junk in bottles that's makes ya smell like a cat's ass. The smell coming off ya is good enough. Long as it don't get out of hand. A woman's the same. She gets a little sweaty, she's getting scrumptious. When ya get busy with her, she's like fancy cork wine. There's some that stink, it's got to be said, but they ain't good looking neither. Looks 'pear to go with a good smell. It's nature saying, she's the one for ya. Your nose'll tell ya. Where's that other jug? This here's empty. Some so full of ideas they're farting 'em out of their backsides. Spend their lives playing at things. Laugh at ya if your grammer ain't perfect or ya don't think like them snotty bastards do. College degrees. A lot of words, that's all. Bluffing, same as erybody else. Looking down on me my whole life but I'm still kicking 'round. That's a kind of luck. Not the money sort. But it'll come. She'll be a easy woman. Like this beautiful sarongee girl on Samoee, name of Laluannee, that loved me and didn't want to marry the chief, so he had me heaved off a cliff to his pet maneating sharks, and she sliced open her big toe and dived in so they'd smell blood and chomp on her so's I could swum away. I couldn't save her. She done the deed. 'Sides, there was another sarongee hiding a outboard canoe to 'scape to a 'chanted island. One thing I know is, don't keep a woman waiting. Or you'll end up waiting. This island was full of them aileens from other space, bigheaded runts wearing 'luminum foil and going to fly us somewheres and 'spermint on us. I told 'em, I'm fine here. But they had their minds set on it, so Nanoopee and me had to 'scape. We run to the canoe and they shone their flashlights that 'fect your brain so it's froze and she went stiff. Didn't have no 'fect on me. My brain can't be changed by nuthin' and no one. It's 'mune 'gainst erything 'cept what I know.

"Nuthin' turns out the way ya 'spect, good or bad. It all runs together, starts looking the same. People waste lots of time figuring that out. Can shoot your mouth off all ya want. Swig left in the jug. I'll finish her off. I'm the only one sitting up. Probly talking to myself. Lots do. They know what they're not saying. It's your near and dear does ya in. They don't mean nuthin' by it. There's a reason either way. It ain't a lie if ya believe it."

Lynch returned to Al's reeking of sour wine, stumbled up the front steps, shirt tail hanging out of his pants, trench coat sleeves tied around his shoulders. The back of his shirt and pants bore patches of brick dust. Steps swayed beneath his feet, far below and suddenly too near and hard, jarring ankles, shinbones, knees. Missing the top step, he skinned a knee, lurched and fell onto the porch. His head crashed into the door frame with an almost nonchalant crack. He lay on his side for several silent moments before his boots began moving in little automatic circles like a windup toy and scraping against the flooring. His hands felt for the frame moulding and gripped it. He rolled over onto his knees. As if climbing a pole, he hoisted trunk and legs until he was vertical. He began pounding on the door with an open palm.

"Mon, 'penup, meehir."

Al opened the door carefully so Lynch wouldn't fall through the opening. He called Speaker, who dragged Lynch over to the sofa. "Yur ah kee. Have supper later. Pork hock and cabbage." Lynch retched, vomited. Speaker turned him onto his side to keep him from choking. A gush before stringy yellow slime dribbled from his lips, making a shiny stain on the carpet. Al left, came back with a pail of water and a sponge. He kneeled, began soaking up the vomit with the sponge and rinsing it in water. After finishing, he stood and looked at Lynch, passed out and snoring. Shaking his head, he picked up the pail.

When Lynch awoke hours later, he smelled boiled cabbage and heard voices in the kitchen. It was almost six and the front parlour was dim. He sat up, his head throbbing, a burning pain in his knee. He stood up, felt dizzy and almost fell back but steadied himself by putting a hand on an armrest of the sofa. Feeling the furniture like a blind man, he got to the stairway and put both hands on the railing and climbed, leaning against it. When he got to his attic room, he twisted the doorknob with a jerk of his shaking fingers and pushed at the door with a sore shoulder. He made the bed in two steps and fell unconscious in a plunge onto a torn mattress.

With memories in aching bone and muscle, he sat on his bed the next morning. Fingering his patchy stubble, he decided to make up for yesterday afternoon by shaving. He would change his shirt, a yellow and green plaid stinking of vomit, for the other shirt the girls had given him, a grey-blue and crimson tartan. In the second-floor bathroom he splashed lukewarm water on his face. With the almost hairless communal shaving brush, he dabbed lather on his stubble and picked up a tarnished safety razor Waste had donated to Al's. Shaking, he cut himself under the lower lip and on the chin. He put bits of toilet paper on the cuts, pink blossoms stuck to his face. Back in his room he put on the new shirt, like the other too large. The creases from the packaging made it appear even bigger. He looked into the cracked bathroom mirror on his way downstairs. Goddam fine shirt, beginnin' a good things.

It was twenty after eight when he entered the kitchen. The smell of coffee brewing on the stove was strong and the bacon and eggs frying in bacon grease made him queasy. Al was at the stove. Speaker and Kevin were seated at the table. Farmer had eaten and was in the garage and Waste had left to scour some favourite places. Speaker and Kevin were talking. Lynch poured himself a cup of coffee. After doctoring it with five tablespoons of sugar and a large dose of cream, he sat down.

Speaker looked at Lynch.

"Such is the perfectibility of man that he can remake himself with a shirt, clothing the old self with the new. And the change quicker than maple leaves, subsumed into their sublime death only once and no gaudier."

Lynch knew Speaker didn't drink or take drugs. Smart people could be a little crazy.

With thumb and forefinger Kevin picked his nose and flicked a lump of snot across the kitchen. He wiped his hand by ruffling his hair. He smirked, pale worms sliding sideways over each other. Speaker was an irritating bastard, always fin de siècle and goddam Götterdämmerung. A nihilist, and yet found spiritual crumbs among the worn slogans strewn across history's table. Ultimately, he said once, everything is a joke. It's only a matter of whether or not you see the point, which is pointless. But he admired selfless acts and individual courage. Mountains of doctrine and scholarly and scientific jargon were nothing to a few glints of precious light. "When I'm ready to reject the whole species, someone does something that makes me hesitate long enough to keep me interested." To Kevin cynicism had become a game and no matter how good he became at it, it limited him, he lacked any feeling for humanity.

He hated Speaker's tenuous and yet responsive link to humanity and never stopped trying to show him up as a dilettante slumming in intergalactic vastnesses of nihilism.

Pushing his lips together and squishing them forward, Kevin glanced at Lynch.

"You're a can of dog food with a new label pasted on it, that's all."

"Dog food's all right when ya need it," Lynch said. "Glad to get it times when I been hard up."

He disliked but understood Kevin in a way he would not ever understand Speaker. Kevin was like Lynch, always out for himself.

"Dog food might be best for you."

"I like lots better."

"Probably shit."

"You'd be 'thority on shit, seein' as it's always coming out of your mouth."

Lynch grinned. Feeling too good to get pissed off 'cause of a squishy-lip turd. Probly cut them suckers on a rusty can lid and poison hisself. 'Less he chokes on his snot first.

Kevin closed his eyes and leaned back in his chair. Al turned from the stove. "Ah, sorry I got no stew beef to give ya tonight. Liver." "It'll taste like filet mignon," Speaker said without raising his head from the book he was reading. From behind closed eyelids Kevin felt a knife sawing into his belly. Lynch slurped his coffee.

Roger Chalmers stood in the apartment foyer Friday afternoon waiting for Carol to join him. Gwen wanted the apartment key, even though she had promised to leave immediately for her cousin's house, where she was supposed to spend the weekend.

"Why do you need a key, then?" he had asked.

"It's a matter of trust, Dad," she had answered, standing a couple of feet inside the doorway. "I'm going right to Nita's place. Aunt Beverley is expecting me. I hope you and Mom trust me not to do anything very bad with so much power."

Her playful tone had placated him. Now Carol came out of the bathroom and kissed Gwen.

"Your father's too trusting."

"What could I do, Mom?"

Gwen wouldn't go to her father for a goodbye kiss. She knew he would come to her. He did, and in stiffly deliberate steps, making an elaborate gesture of reaching into his coat pocket and taking out the same apartment key she was customarily given when they weren't home and Madeline or another girlfriend was sleeping over. He presented it, bowing slightly, and taking it she made a curtsey. Bending, he kissed her on the cheek.

"I don't know how we did it but we raised you with hardly any help from nannies. We've always been proud of that, and I guess if we can't trust you, that goes against all we've tried to do."

"We'll be phoning Nita's every night," Carol said. As she was closing the door, she stopped and took an envelope from her purse and held it out to Gwen. "Here's the letter you wanted for that homeless guy you mentioned. I phoned Harvey Stein, who's in charge of renting suites there. He said he could see your friend at ten on Tuesday morning. His office is on Main, three blocks from the apartments. I put his address and office number on the front of the envelope and made some suggestions that should help, so remember to give your guy this."

After the door closed and the sounds of her parents talking and moving suitcases faded behind the elevator doors, Gwen listened to the silence. The apartment was hers for three whole days, not to cause trouble or waste time but prove that Lynch would cooperate when he knew someone was trying to help him and he could see the immediate and practical benefits of cooperation. They had been playing, this was real. And she had to admit to herself an increasing interest in meeting Lynch's friends. She phoned Madeline, who answered immediately.

"Have they gone?"

"Yeah. I'm getting goosebumps. About this weekend. We don't even know who'll be coming. I don't, anyway. We'll buy some food when you get here. He'll be here by seven. I have to be at Nita's by eight. Or my parents will fizzle into blue fits. They're going to call there every night."

Madeline arrived at four-thirty and they did some quick shopping.

Because the shirts had shrunk their charity fund drastically, they had thirty-seven dollars spending money between them. Forced to scale down their plans for a vegan buffet meal for Lynch and his friends, in the organic section of the local supermarket they bought a bag of nacho chips, a carton of apple juice, two packages of multigrain crackers and a block of soy cheddar. As a concession to weaker souls, they foraged elsewhere in the store, selecting torpedoes of pop and a package of chocolate chip cookies. Gwen decided that she would leave in strategic places around the apartment a few pamphlets on veganism and important health supplements. She would also empty the liquor cabinet, hiding the bottles in a safe place. With trust there were obvious limits.

Lynch was late. Gwen looked at her watch, a birthday gift from her parents. It was seven-forty. She tapped her fingers on the armrest of the chesterfield. She glanced at Madeline in the loveseat. Neither said anything, neither was surprised. Gwen knew she could phone her cousin, offer an excuse and take her parents' call at the apartment the first night. They would understand, packing and moving took time. Stupid old man. Couldn't do anything right. A wish to be rid of him had been growing. Getting him a pensioner's apartment would free them. Why was it so hard to help someone? She let out a ragged breath, shrugged.

A few minutes after buzzing the suite intercom at five after eight, Lynch rapped on the door. A call had been made to Nita and Gwen had spoken with her parents for several minutes. She and Madeline made faces at each other before Gwen went to the door. He stood in the doorway in his boots, jeans, trench coat with traces of vomit stains, and the grey-blue and crimson shirt. She noted his haphazard shave, the bits of stubble under his chin. A vague smell of soap mingled with his body odour. A quick wash with a wet towel and wispy suds had removed some of the dirt from his face and neck.

"Come in." Gwen hoped the note of bored sarcasm conveyed the point.

Lynch said nothing. He swaggered through the foyer and into the living room, looked around intently, as if he had never been there before. Nose up, he appeared to be deciding whether or not he approved. A long minute of this before he looked at Gwen.

"You can sleep here," she said, pointing at the chesterfield, covered with two sheets, and at one end was a pile of blankets topped by a pillow. "There's plenty of food in the fridge. If you're bored, there's television. Please don't break anything or leave a mess."

Lynch stared at her blankly. Gwen wanted to ask when he would be inviting his friends. But she wouldn't show eagerness. He would take advantage of any interest beyond the perfunctory.

"About your friends. Do you know when you'll be inviting them? How many there'll be? The apartment is only so big. And I don't want them bothering people at night with loud noises."

"Aready told me. 'Bout taking care of your property."

"We might like to meet them."

"That so?"

Stalemate. Be authoritative, take the initiative.

"I'll phone at ten tomorrow morning. Let me know if they'll be coming tomorrow. We'll be back about five. I'm keeping the key. You'll have to stay in the suite. If you leave, anyone will able to walk in. We're going."

Gwen glanced at the loveseat. Madeline was staring straight ahead, taking no interest in the conversation. As if on cue, Madeline stood up, went to the foyer closet. She took her coat from its hanger without looking and slipped her arms into it. As she went to get her own coat, Gwen looked back at the dim figure of Lynch. He stood in the shade cast by a table lamp. He was darker and more indistinct, a shabby dwarf, a sinister gnome. She fought an idea before it fully formed.

"Phone you from my cousin's around ten," she said. "Better come and lock the door."

There was no answer. She picked up a small valise she had packed and set down by the door. Expressionless, Madeline opened the door and walked out. Gwen followed and looked back and saw Lynch walking towards the doorway, taking his time. She shut the door, heard the click of locks as she and Madeline waited for the elevator.

They said nothing on the way down. Gwen wondered again why it was so difficult to help people. The hope that tramp would appreciate their efforts fought a growing tiredness, a wish to be rid of him for good. Standing beside

Madeline, she ignored her silence. When Madeline gazed ahead in that dreamy way of hers, she could only be pondering something and would eventually come out of her trancelike state. Sometimes Madeline would tell her what it was about and sometimes not. Gwen never probed on those latter occasions. Now she lapsed into her own daydream. Ever since Madeline had told her about Lynch's friends, she wanted to experience some of that delving into the social depths. Maybe some of them would accept help more readily and less strenuously than Lynch. No, she needed a rest.

Madeline was thinking about Speaker and her father. Each spoke as if he knew the only and complete truth, her father about being a father, and Speaker about helping people. But her father couldn't stay married to her mother and Speaker couldn't help anyone, not even himself. Men, she decided, have a need to be right and women have a need to be sure. Men like Speaker enjoyed arguing. They turned it into a contest. Power and authority meant everything to a man. Love could only be play: gift-wrapped chocolates, honeymoons, wheeling the baby on Sunday in a stroller, trying to get the panties off the secretary. Daily love was beyond a man. Only women understood, and that was why they were always trying to be certain about him, to find out how good he was at it. He could never be as good as they were but they looked for someone who might last a while, maybe many years. Madeline remembered her father's ridiculous attempts to deny he was involved with another woman. "Got to replace that shower head," he would say, "don't know when." Or worse, "Nothing like a home-cooked meal." Madeline saw a photograph fall out of his wallet before he could grab it and stuff it back among his credit cards. The woman was young, with full lips and large eyes. He had been taking money out, handing bills to Madeline, when it tumbled out with the cards. That brassiere in the glove compartment. He had wanted to consult a map on their way to a park and out had come the pink diaphanous cups, the slender straps. "The stuff people drop through your window," he had said. "Should've tossed it out, but don't want to be a litterbug." What was the penalty for littering lies? She wanted her father to be different but knew he couldn't, would never go back to her mother and make the family whole again. He seemed greedy, as her mother appeared too ready to blame him for everything. Madeline never blamed herself for the divorce, though she had heard some children do. Some people wouldn't admit that they weren't the best parents. Hers, wow, did she know them.

Speaker? She was almost ready to admit she liked him, though more idea-crazy than most men. If liking could have some pity in it and a lot of curiosity, she did. What could she do but recognize there was more than one feeling to it?

Within two minutes of locking the apartment door, Lynch had found the hidden bottles. After opening the liquor cabinet, he had gone straight to Gwen's bedroom and searched the shelf in her closet and taken down a bottle of single malt. He was sure enough to have carried a hassock with him so he could reach that high. As he stood with the bottle of Scotch in the middle of the living room, he glanced around at the furniture. Coltsfoot end tables, a richly-inlaid coffee table, an ottoman, an expanse of couches, and through French doors the dining room suite and buffets and cabinets: crystal, porcelain, striped satin, brocade, velvet, watered silk, oak, burled walnut, teak and mahogany surrounded him. Lamps with tall shades lit the room quietly and a crystal chandelier hovered majestically and expensively over the dining room table. Before taking a gulp from the neck of the bottle, he gargled the phlegm in his throat and spat on the carpet. The shiny slickness lay there, a viscous gob on the cream pile. He wanted to pee too but didn't because the girls would be returning tomorrow. Maybe before they came back on Sunday. He remembered hearing years ago that some British thieves, when they robbed the homes of the wealthy, would defecate on expensive carpets. "Piles of steaming shit right there on the rug," Lynch was told, and thought it was a good idea but had never done it. After taking a few swigs, he went to the bedroom closet and grabbed some bottles and carried them into the kitchen. He found the pop bottles in the refrigerator and emptied them into the sink and refilled them with the finest whisky and Armagnac and cognac. He refilled the liquor bottles with tap water and put them back on the shelf. After putting the pop bottles in the refrigerator, he headed for the chesterfield with the bottle of single malt under his arm. He kicked off the blankets and pillow, plopped onto the cushions and drank until he passed out.

Gwen phoned in the lobby for a taxi. As she put her phone back in her jacket pocket, she looked at Madeline. Her daydream was over. She was tired.

"I'll be glad when this is finished, Gwenner."

"Me too."

Gwen did not sleep well at her cousin's that night. She had fended off Nita's questions about what was happening that weekend. Nita might want to come along if she knew, so Gwen made up an excuse having to do with being vegan. It was close enough to the truth, that she and Madeline were going to a vegfest, that she wouldn't be caught out in a lie. But worrying about Lynch was what kept her awake until late. She didn't think he was intimidated enough by her warning. She hurried through breakfast, sidestepping her aunt's and cousin's questions and called at a quarter to ten. Each ring seemed to come from further away. She was losing control. She phoned Madeline.

"He's not answering."

"Maybe he's sleeping and can't hear the phone." Madeline didn't believe this.

"He knew I was going to call. I'm going over there."

"I can't come now. I've got to help my mom clean up. You know her." The last sentence was whispered.

"That's all right. I'll call from there."

Gwen phoned for a taxi. Her anxiety mounted with the elevator and she ran to the door. It swung open to her touch. She hurried in, her eyes checking everything. Near the chesterfield there was a heap of blankets and a pillow on the carpet. Nothing else appeared to have been disturbed. Lynch wasn't there. She thought about what to do. She heard him at the doorway. He had been reconnoitering suites for two hours.

Gwen whirled on him, hands on her hips.

"You were supposed to stay in the suite."

"Got antsy, so I was getting some exercise. I come back. Going to call my friends. Be here tonight. Want to see 'em, don't ya?"

"Don't do this again. You've got to stay in until Monday morning. Unless Madeline and I are here to lock the door. Promise?"

"Yeah." He eyed the telephone on the writing desk, next to the archway into the kitchen. "Ya coming, Al?" Lynch was alone and talking on the phone a few minutes later.

"Ah, no wee. Who'll look after the house? Farmer won't be coming, that's pretty sure. He stays in the garage till bedtime."

"Lock her up. Nuthin's going to happen. You'll be back in no time." Lynch knew Al never went anywhere without a gift for his host. It was usually a bottle.

"Wee'll see."

He did come, arriving with the others around seven, and brought a bottle of rye. Slipping away, Lynch hid it on the shelf in Gwen's closet. Speaker and Kevin had been dragooned into coming by their generous landlord. With them were Speckles, middle-aged and balding, whose nickname derived from his freckles and glasses, big John O', the O short for O'Halleran, huge hands and tiny eyes, and thin, sallow Warts, so named because of the growths and lumps on his face and neck. Speckles, a railway diesel mechanic until a divorce led him to quit, talked about machinery. John O's job as a longshoreman had been a casualty of his drinking and fighting. He would flick an enormous thumb through closed fingers when he needed a drink. "He wants a light," Kevin would say. After quitting the railway, Warts had quickly gone through a number of odd jobs, including fry cook at a waterfront café. Fidgety nervous, the only thing he could be absolutely sure about was having an ulcer. Waste was scavenging that night and Farmer hardly ever left the garage.

"You guys have a good time," Lynch said when they were in the foyer. "There's grub in the fridge, and them pop bottles don't have no pop in 'em."

They followed him into the living room. It had the desired effect.

"How'd ya get to stay in a place like this?" Warts said. "I bet it's expensive to keep, but I guess not if ya got loot. Got to have plenty, more than I seen, more than most seen, and that's not nearly what these people here have." Nobody ever answered Warts. He usually answered himself and covered all other possible responses.

John O' flicked his thumb through his closed fingers and looked towards the kitchen. "In there?" he asked of no one, went and poured and downed two stiff shots of whisky. He returned with the bottle and a half full glass and sat on the chesterfield. Speckles went over to the computerized thermostat. It was on the living room wall nearest the foyer. He pushed a few keys on the pressure pad and sat on the chesterfield. Speaker was examining volumes in a mahogany bookcase set against the wall behind the loveseat. The wood shone with a deep port wine lustre, the doors had glass panels and brass fittings. Kevin had gone to the kitchen. He swore as he fought with the plastic wrap on the soy cheddar, with one finger began pulling out drawers and searching for a knife.

"Quite a place, huh, Al?" Lynch said.

"Ah kee." Al shook his head as he stood at the entrance to the living room.

"Sit on that loveseat over there. That's what I heard them girls call it."

"Luffseat? Girl-wimmen?"

"It's all right, Al," Speaker said as he perused a book. "That's a fancy name for an undersized couch."

"It's a sofa with a cushion missing," Warts said, "and that means it's not a sofa or a chesterfield, if they're the same or different, not those but like them, either one if it had that third cushion it doesn't have."

"Who's missing a cushion?" Kevin said from the kitchen, mouth full of soy cheese and multigrain cracker. A little later, "So this is vegan cheese. Worst tasting shit I ever ate. Unless you like chewing on plastic."

Al edged over to the loveseat and after prolonged scrutiny sat on the corner of a cushion. Shoes tapping the carpet, he glanced at the armrests as if they were going to seize him.

"We've seen the place, so why don't you tell us why we're here?" Speaker said to Lynch.

"That girl ya met at Al's be here in a bit. Wants to meet the guys again, and so does her pal that lives here and ain't seen none of ya yet. They're helping me get a place. So I got to coperate."

"By living in this pesthole."

"Be leaving us?" Al said.

"Looks it."

Half an hour later Gwen and Madeline hurried in, faces pink from rushing up the fire stairs. The taxi had crawled through traffic and waiting for the elevator to arrive was too much when they were so close. They would be visiting a school friend and staying until eleven at the latest, Gwen's aunt and Madeline's mother had been told. A quick call and Kelly Bakewell agreed to soothe any anxious relatives who phoned. Madeline recognized Speaker, Al, and Kevin, who had come in and was sitting on the carpet, his back against the loveseat. The others looked uninteresting. Gwen picked out Speaker from what she had been told about him. He looked intelligent but somehow flawed. And the little man was peculiar, a parrot without feathers or beak and trying to guess what was going to go next. The group as a whole was not impressive. A bunch of strange guys.

"Lynch says you wanted to inspect us under your social sciences microscope," Speaker said after the introductions.

"We wanted to meet you, that's all," Gwen said and saw no sense to any of it. Why was she there and what were these men doing in her parents' apartment? But what was wrong with knowing about people who needed help? Curiosity wasn't a bad thing. If someone needed a reason, that would be good enough.

"You could've met us at Al's," Speaker said. "I realize those streets aren't safe for you. There are taxis. Lynch brought your friend and she escaped alive."

He grinned at Madeline, who allowed herself to return a slight smile.

"Maybe I wanted to show you that we're interested in others." The less fortunate, but she couldn't say that.

"Show, or show off?"

"I wouldn't do that."

"You could be unconscious of your real motive."

"I could be unconscious of anything."

"You've met us. You must have a first impression."

"I don't know."

Gwen felt as if she were taking an oral examination. Madeline was right. Speaker was unusual, an uncompromising interrogator and yet always polite. He didn't talk down to her and Gwen appreciated that.

"You like us?"

"That's silly."

"You don't like us."

"That's silly too."

"Somebody else take over. I've got a book I want to look at, if that's all right with you."

Speaker held up a volume of classical philosophy, had been surprised to find it there. He hadn't decided if the bookcase and contents were purchased for display.

"Of course," Gwen said. Was he saying, if you don't mind my being able to read classical philosophy?

"Ya might get to like us," Warts said, "and might not, it's up to you, not us, but we'd be influencing that opinion, if you're not prejudiced, and I'm not saying so, but say you're not the least little bit that way at all, your opinion is your right, so if ya don't, that's fine."

"Clarity personified," Kevin said. "A bunch of social outcasts being feted by two girls and we're asking if they like us. How do we rate in two teenagers' popularity poll: above or below rock stars and TV hunks? Are we more exotic than teachers and Hollywood hams they dream about or are we circus animals waiting for some paltry peanuts of pity? Unfortunate alliteration."

Speaker knew the gibes were aimed at him. But this wasn't a good time to settle with Kevin.

"Good stuff," John O' said, referring to the contents of his glass. "That pop ain't bad," Lynch said, but Gwen knew the glass contained liquor. She couldn't do anything about that now and wasn't very upset. She had half-expected Lynch to do something. And her guests didn't look as if a couple of drinks would make them wild.

"Nice thermostat," Speckles said to her. "I could use some juice."

"There's apple juice in the fridge. We have a carton and there's a can in the freezer. There's a filter under the sink, so the tap water is safe." Was she showing off? Speckles left for the kitchen. That filter would be worth a look. Maybe it was a four-stage reverse osmosis job.

"Filtered water, great news for the millions drinking sewage," Kevin said but no one paid any attention.

"Is there anything you want?" Gwen asked Al. "There's nacho chips." He stared at the girls as if expecting them to devour him. He seemed to be trembling.

"Got to be going, anywee, thanks."

Warts left for food, John O' lapsed into a doze, Kevin stretched out on the carpet and Speaker sat on the loveseat. Gwen and Madeline sat on upholstered armchairs opposite the chesterfield and on either side of the loveseat. A silent minute was broken by a few snores and sounds from the kitchen. Lynch had disappeared but no one noticed. After reading for a while, Speaker looked over at Gwen. She and Madeline had been glancing at each other surreptitiously. They stopped, fearing an attack of the giggles.

"You really think doing this helps anybody?" Speaker said to Gwen. "I don't know what you've got planned for him, but outside of that, do you think you'll learn anything or coming here will change us?"

"I don't know," Gwen said, "but at least we're trying."

"You mean well, but how much is for you and how much is for us? The way we live shouldn't lead others to think we're lazy, useless, immoral or garbage. In this society if you don't hold an acceptable job you're automatically considered inferior, whatever the reason, and the rest of you is forgotten. Maybe you should try to change society's view of those who won't or can't conform to the idea that the job is the man or the woman. And too many jobs exist to make mindless consumers, plunderers of the planet's resources who think in such short terms the average bug is a Socratic philosopher."

"You really love ideas, don't you?" Madeline said. "What's important is that people who have money should help those who don't have any, and you don't need to talk all day about it."

"I don't have to make excuses for helping people who haven't got what I have, thanks to my parents," Gwen said. "And that doesn't mean I'm thinking about myself. I'm doing what I can. Only because I can."

"You're selling salvation, innocently of course, but you're selling it and I don't want it."

"First person singular, finally. You're speaking for yourself. You should take your own advice. Try to see that helping isn't the whole person, it's part of being a person."

"Don't attempt to trap me. I'm not a welfare case. A problem to be solved. I think."

"Maybe that's your problem," Madeline said.

"Thinking is never a problem. Not thinking is."

"You talk like an essay," Gwen said. "Full of sayings. Deep thoughts. That bores me."

Kevin's voice, insinuating, rose from the floor.

"I wonder if you two will be singing like this in a year or so? Sit in the same room with us? You won't want to be within a mile of us. Panting virgins with boyfriends in fast cars. Itching and throbbing in the tiniest places. Of course, some of us find it hard to wait. You with your pissass opinions. Very trusting. You should know that some guys like the hairless innocence of girlhood, the smooth sweetness. Or a bit of delicate fuzz. Is the door locked?"

"Shut up," Speaker said.

"Don't pretend you don't find them more than politically interesting. Are you a member of the blonde or brunette party, or a flaming redhead?"

"I said shut up."

"John O', wake up," Kevin said. John O' roused himself, looked around. "What?" He sounded groggy.

"You like young stuff, right? When's the last time you had a nice piece of tail like this, fresh, untouched?"

John O's tiny eyes focused on the girls, who sat rigid in their chairs.

"You guys in the kitchen, come in here," Kevin shouted. He was sitting up now on the carpet. Speckles and Warts walked in and stood behind the chesterfield. Kevin looked over at them. "Why don't we let these bitches know how little pussy we get and that it's ugly, bought cheap, diseased or crazy." He turned to face Gwen and Madeline. "Want to help us? Take your panties off. A bunch of happy tramps will leave this place tonight. Then you can forget all about helping poor homeless guys. You'll have done us a big favour. You'll be the last good fuck any of us ever get. You can go and live your rich, successful lives without any illusions about us. Look at these guys watching you. Didn't think this would happen, did you? What did you think you were doing, handing out easy charity? We live our whole lives without you. You think you can come and tell us who we are. What we should do? We've already been told. By the real powers in this society. People like the rich bastards in this building. We're shit and we know it. Strip off and get those legs open. Good party night, Saturday. Why should we be left out? Right, you guys?"

"You'll be charged with the rape of juveniles under the age of consent," Speaker said.

"Bullshit," John O' said. "Who's going to tell? You? Better not. I'll fix ya."

"We're practically invisible, anyway," Speckles mumbled.

"They're old for young girls," Warts said, "but not so old that you could say they're women."

"Get a bed ready," Kevin said. He was looking at Speckles and Warts. "Strip off the blankets. John O' and I'll bring them in."

"The wimmens," Al screamed. He leaped up and ran for the apartment door like a parakeet in flames.

Speaker leaned over on the loveseat and with a quick movement of his wrist stabbed a hard corner of bound morocco into Kevin's eye. He shrieked and fell sideways, cupping his hands over the eye and drawing himself up into a ball on the carpet. He moaned and swore. The others watched him.

"He's an asshole," Speaker said. "You wouldn't have gotten away with it. I know him. He'd deny he got you started. Somebody find Al."

Speckles and Warts went to the open door. He was in the hallway, huddled in the furthest corner. They brought him back to the doorway, where John O' joined them, hands in pockets. "We'll go now," Speckles said to Speaker after taking a couple of steps towards the living room. "Thank them for the evening." Speckles shrugged. The four went to the elevator, Speckles and Warts on either side of Al, escorting the small, trembling figure, and the slouching John O' following.

"You should get that eye taken care of," Speaker said to Kevin.

"I can help."

Her fingers finally unclenching, Gwen stood up, the muscles in her legs like kelp swaying in water. She went into the bathroom and returned with some bandages and a towel soaked in cold water. Kevin was sitting up now, a hand still over his eye. She held out the towel.

"Put this on it."

He pushed her hand away, pulled himself up by holding onto the loveseat with his free hand. He staggered to the doorway. Madeline took a couple of deep breaths. Gwen thanked Speaker. Refusing with a smile her offer to let him borrow the book he had been reading, he handed it to her. "Helping isn't easy," he said and left, catching up with the others on the street. They walked back to Al's, except for Kevin, who had disappeared.

Chapter 7

A block from Al's they smelled smoke and heard the heavy roar of big diesels. Rounding the final corner, Speaker was first to see the flames. Like scarlet wings of trapped birds, they beat against windows on the lower floor. Smoke poured out of the upstairs windows as if they were chimneys and rose in black columns into the night sky. Two fire engines blocked the street and overlapping lengths of hose snaking from hydrants lay around them. Firefighters in yellow slickers and hats were directing streams from brass nozzles at the burning house. An ambulance was parked a little further down the block. Al, already suffering from nervous exhaustion, fainted. Speckles and Warts carried him to a front yard several houses away. They laid him out on the grass. Speaker recognized Sylvia in the crowd of onlookers that stood in a semicircle outside the fire engines. Motorcycle police kept them back. He called to her and she came over. She was wearing a duffel coat that had belonged to her husband.

"What happened?"

"All I know is what I heard from a cop. Somebody broke in and a fire started, they don't know how. Farmer's hurt. They found him in the upstairs hallway, lungs full of smoke."

From around the far side of Sylvia's house, being hosed down to keep it from catching fire, paramedics carried a stretcher. A blanket covered the body on it. One of the men opened the back door of the ambulance and they slid the stretcher inside. As the ambulance left, flashing lights warned the crowd to make way. A side wall of the burning house collapsed with a groaning crash.

Sparks burst upwards, a constellation disappearing in seconds. Wood smoke mixed with the oily smell of asphalt shingles hung in the windless air.

A couple of hours later the house was a damp ruin. Scorched timbers stuck out at angles, seemed the keel of a beached and derelict trawler. The figure of Waste appeared among the ashes, black coat and wide-brimmed hat, sack in one hand and stick in the other poking among the warm debris. A piece of burnt blanket, partially melted pots, chipped and discoloured crockery, and spoons and knives and forks in various states of mutation were the harvest, along with some personal items and souvenirs belonging to the many transients who passed through. Waste was there at the behest of Al who, when he regained consciousness, had managed to tell Speaker to inform the police that the proud scavenger was gathering up any salvageable goods for Al and the other inhabitants of the house.

"That was the hardest to find," Waste said later as he drank tea at Sylvia's. Al and his former guests had been invited. Rowser, her brown and white cocker spaniel, kept barking and running back and forth between the kitchen, where everyone was, and the dark cover of the front parlour. "Be quiet, Rowsie," she would say every so often in a halfhearted way among the rattle of cups, saucers and spoons. She had put out a platter of cinnamon toast to accompany the tea and was receiving compliments.

Warts held up a crust.

"Almost for sure the best I ever tasted. Hard to make. Some say it's how much cinnamon, and others the right amount of butter, or it could be how toasty your bread is. Because it should be crunchy and not too chewy, but that's a personal thing. I've eaten crunchy and chewy at different times. . . ."

"Eat the goddam toast and shut up," John O' said. He glanced at Sylvia. "'Scuse me, excellent." Sylvia vouchsafed a smile.

"Too bad what happened to Farmer," Speckles said. "He should've been in an institution."

"Al's was an institution," Speaker said. "Without the white-coated attendants, drugs or straitjackets. A place to stay. That's what people need. Even those like him."

Sylvia looked at Speaker.

"What are you guys going to do? I can put you up for a couple of nights, but I can't start running a boardinghouse."

"I can stay at my brother's, in his basement," Speckles said. "I keep out of the wife's way."

"That was the shack by the old city dump for me," Waste announced, "before, now, and for as long as needed." He stood up and left without another word.

"One of my drinking partners will put me up," John O' said. "Better get going." He and Speckles left together. Sylvia gave each a bag of tomatoes.

"Don't know," Warts said, fidgeting in his chair. "Could have something soon. Right now I got to wait, not for long maybe if things work out. And I'm almost absolutely sure they're going to."

"Stay here with Al and me, if it's all right with Sylvia, seeing that three of us have already gone," Speaker said, looking at Sylvia.

"You bet," she said. "I'll get some blankets."

She headed for the linen closet upstairs. Rowser was behind and tried to rush past her up the stairs.

Al and Speaker slept on the sofas in the front parlour. Speaker wanted to be nearby in case Al panicked during the night. After debating with himself about possible options, Warts was ordered by Sylvia into the sewing room, off the kitchen. He slept on an old couch much favoured by Rowser, who wouldn't give it up finally without a lunge at him. As Speaker was falling asleep, he could smell smoke from the ruins next door. It seeped around the wood frame windows, the curtains and heavy drapes. He wondered about Al. Al certainly didn't have enough money or stamina to rebuild. That bastard, Kevin. It's always a surprise, seeing how much hatred a spiteful man has. Speaker grinned in the dark. They were warned about Lynch. They wouldn't listen, were too busy trying to save him from what nobody could. Lynch could only be himself. They saw something wrong with that, and maybe there was. But the reasons went back further than any moral relativity could justify. Living your own life is a basic right, and about the easiest to deny others.

In the four years since her husband had died no man had slept in Sylvia's house, and now there were three. She lay in the dark, looking sideways at her bedroom window full of stars and thinking about the men she had invited into her house that night. Well, and whatever that was on the sofa opposite Speaker. The guy in the sewing room was a joke and so was the wooden one with the thick glasses, and John O' with those filthy gorilla fingers and cracked nails of his and eyes like someone drilled a hole on each side of his nose. A little more hair and a banana and the apes would think he was one of them. That Waste was a nut like Farmer and he stank. Speaker didn't look weird except for his ponytail and those worn-out clothes. He had no money, and why didn't he have a job? What was he doing with crazies and bums, and assholes like that Kevin, who'd said to her over the fence, "You're the hairy lady in this circus." Where were the eligible men in the downtown eastside for a striking, smart, older woman who didn't look near her true age? Not the creeps wanting to screw her for a night or get a kinky high from a woman with hair on her body, or the bastards wanting to marry her to grab her house, but a guy who could be trusted. She yawned and she was asleep above the men, her breath misting a star-filled garden of dreams.

A cat wandered close to the warm wreckage, sniffing cautiously and then picking with a discriminating paw at some blackened cans. It had only been hours since Farmer's death. He had gone to the garage as usual after dinner, and on this evening after Al had told him that he would be leaving for a while. Farmer stared after hearing the words, and Al tried assuaging what he assumed were fears. "Don't worry, wee'll be back in a wee bit, Farmer." Farmer never worried. All he knew was that if he sat in the car, everything would be fine. He had enough Balvoline. So why would anything go wrong? But tonight after everyone had gone and the house was silent and dark except for a light on the front porch and as Farmer sat in the garage in the front seat of the old car surrounded by nothing that worked and the smell of old leather, with only a forty watt bulb on a cord dangling from a beam, he heard the side door, the one he had used an hour earlier, open behind him. He turned his head. They were there. Sixteen or seventeen years old. Staring his way. They wore jeans and denim jackets, had closely cropped hair and spoke in low voices.

"Fucking crazy." One was skinny and splotched with pimples.

"Fucking looks it." The other was stocky, with a pushed-in face.

They began an assault on the workbench and drawers and the boxes scattered across the floor and threw aside what was under the cobwebs and dust. They found nothing but broken car parts, licence plates, rusty buckets and old tools.

"You got your Balvoline?" Farmer shouted.

"What the fuck's he talking about?" the stocky one said.

"You'll never have enough." Farmer got out of the car.

"The house," the skinny one said, grabbing a fifteen-inch pipe wrench. The other one picked up a balpeen hammer. They came around the side of the car. Farmer blocked their way to the side door. The skinny one raised the wrench and Farmer slapped it away with a sweep of his hand. It banged against the hood of the car, the scraping slide of heavy dropforged steel ending with a clattering clunk on the concrete floor. "Hit the fucker," the skinny one yelled. The other swung and clubbed Farmer on the side of the head. A bruised swelling appeared on his temple but Farmer didn't seem fazed. He yanked the hammer away and dropped it. The skinny one ran past him and out. Farmer gripped the other's arm and squeezed until he screamed. The skinny one returned with an axe handle that lay against the garage and swung at the side of Farmer's head. Knocked sideways and dazed, Farmer loosened his grip and stared ahead blankly, blood in drips from the tear in his ear. They ran into Al's house, kicking in the back door, turning on lights through kitchen and front parlour and not finding anything.

"Up there," the skinny one shouted.

They ransacked the bedrooms, finding some coins and a strapless wristwatch without a crystal. They heard Farmer in the kitchen. He had staggered in, heard noises and was lurching towards the stairs. They were coming down as he started up. They jumped and their weight knocked him off balance and the two rode him to the bottom. They got up, kicked him in the head and throat, blunt boots ramming into his face, the red bone showing through gashed skin. A ragged gap in his cheek exposed his upper jaw and gum, a swollen tongue half torn and bloody teeth smashed into jagged angles. He could barely breathe through his crushed windpipe. They ran back into the kitchen as he reached for a banister and slowly hoisted himself up to the first step, crawled like a wounded turtle upwards until he reached the landing, rolled over and lay flat on the hallway carpet. He could look up. The ceiling bulb was a yellow blur, the white plaster dim from decades of cigarette and kitchen smoke, grime and soot. Inside he found the words.

"Bal, bal, bel, bel, bell." The painful syllables came out. The vowel changed, it swung, the clapper struck. He heard the sound, sweet and sonorous like a call from another place as it rang out over the countryside he knew as a boy, a vast horizon of wheat fields and barns, of streams and quail, and all flaring with sunset like a falling mouth of bronze.

"Fucking assholes, fucking shitheads got nothing." They were throwing things against the kitchen wall and through the windows. The skinny one picked up a butane lighter on the table and set fire to the window curtains and the heavy velvet drapes in the front parlour. "Burn, you shithouse." He ran back into the kitchen. "Fuck off." They left by the back door. Passing the garage, the skinny one lit a pile of oily rags inside the open door and within minutes both house and garage were bonfires. The smoke rose and Farmer smelled it. It choked him, filling his throat and lungs, and brought tears to his eyes. He couldn't see. He didn't hear the fire engines arrive, sirens piercing the night.

"Where is he?" Gwen was venting the tension of the past hour, jumping with her legs together, hands on hips.

"You look funny." Madeline giggled, fingers still clutching the armrests of her chair.

"Let's get him." Gwen's grin was a mock scowl.

They searched the apartment. Lynch had left and taken one of the pop bottles. He had gone to case more suites, planned to slip back in an hour. He took a couple of swigs before climbing the fire stairs to check the apartments on the upper floors, having left these for last. An hour later he had found three more on the twelfth and two on the fourteenth certain to be empty Sunday. As usual he would knock and wait, knock again and after the second silence pick the lock. When a door opened, he would say his dog was lost and ask if the person heard it barking in the hallway. On the twelfth floor a middle-aged woman came out of the suite next door. Holding onto a doorknob, Lynch pretended he fell and was trying to get up. The door opened as he was pulling himself up and he fell backwards onto the hallway carpet. His leg kicked the pop bottle, placed nearby, and it rolled away. He looked at the woman and the decrepit man who had opened the door. "Have you kind people seen my little dog?" The woman's nose wrinkled as she smelled Lynch, whose stink was scented with expensive brandy. Ignoring him, she walked to the elevator. The man, who had forgotten to put in his false teeth, mumbled something and shut the door. Lynch was on his feet as fast as he could manage, moved over and crouched beside the doorknob of the next apartment.

Forty-five minutes later he came up the fire stairs and onto the fifteenth floor, saw the oak doors of the penthouse suite. They faced the elevator doors in a small, silent hall. He put down the pop bottle and tried the doorknob. Rich bastards leave long weekends. Some don't even lock up. Don't bend down if ya don't have to. But the door was locked. He took the ring of keys from around his neck and picked the lock. He stepped inside the suite. In the darkness urgent hurried noises. The outlines of an enormous living room gradually appeared, potted plants in the corners, lots of furniture, pictures on every wall and a window on the opposite side of the room from him with a panoramic view of the city lights. Some careful steps and he saw to his right a door at the end of a hallway. Light shone from under it. The noises were coming from there and seemed louder now, the grunting of a man and softly shrill cries from a girl. Then silence.

"Daddy?" It was a young girl's voice, her foreign accent evident despite the high pitch and light pronunciation.

"Yes?" The man's voice was deep and low.

"Was I naughty?"

"Yes, you were."

"Will I be punished?"

"Yes. But Daddy is resting."

There was a smack and a wincing scream.

"You're supposed to say, 'You never need a rest, Daddy.'"

"I forgot." There was fear in the girl's voice.

"Don't forget. Then what are you supposed to say?"

"I don't know." A harder smack, the girl wailed, the wails becoming sobs.

"What are you supposed to say?" The man's voice had no anger in it.

"I don't know." There was panic in the girl's voice.

"Yes, you do—remember." It was a final order.

"You don't need a rest, Daddy. You're always ready to punish me again."

"When Daddy is resting, what do you do?"

"I make Daddy happy."

"Make Daddy happy." After a few seconds the man was grunting.

The girl gagged.

"Harder. Get more of it in."

"But I choke."

"Harder, and more, or Daddy will be angry."

The man began to make humming sounds. They broke into stuttered fragments. These stopped and the girl gagged and vomited. The man moved heavily on the bed.

"You're still not good enough for Daddy."

"I'm sorry, Daddy."

"Daddy will have to punish you for this. Wipe yourself."

The door opened and Lynch dropped down behind a sofa. The man who opened the door was naked, bulky, with pink skin and was bald except for a fringe of white hair. He walked to a door next to the bedroom and opened it and turned on the light. He peed, took a jar of Vaseline from the medicine cabinet and came out of the bathroom. As he turned out the light, he glanced into the living room. Passing the bedroom door, he pushed it with his heel but it didn't close completely. Lynch looked around for something valuable he could carry away. It was easier to see because of the light coming from the partially open door, but he hadn't taken anything yet. Lynch's instinct had told him to wait. As he looked around in the better light, he saw objects taking shape and could glimpse the man and the girl.

"Put some on Daddy," the man said in his heavy, unhurried voice. Part of his bulk was visible as he lay on the bed, feet towards the door, the naked girl working between his splayed legs. She looked about five, was dark-skinned and had long straight hair. She worked quickly yet awkwardly, crawling over his flattened thighs after finishing.

"Put some on yourself. Not there, up in there. Hurry. Or Daddy will be angry."

Penis erect, the man got onto his knees. He turned the girl so her rump was facing him. She was on her hands and knees, her rump raised high, her long hair covering her face. He spread her buttocks and began to work himself into her. She flinched and his grip on her pelvis tightened as he pushed. He pulled back before pushing deeper and deeper, back and forth, groaning. As his shoves became harder and faster, the girl began to scream. He seized her throat and squeezed before picking her up by the thighs and ramming her as hard as he could. Blood soaked his white groin hair and smeared his belly. She wasn't screaming any more, had become a limp bag of flesh he kept jamming himself into until he collapsed on top of her. He pulled himself free. Blood seeped out from between her buttocks. He turned her over. She didn't move, her head lolling to one side, mouth open. Grabbing her hair by the roots, he yanked it and wiped his hand on the bed sheet.

"Bitch. What a mess you've made. Couldn't even remember the words. Not worth the price."

He went into the bathroom. Lynch could hear water running. The man came out drying himself with a towel and sat on the bed. Careful not to sit near the girl, he picked up a telephone on the night table and slowly punched in numbers.

"This one didn't work out. You'll have to make the pickup now. Let yourself into the building. You've got both keys. I'm leaving."

Lynch had recognized the man. Crouching behind the sofa thirty feet away, he knew escape was becoming more difficult. But he figured he still had a chance to take something. He could see a pile of clothing on an upholstered armchair a few feet away. Nearby was a briefcase on the floor. But they were closer to the bedroom than the sofa. He crept out, keeping low and silently cursing his back. The creaking of his knees sounded like the turning of dry hinges. Lights came on, filling the living room with a brilliant glare. He was a foot from the armchair and several more from the pink man, still naked and now standing at the head of the hallway. Lynch blinked and the man grinned, a grin people think they see on wolves. Lynch knew that the man could outrun and overpower him. But the man's nakedness gave Lynch one advantage. Fuckin' cocky shit—the thought and run at him simultaneous. He slammed a boot down hard on his left foot and then the right. The pink man swore in pain and made a grab for him but missed. Lynch didn't have time to congratulate himself for shoplifting steel taps five months ago and nailing them on his boot heels. On the way out he snatched a handful of clothes and half dragged the briefcase after him. Instinct. There might be nothing of value in the case and it might bring only a few dollars. But the pair of pants or whatever he clutched as he dashed headlong for the fire stairs would not have to be stolen somewhere else.

Fifteen minutes after the fire door had closed, the pink man hobbled into the penthouse hall in a dressing gown and glanced impatiently at the elevator doors. One of his feet seeped blood between crushed toes and the other had swollen, a large purple bruise on the instep. He breathed heavily from the pain but his face showed nothing. The elevator doors slid open and a pockmarked, narrow-faced man came out carrying a suitcase. He wore a dark suit but no tie. He went into the suite without a word when the pink man motioned him inside. A few minutes later the oak doors opened. The man with the suitcase was carrying it less easily, its sides bulging now. The pink man wore an overcoat that wasn't long enough to hide his naked legs. He limped in bedroom slippers. The man with the suitcase got out of the elevator in the lobby and hurried back to the visitors' parking lot. The pink man rode down to the underground car park and hopped to his limousine.

As Lynch was in the master bedroom closet hiding the briefcase and clothes, which turned out to be a jacket, shirt, undershirt, shorts, socks, tie and a pair of pants, he heard the girls returning and he had to rush back into the living room. Gwen noticed he was out of breath.

"Where have you been? We've been searching for you."

"Looking the place over, getting used to it. Why'd ya leave the door open for, so burglars can walk in?"

"That's a funny thing for you to say."

"Lots of perverts too." He went to shut the door.

"Like your friends. One of them tried to get the others to rape us. That guy called Speaker stopped them. No thanks to you."

"What'd ya want me to do? I can't be 'sponsible for all them bums at Al's. I done what ya wanted. Ya wanted to see 'em."

"We wanted to live through it."

"Where did you go?" Madeline said. "You look worn out."

"Told ya, keeping busy. Need sleep bad."

"I don't know whether to trust you the rest of the weekend," Gwen said. "You're never here."

"Before ya had me locked in them crummy places downstairs. Seen what I wanted to, so I ain't going nowheres."

Gwen considered throwing him out, but that would have been admitting defeat. She looked at her watch.

"It's almost twelve. We're going. If this happens again, you'll have to leave. I don't care what your excuse is. Late tomorrow afternoon we're going to show you the pensioners' apartments. On Monday you'll have to go to your friend Al's place because my parents are coming back. I'll give you a letter to take on Tuesday morning to the office on Main where you go to apply for a suite. We can't go with you. We've got to go to school. Give your letter to the guy in charge of the suites. He'll take care of you."

As soon as they had gone, Lynch was crouching on the floor of the master bedroom and picking the lock on the briefcase, a simple push catch. The tan leather sides of the case flared in accordion pleats at the bottom and it had two leather handles, gold-plated hinges and fittings and a wide strap sewn on one side and going over the top to the other, where it was fastened with a gold-plated lock. After picking it, Lynch could see on the rough cowhide under the strap stamped initials, C.K. He poured the contents onto the carpet, scattered them and swore. There were more than a dozen contracts, a flash drive, a couple of notebooks, ballpoint pens, a nail clipper and a package of breath mints. He put the pens into his trench coat pocket, stuffed the rest back into the briefcase and returned it to the closet. He looked over the clothes. They were useless, much too large for him. After some swigs from Al's gift, he peed on the carpet. His aim was poor and he drenched a pant leg before slumping onto the bed, passing out.

Speaker woke up before eight on Sunday morning. He smelled bacon and eggs and heard the sizzling from Sylvia's big cast-iron pan in the kitchen. He looked over at Al, curled up feet to chin at one end of the other sofa. Al had kicked all of his blankets onto the floor. Speaker yawned, stretched and got up, still vaguely aware, despite the food odours, of the smell of wood smoke from next door. He walked into the kitchen. It was smaller than Al's had been, and cleaner, with no garbage in sight and no flies. Along the north wall, beside the hallway, were the refrigerator and the electric stove. Along the east wall of the north-facing house were the sink, counter and a row of cupboards overhead and under the counter. The southwest corner was the eating area, with an oval maple table and six chairs. Sylvia had revarnished the chairs. The tablecloth was red and white checks and there was a clear sheet of plastic over it. She looked up when he came in. She had put on a freshly laundered housedress and apron.

"Thought I'd wake you guys up this way," she said. "Leonard used to like bacon and eggs for breakfast on Sundays. The rest of the week was porridge. Hope you like this."

"Smells great. I'll get washed."

Warts opened the door of the sewing room and stepped out. He rubbed his eyes with the back of his hand.

"I slept like the dead. Not like them or I wouldn't be here. But like I was dead, like you couldn't wake me. You could. But it would've have been tough."

"You like bacon and eggs?" Sylvia kept her back to him.

"I shouldn't because of my stomach. Ulcer. Like the Devil's pitchfork. But when something smells good, though, what can you do? A lot would be crazy. But a little would be all right. If I eat slow."

"You want to eat or stand there talking like a fool?"

"Wash first," Warts mumbled as he headed for the bathroom. "Got to wash. Get at least some of the dirt off. Not all, of course. But you can try."

Speaker finished in the downstairs bathroom and Warts went in and Speaker checked on Al. He seemed to be stirring.

"How do you feel, Al?"

"Ah kee."

"Feel like eating?"

"With the wimman?"

"This is Sylvia's place. Next door. It was nice of her to let us stay here last night. Why don't you show your appreciation by eating some breakfast?"

"Ah kee." Al put his feet on the rug. "My place." He couldn't say any more.

"Don't think about it, Al. Things will work out."

Warts came out of the bathroom and they went into the kitchen. Al took the chair nearest the back door. Speaker sat next to him, leaving the chairs nearest the stove for Warts and Sylvia, so Al wouldn't be too close to her and afraid to eat. "You're not used to being served, are you, Al?" Speaker said as she approached with her arms and hands full of crockery and utensils. Al shook his head, glancing up nervously. Sylvia grinned to put him at his ease and set down plates, cups and saucers and the rest and went to get the food. There were platters of toast, eggs and bacon, a butter dish, a creamer, a sugar bowl, a bottle of ketchup and a pot of tea.

"This is great," Speaker said after a mouthful of egg and toast.

Ketchup on his lips, Warts nodded, deciding not to speak after a look at Sylvia. Al nibbled on a slice of toast Sylvia had buttered for him.

She was wearing her best slippers, the ones with fluffy balls on them, a gift from Leonard. She hadn't worn them since he died. There hadn't been much company, mostly neighbourhood women with boring gossip and endless complaints about their health. Did anybody notice that her apron was fresh and she had fixed her hair? God, she was really getting silly. Why would they notice an older woman? They liked the food. Couldn't do this for long. A while since men were in the house, even a son of a bitch like that Dan, who expected to hop into bed if you please the very first time he was asked to come over for a cup of tea. Didn't even wash. Filthy clothes. Grabbed with his fingers all yellow from cigarettes. Hurt right through the wool pants. Deserved that slap. Was going to hit back. Good thing Rowser was there. Got him on the ankle. Enough time to get the butcher knife. That stingy Ralph.

He only wanted a wife so he could get a house. Wouldn't bring a decent box of chocolates. Hard candy. Ate a whole cucumber pie. Dug in with his hands. Got rid of him by hinting about dinner at the Golden Gondola. Said he didn't like Italian food. Wouldn't pay for it, that's what it was.

"If I may speak for us guys, thanks," Speaker said. Chewing on another slice of buttered toast, Al glanced up. Sylvia waved a hand at her guests. "Forget it." Warts belched, a foghorn calling for its mate. "Pardon me. Too fast." They heard Rowser barking. He had been let out an hour ago and wanted back in. Sylvia got up and opened the back and screen doors. Rowser went and sat near Al, looking up at him and wagging his stump of a tail.

"Is it a wimman-dog?" he asked Speaker.

"No," Sylvia said, "he's a guy dog."

Al patted Rowser's head and he wagged his tail harder.

"Guess he likes ya, Al," Warts said. "Dogs like me usually, but some don't and I got the scars to show it. I get along with most of them, except abused ones, and who can with those poor things that are so scared they'll bite anybody. Not guard dogs and mean dogs, of course, and some big ones. Dogs like me, mostly."

"Ah kee, wee're friends." Al stopped petting Rowser, who went over to Sylvia and lay down at her feet.

"We've got to start looking around," Speaker said to Sylvia. "We shouldn't abuse your hospitality."

"I'm happy to have you guys. I don't see why you can't stay here while you're looking."

"Thanks. Mind staying a little longer, Al?"

"Ah kee, with the doggie."

"What about you, Warts?"

Warts looked at Sylvia, avoiding her eyes.

"A little longer be all right. You're not rich. Not exactly poor either, living in a house like this. But we're not going to be eating much. Or use a lot of hot water, shaving once a. . . ."

Chapter 8

Drenched in pee and whisky, Lynch woke up late on Sunday morning. When he had passed out, what was left of the bottle had spilled on him. Groaning, he sat up and the bottle rolled off his chest. He tried to grab it and missed and it fell onto the carpet and he knew by the hollow thud that it was empty. He took off his clothes and wiped himself with a bed sheet. He looked in the dressers, took out a white dress shirt, and from the closet a pair of grey flannel pants. He put them on, rolling up the cuffs on shirt and pants. Fancy duds. Good as that shit I stole. Them bitches be sprised. Out of here 'fore they get back. Sposed to call them guys. Morning? Noon? Time? Ten on that fucking clock. Doughnut's fuckin' card? Got to be in the shirt on the bed. Fuckin' nuthin' in the pocket. In the other shirt. At Al's. No fuckin' time to go get it. Phone the grage. Could be waiting there. Sunday. Be closed, anaways. Them fuckers' names? No Doughnuts or Zimmo in the phone book. Who'd know? Nobody at Al's. Studer the fence. They unloaded with him. He'd know the number. Called Studer cheap. Asked him for a loan. Bastard wouldn't. He wouldn't 'member that. Months ago. Let him know it's 'portant. He wouldn't cross them guys.

The telephone rang. It was Gwen.

"We'll be over late this afternoon. Be ready."

"Ya can't come."

"Why not?"

"Don't feel good. I can't see that place. Not today. Monday be better."

"We can't go Monday. I've got to clean the apartment before my parents get back."

"I'm sick."

"Have you been drinking?"

"I caught something. Got to sleep it off. Come by later. 'Bout seven."

"It'll be almost dark. It wouldn't be safe for Madeline and me. And we want to have a look at the outside. Can you be ready by four?"

"That'd be 'bout right."

Lynch dialed Studer's number, well known to thieves in the downtown eastside. Studer hung out at Pop's Billiards, on the second floor of the Commerce Hotel. He hardly ever left the building and never in daylight, rented a room there. Grey face, lanky frame and sparse strands of flat hair, he rolled up his shirtsleeves to the armpit and usually wore a green visor. He spoke carefully and could make one word say everything he wanted.

"Yeah. Yéah. Ya-ya. Yee-ah. Ohya. Yaha. Yaaaah. Ya. 629-4920. Yi."

"What the fuck kept ya?"

"Couldn't find the card ya give me, Doughnuts. It's in my other shirt. At Al's. Couldn't 'member your number. Had to call Studer over at Pop's."

"That shirt's gone. Al's burnt down last night. We quit late, saw the smoke and had a look. Be there in an hour."

Lynch hung up and swore. He was thinking about the thirty dollars he hid at Al's. But he wouldn't need it. Or his few clothes there. His cut from the stuff was going to set him up. The other guys would be on the street. He remembered that the caretaker's suite was near the exit doors. The caretaker might see them and get suspicious.

Maggie MacDiarmid answered the door. As usual, she had gone to church with her husband that morning. She was cleaning off the table after they had marmalade and toast with their tea. He was dozing on the sofa in the living room. Lynch stood before her in Roger Chalmers' white button-down shirt and grey flannel pants, his voluminous black coat, and around the shirt collar had thrown a loosely knotted plaid tie Gwen bought her father one Christmas but he had never worn. Lynch appeared to have shrunk several sizes smaller. His fingertips were barely visible and boot toes bulged under rolled-up cuffs.

"What was it ye wanted?"

"I got to see the caretaker. Got a problem in 206."

"I'll get him for ye. I see you're wearing plaid."

"Huh?"

"Your tie. Are ye Scottish?"

"I never said no to a Scotch."

"Ye mean Scot. What's your name?"

"McLynch."

"Are ye Irish?"

"I'm mixed Scotch and Irish. It's a small clan. We only got one bagpipe. Can't even 'ford none of that tart stuff."

"Hee, what's that aboot a tart?"

"Them woolly skirts with the big safety pin."

"Ye mean kilts."

Funny wee man. That's for certain.

"Are ye a God-fearing Christian?"

"When I'm scared enough."

"Ye know, there are things going on in this building we Christians should poot a stop to. I'm talking aboot those whoores that pretend they're innocent little girls."

"I got that problem I told ya 'bout."

"I'll get ma husband. Do ye know them, who they are, who's their pimp?"

"I don't know nuthin' 'bout 'em."

"Wee'll, I think action should be taken by people like us. If we don't, who knows what'll happen? The place will be Sodom and Gomorrah. And there's Armageddon to consider, too. How'll we be found at the Last Judgement?"

"I got to see your husband."

"Ye must have quite a big problem not to want to talk aboot the Lord on Sunday."

"Yeah. Get your husband, will ya?"

She stared at him. He wasn't properly shaved on the Lord's Day, his clothes certainly ill-fitting. Had she made a mistake in thinking him one of the righteous? Did he know more aboot the whoores than he admitted? He could be a customer. She remembered the tramp her husband encountered in an empty suite. No wonder he didna want to talk aboot the whoores. She closed the door halfway and hurried over to the sofa.

"Ian," she whispered harshly and shook him by the shoulder.

"Wha'?"

"There's a wee man at the door who says he's got a problem, and I think he's the one ye found sleeping in that suite."

MacDiarmid rubbed his eyes and sat up. He had been dreaming. He was in a piping contest and being admired by a lovely girl in Highland dress as he played his set of pipes beautifully. Above her kilt she was bare, and so was he above his. His chest was hairy and he had a full head of hair.

"What are ye talking aboot?"

"I tell ye, he's that man."

"You're daft. He wouldna come back."

MacDiarmid went to the door, opened it wider. He eyed Lynch carefully, decided that his wife was imagining things.

"What's the trouble? Are ye a tenant here?"

"Some friends are letting me stay in their place till they get back Monday. Been here a couple of nights. I was out today. When I come back I seen the place been broke into. The lock's busted."

"I better phone the police."

"Call up there. They busted up the 'partmint."

"What did they do?"

"Lots of stuff. Holes in the wall and erything."

"Ma God."

MacDiarmid shut the door quietly behind him and they rode the elevator to the second floor, Lynch letting the caretaker hurry ahead of him to the apartment. The door was slightly open. MacDiarmid pushed it and stepped inside the doorway. Lynch waited until he heard the caretaker's body hit the floor. Zimmo was standing over the unconscious man, a short length of pipe in his hand.

"Works every time."

"What took ya so long?" Doughnuts said.

"His wife's a yapper. Had to keep asking her to get him."

"We'll tie and gag him and dump him in a closet," Doughnuts said to Zimmo.

Ten minutes later the three were downstairs outside the open exit doors. A white van was parked beside them. Doughnuts and Zimmo had met Lynch at the entrance after Lynch phoned about the caretaker. They drove around to the back after dealing with MacDiarmid. The mechanics were dressed in white coveralls, like professional movers.

"We only take the best and it can't be big," Doughnuts said to Lynch. "Cameras, smartphones, notebook computers, desktops, printers, calculators, money, wallets, credit cards, jewellery, watches, anything gold. No big screen TVs, paintings, clothes, furniture, statues. Stuff goes in those bags Zimmo's getting out of the van. We take a couple of hand trucks to stack the bags on. We move fast. Five minutes each place. Take us to the best one on each floor first. We start low, work our way up. Come down when all bags are full. We go back till the van's packed. Don't rush. Look as if you're on a job. Somebody talks to ya, answer. Don't yak. Building looks pretty empty. Let's go."

On the first six floors they didn't see anyone, and on the seventh a man waiting for an elevator didn't even glance at them. When on the tenth a middle-aged couple saw Lynch picking a lock as the other two stood by, they kept talking as they passed. Their only trouble came from Maggie MacDiarmid. On their third trip to the van, Doughnuts slipped and banged his hand truck loudly against one of the exit doors. It had been over an hour since her husband left, and Maggie was pondering what to do. When she heard the noise, she came out of the caretaker's suite. She pushed open an exit door and saw Lynch passing a bag into the van. She rushed over.

"Where's ma husband?"

"Tell her he's phoned the cops and he's waiting for 'em," Doughnuts whispered, leaning close to Lynch so she couldn't hear.

"He called the cops. Waiting for 'em."

"Why didna he come back and tell me?" She had seen Doughnuts leaning towards Lynch and heard whispering.

"'Cause there's lots of stuff busted. He's trying to fix it."

"He canna fix a thing afore the police, the claims adjuster, and the owner, the tenant or sub-lessee sees the damage. His tools are in the storeroom, anywee. He would have to go down for them. He would've come by and told me."

"Why don't you go talk to him?"

"Think I weel. Your suite number's 206, ye said."

"Come with us," Doughnuts said. "We're heading up there now. Give ya a ride." He motioned for her to sit in his hand truck.

"I wouldna accept a ride from you."

"What'd ya mean?"

"I want nothing from a Catho-lick Eyetalian."

"Ya might get something ya didn't expect."

"Your threats are stupid. I dinna like what's going on here. Dinna think ye can get me upstairs like ma trusting husband. If you've done anything to him, you'll pay. I'm phoning the police."

She ran back to her suite but Zimmo was quicker, got to the open door before her and stood in the doorway. Doughnuts was behind her and shoved her into his arms.

"Hey, she's a big broad," Zimmo said. "I like big broads, can take my weight."

He spun her around so he was behind and against her.

"Get away from me," Maggie hollered, jabbing an elbow into his ribs. He winced. She shot the same arm forward and hit Doughnuts on the jaw. He fell down but grabbed her legs. Zimmo put an arm almost around her waist and the other around her neck and held on. She tried to kick Doughnuts but his grip was too strong. Her ankles squirmed within his locked elbows.

"What'll we do with her?" Zimmo said. "Too bad we got no time for fun."

Doughnuts grunted. He jumped up, avoiding a kick and butted Maggie between her nose and right eyebrow. She began bleeding from her nose. Dizzy, she slumped in Zimmo's arms. He dragged her over to the sofa. Doughnuts brought some rope from the van and tied her hands and feet, and so she could breathe didn't gag her. He wedged wadded toilet paper into her nostrils to staunch the flow of blood and then rolled her over onto her right side so that she faced the back of the sofa and tilted her face an inch from the cushion. When they went back to the van, Lynch was inside resting on the bags.

There were three floors left, including the penthouse. Lynch hadn't mentioned what happened and was uneasy as they worked upwards towards it. He wouldn't be alone. Maybe this afternoon it would be empty. Lots of good stuff there.

Maggie regained consciousness and felt a weight between her eyes, as if huge fingers were plugging her nose and twisting it. She remembered, screwed up her face a bit. The fingers became a sharp blade slicing down through cartilage and made her weak. Her eyes focused on the rough cotton and polyester weave of the green sofa fabric. An ache in her right shoulder bothered her. When she tried to shift her weight she seemed to have lost her hands, then felt the rope around her wrists at the small of her back. An attempt to move her feet found the rope around her ankles. Neither rope was tightly wound but there were several coils of it. She was thirsty and her mouth was dry. After straining against each rope, she licked the crust of blood on her lips.

Is God punishing me? Have I been remiss in ma Christian duties? I read Scripture every day. I poot as much as I can in the plate every Sunday, too much according to Ian. I'm going to help with the church bazaar in October. Reverend Finnerton says ma attendance is best in the whole congregation. I help Ian with his work. Vacuum miles of carpet in the building. Look after those plants in the lobby. A jungle there. One with thorns. Stabbed ma finger cleaning it. Sharp. Went so deep. Blood welling up like a red oil and running like a snake along ma hand. Sucked it. Warm and salty. Is He trying this way to teach me a lesson? Am I too proud? This humbles me surely, Lord, for whatever I have done. They didna touch me, that dark one, hair all over his hands. Doing this to me. What'll ma nose look like now? That girl, Sally, broke hers playing grass hockey. Ugly bump on it afterwards. Ian won't notice. What did they do to him? I don't think they're murderers. Is he tied up? Ye stupid bugger, it's your fault. I'll take ye by that tuft of hair and throw ye away. I told ye the wee man was the same one ye told me aboot. Couldn't ye see it? I never saw him but I knew it. Him and his little whoores are part of a gang. And ye went with him. Perhaps he's not tied up. Perhaps he's with the whoores, enjoying himself. And I'm hurt here and left to die. He planned it. To get rid of me. Couldn't do it himself. Gutless. Hoping I'll die and he'll have all the young girls he wants. That won't be many. Hardly touches me. He's daft aboot girls. Perverted. Oh, God, I'm being tempted by bad thoughts. Ian wouldna do this. He's probably dead and I'm being tormented with hate for him. Ian, if you're dead and listening, I didna mean what I said. I'll free myself and get the police and they'll find you're murderers. I'll not forget ye. The holy martyrs suffered more and never lost faith, and I mustn't.

Maggie took a couple of minutes to muster her strength before she bent her knees and pushed with her aching right shoulder. Using her feet as a pivot, she rolled onto her back. She groaned at the effort and lay there a while breathing heavily through her mouth. She swung her legs onto the floor and sat up. She felt dizzy and her swollen nose, with toilet paper still firmly wedged in the nostrils, seemed more like a throbbing foot. She swallowed a thick gob of blood and mucus, felt like vomiting but fought the nausea and began working at the coils around her wrists. They wouldn't loosen, so she tried those around her ankles. They had more give, and she kept twisting her feet to loosen the knot. It gave, but slowly, and she rested after bursts of twisting. Twenty minutes later it had slackened enough for her to pull her feet free. She stood up and dizzy again sat down, her mouth open and breath forced, throat like sand, her shoulders and wrists cramped and almost numb. She waited for a few moments, got up and went to the apartment door. With her back to it, she put her fingers around the doorknob and turned it. She kicked the door open and looked up and down the hallway. It was quiet and empty.

Twenty-five minutes earlier, five minutes before Maggie MacDiarmid had regained consciousness, Doughnuts and Zimmo had driven away. The last floors had been as easy as the others. The fourth trip back to the van was their last. Lynch had decided not to risk the penthouse.

"Been up there?" Doughnuts said after they finished with the fourteenth floor.

"Heard something. Didn't go in."

"Let's take a look."

"We got plenty."

"Worth a look if they're out."

"You guys go. I'll look after the stuff."

"We all go."

They wheeled the hand trucks into the elevator. With his elbow Zimmo jabbed the floor button. A silent ride up to the fifteenth floor. The oak double doors were wide open.

"Ya see," Doughnuts said. "Never know till ya look. Somebody was careless. Let's go."

"Wait for yas here," Lynch said. Shit. Was last night. How'd they know?

Zimmo moved behind Lynch. Doughnuts stood in front, facing him. Too small and tired to fight or run, he couldn't have escaped. They had a reputation. They had crippled guys who hadn't kept their word or owed money and hadn't paid. There were rumours of a couple of contract killings because money was held back in drug deals. That was it. The pink man was powerful. More powerful than Lynch had thought. His bad luck to be found in the same place twice. This was easy. Delivering one beat-up tramp. They even had time to go through the suites before they did their second piece of business. Whoever waited on the other side of that doorway was there to kill him but wanted to talk, or he would have been killed in the van.

Doughnuts turned. They walked through the doorway, leaving the hand trucks outside. The drapes were open and the sunny living room now showed itself to be full of black leather sofas and chairs. To the left were dark cabinets and a stereo against one wall. To the right a bar and four stools took up most of the other wall. Behind it were two shelves filled with liquor bottles, crystal decanters and a row of glasses, including shot glasses and a couple of brandy snifters. The potted plants Lynch had seen last night were actually vases full of pampas grass and the pictures oils of northwest seascapes. He noticed none of this, instead was looking at the man who had walked into the living room almost as soon as they had. Tall and bald but tanned, not pink, he was wearing a black suit and tie and a white shirt and black shoes. He motioned with his hand for Doughnuts and Zimmo to leave. They shut the door behind them and he came over to Lynch. More than a foot taller, he stared down, casually alert, as if bored with such small prey.

"Where is it?" A flat voice.

"What'd ya mean?"

Lynch knew he would be killed as soon as he told where the briefcase was. A simple fact and accepted the way he accepted bunions and a cold wind.

"You want money? You'll get money. After. Where is it?"

"Tell me what ya want."

The man hit Lynch across the face. He used the back of his hand. The blow wasn't hard, and not the hardest Lynch ever received, but it was hard enough to knock him off his feet. He got up slowly and backed away.

"Where is it?"

"I give it to someone. Guy I owed a favour. I took some pens, nuthin' else. Ya can have 'em back. Got no use for the rest."

"Who is this guy?"

"A bum."

"Where is he?"

"He don't live in one place."

The man moved towards him and the hand struck again, harder. He was knocked back, his feet in mid-air as he landed on the carpet. The side of his face was numb. He didn't want to but got up, afraid he might be kicked. As he stood up, the man stared but not at him. He raised a hand to scratch his chin. Lynch jerked his head away.

"Take me to him," the man said, grabbed Lynch by the shoulder, swivelled him around to face the door and pushed him. He stumbled and lurched towards the elevator.

"Call duh polith. Ba hubband burdud. Liddow mad food hib. Died be ub."

Maggie MacDiarmid, hands still tied behind her back, ran towards two widows chatting in the lobby as they waited for the elevator. Her face and blouse were smeared with dried blood, nose swollen into a knob. Thirty minutes later Ian MacDiarmid's hands and feet were being untied by a policeman. He was brought down to his own suite for questioning and saw his wife lying on the sofa, head on a pillow. A paramedic was attending to her nose.

"Toad hib id wad hib," she said to the policeman who was questioning her husband. "Liddow battard."

"What's his name?"

The man guided his sports car through traffic towards the downtown eastside. Shifting smoothly, he passed cars and changed lanes. Like a racehorse being given its head, the black car slipped sideways into openings with inches to spare and surged ahead. The turbocharged flat six at the rear was a roar of threshing oil-slick metal.

"Binner. 'Cause he lives in 'em."

"Where?"

"Back of pubs. Main Street."

"I drive down the alleys. You see him, we get out and look. I've got a collar on you and I'm holding the leash. You try to run, I pull you back hard and hold you up by that leash and collar till you choke."

Lynch hadn't seen Binner for months. He didn't know why he thought of him when forced to come up with a way out. He had no idea what he would do when they found him. Younger than most of the people Lynch knew in the downtown eastside, Binner was twenty-five and had been in a mental institution for five years until he convinced a psychiatrist that he no longer believed himself to be the legitimate heir to Zurbar, Emperor of the Pleiades. He did not say that he had replaced Zurbar, who had been deposed by a popular revolt. He would look up at the stars on clear nights and talk to his subjects. On cloudy ones he would speak to himself of isolation and exile. Whenever he spoke to others about his homeland, he would say it spanned many solar systems of beautiful planets, all high and cold desert and mysteriously fertile, and that his subjects "loved the cack-teye" or they would have joined him here and made him ruler of the earth. Living mostly on garbage he found in nearby dumpsters, he was helped regularly by Slouch Annie, who wheeled her shopping cart through the downtown eastside every day, searching through garbage cans, dumpsters and heaps of trash and sleeping in doorways. Years of pushing her cart with her arms straight out in front of her gave the short woman a hunched back and her name. A pale blue woollen cap pulled low over her grey hair, a heavy wine cardigan frayed at the cuffs and covering most of her grey and rose print dress, she trudged in black boots and two pairs of work socks behind her cart through alleyways, always managing to save for Binner something from among her choicer pickings. The few remaining slices of a day-old loaf of bread. A squashed chocolate bar. She would knock on his dumpster behind the Huntington Arms hotel and pub and throw food in when he lifted the lid. There were two dumpsters at the back of the hotel. The one beside the service entrance was used daily but the other, a battered wreck unused for years, was near a corner of the building. Binner lived there. He would peer over the edge, smile benignly at her and tell her that she knew how to treat a ruler. "Yup," she would say, grinning, showing her crooked stained teeth. He would say that his people wanted him to return but he would be staying a while longer because some matters of policy remained to be determined. "Yup," Annie would say and push her cart down the alley.

Another friend was Indian Red. His fair complexion and red hair made some whites doubt he had aboriginal blood. "You got light skin" was a common response in pubs or at the park where he played softball on summer evenings. "Yeah," he would answer, "because one of you raped a squaw who was my grandmother." "You know why we're friends?" he once said to Binner. "We both lost a home. You out there and me down here." He worked as a bouncer at the Blue Anchor pub, did odd jobs and rented a room in one of the decrepit skid row hotels. But he felt safer on the streets. "The smell is better and you can see trouble coming."

The car glided down an alley behind Main, giving Lynch a personal tour of his own life. The evening was muting into shadow the bleary yellow and sooty red bricks of back walls of hotels, pubs, restaurants and stores, dimming exits and service entrances. An orange or a blue dumpster was behind most buildings. Men sat on the asphalt pavement, backs against a dumpster or the leaning mast of a telephone pole rigged high with drooping wire and cable. Most of the men were holding a paper bag with a bottle in it. Lynch recognized some of them. He knew where Binner's dumpster was and was stalling, trying to figure out how to save himself.

"Is he in that one?"

"Nah."

"You better not be playing."

"Don't see him."

"You're going to run out of alleys and I'm going to take you somewhere."

"Can't see him if I don't."

The car slipped out of the alley, cut across traffic and slid into another alley. The man downshifted and the car crawled.

"See him?"

"Orange one."

"Remember what I said."

The man braked and shifted into neutral, put on the emergency brake and left the engine running. They got out and Lynch went over to the dumpster and stood on tiptoe to look inside. There was no one, only a clutter of cardboard boxes and bundles of paper. Lynch turned away as the man came up behind him.

"Not here. Other one."

Lynch hurried over to a blue dumpster. The lid was down but not completely shut because of the mass of garbage inside. He pretended to examine it closely. A girl's face on the side of a carton stared at him. The face of a missing child or a label in shadow.

"Not here neither."

"I could see that from over there. You are playing."

"Eyes no good." Lynch's eyesight was excellent.

The man drove through a third, crossed over to a fourth alley, where a head was sticking out of a dumpster.

"That's him," Lynch said, pointing before the words came out.

"Let me talk. If this works out, there'll be something coming to you."

Lynch lagged behind the man as they walked to the dumpster. Binner ducked when he saw them. Royalty shouldn't wait on ambassadors. They must announce their presence and he should respond in the proper manner after the proper delay.

"Hey, you," the man said. "I want to speak to you."

There was no answer. He banged his fist on the dumpster and looked inside. Binner was sitting in a corner, staring ahead with what he would have called a regal look. The man saw an emaciated hollow-eyed figure with scraps of beard, rags for clothes and an empty look on his face.

"I said I want to speak to you."

Binner kept staring straight ahead. Lynch knew that he would take his time before answering.

"What's wrong?"

"Dunno. Never seen him like this."

"You talk to him."

"Said you'd do the talking."

"I said talk to him."

Lynch put his hands on the top edge and hoisted himself so he could look inside, his toes barely touching the asphalt. Binner was almost ready to talk. Lynch waited a few seconds. Binner looked up and smiled.

"Hi, Binner. How ya doing?"

"Pretty well, considering the state of international relations. My subjects want me to return."

"Are ya going?"

"Not yet. I have problems to consider. Foreign affairs, for one. The distances are so great, as well."

"'Bout that briefcase, Binner. Ya know, the one I give ya for them 'foren 'fairs."

"I don't think I remember."

"It was very 'portant for your people."

"I must have it somewhere."

"Look, will ya?"

"Help him," the man said.

"My bones is stiff. Can't jump in like a kid."

"Get in or I'll throw you in."

"Gimme a hand up."

The man stooped a little and Lynch put a foot in the man's cupped hands and hoisted himself into the dumpster. Binner was sorting through the bundles of paper around him.

"Find it, Binner?"

"Not yet. This is wrong. I should remember something that important. My subjects expect so much from me. Not that they shouldn't. If I fail them, who else is there? The pressures on an emperor are not well known or understood. Presidents and prime ministers get all the attention. As if only they've got troubles. But we monarchs have as many."

"'Course," Lynch said, throwing around paper and boxes.

"What's going on?" the man said. "Got it yet?"

"Nah."

"This is a major failure," Binner said as he sorted through supermarket flyers and bills of lading. "This disheartens me. My subjects may be discouraged by this. And I may never be able to return and face them. It must be here. The sky promises to be clear tonight. Perhaps my subjects have some knowledge of this and can give it to me. I can relay it to you through the proper diplomatic channels."

"What's he talking about?" the man said. He leaned over the edge of the dumpster and saw the two attacking the garbage.

"'Bout getting help."

"We don't need any."

"But my subjects are often of invaluable help. We surely can avail ourselves of it in a matter as supremely important, one may even say crucial, as this one."

"He's crazy and you knew it."

"I give him the briefcase."

"Get out of there."

"You have absolutely no right, sir, to obstruct an ambassador in the lawful course of his duties. Diplomatic immunity protects him, and you must observe the proprieties."

"Get out," the man yelled at Lynch.

"Nay, varlet," Binner said in a voice still calm and authoritative. "Ye shall not transgress the immaculate order of God and royal sovereignty. Else all shall fail. That is worth fighting for. If we fail to stand for that, what are we? Apologize at once, and ye shall do a fitting penance. A pilgrimage, I think."

"Shut up or I'll shut you up," the man said in a quieter voice. But his yelling had attracted the attention of others in the alley, including Indian Red. He was on his way to the Blue Anchor and was cutting through the alley. He usually stopped and said a few words to Binner.

"What's going on? Hi, Lynch."

"Hi, Red."

"Nothing is going on," the man said. "We made a mistake."

"A mistake?" Binner said. "The violation of an imperative, an entrenched prerogative. The overriding of convention. The denial of the social order. Regarding civilized procedure with derision and contempt."

"You rile this man up? Can't you see he's different?"

"Let's go," the man said to Lynch.

"What's the trouble, Lynch?"

"This guy wants me to go with him. I don't wanna go."

Red stared at the man.

"Why don't you get going, mister?"

The man turned and began walking back to his car, glancing at three men a few feet away sitting in a semicircle and passing around a bottle. Another bottle lay on its side nearby, empty, the green glass almost black in the fading light. By the pockmarked brick wall of a porno theatre a man had passed out, was on his back, head to one side and mouth open. A little further a man who had loaded sacks of rice from a van onto a hand truck was wheeling them into the back of a café. As the man walked, Lynch climbed out of the dumpster. He scrambled over the top and let himself down, holding onto the edge, boots scraping the sides. The man was at the car now, opened the door and reached in towards the glove compartment. He came back out with a gun but Lynch was already running down the alley. The man dove back into the car as Red stepped in front of it. Red could hear Lynch's boots clumping behind him and getting fainter. The car jerked forward before the man instinctively hit the brake pedal, as Red knew he would. He jammed the accelerator to the floor but the body in front of him disappeared as tires screeched and the car flashed past through empty space. In the quick silence afterwards Red got up feeling an elbow and went over to the dumpster. Binner was sitting in a corner, talking to himself about coping with the unforeseen and long-term consequences of the missing briefcase.

"Consult. That's what we have to do. And the intragovernmental bodies exercising a supervisory capacity in this matter must be impervious to outside influence. We can't have any accusations of favouritism. The investigating committee will have the authority to subpoena records from anyone. All legal protection must be temporarily suspended. Any rights not waived will be taken under advisement for the perusal of the next plenum session after caucus, de facto per diem ex cathedra."

Binner looked up and smiled and held up a hand, as if to say, I'm busy now.

Chapter 9

On Sunday Gwen and Madeline planned to attend a vegfest before meeting Lynch later. But there was a hitch. Gwen phoned in the bathroom at her aunt's. She whispered.

"Nita and her mom are coming. I shouldn't have mentioned it. I couldn't say no. We'll be at your place at eleven."

Aunt Beverley drove an SUV. She was a big woman with pudgy hands. She steered with her palms. Nita sat in front with her. Gwen and Madeline sat in the back. Nita was seventeen and big like her mother. Madeline saw the tattoo on the inside of her left arm.

"Is that a seahorse?"

"Yeah. That's the name of my old boyfriend underneath. Got it before we broke up. Never do that again. Got to meet another guy with a four-letter name I can put over his."

"You could add other letters, or turn it into something like seaweed."

"Like to do that," Nita said and laughed.

"Never been to a vegfest," Aunt Beverley said. "What's it like?"

"You've got to pretend you like the food."

"Mean it's crap?"

"Put it this way. We're doing it for the animals."

"Everything is overpriced," Gwen said. "Don't eat the tofu omelette. It tastes like a pencil eraser. If you like real cheese, you're not going to think much of soy cheese. Same with vegan butter."

"Why do you go?"

"Show solidarity with other vegans," Madeline said. "Share the pain. And the gain. It's a small price to pay when you think about what the animals go through."

"I'm starving," Nita said. "Isn't there anything there?"

"The ice cream isn't bad if you get one with lots of fruit," Gwen said. "The chocolates are safe."

"Don't believe what you hear," Madeline said. "The louder the yum yums, the worse the stuff is. I'm wired after. High on sugar."

"Anything else there?"

"Make-up. T-shirts. Sandals. Tank tops."

"Is it free?" Aunt Beverley said.

"This one is," Gwen said. "Some places in other cities are starting to charge admission. They charge big prices for the stuff. But they're saying the rent for the grounds is high. For some people it's nothing but selling stuff, and the animals are only an excuse."

The vegfest was in a small marine park on the west side. There was an avenue of grass between two rows of booths. Behind one row was a picnic area with trees and behind the other the beach. At the entrance to the rows a banner hung between two poles declared: "A Celebration of Vegan Life Is a Celebration of Animal Freedom."

Near the banner stood Gordo, a bodybuilder and fitness trainer. He had muscles like balloons, horse teeth, a shaved head and a close-trimmed beard. Gwen and Madeline had met him at other vegfests, where he would chat with girls and have his picture taken with them. Gordo recognized them and came over, muscles straining against a tank top and shorts.

"It's Gwen and Maddy, right? Hi."

Gwen introduced her aunt and cousin. Gordo gave Nita a toothy grin and a side view of his bulging biceps and her eyes swam and she began playing with her hair. An exchange of pleasantries and Gordo asked about a photo with Aunt Beverley and Nita. Nita was eager and Gwen used her smartphone. Spotting some girls at the other end of the booths, he left. Nita in a daze, her eyes followed him. Aunt Beverley made a face.

"He hasn't got the brains of a package of Smarties."

Gwen bought a bag of kale chips and a passion fruit drink, Madeline a slice of layer cake and a flaky pastry with pecans and sweetened with agave nectar and Aunt Beverley and Nita sampled fake meats and bought vegan burgers. Everybody sampled spicy Asian dishes but didn't buy any, or any of the pizzas on offer. Gwen and Madeline met some friends from school. They talked about the coming year.

A half hour later they had visited all the booths on the park side and were making their way along the beach side and heard an argument. Vegan Slut was visiting the city and making a personal appearance at a booth selling her make-up, soap, deodorant and toothpaste. She had been signing autographs for her fans when a man who had been drinking the organic wine being sold at the vegfest stumbled against her booth. He knocked over a make-up display and fell down and she swore at him. He got up, black lipstick stains on his shirt, and tottered in front of her, trying to focus on the dagger stuck through her heart.

"I grow the food you eat. I was growing organic produce on my farm thirty years ago, before this vegan shit came along. Yeah. No slogans, T-shirts or vegfuckingfests. No doctors selling the organic diet. Weeding by hand sometimes, down on my knees. Experimenting with what would work. Talking with other farmers. If one of us got sick, the supply of organic wheat or rice or beans or oats interrupted for the whole country—whole continent sometimes. Who cared? We cared. Or none of it would've ever happened. And you come along making nothing but money. Never got your hands dirty. Never grew a thing except your bank account. Flying around the world and selling yourself while you're saving the animals. Convenient. Conferences and panels bankrolled by vegan supplement companies. And the vegetable oil companies and the sugar interests love you, honey. Oh, I know I'm not supposed to eat it but can I say it? Speaking for those who can't speak for themselves. You're speaking for yourself. I got to get back to my farm and grow some vegetables. Try to save what topsoil I've got. If we save every animal on the planet and lose our topsoil, we're gone. The tie-in between erosion and herbicides doesn't get any coverage in the media, and I wonder why? Go sell your lipstick."

He moved off, vanishing into the crowd.

Nita had wandered away and her mother was searching for her.

At a booth selling pizza Vegan Kylie, an Australian You Tuber popularly known to her male fans as the "Aussie Angel," was sampling various offerings. Blonde hair framed her soft face and large eyes, and her voice exuded soft-hearted femininity. There were tears in it when she talked about slaughterhouses. Marriage proposals and declarations of love filled the comments on her videos. Her boyfriend, Gavin, was with her. His nickname among envious males was "Yis, Kylie." They were tasting the mushroom, broccoli and vegan parmesan pizza as Gwen and Madeline approached. "None of that bloody cow puss for me," Gavin said.

"Milk isn't cow puss," Gwen said, stopping.

"What the bloody hell is it?"

"It's protein, fat and water. It gives a calf life."

"They drag the poor thing away before it sees a teat. Turn it into veal. And the mom's a bloody milk machine. Learn something, why don't you?"

"That doesn't make milk puss."

"Hey, listen to her. Fyi, puss, shit and blood get into milk."

"At a well-run dairy that doesn't happen. And milk in most places is rejected when it doesn't meet the quality standards. It's in places where farmers are allowed to feed cows sugar, feathers, old fast-food oil, gum and candy that you have to be careful. You can't lump all dairy famers together."

"What're you doing here? Spreading dairy industry propaganda."

"I'm a vegan but I don't believe in propaganda. From anybody."

"I know what's coming. You're going to tell me eggs aren't chicken periods and cholesterol bombs and honey isn't bee vomit."

"Calling eggs 'chicken periods' is like calling milk 'cow puss', an appeal to emotion. You're trying to disgust people. There's two kinds of cholesterol, HDL and LDL, and two kinds of LDL, types A and B. Only type B is dangerous and eggs don't raise it. They raise the good kinds. Cholesterol doesn't cause heart attacks, inflammation does. Bees have two stomachs. The honey stomach is for nectar. They add enzymes, turning it into honey, and the honey is stored in cells in the hive. It feeds the colony during the winter.

It's food, not vomit. Would you eat what somebody puked up?"

Kylie stepped in front of her boyfriend.

"Don't you believe in saving the animals? Do you know what goes on in slaughterhouses? Haven't you seen movies online that show the terrible practices? The pigs squealing as they are asphyxiated. The lambs trembling as they bleed to death. The debeaked chickens that can't move in their cages, almost no feathers. Take them out and they're so weak they fall over. Only heartless people would want to support that."

"Save your tears for your fans," Madeline said. "We go to pig vigils and march in animal rights parades. We want to put slaughterhouses out of business and close feedlots. We don't make money from the cause, we spend money supporting it. It takes more than selling T-shirts and diet books online, giving talks at health spas or eating pizza at a vegfest to get things done."

"Hey, I heard a good one," Gavin said to some in the crowd that had gathered around. "How do you keep the carnivores away? Tell them you're not a raw vegan, you're a cooked vegan. Get it?"

"Shut up, Gavin," Kylie said.

"Yis, Kylie."

Aunt Beverley returned with her daughter.

"She was looking for Mr. Muscles. I had to find a toilet. Those burgers were a bit rubbery. At least we ate healthy."

"Maybe not so healthy," Gwen said, "if the soy or pea or black bean was GMO instead of organic. Most of the non-organic is genetically engineered to absorb large amounts of herbicide that will kill everything else, and you get some of it."

"I'm going back to beef," Aunt Beverley said.

"Feedlot cattle are fed GMO crops like corn and soy," Gwen said. "The best beef is grass-fed and organic, if you can afford it."

"Never thought I'd hear you recommending that. You don't eat any meat or dairy, so how do you get your protein?"

"Peanut butter and wholegrain bread. Peas and rice or beans and rice. Multigrain cereal with almond milk. Everything organic."

"Organic's expensive."

"Yeah, but we get allowances and we shop around for sales. Good meat costs more than what we buy."

"If I were your mother, I'd be worried about you two."

"My mom's been having galactic fits since I went vegan," Madeline said. "Threatens to force-feed me if I don't quit."

"I get daily lectures," Gwen said.

"Judging by the people I see here, I don't think much of your vegans," Aunt Beverley said.

"Some of them are phonies. Trying to make money. Others are like us. Want to do something. We've met some good people."

"Maybe you're trying to grow up too fast, taking on too much at your age?"

"Have you been talking to my mom?"

Aunt Beverley grinned.

"You have."

"Well, Gwen, you can't expect her not to worry about you. You may be very intelligent but this may be something you should think about later on when you're older and more capable of handling the stress."

"I think I'm capable now, Aunt Beverley."

Gwen looked at her watch.

"It's almost one o'clock. Let's get seats for Dr. Todd's talk. He's a vegan doctor on You Tube. He's flown in from back East, never been here before. Said on his last video he's going to stay for a while."

Her aunt gave her a do-we-have-to? look.

"He won't speak for long," Gwen said.

An open-air tent had been set up at the far end of the beachside row of booths for the featured speaker at the vegfest. There were plenty of seats available. They sat at the front. Dr. Todd was talking with Vegan Kylie at the side of the stage, near a display of his latest book, *Veganism, Apocalypse of Truth.*

"What's he doing with her?" Gwen said.

"Maybe they're——. Nita made a circle with her thumb and forefinger and was poking her other forefinger through it.

"Grow up," Aunt Beverley said. She put on her glasses, studied the doctor.

"He's wearing a rug. You can see where it meets his hair. Looks as if he's had a facelift, too. Skin looks stretched."

"Botox, anybody?" Nita said.

Vegan Kylie and Dr. Todd walked up onto the stage and she went to the standing microphone. Gwen and Madeline turned to each other with disgusted looks. A delicate voice floated out to the audience. Vegan Kylie looked as if she were praying.

"This has been a rare opportunity for me to meet somebody I've admired for many years. An advocate for animal rights for more than a decade. A fighter for truth and justice, reviled by many in the mainstream media, who want to keep the present slavery going. But that is going to change. And we're going to change it."

She waited for applause. It was sporadic from the small audience. Gwen and Madeline didn't applaud. Vegan Kylie turned the microphone over to the featured speaker. They said something to each other, their heads staying close for a few moments.

"They kissed," Nita said.

"No, they didn't," Gwen said. "She bussed him."

"Well, a buss is a real kiss."

"Nothing about her is real."

"He looks too well fed to be a vegan," Aunt Beverley said.

"They got a thing going," Nita said. "Probably meet up later."

"Grow up, Nita."

Dr. Todd's voice boomed out over the audience.

"Fellow vegans, we are on the march. It's only a matter of time till the world listens to our raised voices. Other visionaries have been laughed at, despised for demanding freedom and justice. We have conquered racism, sexism, genderism and ableism, and now it's the turn of speciesism."

"Speciesism?" Aunt Beverley said. "What the hell is that?"

"Listen," Gwen said.

"Animals have a right to live their own natural lives. Not as our slaves, providing secretions and body parts that kill us and mean slaughter for them.

But as free life, to be what they were meant to be. Follow their own, their predestined natural paths."

"Does that go for snakes?" Aunt Beverley said. "I hate snakes."

Gwen and Madeline glanced at each other.

"I can see by the turnout today that our movement is growing. I'm happy to see so many young people in our ranks. The message is spreading. Keep spreading it."

"Yeah, keep spreading it," Aunt Beverley said. "I can smell it from here."

"Please, Aunt Beverley."

"Oh, sorry. I don't want to ruin it for you."

"Remember, to be a vegan is not good enough. Be an active vegan. Get involved in cow saves, pig vigils, marches, demonstrations, conferences, and boycott the producers of animal products. Tell your relatives and friends the truth. Remember we all were once meat eaters. We had to come to the realization we were committing a crime by taking from animals what is not ours to take. So be patient in converting those that need to be shown the truth. The message is powerful and it will get through finally. Our fellow creatures are not pork chops, beefsteak, milk, eggs, liver, kidneys."

"That reminds me, have to pick up some steaks," Aunt Beverley said.

"I don't care about the arguments that go on endlessly about whether we have the gut of a carnivore, herbivore or omnivore. Comparing lengths of the gastrointestinal tract to prove something. Our gastrointestinal tract is unique to us, as is our brain. Or the argument about whether we have the teeth of a carnivore or an herbivore, flat molars, fangs, worn-down bicuspids, et cetera. Or the one about our stomachs: we have one, a cow has four, or does it have one with four parts, for chewing its cud. None of that is what we're about. We're about saving the animals. Whatever humans have been in the past, whatever habits they had then, are history. It's what we are now that's important. You can thrive on a plant-based diet. So many vegans are proof of that. Agriculture and food science have advanced to the point where we have an abundance of plant-based foods to supply all our needs. And we have the latest technology, the means to bring it to us from all parts of the world at our convenience. So what is the excuse for eating animals? Absolutely none."

"Talk about going on endlessly," Aunt Beverley said.

"Mm, bacon," Nita said.

"I deal with these and other issues at much greater length in my books and videos, all available on my website. There's *Plain Talk for New Vegans*, for those wanting comprehensive answers to their questions, and my autobiographical trilogy, *Vegan Beginnings, Vegan Struggle* and *Vegan Triumph*. Among important videos are my address at last year's animal rights conference in Los Angeles and my speech at the animal rights march in London in August, and by the way my latest book, *Veganism, Apocalypse of Truth*, is on sale right here at a special vegfest price. I will autograph all copies. And here's some exciting news. My line of vegan supplements, including herbs, will be available this winter. My website will keep you posted."

Fifteen minutes later Dr. Todd concluded his remarks.

"We may once have been hunter-gatherers, as before that we were frugivores. We've had to adapt to changes in climate and availability and kinds of food. This time we're going to adapt, not for a biological or climatic reason, but a moral one. Meat and dairy won't kill you, at least not right away. (Pause for laughter, and the single laugh coming from the back of the sparse gathering sounded hollow.) But we won't spend time arguing with carnivores about the effects of animal foods on our bodies. It's the moral issue that concerns us. As long as one sentient creature dies to provide food for us, our job is not done. Spread the message. Go vegan, save the animals."

The applause was sporadic, Gwen and Madeline trying to make up for the lack of enthusiasm by clapping hard and long.

"Crowd doesn't have much energy," Nita said. "Wonder if it's the veggies, or they're tired from farting after all those beans?"

Gwen and Madeline wanted to speak with Dr. Todd for a while. Nita had spotted Gordo, a late arrival, in the audience and was eager to talk with him. Aunt Beverley said she'd wait for everybody. But she had to shop so she couldn't wait long.

"I suppose you want to buy a copy of my new book?" Dr. Todd said on seeing them walk onto the stage.

"We've already ordered it online," Madeline said, lying. She and Gwen had discussed this earlier. They knew from what they had read online the new book was a rehash of the old ones, and they had a couple of those. Dr. Todd suspected the truth. But they were fans.

"We wanted to tell you we enjoyed your talk," Gwen said. "We've watched all your videos."

Gwen couldn't help noticing he was overweight. And Aunt Beverley was right, he was wearing a toupee. About the facelift, she wasn't sure. But he wasn't a pop star, he was a doctor. But shouldn't a doctor look healthy? Big belly. Round face. Dr. Todd probably travelled a lot, going to vegfests, marches and animal rights conferences. A popular speaker. Putting out vlogs. Writing books. Wearing himself out. Jet lag, airline food and restaurant meals. That was it.

"What do you think about spirulina and chlorella?" Gwen said. "We were thinking of taking them but we heard the vitamins and minerals aren't bioavailable. And that they're not human food. And you could get liver cancer. Is that true?"

"Isn't it really pond scum?" Madeline said. "Floats on stagnant water. We heard companies don't clean it. It's raked up, dried and put into bottles. The workers drop cigarette butts into the water and birds crap into it as they fly over."

"Don't listen to false rumours. Do you think producers of health supplements, of all people, would sell polluted products? I take them and am perfectly fine. And I will be selling them as part of my new line of vegan supplements."

"We've seen videos of ex-vegans saying their health fell apart," Madeline said. "Cracked teeth, backaches, inflammation in their joints, couldn't sleep, couldn't remember anything, depression, anger, anxiety, no energy."

Dr. Todd cleared his throat.

"They probably weren't doing it right or hadn't finished detoxing."

"That's what they said vegan doctors and friends told them. How could none of them be doing it right when they followed all the advice? Some had been detoxing for years. How long does it take to detox?"

"I wouldn't believe them. I think those people are looking for attention.

Veganism is the coming thing and they want to get in on it somehow, so they complain. There are people out there who are ready to blame their neuroses on anything. Their problems are rooted in other causes and they don't want to admit it. Easier to blame it on vegans and veganism. We're a convenient target."

"One guy was chewing on a muffin and a few of his teeth came out in pieces. That had to be the hardest muffin ever. One of them couldn't get out of bed. Couldn't put on his pants. Another couldn't sleep for weeks. A woman couldn't remember why she'd gone to a room. One couldn't get off the toilet. Everything came out undigested. Some couldn't do anything, walked around like zombies. Are they all liars or crazy?"

"I can't address all their problems. It seems to me the Internet has become a place where weird people gather and tell strange stories to get an audience. And the stranger the story the bigger the audience they get. You shouldn't believe that stuff."

No one else was waiting to talk. The tent had emptied. The only person still seated was a bored-looking Aunt Beverley. Nita had been outside talking with Gordo. But she was returning because one of Gordo's girlfriends had shown up. Dr. Todd glanced at his watch. Couldn't keep her waiting. What was that address? Got her phone number, anyway. A man must get what he can. Get rid of these girls.

"Sorry to run. I've got an appointment."

"You think we're too young to be vegans?" Gwen said.

"No one is too young. I've got to be going."

He went over to the display of paperbacks and threw them into a suitcase and trundled off the stage with it.

"He's overweight," Madeline said. "Didn't notice it before."

"Me neither," Gwen said. "It's probably because he sits behind a desk when he's interviewing."

"What would he eat that would do it?"

"Macadamia nuts? Olive oil?"

"He doesn't believe in any oils, not even olive oil."

"Must be the nuts then. Maybe he chews on them when he's travelling."

"He didn't want to talk with us. Left in a hurry."

"Maybe he's after more nuts."

The four left the tent and walked between the rows of booths.

"What a pain in the butt," Nita said.

"I hope you didn't give Mr. Muscles your phone number, Nita," Aunt Beverley said. "With those biceps he's probably on steroids. I had enough trouble with your last boyfriend, that biker. Swastika on his helmet, wheelies in the driveway."

"He's got a steady. They're engaged."

"Gwen, Maddy." A woman off to the side was waving.

It was Kendra Meers. In her late twenties, she was thin and had large eyes. Her ears stuck out and she always covered them with her hair. She was with her boyfriend, Innis Bunce. Spaghetti arms dangled from his T-shirt and legs like hairy thistles sprouted from his shorts. They had met Gwen and Madeline at a vegfest eight months ago and recruited them for pig vigils and animal rights demonstrations. Kendra waved them over.

"Gwen, Maddy, we're staging a demonstration at The Hunters' Club tonight. It's a new level of activism. Protesting at places where carnists feed. You in?"

Gwen and Madeline looked at each other. They nodded.

"You know where it is?"

Gwen nodded.

"Be there by six. Bring signs or you can make them there. We have blank placards. And pens."

"What was that all about?" Aunt Beverley said when they returned.

"Nothing," Gwen said. "They're old friends. We're meeting later on for a vegan event. I'll check my parents' apartment before we go. I'll be at your place about eight."

"Weirdos," Nita said. "Need some meat."

Gwen and Madeline glanced at each other.

Aunt Beverley and Nita left early to go shopping and at half past three Gwen and Madeline took a bus to Glen Loughran Tower. On the way they talked.

"It should've been called a junkfoodfest," Gwen said.

"A sugarfest," Madeline said. "I won't break our vow not to eat meat or fish, but I'm weak around cream cheese."

"I won't break it," Gwen said, "but I get jumpy around butter."

"My mom was making an omelette last week. With butter and Parmesan."

"'Would you like some, Madeline?'"

"'No, Mom. You know I'm a vegan.'"

"'I put in four eggs. I can't eat it all.'"

"'You did that deliberately to get me to eat some.'"

"'Have a bite, a taste. It smells so good.'"

"I went to my bedroom and shut the door and after she's finished I can hear her put a plate down on the floor. I hear a kitchen towel flapping as she's trying to get that gorgeous smell under the door. 'Go away, Mom. I'm trying to stop an animal holocaust.'"

"Must be hard. Your mom being a gourmet."

"Yeah, you're lucky. Your mom can't cook."

"I'd cook for her and my dad but they won't eat what I do. Even kale chips."

Chapter 10

"Why do you live the way you do? Could've gotten yourself a regular job and had a family."

It was early Sunday evening. Sylvia and Speaker were talking in the kitchen. She leaned forward slightly in her chair as she spoke. Warts had gone out hours ago. Al was in the front parlour looking at some old colour postcards Sylvia had put on the coffee table for him. They were shots of the downtown business core in the Forties and Fifties: granite neoclassical bank façades, art deco office fronts, red-brick department stores with display windows, restaurants with neon signs, scarlet and cream trams and trolley buses, long-nosed cars, and street crowds wearing fedoras and full-length coats.

Speaker had spent the day looking for places for himself and Al. There hadn't been much, only homeless shelters. Hotel rooms were too expensive for more than a few nights. He had little money and he wasn't sure what Al had left now besides a vacant lot. Selling it would bring enough to supplement his pension cheques—did he get more than one?—amply for quite a while. But he needed a secure situation. Wouldn't last in a hotel room, even if he rented one by the month. Word would get around. Take everything he had. Get mugged in his room. Maybe murdered. Welfare would probably sell the lot and put him in an institution. That would only be a slower way of killing him. He never mentioned any relatives. Too big a problem for Sylvia, even if she were willing.

"I said, why haven't you got a regular job and a family?"

"Sorry, I didn't hear you. I've never listened to commercials for fantasies about a false permanence."

"What's that mean?"

"I don't see people as jobs, marriages, money or education. They're common nouns, bubbles on a wave heading for the beach. I think of the wave, not the foam. And of all the other waves that have gone before, and those that'll come after."

"So you never wanted a wife?" Sylvia sipped her hot tea as delicately as she could.

"Only make her miserable. No steady income. Don't want to mow suburban lawns, barbecue or shop at a supermarket. Or give an employer my time."

"You'll be a lonely man. That's for sure."

"Some of the loneliest people have families. Or had them."

"Maybe you should've been a university professor." Sylvia moved her cup around in its saucer.

"I was self-incarcerated in academe. Became a graduate student and an instructor, one of the sixteen thousand species of beetle on campus. Each busy digging into the dirt of its own truth, with proper academic deliberation. Each ponderous step documented for some fancied posterity that supposedly will have nothing better to do than examine a pullulating mass of archaic arcane verbiage. I was involved in the biggest make-work project in history. Everything cloaked in the sanctified concepts of academic freedom and tenure. Or don't bother me and I won't bother you and we'll get to keep on pretending that we're doing something significant."

"People learn things at universities, don't they?"

"It's teaching to teach teaching, instead of how to think."

"You should teach people how to think, instead of spending your time with a bunch of bums."

"People don't want to think. Don't have time. Too busy making money. Thinking humbles you. You forget what you're supposed to buy. Everything's for sale. Except a passionate intelligence."

"You're wasting your life."

Sylvia reached over and picked up the teapot and refilled their cups. She added a drop of cream to hers. Passionate intelligence? Passion was about sex and love. Not about thinking. People were passionate about God, about helping others. Nothing wrong with that. But passionate about your brain?

"We're all wasting our lives. Some of us know it."

"I suppose I'm one of those who don't know it."

"You're probably better off for that."

"That's the first thing you've said that's upset me, Speaker."

"Didn't intend to. Sorry. Can you live with the idea that everything is dissolving? You're a drop in an ocean of nothing."

"I can't dissolve in nothing. Even I know that. And I believe I have a soul and that it's more important than my body. Only fools think there's no room for God in the universe."

"And I'd never deny you your right to think so. I'm against the destructive arrogance of the self-important who run the place."

"You're smart, but you don't know people. A few are like you and some could be like you, but most can't. If those of us who aren't like you tried to copy you, the rest, who didn't want to, and there'll always be more than enough, would grab everything and wipe out the ones like you or make slaves out of you. It's people like me in between the thinkers and the bullies who keep things going, but who never get any credit. It's a guaranteed mess but I don't want your way."

"I'm a special kind of fool. That's why I live down here."

"What about me?"

"You give most of the food you grow to charities. You give money, donate clothes. You take in battered women. You're a saint in gumboots. Best of us all."

Sylvia put her cup into its saucer slowly and carefully, looking down at the simple operation as if she had never done it before. The back door was open because of the warm evening. Facing that way, when she looked up she saw a dark form lurch against the screen door before slumping onto the porch. The hunched form made harsh breathing noises. Speaker went to the door and turned on the porch light.

"It's Lynch."

He opened the door and Lynch scrambled in, collapsing onto a chair. He looked shrivelled in his baggy clothes. Sylvia brought him a cup of tea and a homemade cinnamon roll. He slurped the tea, put the empty cup on the table, pulled a chunky curl off the roll and began to chomp on it. When he spoke, bits of roll flew out of his mouth.

"Guy's after me 'cause of something I took."

Speaker sat down and leaned forward, hands on his knees.

"Who's after you?"

"Dunno. It's 'cause of a briefcase. Picked it up in one of them 'partmints. Nuthin' in it 'cept paper. Took some pens. Told him I'd give 'em back. Knew he'd kill me soon as he got hold of it. Said I give it to Binner. We went and seen him. I run away and come here."

"How did he find out you stole it?"

"I had some bad luck."

"Where's the briefcase?"

"In that 'partmint. One you guys were in. Staying there by myself. Sposed to meet them girls today. I didn't show. Parents coming back tomorrow. Place's empty right now. Got to hide somewheres."

He looked at Sylvia. Speaker leaned back and frowned.

"You can't leave that briefcase where it is. Those girls would be in danger if whoever's after you traces it to that suite. If the girls find it, they'll go to the police. They'd have to implicate you. You've got to get it tonight. I'm guessing you've got a way of getting back in. I'll go with you."

"Let 'em do what they want with it. Nuthin's going to happen to me."

"If you want to stay here, you'll do what Speaker tells you," Sylvia said.

"Aw shit. I run all the way over here. Now ya want me to go back to where this guy's waiting to kill me. I only got so much luck, ya know."

"Considering the way you look and the way you live, I'd say you got all your luck still coming to you."

After they had gone, Sylvia went into the front parlour. Al was staring at a postcard displaying a photograph taken in the Forties of the Great Northern station, a railway terminal of red brick and white stone and a landmark in the downtown eastside until it was demolished in the Sixties. Al saw her but pretended he didn't. "I see you like them," she said. He reached over, patted Rowser on the head. "Ah kee." Rowser wagged his tail slowly and got up and went to Sylvia. She rubbed his side with her slipper and returned to the kitchen.

"Algernon." The sharp-faced woman with her hair pulled back in a bun was standing a few yards away on the platform, a black coat over a grey dress with a white lace collar, stockings grey and her shoes heavy and black. "Get over here," she said to a small white-haired boy of seven who was gazing at the two drive wheels of a steam locomotive. The wheels were taller than he was, their rims painted white. The connecting rod, a beam of shiny silver steel, ran laterally from the wheel journals to the piston housing, black and low at the front. Water dripped and steam escaped in wisps from an outlet valve. With its gloss-black cylinder-shaped boiler and its cab window high up, the locomotive seemed impossibly massive and powerful to the boy. But it was the whuffing chuffing smoke from the stack that thrilled him, exhilarating and slightly scary as the engine entered the marshalling yards and slid into the depot, bell clanging, headlamp bright, steam spurting from its sides and the tracks groaning and screeching with its weight and the weight of the long line of swaying coaches.

The boy had accompanied his aunt to the Great Northern station. She had seen off friends leaving for the Middle West. He had taken trains with his parents. They had let him look at locomotives and walk along the platform, as long as he didn't stray away from them. He ran up to her and was going to say, "Sorry, Auntie, I was looking at the train," but she swung her purse and knocked him down, a corner of its metal clasp hitting him on the side of the head. He lay on the platform, his right knee hurting from the fall. Several people looked but didn't say anything. When he got to his feet, she reached down and grabbed a shoulder of his coat and yanked it, throwing him ahead of her. He stumbled and fell again, got up and walked, knees shaking. He knew his aunt would beat him that night with a piece of kindling. He would get no dinner. His final punishment, to be kicked by her black shoe into his dark room upstairs.

His aunt called him "Algernon" only in public. In her house "idiot" or "half-wit" were sneered or yelled at him. He would stay out of her way as much as possible. At mealtimes he would look down at his plate and avoid her face, its thin lips, flat grey eyes and bloodless skin. Once she caught him staring and guessed somehow he was looking at the fringe of dark hairs on her upper lip. She picked up a soup spoon, reached over and flicked her wrist. The edge of the spoon hit him on the lower lip and chin, the blow jarring his teeth and cutting the inside of his mouth. His lip began swelling and blood dribbled from his mouth. "Don't you dare bleed on the tablecloth," his aunt snapped at him. He sucked on his lip, swallowing the blood.

His aunt had never married, inherited her house from her mother, his maternal grandmother, caring for the senile invalid until she died. His parents died two years later in an apartment fire when he was five, his rescue by a firefighter the subject of a newspaper story. Because his Aunt Irene was his closest living relative, the boy was sent to live with her. She took him in as her Christian duty, being a regular churchgoer. She sang in the choir and held weekly teas for church members. He would be dressed up and told to sit quietly in the front parlour and not say anything as the ladies chatted. He knew he had to obey her instructions, having learned that disobedience brought a slap from that narrow cold hand or blows from a piece of kindling. At the first tea he had sat next to the sideboard and listened to eight ladies, all middle-aged, pass off gossip as information and vindictiveness as religion. After an hour and three tall glasses of water from a pitcher on the sideboard, the only drink allowed him at these gatherings, he needed to pee. A half hour more and the warm stuff began to trickle down his pant legs onto the shiny oak floor, forming a pool at his feet and becoming large enough to reach her favourite Turkish rug and soak slowly, darkly into it. Eventually one of the guests glanced in his direction and saw the wet floor. She nudged his aunt. He never forgot his fear as his aunt's head turned and her eyes saw what had happened. She put her cup into its saucer and carefully put the saucer on the table between the teapot and plate of thinly sliced pound cake, excused herself, rose from the sofa, hands smoothing her shark grey taffeta dress, and came over. Wiry fingers snatched his ear and twisted it as she pulled him after her into the bathroom. "Take off those clothes," she hissed, shut the door and went back to her tea. He waited two hours, sitting naked and trembling on the toilet until the guests had gone and his aunt had finished cleaning up. She returned holding a large steel ladle. She didn't say anything, began swinging at him, hitting wherever she could until he was bruised and cowering in a corner of the bathtub. She filled the tub with hot water. As the boy cried and leaped to escape the stinging water on his swollen and bleeding feet, she picked up a large brown bar of laundry soap. The hard edges of the new bar rasped his skin. Fingers clutched at his hair, suds stung his eyes and mouth as he tried to breathe, only swallowing soapy water, choking, bursts of screams escaping. "Cry and I won't stop," she promised in her rigid voice. Only when he was shivers and whimpers did she toss the soap aside and rinse him off.

A few minutes later Sylvia returned to answer the front door. "They bring back the past, don't they?" She turned on the porch light, lifted the mail slot and peeked. It was Warts.

"Hi," he said as he walked in and glanced around. "Where's Speaker?"

"Gone somewhere with Lynch."

"Yeah? Where?"

"He can tell you when he gets back."

"So you're kind of alone. There's Al over there, but that's sort of being alone, almost."

Sylvia walked into the kitchen and he followed.

"Speaker find a place?"

"No."

"Me neither. But I got a chance in a couple of days or so to get something. Not absolutely, but pretty good. So how are you?"

"All right."

"Yeah? Guess Speaker be away for a while. More than a bit. Not all night, of course. But most of it."

Warts sat at the table. Sylvia put away plates, cups and saucers she had washed earlier and began cleaning the kitchen counter.

"Had this place long, Sylvia?"

"Twenty-five years."

"Yeah? Married, weren't ya?"

"For twenty-seven years."

"That's a long time. Not so long if you're happy with somebody, of course. Not many have that kind of happiness. You probably did, I guess. So you been a widow for a few years, I suppose."

"Yes."

"That's more than a bit. And you're not that old. To be a widow, I mean. You could get married again. Or maybe you're not interested. Some women aren't and I don't blame them. They want their independence these days. Even old women. Older, I mean. Not like the past, when a woman had to get married to get somebody. Who cares these days? I agree. Nobody else's business. Marriage is only a ring. Own this house, I guess."

"Yes."

"Nice place. Clean. Plenty of room here. Big garden. I noticed today. First time I looked close. Seen it from Al's but never realized. Saves quite a bit on the food bill. That helps, of course. Got it beat here. Need nuthin' else, I guess. No help. But I don't think there's no one that don't need help sometimes. Especially a good-looking woman."

"Look Warts, I'm tired. I'm going upstairs. I gave Speaker a key to get in. Leave the front porch light on for them."

"Sure."

Sylvia's outline dimmed in the dark hallway, disappearing as she turned to climb the stairs.

That one wouldn't make a wife. Thinks she's too good. That's why she hasn't got a man. Wants to be her own boss. No wonder her husband's dead. Couldn't take it, had to get away. Who wants a woman that wants her own way all the time? Alone for too long, used to it. Afraid to lose what she's got. House, money from her husband. Didn't John O' say he had a store? Robbed a couple of times. Beat up once. Older guy. Crazy about her. Guys all whistled at her years ago. Thought she was hot stuff. Older than me by quite a few years. Too old. She'd be lucky. Who wants her? Nice house. Not beat up like Al's. Al's? That's gone. Wonder if she wants the kitchen lights off? Got to sleep in that little room. Couldn't live with that one. Order ya around. Lines on her face. Puffy. It would be how old? Well built. Throw some paint on the siding every few years and that's it. Doesn't need it yet. Basement windows spotless. She's cleaning all the time. Don't see beams like that in a basement any more. Six by six. Yeah, she's had it, that's for sure.

It was almost eleven when they arrived at the suite. Grunting, Lynch got down on his knees in the master bedroom closet and reached into a far corner behind some shoes. He pulled out the briefcase and handed it to Speaker. "There's nuthin' in it 'cept paper, like I told ya." Speaker took the briefcase over to the bed and sat down. He turned on the night table lamp and took several bundles of paper out of the briefcase. Some were employee contracts with the staff at a local television station. There were reports on newspaper advertising revenue. He turned the briefcase over and dumped the rest of the contents onto the bed. Legal papers, more reports, and the notebooks, flash drive, breath mints and nail clipper Lynch had seen. Both notebooks had coiled wire binding at the side and black manila covers and ruled white pages. In one he saw a list of men's names printed with a ballpoint pen, with local telephone numbers beside them, and finally a number without a name. In the other notebook more names and numbers, again printed with a ballpoint pen in black ink, and beside them the names of other cities, many overseas, and on a separate page what seemed a code in numbers and letters. In this notebook were quickly jotted comments beside some of the names. "Always fresh supply." "The customer is always light." "Watch for stitch jobs." "Has shaved them—one had real tits." On the first page of both notebooks were the initials, C.K., with decorative doodling around them. Speaker stared at the initials. They were in the same large, blocklike handwriting as the comments. He put the notebooks and flash drive inside his sweater, into his shirt pocket, and everything else back into the briefcase. He glanced over at Lynch, sitting on the floor, his back against the wall and staring into the wreckage of the day. Lynch was tired of waiting his whole life. Speaker was a blunt reminder.

"No wonder you're in trouble. You've stumbled into a big man's private playpen. Sex with baby girls. His initials are in the notebooks, and names of guys like him."

"What're ya talking 'bout?"

"That man wouldn't be after you if you didn't know more than you're telling me. It's more than a briefcase."

"I seen something."

"He killed a girl?"

"In that penthouse."

"So you're the single witness and the guy you saw is the owner of this briefcase and someone's been hired to kill you and get it back."

"That's why I got to stay at Sylvia's."

"Did he see you with anyone?"

"Binner and Indian Red, and Binner's loony and Red don't know nuthin' 'bout it."

Speaker tapped the briefcase. "We'll take this with us."

"What're ya going to do with them books?"

"Nothing, yet."

"Guy's rich, pay big to get 'em back."

"You want to outwit a man who's paying to have you murdered?"

"You're smart. You could get money from him without neither of us getting hurt."

"You want me to help you blackmail someone who's trying to kill you because you found out he's raping and murdering girls? You don't think he should pay another way?"

"Ya mean go to jail? They'll never get him, he's too big."

"You could be right."

"So how 'bout making him pay off? One big wad and we beat it."

Speaker looked closely at Lynch. His knees were drawn up to his chest, scrawny hands playing with frayed bootlaces. The small face was blurred in semi-darkness. He seemed a prematurely old child shrivelling into self-absorption, oblivious to anyone else's need or pain and to any sense of wrong. Why aren't moral philosophers more realistic? Why do they offer easy examples to illustrate their generalities, as if personal and social behaviour are explainable by games of logic. If this is so and that's so, then this must be true. But wait. There's a fallacy here, an incorrect assumption, a misunderstanding, a contradiction, a sneaking prejudice. Clear it up and you solve the problem. Syllogistic simplicity. As if the mind were a computer chip, an embedded silicon roadmap instead of neurons and synapses, soft tissue washed by blood. We've done so much to get away from the smell of humanity. Brain prejudice, the body's betrayer. Generalize. Try to find better and better ideas. The only problem is, they explain so well that human behaviour becomes secondary to an idea explaining it, and that's called theory. Philosophers would never understand Lynch, any more than he could understand them. Neither type of mind could grasp what the other was thinking. Social workers, psychologists, the police, politicians, lawyers and judges and the media were other groups with their own ways of sorting out people like Lynch. Each had a formula that served its view, instead of trying to accommodate an individual's perception of his or her self. It came down to a job, a task narrow enough in scope so you could get paid for doing it and justify yourself to a society basing itself on the indefinite article: I am a doctor, I am a computer programmer, a managerial consultant, a systems analyst. The technical parameters of tasks made them easier to do and to justify payment for doing them. Quantifying operations involved in tasks made for quick and objective evaluation of each operation. Tot them all up and the task was done, the job complete. As for the subject, whether you saved or condemned him, no one could criticize you for not having done your job. And the job could never be wrong. When mistakes occurred, it was because employees were not perfect. Somebody failed somewhere and would be disciplined, perhaps merely retrained. Where necessary, changes would be made to prevent the same mistake. Lynch was material for a job whenever he bumped up against a social barrier. He was somebody's income or promotion or future or publicity or failure. Sociopath, tramp, criminal, victim: these were labels that subsumed him and any thoughts or feelings that made up the person. He became part of someone's job-identity, his meaning and significance confined within the perspectives of the job. Restrictions of time or money or personnel meant that he was a few minutes worth or dollars or people or prescribed solutions. His only potential was more of these, his only value what they meant as expenditures. Whether he was grateful or hateful was irrelevant. Someone would have the job in any case. There was a job for anything Lynch did or didn't do. He was penned into the downtown eastside, and his solipsistic schemes were delusions to a psychologist, potential trouble to social workers and the police, a trial date to judges and lawyers, election promises to politicians and news in media ratings battles. He was a rat in a warehouse, roaming inside the walls and unaware of name brands as he gnawed through cardboard and plastic packaging.

"Missing a big chance, Speaker."

"It wouldn't be nearly as easy as you think to get money from this guy, and if I helped you get it, it would have the smell of raped and beaten and dead girls on it and I'd like to think I'd never despise myself that much."

Lynch got up, pulled his old clothes from under the bed and changed into them. Speaker turned off the table lamp, picked up the briefcase and went to the door and switched off the bedroom light. They used the fire stairs. There was no one in the lobby. It was close to midnight when they left.

Gwen and Madeline had arrived at Glen Loughran Tower at five to four that afternoon. They saw a patrol car outside the entrance and two officers in the lobby. After identifying herself, Gwen was told that some apartments had been burglarized. The extent of the robbery wasn't known as yet because many of the tenants had gone away for the long weekend. The police had been knocking on doors and trying locks, but it was difficult to tell in some cases when they went inside what had been stolen. She wasn't told about the MacDiarmids. They had been arguing so much that the police didn't know what to believe. The battle hadn't finished.

"The wee man must hae hit me from behind with something and tied me up so he could rob that suite," Ian MacDiarmid said to an officer.

"There were three of them, ye stupid man," Maggie shouted. "That wee devil, a dark one with evil eyes and a big heavy bruiser. They would hae stolen the whole building but for me. Tried to subdue me, but God gave me the strength to survive."

"I only saw one," her husband said lamely, a bandage wound around his head.

"As if I dinna hurt enough. Could the wee man hae smashed ma nose?

They had a van and were carrying cartloads of stuff out the exit before they saw me. That dark one tried to get me to ride in his cart but I wouldna be forced onto it for anything."

Gwen and Madeline had hurried up to 1108, found the door unlocked and rushed in but nothing appeared to be missing or disturbed. Lynch had told Doughnuts and Zimmo that the girls would be coming later, so Doughnuts decided they should only take things Gwen wouldn't immediately notice were gone. She would be there in hours and he wanted the discovery of the burglaries to be delayed as long as possible. And he didn't know how much time the man in the penthouse would take with Lynch and whether Lynch would be killed there or not. If the body was found in the building, being identified as accomplices was a possibility, so getting far away fast had to be a priority. They took Carol's gold necklace and emerald ring. A large, square-cut stone set sumptuously in four gold claws, it gave off a dazzle like a tropical rainforest pool distilled into a single drop. The boxes were returned to the wall safe, opened easily by Lynch. His scrawny fingers twiddled the combination lock as a grizzled ear listened for the tumblers to click. The other two had watched, impressed.

"We won't see him any more," Gwen said, plopping herself down on the chesterfield, her feet in the air as she landed. "I found out if I could trust him."

"Think he'll be arrested?" Madeline said, sitting on the loveseat.

"Who cares? I kept hoping he'd appreciate what we tried to do for him."

"That's over. We could be called as witnesses if they catch him and he mentions us. To get us to save him. What'll we say?"

"That we gave him a place to stay because he was supposed to go for an interview so he could get a pensioner's apartment. But he disappeared and we don't know if he stole anything—ha."

"Think your parents will get mad?"

"For a while."

"My mother will give her usual, 'I told you, Madeline, you never listen to me, you do these crazy things, when will you learn?'"

Gwen stood up. "Picked the wrong guy." She took off her corduroy jacket, undid the sleeve buttons on her blouse, rolled up her sleeves and pulled her blouse out of her jeans. "I'm going to start cleaning." Madeline got up and took off her jean jacket and gave a flip with the back of her hand to her ponytail. "I shall vacuum." She got the vacuum cleaner from the foyer closet and began thrusting it along the hall carpet like a blind fencer.

Gwen went into the kitchen. There was a pop bottle upside down in the sink. That morning Lynch had finished what the others had left from the night before. Gwen picked it up, smelled whisky. She knew from where. Something else to explain. Chunks of soy cheddar lay scattered all over the counter. She shovelled them with her hand onto the plastic wrapping, threw it into the garbage pail under the sink and opened the refrigerator door. Lynch had left something. On a dessert dish were coils of a small black turd.

Gwen and Madeline left Glen Loughran Tower at five thirty, taking a bus to The Hunters' Club. A half hour earlier the patrol car departed. The caretaker was told to report suspicious persons. The police would be returning tomorrow to continue their investigation. A notice posted in the lobby asked returning tenants to report any missing property to the police at the number given below. When Speaker and Lynch arrived, the caretaker was asleep on the sofa. Maggie was in the bathroom examining her nose.

About fifty protesters had already gathered at the restaurant when they arrived. Many were holding signs. "We are speaking for those who can't speak for themselves." "You're eating the corpses of sentient beings." "Carnivore=corpse eater." "Come out of the cave." Gwen and Madeline made signs at the apartment. Gwen's read: "Give Life, Go Vegan." Madeline had written: "It's cruel to eat what you don't need to live." Underneath she had drawn a lamb's face.

Kendra took charge of the protesters.

"Line up along the sidewalk. Show your signs to those inside. The cops might be here. Don't give them any excuse to arrest us. We're peaceful demonstrators exercising our right of free speech in a democracy. Don't block the entrance. Allow people in and out. Don't get into a fight with a customer or a pedestrian. If anybody is abusive, don't lose your temper. We're here to protest and to answer questions. Mainstream media wants the public to think we're a cult. We've got to tell people why we're here. Get the message out. Educate them."

The Hunters' Club was on Hornby Street, in the downtown business district, an upscale restaurant catering to a clientele fancying boar, moose, deer and buffalo. The owner was Rudolf Stoeffel, a large man with red cheeks and a white mustache. The restaurant was three years old and popular. Reservations had to be made two weeks ahead. It was closed on Mondays, and all of August, when Stoeffel went back to his native Austria. The interior was late nineteenth century saloon, with hardwood floors, wall panelling, tables, bar and timbered ceiling, and the lighting fixtures brass. On the walls were Victorian photographs of hunters with their kill. The bartenders wore handlebar mustaches, pinstriped shirts and celluloid collars. The waitresses dressed in long skirts, high-button shoes, mutton-sleeved blouses and wore their hair upswept. The aroma of roasted meat permeated the air.

Kendra picked Sunday because it was usually a slow news day, so there was a chance of making the late news. She had alerted the television stations and the socially active You Tubers in the city. Smartphones ensured there would be the Internet for prolonged exposure. Another reason for Sunday was the business district wouldn't be congested with commuter traffic and aggressive pedestrians. The protesters would be seen and heard and not obscured or harassed by hungry stockbrokers.

Gwen and Madeline, the youngest of the protesters, took their place along the sidewalk, facing the restaurant and holding up their signs. They were near the entrance, a wooden door with a brass doorknob and knocker. It was still light enough to give them a fairly clear view of the interior through the large wood-framed plate glass window. A waitress was carrying plates to a table. Customers at another table, close to the window, were staring at them. They waved their signs. The customers kept staring, as if trying to read them.

The door opened and two men came out. They were heavyset, had short beards and were wearing business suits. They stopped and looked at the demonstrators. One spoke to Bunce, the protester nearest them.

"What are you doing here? I don't go to a vegan restaurant and hold up signs. I don't call you names. I respect your right to eat what you want, so why don't you respect mine?"

"Our food doesn't come from dead animals. We don't kill living creatures to eat."

"I'm doing nothing wrong. Men have been hunting for hundreds of thousands of years. That's what's made us what we are. I'm a hunter and the animals I kill feed on grass in the wild. You people are trying to make us out to be criminals. We kill quick and we eat the animals because they nourish us. If we don't kill them the wolves or cold or sickness or hunger will. We cull the herd."

"Why don't you make it more equal and hunt with a spear?"

"I've hunted boar with a crossbow."

"However you do it, you're robbing the animals of their lives. There's plenty of food around now without having to kill animals."

"Fruit and veggies? If you want to climb back up into a tree and eat bananas, go right ahead. But some of us aren't going to fall for your bullshit. We need meat. Animal fat and protein build our brains. Autopsies show vegan brains shrink more than vegetarian brains, and those of meat eaters shrink the least. That's why mothers feed breast milk to infants. You dimwits feed your kids soy milk. Those that don't die have permanently impaired brains. Like their parents. I'm not destroying the ecosystem. I'm doing more for it than you with your soy garbage. How many acres of rainforest have gone to plant soy? How many species have gone extinct?"

"Not as many acres and species that have disappeared to raise cattle for hamburgers."

"If you ever make hunting illegal, you'll have to come after me and take my gun away. It may come to that. With so many virtue-signalling politicians, it's amazing they haven't all got broken wrists. What gender are you? Confused? Considering? Or maybe clueless?"

"Getting personal. That's what people do when they have no counter argument."

"Your vegan bullshit won't work with me. I'm based. I took the red pill. I don't like being singled out as a murderer for doing something that's good for my body and good for the environment. Why don't you go demonstrate in front of a fast-food franchise? Seems to me you picked the wrong target. Maybe on purpose. It's easier to pull your shit off on a small business. The owner hasn't got the money to fight you and he's got fewer customers to scare away. Put him out of business and you've won. And the franchise giants are good to go. Think maybe I'm right?"

"Keep eating animals and you'll always be wrong. And in case you haven't heard, fast-food franchises are starting to serve vegan burgers. You cavemen are caught in a time warp. You're on your way out."

"I'm wasting my breath. You're brain dead."

The men walked away.

A quarter hour later a car slowed down as it passed.

"Here little piggies. Have some water, oink oink."

A hand holding a squeeze bottle appeared at a window. A spray drenched some of the protesters.

"It's pee," a girl yelled, dropping her sign. Napkins and a water bottle were passed around.

"I've got your licence plate," Kendra shouted, holding up her smartphone as the car had raced away.

An hour went by. Some of the protesters went to the restaurant window and held up their signs. Stoeffel appeared at the window and wagged a finger at them. No one from the media came to cover the demonstration and Bunce wasn't happy.

"Where's the fucking coverage? We let everybody know. What the fuck is wrong with them? They all on holiday?"

A man walked in front of the protesters.

"I'm eating a bacon double cheeseburger."

"Good for you," Bunce said. "You can think about that while you're waiting for your quadruple bypass."

"I'm enjoying this."

"Enjoying the growth hormones, antibiotics, pesticides and herbicides?"

"Delicious."

The man finished and smacked his lips.

"I think I'll get another one. Have a great time with your tofu, spinach and boiled kale."

Bunce shook his head.

"Oh fuck, here comes Quentin. Of all the useless assholes to show up.

Nothing but a narcissist. Why tell him, Kendra?"

"I didn't."

"How did he find out?"

"Ask him, why don't you?"

The man approaching the demonstrators was thin, his beard wispy, jeans ragged, and he wore a black leather vest but no shirt. He was half bald, the hair on the back of his head growing halfway down his back. He was holding a sign. "I'm a believer, think you."

"What's wrong?" Gwen asked Kendra.

"He's got a You Tube channel, but all he does is talk about what he's into, like one week the only thing to eat is papaya and the next week it'll be coconuts and two weeks after that he'll be into sungazing or astrology or flat earth shit. He's always high on something but nobody can figure out what. He's a freak show. Nobody takes him seriously."

Waving his sign, the man approached Kendra.

"I love you one hundred per cent."

"I didn't think you were one hundred per cent anything, Quentin. What's the magic fruit for this week?"

"Not a fruit—lettuce."

"On a diet of lettuce?"

"Massaging my gums with it."

"What does that do for you?"

"It's a spiritual experience. I can see you smirking. You think I'm kidding. I'm serious."

"That's your trouble, Quentin. You're serious, all right. But you don't pick the right things to be serious about. You're wasting your time."

"Wasting yours, you mean. Self-important, you and Innis, saving the animals. I agree. That's why I'm here."

"I haven't time for this, Quentin. Get in line with the others or go home, please. By the way, read your sign. You've misspelled 'thank.'"

"Haven't. I've left out the question mark. Not to give away the meaning. See it, don't you? For deep thinkers. I feel what you feel, but not in your way. That make me wrong? Or you?"

"Why complicate things? Stand with the others. Hold up the damn sign. Though I don't think anybody's going to guess your deep meaning. Try to remember. You're here for the animals. Like the rest."

"How can you be so right, Kendra? You're the girl missing from my life."

"Something's missing. I don't think it's me."

"I can see it's open season on men as well as meat."

"Not all men, Quentin, and you're not all men, or maybe I misspelled that?"

"Ouch. I shall do my duty."

He stood near Gwen and Madeline.

"Is this all we do?"

"Being here is what's important," Gwen said.

"Thanks for telling me."

"I haven't told you anything. I've reminded you."

Gwen stared straight ahead and he took out his smartphone.

"Need something for my next vlog. I'm a vlogger, or vloggist. I go vlogging, or maybe it should be vloggin, for my vlogees. Catavlog my vlogs. So they won't get vlost. I used to blog but everything got all blogged up. Now I can see what I'm doing."

"Are you here to show off?" Gwen said.

"I came to see if activists can prove veganism isn't a cult-de-sac."

"Your cheap jokes don't impress us," Madeline said.

"You guys are getting in a lot of practice early at being little bitches."

"It's easy with you."

"I'm getting out of here. I don't suppose they'd make me a salad in there. I'm not fussy. Something free of meat juices I could eat off the premises. They've got a special on romaine this week at the local Asian market, anyway. I'm gone. Don't step on any caterpillars. You're squashing a butterfly."

He put his phone in his jeans pocket and dropped his sign in the gutter.

More customers left the restaurant. They walked away without looking at the protesters. Madeline saw someone before the door closed again. She put her sign on top of her head and bent it down like a sun visor.

"He's—in—there."

"Who?" Gwen said, straining to see as the door closed.

Madeline couldn't speak. She turned her back to the restaurant. Stared at traffic. Gwen understood.

"He's in there?"

Madeline nodded. They both looked at traffic. Kendra noticed. She came over.

"What's wrong?"

"Dr. Todd's in there," Madeline said, staring across the street as Gwen scuffed the heel of her sneaker against the curb.

"You sure?"

Madeline nodded.

Kendra thought for a while.

"Here's what we'll do. The three of us are going in there like we're customers. You guys confront him and I'll get everything on my phone. Go in ahead. Be my shield."

They put down their signs and went to the door. Gwen opened it and they stepped inside. A waitress walked over and opened a book on a small high desk like a lectern and smiled at them. She waited but they walked past. She had to raise her voice.

"Do you have a reservation?"

"We were passing by," Gwen said, stopping, "and I recognized my uncle through the window. I'd like to go and say hi. We'll leave right away. We're tourists."

"All right, you can go. Make it quick. This is a restaurant. Your friends will have to stay here."

"What is this, a hospital?" Kendra said. "She wants to introduce us, if that's all right with you."

Before the waitress could answer, they headed for the back. At a corner table sat Dr. Todd with a woman with plenty of cleavage in her blouse and leg to her skirt. A rich socialite, she had made reservations weeks ago, knowing when the vegan guru would be visiting. Sitting next to each other and against the wall, they had been eating and drinking and planning. They were laughing now about something as the three approached. Kendra stayed behind the others, hiding her phone in her palm. Gwen pointed her finger at the doctor.

"You carnivore. We believed in you."

Madeline leaned over the table. Her voice brought the restaurant to a halt. "There's blood on your lips."

Drunk and stunned, the doctor stared, wondering who the strangers were. His companion looked around for an escape. Kendra recorded it all. The doctor managed a stupefied grin but Kendra put paid to that, waving her phone.

"We're splattering you all over the social media. You're going viral, carnist."

On their way out a bartender moved to stop them.

"Fuck off," Kendra said. "You want an assault charge filed against you for molesting girls?"

The bartender stepped aside.

The demonstrators had been there for two hours. Kendra decided it was time to leave in case the police showed up and confiscated her phone. A charge of trespassing wasn't likely, nor one of harassing customers, and Dr. Todd wasn't going to press charges, but why take a chance? They had made their point and there was next time. The protesters broke up feeling a mix of accomplishment and disappointment. There was a long way to go. Gwen and Madeline were still in high dudgeon about Dr. Todd. But Kendra said that slice of animal muscle he chewed on was going to be a lot more expensive than he imagined.

Chapter 11

Returning to Sylvia's, Speaker and Lynch took side streets and alleys, trying to avoid being seen, Speaker thinking about what to do with the notebooks. Mail them anonymously to the newspaper? That man owned the newspaper, the only one in the city. He owned one of the four television stations. None of the others would touch the story. They wanted fake news, fake scandal, or perversion on a scale they could handle. An interview with the mother of a runaway teenager whose naked body minus her sex organs was found in roadside bushes in a park. There would have to be some explanation sent along with the notebooks. How much could he say and be anonymous? And what about Lynch, witness to a murder? There was little chance of him testifying. Change his story to save his life. Or take the first bribe he was offered. In his world justice was for the rich, the poor survived. The police? They'd send the notebooks up the pipeline and somewhere up there would be someone who'd love to do that man a favour. The notebooks would disappear. If they didn't and if in the unlikely event Lynch came forward and was found to be a credible witness and charges were laid, what would happen? Without the body of the victim and evidence at the scene of the crime, and with the only witness a tramp in the middle of committing a burglary, a conviction for rape and manslaughter would be inconceivable, and knowing that, why would any prosecutor plea-bargain with Lynch? That man's pack of lawyers would portray him as a victim of blackmail by perverts trying to destroy him for his anti-porno, anti-pervert media campaigns. Lynch would find himself faced with countercharges of breaking and entering, theft, the fabrication of evidence, forgery and extortion and would end up in prison and have his throat cut by somebody who owed a favour to somebody who owed a favour to that man. Having been exonerated by the courts, that man would appear in front of television cameras with his wife and thank her for supporting him throughout his ordeal. He would demand a police investigation into the cabal of perverts trying to destroy him. For a while there would be official noises in that direction, yet another favour. Media probes, if any, would die out. But the notebooks did exist, were an accusation directed at that man and anyone who knew about them and ignored them. And what was on the flash drive?

Lynch straggled along a few steps behind Speaker, limping on tired feet, stringy calf muscles aching from his hectic running earlier. His throat was dry, burning for a drink. Get older. Nobody helps. Ya plan something. Keep from freezing and starving. The bastards take it from ya. Can't trust no one. End up getting killed. Come up with a idea. Get nuthin'. Got 'em into them 'partmints. Good stuff. This fucker. Too smart for hisself. Don't know how to take 'vantage. Slow down, ya stupid bastard. Get there going slower too. Fuck off out of here. Stay at Sylvia's till this blows over. Cooks good grub. Lots of meat in her stews. Been by herself a while. Give her a whirl. Not so busted up. Piss. Alley somewheres.

A block from the house Speaker stopped and waited for Lynch. They crossed over to the other side of the street because Speaker wanted to get a clearer view of Sylvia's house as they approached it. No lights were on. It was tall and gaunt against a clear but moonless sky, a black pointed slab in a row of them on a forgotten street. He stopped again, looked around. It was almost one. The cars parked along the road were dark. Lynch squatted, taking advantage of the delay. Seconds later something feathery brushed against his hand. He jumped up, feeling the strain in his legs.

"Shit."

"What's the matter?"

"Something touched me."

"Not the love of humanity, was it?"

"What'd ya mean?"

"It was a cat."

A large grey cat with cavernous eyes was in the middle of the road, having scurried away when Lynch had yelled and straightened up. It paused and looked back, ready to run or stay, its plume of tail waving slowly, whisking the cool night air.

"I'll kill the fuckin' thing."

"It was marking you, claiming you as part of its territory."

"Scared the shit out of me."

They crossed the street. When they reached the sidewalk, they could hear Sylvia yelling. A light went on in the downstairs hallway. The front door was jerked open and slammed against the wall. The bulky figure of John O' tumbled down the porch stairs. Holding a shoe in one hand and with his other hand against his head, he bulldozed through the half-open gate and fell, his knees hitting the sidewalk. Waving a crowbar, Sylvia appeared in a diaphanous white nightgown. With the sweep of a murderous hand she slapped on the porch light, Rowser beside her, barking nonstop in the echoing night.

"Breaking into my house. Some thanks I get for helping you."

She slammed the door shut. The porch light stayed on. John O' stood up and dropped his shoe and jammed a foot into it. He wiped blood off his forehead with the back of his hand. Checking for loose teeth, he felt his jaws. There was a tear in one of his pant legs. He explained.

"Got here a little while ago. See if you guys had any luck finding a place. I knock. No answer. I go 'round the back, door's unlocked so I let myself in. Dark in the kitchen and don't want to wake nobody, so I didn't put a light on. Forgot that goddam dog of hers. Barks like crazy, grabs onto my leg. Next thing I know she's coming downstairs hollering. Light comes on and I get smacked on the head. 'Fore ya know it, I get another on the jaw. I got out 'fore she killed me. She's got a wallop. I didn't mean nuthin'."

"You entered a woman's house without an invitation, and I find it hard to believe Sylvia would leave the back door unlocked," Speaker said.

"It was nuthin'. You trying to make it something?"

"If I did, you'd show me where I was wrong."

187

"Clout ya? I'd kill ya if I did."

Lynch snickered.

"Too bad ya didn't find her purse. But ya got to see her in her nightie, enough to keep ya awake."

"Shut up, Lynch. I'm not in the mood to put up with you."

Throwing his arms out wide, Lynch began tapping his boots on wave ruts in the worn asphalt of the road, a tattered scarecrow dancing away the night.

"She outhit ya, big ass."

"You old shit."

"It's me, Sylvia. I'd like to suck your big tits."

"I'll kick your ass up your backside."

"I'd like to get my teeny weeny inside ya, Sylvia, if I can find it."

"I'll get you."

"Ya won't get me any more 'n ya got her or her money, blubber guts."

"Stop it, you two," Speaker said.

"Keep out of this," John O' said as he tied his shoelaces.

He straightened up and ran towards Lynch. Tired as he was, Lynch raced away from the waterfront brawler, who began to wheeze as he chased Lynch down that block and into the next one. At the end of the second block Lynch made a wide turn and scuttled back. He stopped, waited a few seconds and scooted around a lamp post on the other side of the street from Sylvia's house. John O' lumbered after him, breath rasping in and out. Streetlight gave his round face and the bulge of his balding head a jaundiced look. Sweat trickled down his forehead and cheeks, beads dripping from his chin. He got to the lamp post and leaned his shoulder against it. In the middle of the road Lynch stopped running and turned around, breathing hard himself and feeling a burning in his lungs. He would suffer for this, with aching cramped muscles and swollen feet, but he didn't care. On this day of failure he was finally getting away with something.

"Get wind enough to swallow a case a beer so's ya can bullshit punks in a pub 'bout how tough ya are."

Lynch turned away, satisfied with this final jab. John O' heaved himself away from the lamp post and made an all-out charge. Lynch was coughing between wheezes and didn't hear him approaching. He felt a huge hand grab his shoulder and twist him around, and saw or later thought he saw the right. But the massive fist didn't land squarely on his chin. John O' was off balance when he threw the punch. That saved Lynch from a broken jaw. He was sent spinning backwards across the road and collapsed, semi-conscious. John O' stood in the middle of the road, bending over to catch his breath. He tried to grin at Lynch sprawled against the curb. John O' only had seconds to congratulate himself before he felt the biggest punch of his life. It blindsided him, lifted him off his feet and hurled all two hundred and thirty pounds fifteen feet down the block. The force of the blow broke his neck and spine. He was dead when he landed.

Speaker heard the car before the collision. It had silently glided around the corner, lights off, and slid nearer to Lynch. The sawtooth shriek of its revving engine and high-pitched tearing sound of tires flexing in a smoking blur before the car leaped at him. But it hit the bending John O'. Roaring off into the darkness, a furious dung beetle was leaving its nocturnal lump in the glare cast by a street light.

Speaker ran to Lynch, who put a hand to his jaw, winced and spat blood.

"You all right?"

"Huh?"

"John O's been hurt. I think he's dead."

Speaker rushed into the road. John O' had landed on his head and fallen over onto his back, legs folding at the knees and collapsing sideways. Dark fluid was seeping out of a crack across the side of his head. It was at a grotesque angle to the rest of his body, as if it were trying to rest on his shoulder. His mouth and nose were squashed together. Speaker didn't bother to check for a pulse. He went to Sylvia's house and turned the old-fashioned key-shaped doorbell ringer. She opened the door after Speaker identified himself. She had put on a pair of pyjamas and was wearing a bathrobe over them. She had been sitting in the kitchen and drinking a cup of tea when the doorbell rang. Barking furiously, Rowser had dashed ahead of her to the door but wagged his tail when he heard Speaker identify himself.

"John O's been killed and Lynch's hurt," Speaker said before Sylvia could say anything. "Car hit John O'. After he punched Lynch, knocking him out of the way. I'll explain later. Call the police."

Speaker went back to Lynch, who was sitting up and shaking his head slowly.

"That bastard really got me."

"Somebody got him. He's dead. Car hit him. It was after you."

"What am I going to do?"

"That guy either found you by accident or knows about Sylvia's. Maybe he thinks he killed you. Maybe he doesn't know about Sylvia's. If the first is true, you're fine. If not, and the second is true, you're safe for now. If neither, you're in trouble. I'm guessing he hasn't pinned you down to her house. If I'm right, you can hide there. I'll explain to her the situation you're in. I'll tell the police it was a hit-and-run."

He got Lynch to his feet and up the stairs and explained to Sylvia.

"I've got to keep Lynch out of this for his protection and ours, too. Hide him. Don't tell the police anything. I'll say that the sound of the accident woke me up. I went outside and saw the body. Woke you. I'll tell them John O' was an acquaintance from next door. They know about the fire at Al's."

"Sure. Don't stand out there. I'll put you upstairs tonight in the spare bedroom, Lynch. Tomorrow I'll fix you up a place in the basement."

"Ya have something for a beat-up man, Sylvia? See, my jaw's swelled up."

"I don't have anything like that. I'll bring you some warm milk. Come on. Take hold of my arm."

"I wanted to go up them stairs lots of times. Never figured it'd be this way."

"Shut up and walk."

After the ambulance had taken the body away and the police had asked their questions and gone, Speaker sat with Sylvia in the kitchen. It was past two. A sound sleeper, Al had woken up when the police arrived and had gone back to sleep. Warts came out of his room, heard only what the officers heard, and went back to bed. An exhausted Lynch had fallen into a deep sleep as soon as he lay down. Speaker told Sylvia what he knew but not who owned the briefcase. She didn't ask, sipped her tea until she had taken in all the rest.

"What are you going to do?"

"I don't know. I'm not sure I should've told you as much as I have. But you should know the reason why Lynch's in trouble. The man after him will come back if he doesn't think he killed him tonight. The notebooks are meaningless to everyone down here except Lynch and me. He wouldn't have caught on if I hadn't explained what they were. That wouldn't have happened if the owner hadn't ordered the hit, overestimating the trouble Lynch could cause. Probably thinks the notebooks will fall into the wrong hands. Most likely they would have ended up in a trash bin. Lynch's almost illiterate. And there's no way he would tell the police about the murder. We're dealing with a control freak with lots to hide. Even from a tramp. Ironic, isn't it?"

Sylvia rubbed her forehead. She had a headache. Too much tea. Four cups. Too much excitement. Rowser barking and she grabbing the crowbar, under her bed in case, but she never thought she'd need it, but it made her feel better, that's all. The dark shape in the hallway, Rowser at a leg, swings at the lump of a head. Conscious of her fear now, she began yelling, angry she could be afraid in her own house. Snapping on the hallway light, seeing John O' heading for the front door as she chased him with the crowbar. Snarling, Rowser still gripping that leg and being dragged along. Sitting at the kitchen table and angry the fear was making her shake, she heard voices outside. But she had been too upset to care what they were saying. She had trusted these men, invited them into her house. The first chance any of them got, he broke in. Couldn't trust them. Get rid of the whole works. An engine howled and tires spun senselessly. Was there a bump? The doorbell rang and she was still sitting, but it made her rush to the door, furious but not shaking now, Rowser at her side. Speaker's news left her wondering what to feel. Finally, she had been told about the briefcase. A powerful and wealthy man, secret notebooks, a hired killer, child rape, child murder. She felt too tired to think any more. If she could get upstairs and fall onto her bed, close her eyes and could dream again what she was dreaming before all this.

"You all right, Sylvia?"

"What?" Speaker's voice startled her.

"You look as if you need sleep. Get some rest. I'm a light sleeper. If anything happens, I'll wake up."

"Rowser always sleeps downstairs. If anything's wrong, he wakes up and barks like hell. I've got deadbolts. Two each on the back and front doors. How did he get in?"

Speaker checked the back door. It was locked but the porch window wasn't.

"John O' must have lifted the window latch the other night before he left, planning to return. Not enough so you'd notice, but enough for him to force the window open."

Speaker refastened the latch and left. Sylvia washed their cups and saucers. Her lime terrycloth bathrobe felt tight around her shoulders and waist. But she felt comfortable. And she was glad she had put on Leonard's old red and white striped pyjamas. She wanted to wear something that would calm her nerves, help her get over the shock of John O' coming out of the night. She wouldn't feel safe in white silk for a while. Maybe not ever. And she wished she hadn't begun wearing those slippers with the fluffy white balls. They looked silly. What was she trying to do? Hide her age? Be someone she wasn't? She was middle-aged or so, didn't shave, wore boxer shorts under dresses and liked gumboots for yardwork. Her one, and it was private, concession to conventional fantasy had been her white silk underwear: brassieres, panties and sheer nightgowns. She had slept only in them ever since Leonard had surprised her with a white silk nightie early one Christmas morning. He added other items regularly over the years. Each had meant nights of cosily provocative love. After he died she continued wearing her white silk things in bed, sometimes one and sometimes all, according to how she felt. She had gotten used to this. And it reminded her of her married life. Now Speaker and Lynch knew what she wore. A special link with her husband suddenly had been made unbearably public. She must look an old fat woman desperately trying to look younger. Pyjamas would be warmer this winter. Leonard did leave four pair, two of them still in packages with the price stickers on them. Why waste them?

Chapter 12

As tenants and owners began returning to Glen Loughran Tower Monday afternoon and evening, the extent of the robbery became known. The police returned and lists of stolen property were compiled. Victims prepared to contact insurance companies on Tuesday. Some went to see the caretaker, demanded to know why there wasn't better security in the building. "One wee man, was it?" Maggie MacDiarmid said to her husband as the total of suites and items rose, along with his blood pressure. "For the love of God, leave me alone" he moaned. "I could lose ma job."

The penthouse suite did not report a theft. No one entered or left it for many weeks after Monday morning. In the master bedroom the bed had been stripped of pillows, sheets and blankets. The fixtures in the hallway bathroom had been scrubbed with soap. All floors had been swept, carpets vacuumed. Clothes, liquor, the contents of the medicine cabinet and several personal items had been taken down the fire stairs in the Monday dawn to an unmarked truck. The bedding was removed in garbage bags. Behind the locked windows and doors of the suite the smell of soap and disinfectant permeated everything. Another world took over, crawling unseen through light and darkness, breeding, feeding on each other, defecating on the furniture and the carpet. Life within stainless steel taps, the slime of holes, plastic night under sinks, inside drains and toilets, floating as scum on quiet lakes in ceramic tanks and bowls, and over the stretching plains of dust, and in the silent wool and polyester forests, was the only life. Never able to claim immortality and silent in numbers and never tired until dead, it crawled on.

And below the level of human notice, in transmutation to soil, mites would find that speck of blood on the mattress.

Gwen's parents returned Monday evening at six. Earlier there were patrol cars outside. An officer told Gwen and Madeline about the mounting toll. They decided to say nothing about Lynch, at least for a while.

"He didn't do this by himself," Gwen said.

"We could tell Speaker," Madeline said. "He might know what to do. I haven't told my mom. I'll have to tell her tonight. She'll find out anyway. It better be from me. Or I'll hear the voice that never stops."

"We can't see Speaker today. I've got to be here when my parents get back."

"Oh, no." Sitting on the chesterfield, Carol was looking at the open jewellery boxes in her hands. An officer had told them in the lobby about the burglaries. Gwen mentioned that Lynch had stayed in the apartment, and some of the rest. Roger had gone into the master bedroom to check the wall safe above the bed, hidden behind Gwen's watercolour of a sailboat in the harbour. Done when she was twelve, the quick brushstrokes suggested the rakish hull, slanting deck, windtaut rigging, and ballooning white spinnaker stretching over foam-crested blue waves. It was all daring forward motion, nothing spared. All Carol saw now was the white satin lining of the boxes. Gwen had forgotten about the safe. Roger tried to divert blame from her.

"I told you to put them in the safety deposit box. We've got no special coverage for jewellery."

Carol knew what Roger was trying to do. Her voice was tight.

"I was going to have them appraised and get special coverage. I couldn't put them away in a box. They were Mom's and Grandma's. I liked to look at them. I wanted to have them close."

Gwen felt like crying. This was worse than when Spots died a couple of years ago, wheezed and fell over onto the dining room carpet and lay there. That one eye she could see was large and shining like the marbles played with by children. The slightly open mouth seemed to grin at her, as if Spots wanted to tell her something. But she knew he was dead. Spots had had attacks of wheezing before. The veterinarian had said that older cats, especially in a damp climate, got congested lungs. There was nothing to do except hope that he would recover. He did several times. But at sixteen he was too old. Gwen remembered her father putting him into a shoebox, head hanging like a doll's as he lifted the body off the carpet. Gwen had wanted to bury him but her mother suggested it was better for him to be cremated at the city pound. Quick and clean, she said. And they had pictures of the cat to look at, including her favourite, Spots wearing a funny hat at her birthday party the day Gwen turned eight. That big orange and white head with the cone-shaped candy-red hat peering over the edge of the table at a piece of cake on the dish in front of him had always made her laugh, and feel sad after he died. Her father never told her that the pound was closed when he got there. He left the box outside the door.

"Why did you think you could trust a tramp?" Carol said in that tense voice. "Did you and Madeline drag him out of a garbage can? But it's worse than that, isn't it? Because he can open safes and pick locks like nobody's business. Why would you let someone like that spend a minute here? Couldn't you at least have asked us what we thought about it? No, that would have spoiled your fun. Your experiment has cost me something very precious."

Roger walked to the loveseat and put a hand on the back, near Gwen's shoulder. He wasn't sure he should be doing this. But he couldn't help himself. Gwen sensed something precarious in the relationship between the three of them, something that hadn't been there before, or maybe it had and she hadn't recognized it. Carol's good-natured attitude towards her husband's doting on his daughter wasn't as easy to maintain as all of them had thought. This was their first test. So much would depend on it.

"She made a mistake, Carol. Gwen tried to be an angel of mercy at fourteen and help a homeless person who turned out to be a thief. She should have let us know. But her mistake came from goodness. That's a compliment to us."

Carol tossed her head back against the chesterfield.

"Some compliment. I lose and you sermonize. Our daughter turns the place over to a thief and you act as if she spilled her cocoa on the carpet. Sorry, Rog. This is more than a prank. At least two dozen suites have been burglarized and who knows how much taken. The caretaker and his wife were assaulted. If someone had returned early, there could have been a mugging, even a murder. How's that consistent with anything we taught her?"

Roger took his hand from the back of the loveseat. Gwen knew her mother had put her away from her and was asking her father to do the same. For the first time, Gwen was not absolutely sure of him. That certainty had never been abused but it had given her a kind of unclouded confidence in her abilities as well as in his love. Carol loved her daughter, but it was a qualified love based on an intellectual appreciation of her that overlay maternal instinct. Gwen was more than bright. She could reason beyond her years. She could play the piano, sketch and do accomplished watercolours. She picked up languages quickly and found computers boringly easy. And she was pretty, even beautiful. Her mother could see no weakness in her and that was comforting but also disturbing. Gwen seemed less like a daughter and more like a competitor, not only for her father's love but also for her uneasy mother's self-esteem. There was a sort of perfection about her, a wonderful completeness unfolding itself without haste. It made less intelligent and average-looking girls and women appear forced, harried bumblers that depended on chance. Carol disliked this, and here was a fortuitous opportunity to attack Gwen indirectly.

Rigid on the loveseat, Gwen stared down at her hands clasped together in her lap. She knew her mother didn't want to forgive, and not because of a necklace and a ring. But she wasn't aware of the envy she aroused in her when Roger kissed Gwen on the forehead or asked about schoolwork, which he did every night over the dinner table during the school year when he was in town and didn't get home late. If he was late he would sit in her bedroom as she worked at her desk, watching her, asking questions, listening closely and commenting on her replies. Their frequent laughter was low and mingled with whispered phrases. To Carol, working in her study, their laughter mocked her exclusion from their conversations. They appeared to have an intimacy she could not achieve with her husband, who told himself that he loved his wife because he made love to her. Over the years the tussle between their bodies had become more like the congenial exercise of scrubbed and scented flesh than an intimate placating of sweated urges. He hardly ever asked with any real interest about his wife's career. There was always the general question, "Everything all right, darling?" The answer was expected to be not much more than, "Fine, honey." She thought of having an affair, had even from time to time tentatively compiled a list of likely candidates, but hadn't gone beyond that. Their nineteen-year-old marriage hadn't settled as yet into that state of dull union impervious to any threat, a type of medieval bond made up of various degrees of stubbornness, realism, acceptance, disinterest, convention, friendship, disillusion and routine and lack of opportunity. That kind of compatible yoke seemed ironic to Carol in an avowedly sexually mature, professedly romantic society, where she saw love and sex sold like name brands.

Both sets of grandparents had loved Gwen with gifts and praise. She was their favourite grandchild. Carol felt oddly irritated that Gwen wasn't spoiled by this attention. "Gwen is such a perfect child you couldn't have botched the job if you'd tried, could you, Carol dear?" her mother-in-law had said. She told Roger and he had said, "She means well, darling. She's proud of her. I'm proud of you both, especially of you as her mother." When she had opened the door to a half-naked Gwen spattered with blood, Carol's maternal instinct surprised her with its force, seeming to freeze her blood one moment and flood through her like molten lava the next and obliterate her. She had hugged and kissed her, but it was Roger who caressed her when Carol went to get towels and blankets. When she returned and saw them holding each other, her husband white with shock and Gwen blindly sobbing, the lava turned to cold acid in her veins. Not surprised at her calmness, Carol telephoned for the police.

"I'm sure Gwen feels bad about what happened," Roger said.

"I'm not sure I want to hear any more," Carol said. She put the jewellery boxes on a side table, stood up in one stiff motion, went into the master bedroom and shut the door.

Gwen turned to her father. "Daddy, I'm so sorry." For years she had called him "Dad." Roger put his hand on her shoulder.

"Your mother is upset. She'll get over it after a while."

Later that evening Gwen phoned Madeline to compare parental reactions. Mary answered Madeline's smartphone, voice cool. "Hello, Gwen. Madeline can't come to the phone." (In the background a whispered, "Why not? A minute, Mom, please.") "She's got to get ready for school tomorrow. I'll tell her you called." She thought about texting or sending email but knew Mary had confiscated the phone and probably had forbidden Madeline from using her computer. She knew Mary's tenacity in dealing with Madeline.

The next morning Gwen and her mother avoided each other. Roger thought of saying something about yesterday as he leaned against the kitchen counter and gulped down a cup of coffee. He had to leave for an early meeting. Carol spent most of the time in her study putting papers into her briefcase. Gwen sat at the kitchen table eating organic seven grain cereal with almond milk. She cooked the cereal for herself, preferring it to her parents' name brand box of sugared flakes. Roger said he would be coming home late and kissed them a quick goodbye. My dicky-bird husband, his wife accepted again. My dad's only another dad, like the rest, Gwen told herself. After he had gone, neither wanted to stay. In the race to leave first Carol won, saying goodbye from the apartment door, and Gwen answered.

At the Laura Peabody School that morning before classes, Gwen looked for Madeline amid the confusion of a first day back after summer vacation. She saw her near the main entrance. It was a few minutes before the scheduled assembly in the auditorium. The assembly marked the beginning of each school year at the ninety-four year old institution, the oldest and largest private girls' school in the city. Renamed "Pisspotty" by some irreverent girls decades ago, the name had been passed down faithfully to kindred spirits in succeeding generations. Gwen waved and shouted to get Madeline's attention in the crush of excited talk and bodies, laughter and bumping, high-pitched giggling and dropped combs, yelling and sleeve tugging, of a few hundred other girls, all dressed in white blouses, black blazers with white piping and the school crest, pale grey skirts, ties and socks, and black shoes. A teacher whose stay there was short said that at such informal gatherings they looked like a flock of juvenile penguins. Gwen made her way towards Madeline after getting rid of Kerstin MacEvoy, who was rumoured to be a transsexual by students who disliked her. Gwen didn't believe this but avoided the stocky pigtailed gossip. Her legs stood like fence posts blocking Gwen.

"So, Gwen. Any news? Alison and Blair are deep. He's definitely quits with Kinsley."

"Hi," Gwen said as she stepped around her.

"She went with him to a party at Sabina's last week. Wow. Hot. Gwen?"

When Gwen got to the broad stone stairs of the main entrance, Madeline saw her.

"I've been looking for you. I'm afraid to ask what happened. Tell me, no, don't. Yes."

"The guillotine, chop. They took my mother's necklace and ring out of the wall safe. I forgot about them. She's really mad."

"I guess she blames us."

"Me, not you. I let him stay there. We've got to see Speaker after school. There's Crittenden. Assembly snore."

According to tradition, the welcoming address in the school auditorium was given by a different speaker each year, but it was invariably the same tediously obvious constructive advice in homilies and platitudes offered with patronizing camaraderie and hopeless attempts at humour. This year's speaker was Divie Smith, named Division Algebra Smith by her father, a famous mathematician and world class chess player who had gone insane and committed suicide in an asylum, trying to subtract his head from the rest of him with a razor blade. Plain and skinny, his daughter never wore anything on her face except wire-rimmed glasses. She inherited his love of mathematics but not his passion for chess or skill with a blade. Her classes were dry affairs, the painstaking repetition of basic principles illustrated with labyrinthine problems. Students were expected to master every part of the course. But she had a bad memory and tended to ask the same examination questions. It had become standard procedure for students to consult a passed down dog-eared file of old exams and memorize the answers. The subject of her speech was the truth of numbers. Blinking, she stood rigid at the podium, her close-cropped hair going grey and a lightweight tweed suit baggy on her frame. Her voice shook a little from nerves.

"Be true to yourself, your parents, your friends and your school the way you must be true in mathematics and your education will add up. If you aren't, you'll be left behind after class trying to find the right answer. A lot of you know how that feels. Not pleasant, is it? The right answer is work. Know and apply your basic skills and a beautiful pattern of truth will emerge. In the same way you see truth in the answer to a math problem. And there is real beauty there, as some of you more fortunate ones know. Laziness isn't the answer. Do the problem over. Think basics. You will find it's not difficult once you do this. Even if you are not blessed with great intelligence, work will get you through. Even in mathematics, though I suppose some of you doubt me. Especially those of you who haven't yet taken my class. There is only one way to a happy and constructive school life. Be honest in your application of your abilities to any problem you may have. Problems are there to be solved. And I'm here to tell you the answer is there. For any problem. And with this attitude, your life here and later on as responsible adults will be more rewarding."

Several older girls at the rear of the auditorium began to chant together in a loud whisper, "Go, Divie," until a teacher who had been stationed at the back wall came over and told the offenders to stop or risk detention. Near the front somebody said "Encore" in a loud voice and two teachers rushed over from a side wall but were too late to spot the miscreant. A large balloon of pink bubble gum burst with a pop. A small girl, gum sticking to her freckles and glasses, was hustled out flanked by frowning teachers. Divie's welcoming address droned to a close and other speakers talked about maintaining school standards and the various academic prizes to be won in the coming year. Near the end a girl slumped in her seat and had to be carried out. She hadn't eaten that morning or slept the night before. Some girls stood up and were told to sit down. Everybody stood as the assembly ended with the school song, the music provided by an old hissing tape piped over the public address system. The students made a ragged chorus, some singing deliberately off-key. Dismissal brought an explosion of noise, shouts and chairs tumbling over each other as a mob dashed headlong for the exit doors.

It was all familiar to Gwen and Madeline, who had attended Laura

Peabody for a few years. They spent the day receiving textbooks, finding lockers, locating classrooms and re-establishing old friendships. Lunchtime meant the assembly line cafeteria experience again, and food most of which they wouldn't eat, intending as in the past to supplement it with their own. As the lunchroom line-up passed the dishes, platters, trays and pots, they saw the slices of green lemon pie topped with brittle meringue, and the spaghetti bolognese, pink watery sauce coating slitherings of fat pasta in a stainless steel trough. They each settled for a glass of apple juice and oatmeal cookies, vowing to circulate a petition demanding much better food. Talking to the tired anemic school nurse, who doubled as the nutritionist, hadn't worked. As ignorant about food as she was about supplements, she had smiled away their complaints.

Stephanie Shove, who planned to run for student council president, stopped by their table. They had the reputation around the school of proselytizing for environmental concerns. Besides circulating petitions to save dolphins, whales and old-growth forest, and raising funds for animal sanctuaries, there was their campaign against speciesism. Unwilling to concede the intellectually avant-garde as beyond her constituency, she nevertheless regarded them as suspect radicals. Stephanie's father was the CEO of an oil company. Holding her tray to one side, Stephanie leaned forward, smiling the smile of an unflappable politician as she looked at what the school's notorious vegans were eating.

"That looks quite nourishing."

"Can't eat anything else over there," Gwen said.

"I suppose it's not gourmet, but the school has a limited budget."

"They could give us something better than that. Organic fruits and vegetables. Whole grains and beans. Wouldn't cost that much."

"Starving people in the underdeveloped world would be glad to eat anything in this room."

"Including the floor tiles and the plastic spoons," Madeline said.

Gwen looked at Stephanie's tray.

"I see that you have the tart of the day. Vinyl strawberry with polyvinyl chloride red sauce. And shaving cream topping in a sawdust crust. You must find that aluminum tray delicious, too."

Smile almost faultlessly in place, Stephanie moved on to other tables.

In the yellow flare of sunlight ebbing westwards on a late afternoon in September, the now familiar blocks of the downtown eastside looked harmless from a taxi. Corner grocery stores tucked into apartment buildings, vegetable markets, boxes stacked outside, one-window cafés, narrow hotels next to vacant lots, a couple of larger hotels with pubs. A block north and one east and they were near the waterfront and railway tracks, could see piers, freighters and warehouses. They recognized the old houses on the south side of Alexander Street. The driver stopped in the middle of the empty road and they got out, Madeline glancing around.

"I didn't see that empty lot last time."

She looked at the pile of charred timbers, scattered asphalt shingles, splintered window frames and collapsed fencing. A woman was in the front yard of the house next door. She wore a russet dress, moss green cardigan, gumboots and a straw sun hat. She was bending over with a watering can and sprinkling potted geraniums along the walkway.

"She's next door to Al's. Oh, my God."

They walked over and Madeline said hello and introduced Gwen. Sylvia straightened up and smiled at Madeline.

"Hello, dear, nice to see you again. Pleased to meet you, Gwen. You're as pretty as your friend. Such creamy skin, beautiful hair. Mine was auburn. Leonard, my husband, used to say it looked like a sunset over the ocean. Have to dye it now. Guess you've noticed next door."

"What happened?" Madeline said.

"It was terrible. Al's burnt down on Saturday night. Farmer's dead. It was probably arson. Some of those guys are staying with me. Talk to Speaker when he gets back. He went to get some groceries. Come inside and wait. I'll give you some of my cucumber pie. One of my favourites."

"We're vegans. We don't eat eggs or dairy."

"Don't worry. I don't use them in this pie."

Sylvia put the watering can down on the front stairs. They followed her around the side of the house, up the back porch stairs into the kitchen. She asked them to sit down, went to her refrigerator freezer, cut large slices of pie and brought them to the table. "It's better when it's cold." They were tentative with the first bite. But the taste of grated lime peel on slices of cucumber topping a frozen banana filling in a flaky crust rid them of doubts. They ate quickly.

"That was great," Madeline said after swallowing her last mouthful. She was a faster eater than Gwen, at least two bites ahead.

Gwen nodded, her mouth full.

"Hm."

"There's plenty more," Sylvia said.

"Maybe a little piece," Madeline said.

"Hm."

"Where's Al?" Madeline asked after she finished.

"He stays in the front room, sleeping or looking at some postcards I gave him. Rowser, he's my dog, keeps him company a lot of the time."

"I guess he's upset losing his house."

"He doesn't say much."

The screen door opened and Speaker came in carrying a couple of bags of groceries. Everybody said hi and he put the bags on the counter, beside the sink, and came over and sat at the table.

"Got everything you wanted, Sylvia, except artichokes. They'll have them next week."

"Thanks. I was telling them about the fire. Not everything, though. Fill them in."

"We've got something to tell you," Gwen said. "Some guys robbed at least two dozen suites in my building, including my parents' place. We know whose idea it was. Where is he?"

"I know about the robbery, I've seen him since, I know where he is and he's given me a problem I've got to deal with."

"The problem has got something to do with the robbery, hasn't it? And it's not whether or not to turn him in."

"That's right."

"I want to see him. He stole a necklace and ring of my mother's."

"He hasn't got anything. He was set up."

"That's what he told you."

"I've got more than his word. The robbery is a secondary matter now. I'm sorry about your mother and the others. I don't think they'll see any of their stuff again."

"What's going to happen to him?"

"He's hiding, afraid he'll be killed."

"Why would he be afraid of being killed? Oh, I get it. That's the problem he's given you. Why can't you tell us where he is?"

"He's under your feet. You shouldn't see him. He's afraid to say anything. He can't get your mother's necklace and ring back for you."

"If he tells the police where the stuff is, they'll protect him."

"He saw something and he took something and somebody is dead because of that."

"I want to see him." Gwen stamped her foot.

There was a muffled noise in the basement. Boots clumped up the stairs. The door opened slowly and Lynch poked his head out and saw the girls. He stared at them before looking at Speaker.

"What'd ya want?"

"We trusted you and you robbed a whole building," Gwen said.

"It was a smooth job. We got away with erything we wanted. I could've been down in Porto Vayartee or them Bahamees or Jamaicee or Barbadee with bikinees or nudees waiting on me. Them locks opened like a easy woman."

"Go back downstairs," Speaker said.

"You're showing off in front of 'em 'cause their people's got money."

"If you don't listen to me, you'll probably end up dead."

"Then ya can peddle that briefcase and them little books and keep all the money to yourself."

Speaker turned away, letting his breath out slowly.

"Do what I said."

"Ya. Back to my hole. People's always putting me in holes, saying stay there and don't make no trouble. Tired of it. Don't care no more."

He yanked the door shut. He banged his boots on the steps as he descended.

"Tell us about the briefcase and the books," Gwen said. "Or I'll report him to the police. They told my father the caretaker and his wife said a little guy was behind the robberies. They'd recognize him."

"The briefcase and notebooks have nothing to do with the robbery. Somebody has already died because of them. John O'. You met him on Saturday with Al and the rest."

"One of those guys who were after us?" Madeline said.

"He broke into my house," Sylvia said, "after I fed him and offered him a place to stay."

"He saved us from a bunch of guys," Madeline said, pointing at Speaker.

Sylvia shook her head and got up, went to the counter and began making tea.

"Tell us about the briefcase and the notebooks," Gwen said to Speaker.

"You're already in trouble with your parents. I don't want to get you into more."

Sylvia filled a kettle and put it on the stove. She dropped a teabag into the teapot before returning.

"Look at what happened because you wanted to help Lynch. Speaker's trying to protect you. It's for your own good. Gwen, dear, you and Madeline won't turn Lynch in if Speaker doesn't tell you anything."

"No. We tried to get him an apartment. I let him stay in my parents' place so he'd want one of his own. Ignored what he was like. I was stubborn."

"I knew you wouldn't. Lynch is in enough trouble. And he got nothing from the robbery. Not that I think he should have. I've known him for years, longer than Speaker has, and all he's wanted to do is steal. It makes him feel good, like he's important. You wasted your time. Reforming him is like trying to make a snake go straight."

Sylvia turned to watch the kettle. Madeline picked with her fork at the remains of her second piece of pie. Speaker was staring at the floor. Gwen looked at him. He seemed resigned to failure, no matter what he decided.

"My mother's a lawyer and my father's a real estate developer, knows lots of people."

Speaker looked up at her and grinned.

"Influence."

"So what's wrong?"

"In my experience people with influence don't help people with none."

"They'll help you if I say so."

"Not only is this beyond people like me, it's beyond them, unless they're the most powerful people in the city."

"We could try."

"So that's it. You two again. Definitely not. I don't trust you. Besides, trying wouldn't be good enough. With this, starting is finishing, one way or the other. Wish I had your pluck, a lot of innocence, a little luck."

"You're almost a poet."

"I'm almost a lot of things."

Sylvia brought over the teapot and a cosy, teacups and a plate filled with cookies.

"Have some tea and cookies before you go. They're tomato cinnamon. Better than it sounds. Leonard said you could shoe a horse with them, they're so big. Used to eat a plateful. His favourites were the green onion and cheddar and the walnut garlic. The secret is how much."

What would the good people do? The ones with responsibilities, high-paying jobs, families, futures, all the prerequisites that supposedly guarantee a successful life. Futures. Speaker smiled. He liked unintentional humour. He was sitting in the front parlour and watching the street. It was twelve thirty. Gwen and Madeline had left in a taxi at six. Sylvia had given each a bag of cookies. Gwen had written the telephone number of her apartment on a sheet from her loose-leaf binder and given it to Speaker. Sylvia had gone to bed an hour ago. She was an early riser. Warts had returned at seven, gobbled a bunch of cookies and gone to bed in the sewing room after summarizing the results of his search. There could be a place to stay in a while if the thing worked out. Not a sure thing but probably almost.

Speaker had silence and time now to decide what to do about the notebooks. He took the sheet out of his shirt pocket and looked at it: Gwen Chalmers, 731-2194. Her handwriting was evenly spaced and clear, as the writing of the young usually is, as if they have plenty of time to say what they want and need lots of room to say it, and everything and everyone can be understood and nothing can be beyond logic, and truth is a certainty like youth and energy. Speaker grinned but had to admit he admired her, she had pluck. What a word to use. Had she understood him? She got the gist but did she make the right inference from that dated word? It applied to her and Madeline. They had an eager determined willingness to try for better. Ready-made heroines. Was "heroine" allowed now? Had it been consigned like "pluck" to the ranks of the outmoded? He saw himself as a caretaker of old words, a rusty knight of philology galloping across the courtyard of an empty castle, his charger's hooves striking out of the stones antiquated sounds that echoed as vanished voices of desire and defeat. No, that was too romantic. A man of ideas in an electronic world would be closer to his truth, an outmoded page turner in a world of milliseconds and websites. He was a thinker in a time when information was sold in more and more compact forms, as various products for ratings, money, propaganda, hatred. Thinking took time, the one thing no one seemed to know what to do with except sell. What do you do with your time? Do you do something once, for the experience, or as many things as possible once or many times, or one thing many times, or nothing? Does it make any difference? Nobody seemed to wonder about this. People were used to fast food, quick summaries, philosophies in a few seconds, a civilization in an hour on television, a writer or painter in a phrase, or worse a quirk, a movement in an aside, pizza history, popcorn society, absolutely everything as a guaranteed freak show they could watch without any need to understand. Be on time, get to the point. But what if there was none?

Speaker grinned. Everything was related, wasn't it? The man who owned the briefcase and the notebooks was in the fast food information business: newspapers, radio, television and Internet. Simple words and simpler ideas, deliberately mishandled and loaded with bacteria. His food was a kind of brain poison. And yet most customers would have enough inherent or inculcated moral sense to be outraged that the man supplying their info-food was brutalizing and raping little girls, had even killed at least one of them and was involved in a ring of men who satisfied lust this way. And for the info-man there was power over the minds of the ignorant as well as the flesh of the innocent. Arrogance was the common factor. But because it depended on weakness in others, this arrogance was itself weak in some fundamental way. It was the self-delusion of the man who is incomplete and who must prey on others, keeping them from being whole. The stupid, the narrow-minded, the young and the unprotected were all victims, and he saw their availability as merely a constant ratification of power. There was a co-dependency between his info-food and his sexual appetite. Enough listeners and gawkers (his newspapers were for looking) ensured the supply of children as well as enabled him to buy the protection he needed, and the girls' tortured bodies were the physical revelation of his diseased vision of informational omnipotence. Screw the public.

Where would he be weak? Official protection through bribery or connivance could only extend so far. It would only take a whiff of that rich blood to get the public's saliva dripping and its fangs to show. In days he would go from invulnerable to everybody's moral dinner. And some of the ones snouting in for the biggest drink of blood and tear of flesh would have known with their fingers between panties and skin a girl's hairless pudendum, would have made that secret pact in the dark to tell no one, would have ignored their violence to tender flesh, and would have convinced themselves of nothing but pleasure in the sore and ripped entrances, the clutch of tiny legs in pain. In public they would be the fathers of trust, the grandfathers of rectitude, the uncles of generosity, the neighbours of kindness. But they and many others would wait to see if he were wounded beyond recovery before they joined in the kill. Personal protection was something else. The father on one of his victims could catch him with a bullet in a vulnerable step between hotel and limousine, studio and rally. But he would be too cautious for that to be likely. And some of his victims had been abandoned or even sold by impoverished parents. Sometimes they were blinded by the light that shines through money, especially the larger denominations, and often pimps and madams posing as intermediaries would lie, promising parents their child was going to be a domestic servant in a respectable household. They would never know the girl was going to be beaten and starved and thrown into a dark room until she died or agreed to work in a brothel, a plaything for well off "sex tourists" from around the world. Words again. Not pedophiles, child rapists, but your average guy in search of thrills. Doesn't the money go into the local economy? Do people really have to know that it comes from an adult male fucking a seven-year-old girl who, because of greed, ignorance and rural poverty and being born with the wrong colour skin, won't live as long as his dog?

Exposure was obviously the key, and it had to be television because he owned the only newspaper. But how would the television stations that weren't his handle the story among wall-to-wall commercials, cliché-riddled movies, sitcom reruns and helicopter news, meaningless jabber for editorial comment and scandal shows that were themselves a not too refined form of sharp-nosed pornography? In fact, wasn't info-man the reductio ad absurdum of modern communications: a selective use of facts that proliferated mass ignorance and bias, an ironic covering up with a thigh in the eye, a crotch splotch, keeping abreast with a thong bikini and an innuendo tickle. The private sacrifice of prepubescent girls to adult males was only another side of an egocentric sexual gluttony, an outlet of pleasure among the drugs of choice.

It was two o'clock. Speaker was tired. The street was deserted except for cats feuding over night territories. He got up and went to the window. He liked watching them. They used cars as observation posts, jumped down and struck with a hiss and the swipe of a raised paw at interlopers. It was an ancient fight, understood by all participants but mice, grey mouthfuls of a night's catch. Cats imposed their own boundaries on streets and yards, ignoring human ones as they ignored people except for food and a roof. They didn't have a dog's notion of property, barking behind a fence for dog food, couldn't be taught to defend the importance of human things. They had never lost the sense that their own lives meant more. In all things that mattered, they were completely independent and completely undependable. In a few hours they would go back to playing their roles of housecat and pussy, being scratched under the chin by a lonely shut-in, or they might have to accept the flat hand of an overeager child pounding their head. But the night was theirs for those that could get out, stretch their haunches on the porch before two-footing down the stairs, sniff at the curbside and twitch a cautious tail into a question mark at what was going to come out of the dark.

Chapter 13

Cats investigate cautiously. Some of the bolder ones approach without seeing a sign of welcome, mewing as they get nearer. Tail raised, they rub against a pant leg, marking another possession. Ten minutes after Speaker left the window, a thin black cat with one white forepaw and a white spot on its face came out from behind the tire of a truck and hesitantly approached a man standing on the opposite side of the street from Sylvia's house. He was tall and bald and wore a black suit. He had parked his car down the block. Cats can make mistakes. When this one came near, a shoe slipped under the cat's arched belly and sent it skidding across the street to the gutter on the other side. It crawled under a car. The man looked at the house again. On Monday night Doughnuts had received a call at home.

"Don't know where he's gone. There was Al's over on Alexander. Burnt down Saturday night. Bum like him could be anywhere. Sleep in the open. Could be in a house around there. I heard some of the guys at Al's found other places. Let ya know."

On Tuesday evening Doughnuts had made a call.

"I asked around. No sign of your guy. Sure he is. I'll ask some more."

Later that evening the man standing across the street drove through the neighbourhood in a rented car. A man in his eighties was sweeping his walkway. Another pensioner was walking a dog. Neither remotely resembled Lynch. As he was driving away from the downtown eastside, he decided to have another look. Near midnight he parked on Alexander Street and waited in the car. He saw Speaker come to the window. The man decided Lynch was in that house. He waited several minutes after the parlour light was turned off and got out of the car. He glanced at the windows of other houses before heading towards Sylvia's. An old-fashioned street light nearby, a globe on top of a cast-iron post, threw a shadow, a black cutout of stem and bud in a yellow circle. He lifted the latch of the gate and swung it open slowly to avoid squeaks. On crepe soles he crossed the walkway and short front yard, opened the side gate, went around to the back and climbed the porch stairs. The kitchen window was low and came part way over the porch. He put a foot on the railing, hoisted himself up, leaned over and looked in. Through half-open curtains he could see the time in blue numerals on the electric stove. They glowed in the darkness. From his jacket pocket he took a roll of duct tape and a glass cutter, taped and scored a half-circle around the latch of the wood frame window, pushed the scored glass with a gloved hand, using the other to pry off the putty with a penknife. The piece of glass loosened and came out after several wiggles. He put it on the window ledge, inserted his gloved hand into the hole, lifted the latch and opened the window and eased himself in from the railing. Unlike the latch the hinges, painted many times, gave a slow creak of stress as the window opened, waking Rowser, who barked nonstop dashing into the kitchen. The man was holding an automatic pistol with a silencer. He shot towards the noise twice, there was a sharp cry. Lights went on in the front parlour and upstairs and Sylvia hurried down as Speaker ran in. He flicked on the light and saw the man with his gun pointed at them. Sylvia saw Rowser on his side on the floor, panting heavily and making wheezing cries. Blood had spattered on the white linoleum and a matting of blood and hair darkened the golden brown of his shoulder.

"You shot Rowser, you son of a bitch. Bastard."

Sylvia knelt, her hands shaking. She wondered where to touch, what to do. She gently stroked Rowser's head. Tears in her eyes, she looked up at the man.

"I've got to get help for my dog."

"Touch the phone, I'll kill you."

The man looked at Speaker.

"I want him."

"He's not here. He left a briefcase."

"Where is it?"

"In the front room."

The man jerked his gun at Speaker and he left.

"It's all right, Rowsie," Sylvia murmured, patting his head, biting her lip. "I'll get help for you."

Speaker returned with the briefcase and held it out to the man. The man took it with one hand, put it against a raised knee and opened the catch. He held it up by one of the handles and the top fell open. He glanced at the crammed contents. A sleepy Warts opened the door of the sewing room. He stood motionless in undershirt and shorts, staring at the man. The man pointed the gun at him. He waved it at the door.

"Come on, get moving. No cops or I kill him," he said to Speaker.

Warts began to shake.

"In bare feet, without no clothes?"

Warts had to put both hands on the doorknob to turn it. The door opened slightly. The man kicked it wide open, shoved Warts in the back with the briefcase and he stumbled out onto the porch. The man followed, glancing at Sylvia and Speaker. When he was out of sight, Sylvia ran for the telephone. Speaker rushed to the front door and opened the mail slot. They were heading up the street, Warts gingerly on bare feet. When they reached the car the man checked the street and motioned for Warts to get in the front passenger seat. The man put the briefcase on the floor behind the driver's seat and got behind the wheel. With no lights on, the car left.

Fifteen minutes later the man parked at the side of a road in the city's largest and oldest park, as old as the downtown eastside. A black phalanx of roadside conifers towered against the night sky. Boughs almost touched the car. There was no traffic. The nearest arc light was twenty-five yards away. The man turned off the engine and lights. He looked at Warts in the darkness.

"You don't know me."

"Never seen ya. Seen lots of guys but not like you. Not that you're so special I'd pick ya out again. I remember no one and nuthin'. Ask around."

"You could recognize me."

"Didn't see ya."

"I saw you looking."

"Wasn't. Not even once. If I looked I couldn't see ya, anyway. Bad eyes. Not blind but pretty near. Can't read a paper. See TV all right, but that's it. Not some of those commercials, only big letters."

"You were looking."

"Wasn't. Honest."

"You were."

"Told ya, can't see. I know nuthin'. I don't know those people there. Only to say hi. Don't even live there. I do, for a while. Till I get a place."

The man reached for something he had tossed into the back seat. Warts felt the end of the silencer pressing against his left nipple, the cold circle of it coming through his undershirt. He had been trembling ever since leaving the house but now it got worse. The muscles in his forearms and thighs jerked as if he were a puppet trying to sit on a car seat. That thing against his nipple kept pushing. He tried to move backwards, and from side to side, but the hardness moved when he did. He wanted to grab the thing and shove it aside. Take it away, take it away. His sensitivity rose to a pitch where he thought he had to do something, even though it could mean his death. The idea of death, though terrifying, was theoretical. Would the bullet go through him, would there be a massive tearing pain, would he die instantly or linger for several seconds, bleeding onto the roadside as he looked up into those black spires, and would Sylvia care when she heard?

Suddenly the relief of the silencer not being against his nipple, though he still felt a ring of cold pressure there. A hand reached over and opened the door. The silencer was there once more, this time a jabbing pain in his ribs. He backed away into the half-open door and fell out onto the roadside gravel. Sand and pebbles rasped elbows and knees, scraping like sandpaper with sharp fragments of stone in it. The pistol whacked his feet, caught between the door and rocker panel. He pulled them free, the corner of the door gouging his ankle. The door closed, the tires spun, spitting gravel as the car passed, flying rocks stinging his face and spraying sand grains into his eyes.

In seconds the car was two red dots and a receding whine. Warts' fear of being shot was replaced by fear of the forest. He limped along the road on his cut ankle, wincing as he walked, carefully touching skinned elbows. The forest was a looming mass on either side of the road, almost shutting out the sky, and the way ahead narrowed into the darkness. The arc lights, each standing within its soft cone of dusty yellow light, seemed impossibly far apart. Every so often he heard movement in the low branches near the roadside and each time he would freeze and listen. But nothing happened and he would begin limping again, at first cautiously and then with more confidence, until the next noise.

I must've been seven or eight when we came here. Grandma, Auntie Florrie, Gus, Shirley and me, down by the beach pool somewhere around here and Auntie Florrie made salmon sandwiches, some cheese too, and the salmon ones were wet, and Gus brought 7Up and something in a thermos for himself. And Auntie Florrie took pictures with that old camera like a black box and Shirley was five and scared to go in the pool and Gus took her by the hand and she was bawling in that little pink bathing suit. Auntie Florrie said, why don't you go for a swim? Nobody learned me. Shirley was crying so bad Gus had to bring her back and Grandma said have a cookie, honey, and Shirley threw it back at her. Auntie Florrie and Gus never got married, did they, taking me with Shirley everywhere. Was Dad dead then? Went to the hospital that last time the year before. Cancer of the something. Cancer of the bottle, I heard Auntie Florrie whisper to somebody, Gus, yeah, Gus. Dad in that bed, looking at the ceiling. Ma nodding. He knows you're here, Fred. Ma was crying all the time after, working, paying off debts. Auntie Florrie looked after me when she couldn't. That fisherman, Slav guy, Step-somethingski. Hand bigger than my head. How's the little boy? I'll catch you a fish bigger than you. Take you a month to eat it. Make you big, Pintsize. How could Ma like him? Spit everywhere, big gobs, and dropping cigar butts and stubbing them out with his boot. Ma would've married him. That storm, Northern Sunspray disappeared, big trawler like that gone. Ma crying again, her face all red.

First time back here. Never liked it except for the beach and the chips. Good with vinegar. Popcorn from those carts, butter can with the long spout. Had to line up for chips at that concession stand. Out of the pool after a dunk, tried to paddle a bit, float, so cold, shivering coming out walking in sandy water and up the concrete edge. Sand all over my toes, making scratchy sounds on the concrete. Vinegar dribbling out of the bottle. Pointed silver top. Square cardboard thing they put the chips in. Sprinkle salt. Eat chips walking back to the blanket. Drops of water like glass half-beads still on my skin. Back too red. Auntie Florrie looking at me, are you burning? Smeared Noxema on my shoulders that night, so cold, medicine smell. Auntie Florrie telling me to stay still.

Shit. Not glass. No. Good. Goddam ankle hurts. Shit. Another one. Can't see here. Road got to end now. Gus drive down here to the beach? Auntie Florrie putting on her lipstick in the front seat. You like the beach, Fred, or would you like to go in the pool next to it? I don't know, but one's deeper and the other's for kids, because I guess it's safer with a wall around it. But if you took the wall away, it'd be the same. Say what you mean, Fred. What she expect from a kid? Ma was the same. Tell me what you want to do. Want to stay with Aunt Florrie for a while, till I get back, or do you want to come with me? I want to go with you, Ma, but not if he's coming. You don't need him. He's not my dad. He always calls me Pintsize. He likes you. No, he doesn't. He wants you unless he gets you because he takes me too, or can make me say I hate him and don't want to go. And I don't. Drowned. Gus dead when his truck went off the highway coming through the Rockies couple of years later. Grandma too by then. Auntie Florrie moved in with us. Got jobs at the cannery. Shirley's going to be something, you watch, Auntie Florrie told Ma. She's going to graduate high school. Ma never said nuthin' about me. Shirley graduated, too. Wanted to be a teacher. Till she met that salesman. Went down the coast. Married there. Auntie Florrie cried all that day she got the letter. Wouldn't visit for three years. Two kids by then. Went down there to stay with her after the divorce. Ma gone. Auntie Florrie phoned me at the stores. Your mother's very sick. Died that night. I didn't know she had a bad heart. Had my own troubles too, Sonia pushing me. You'd better decide. Say it, dammit. What could I say? Let's get married later, when we're sure, because now maybe we aren't, because if you're sure without getting married, you're ready and that's good, and you can, but if you aren't sure and you do, you have to get sure later on after marriage to make it work. But probably not, unless we'd be thinking that we'd got married to make certain we were sure, and that's pressure to force us to be happy, and you can't force it, unless you're willing to ignore happiness because you're married. I couldn't make it plainer. She liked that delivery guy better, anyway.

No end to this shitty road. No one. Deserted. Everybody gone. Don't even know Auntie Florrie's address down there. Wonder if she's still alive? Shirley probably ignore me if I called. You're the ugliest man ever. She was a kid when she said that. No, in high school. Who cares? No looks. No seniority. No pull. I can't keep ya, Fred. You're sleeping all the time among the stores. Guys can't fill their requisitions. Trains got to run on schedule. You want to be a labourer, work in the yard, I'll talk to Scottie. I can transfer you there. And don't talk to me. I haven't got ten years to hang around while you make up your mind. Time for his nephew. Ends up with my job. I'm supposed to pick up scrap on the rip track.

The road turned and dipped and the forest thinned to grassy hills and hollows with a scattering of maples and oaks. Warts felt more exposed. He hurried between trees on the dewy grass until he neared the edge of the park, where the road went past some apartment buildings. There was a telephone booth in front of the entrance to one of the buildings. Walking in a crouch to within ten yards of the booth, he hid behind the massive trunk of a broad-leaved maple. Hungry and cold, he tried to concentrate. Would the operator make a collect call if she had Sylvia's number? What was her number? Would the house number be any good? The number of the house? As he shook from cold and indecision, he saw somebody walk out of the entrance. A pudgy man in a blazer and flannel slacks stood inhaling the ambient temperature. Warts leaned out from behind the maple. "Pardon me, sir, I need help." The man stared for a few seconds before going back inside.

Warts figured the man was going to phone the police. It was after five and getting light. He would be spotted easily. An alley facing the park divided two rows of small apartment buildings. Behind each building were garbage carts. He limped across the road and into the alley shadows. He saw something nearby move, a lump behind a cart. It was bigger than a skunk or raccoon.

217

The lump straightened up into a man and stared, picked up a sack and walked towards him. Tired, Warts rested on his good foot.

"That you, Warts?"

He couldn't see the man clearly yet but recognized the voice, clipped, economical with words.

"Hi, Ray."

It was Raymond Yang. He called himself "the only Chinese bum in the city." Once an accountant with his own office in the financial district, he was engaged to the daughter of a Hong Kong banker. She was killed in a car accident two hours after they announced their engagement. He had been driving after too much tequila, a drink he never tried before. He lived now in a rented room and roamed alleys in the downtown business area and nearby apartments, going as far as the park. His family gave him money when he would accept it, although his patriarchal grandfather never forgave him for giving up accounting and disgracing the family. He met Warts through Waste and over the years they had talked about stocks. Warts was always planning to invest in the market when he got enough money, unless of course something else came up. It always did.

"Where your clothes?"

"They're at Sylvia's. Staying there after Al's burnt down. I wake up, hear noise, come out of my room and see this guy with a gun. Takes me hostage and dumps me out in the park. Somebody over here saw me. He's calling the cops."

"Take my coat. Keep it till I see you."

Yang took off his overcoat and handed it to Warts, who slipped it on his skinny frame. They were about the same height and weight.

"I got to phone Sylvia and let her know what happened. You got change?"

"Yeah. Hurry, the cops."

They walked out of the other end of the alley. It was still dark enough so that only the observant would have noticed that Warts was limping badly on bare feet. Two blocks from the alley there was a telephone booth. As Warts picked up the receiver, a patrol car went by.

"It's me, Warts," he told a sleepy-voiced Sylvia.

"Oh, you're all right. We were worried."

Warts would have liked to hear "I" but she did sound relieved.

"I need my clothes."

"Speaker's here. Tell him where you are he'll bring them."

They waited behind an all-night restaurant, sitting on a grassy embankment bordering the parking lot. They could smell hamburger grease and chip oil. Warts was thirsty. Yang took a bottle out of his sack and filled it from a hose at the gas station beside the restaurant. It was warm and smelled of rubber. Warts drank in gulps and choked a couple of times. Yang reached deep into the sack, took out a crumpled package containing some digestive biscuit crumbs and handed it to him. He shovelled them into his mouth, coughed as dry crumbs rasped his throat. He took a swig from the bottle. The patrol car returned and they got to their feet. After it passed, they sat down. Speaker arrived forty minutes after Warts phoned. There were few buses at that hour. And he'd had to walk two blocks from the bus stop. He was carrying a shopping bag with Warts' clothes in it. Like Sylvia, Speaker hadn't slept all night. Warts put on his socks. The soles of his feet were smudged and stained with dirt, wet grass, oil and road tar. There was a scab forming on the cut on his ankle and he winced as he put a sock over it. He took off Yang's coat and handed it to him. He put on his black polyester pants, white shirt, black shoes with crepe soles and brown ultrasuede jacket with leather trimmings and sat down.

Speaker wanted to get some sleep and figure out what to do with the notebooks. He had stuffed them and the flash drive under the cushions of the sofa before taking the briefcase into the kitchen. It wasn't something he thought about. He simply did it. Sylvia and the others had to be told. She was feeling much better after finding out from the veterinarian at a downtown eastside all-night clinic that Rowser had lost blood and flesh but the bullet had passed through, hadn't hit a bone or anything vital and he would recover. Sylvia had cried at the news and again when she left Rowser at the clinic. Speaker had gone with her in a taxi. It was almost dawn but he looked at Warts' tired face and sat down next to him. He waved a finger at the restaurant and the pumps.

"Which one is the gas station? Drive in, fill up. Pick up your grease and oil. Fart high octane all the way home."

They laughed and Warts' laughter turned to sniffles. He wiped his nose with the back of his hand.

"I was walking out of that park, thinking I got no one, nuthin', might as well be crazy or dead so's I don't know what's happening, unless being crazy makes ya more and more nuts, or the dead are still here some way because they're so upset by what happened when they were alive they can't never leave. Maybe there's no escape."

Speaker stretched out on the grass. He looked at the random clouds. The stars were becoming dim. On the horizon the blue edge of night was fading.

"Liquor is a bad liver and hangovers, drugs are an overdosed dream, sex is waking up alone afterwards, but love, love is a woman who smiles so beautifully it doesn't matter what you believe about anything else as long as you can see that smile."

"I saw it," Yang said.

Warts yawned.

"See what?"

It was half past six when Speaker and Warts returned. Sylvia had gone to bed and was in a deep sleep. She had given Speaker a duplicate house key. Warts fell onto his bed and passed out. Al had woken up during the confrontation in the kitchen, hid behind the sofa and had fallen asleep when the house was quiet again. Still traumatized by the fire, he was only vaguely aware of what the others faced. Lynch heard everything, had come up after Warts' hasty departure and Speaker and Sylvia had taken Rowser to see the veterinarian. He took some tomato cinnamon cookies and returned to the basement. Speaker didn't want to think about the notebooks. If he could only fall asleep, he would have enough energy later on to reach some conclusion. He took off his sneakers and lay down on the sofa as morning light came through a vee where the drapes met.

As Speaker tried to sleep she was there, a naked curl in a suitcase shovelled with tons of debris by a bulldozer blade at a waste site, her squashed remains packed down under tread and already in its wake the pecking gulls and nosing rats. It's either something or it's nothing. It's a choice, and he knew he'd have to make it. What did his life mean? No more than hers. Somebody he'd never met, but so much was about people he would never meet. And many of them were dead. But he knew them and they had become part of his life. None of the words were any good: sympathy, pity, responsibility, guilt. Something in the blood had made him do all the good and crazy things he'd ever done. It would tell him right and wrong, and it was never a logical reason, but the one he knew he couldn't escape. It was what he shared with her, the battered heart, the blood-washed brain, the pulse hammering out the rhythm he couldn't forget.

Chapter 14

"There's a man asking for you," Carol told Gwen that evening. She poked her head into Gwen's bedroom, phone in one hand and the other covering the mouthpiece. She spoke nonchalantly, hiding any interest in who this older man was. She was sure he wasn't a teacher. He sounded too intelligent. Gwen knew who it was, surprised she wasn't surprised he had called so soon. She felt important and justified. He wasn't one of those conceited guys who had to be right. She turned from where she was lying on the bed.

"Thanks, Mom. I'll take it here."

Carol shut the door. They were still only civil to each other. Roger was the problem. Gwen never had any intention of coming between her parents. She didn't know how much suppressed jealousy there was in Carol. Roger's attitude towards Gwen was doting adulation. Carol had to watch and bear it. She wanted Roger to let Gwen go, free her to grow up as she wished. Carol saw Gwen treating him with good-humoured tolerance and this irked her. Her husband was her daughter's play-hubby, and so what was she?

"Hi," Gwen said, trying to hide her satisfaction.

"Things have gotten dangerous here. The man after Lynch broke in. He had a gun. I said he'd gone and gave the guy the briefcase, but kept some things. He took Warts as insurance, released him later and he's here now. I don't know what that guy's going to do when he finds out he didn't get everything. I'm not sure if doing something about what I've got will make things better."

"That guy's decided for you. Phone the police and tell them that there's been a break-in and you need protection. They'll send a car around for a few nights and that'll scare him off. I'll talk to my mom tonight and get back to you. My dad's working on a project out in the suburbs and he's sleeping over at a friend's."

"Mom?" Gwen's voice was hesitant as she entered her mother's study. Carol was seated at her desk, glasses on her forehead, one hand rubbing the side of her face as she leaned her head that way. She was tired and wanted to go to bed early and sleep away the endless work, the stolen jewellery, her husband's fatuousness, her daughter's strength.

"What is it, Gwen?"

Her voice was distant but not unkind. She didn't want this formality between them to get worse.

Gwen advanced cautiously into the study. It was a large room, with the best view in the apartment. The big window in front of the desk looked out over the downtown core and the harbour. On the other side of the harbour were the North Shore mountains, beginning almost at the water and rising blue to flint-edged summits, dapplings of snow whitening them in winter and on the forested flanks white powder on a blue sweater. Now in late summer there was no snow and the peaks were hatchet blades and blunt edges. In the evening everything disappeared with slow finality from grey to blue-black. And in between the light threw its ascending silk bands one after the other across the sky: golden peach, scarlet, bronze-orange, rose, fading lime, a rinse of yellow and a bluish white fading before the deep blue resonance of mid-evening. The water was a sunpath of copper flakes cupped in waves until they became bits of slippery pearl glow fading into the purpling mass. Gwen would watch the sunset if her parents were out. She let the colours sink into her as a silent prayer, a memorial service for the day. She would hold her raised hands together in front of her and stare at the approaching darkness.

The study furniture was standard. Carol did most of her writing at a large oak desk, in longhand with a fountain pen. She sat in her wooden swivel chair, for many years her father's. A computer, printer, disk file, and computer paper were on another desk, steel and smaller. Steel filling cabinets lined one wall and bookcases at right angles to them another. Three leather chairs took up much of the remaining space. On the oak desk were framed photographs of Gwen and Roger. The cabinets were crammed with files in bulging manila folders, and on top stacks of computer disks and a box of labeled flash drives, and the bookcases, besides holding law books, were jammed with bundles of legal-sized paper tied with string, and more manila folders. Roger worked there, more than half of the material in the filing cabinets his. He used the computer desk, uncomfortable about the other one, and never sat in the swivel chair. Carol's father had presented it to her when he retired after a career as one of the most successful criminal lawyers in the city's history.

Carol hadn't turned around when she answered Gwen, who spoke to her mother's back and leaning head. She took a few more steps and quickly sat in one of the leather chairs. Her mother turned around and she saw a slight smile. It was Carol's long-suffering smile but better than the back of her head and the baggy sweater.

"Mom, I have to talk about something. The man who phoned has a problem. I don't know exactly what it is, but somebody has been murdered. And a lot of people are in danger."

"Why doesn't he go to the police?"

"Because it's so big he's afraid of what'll happen if he does."

"The guy sounded intelligent. But getting you involved isn't. I suppose you met him through your tramp. You've got to be more careful. You and Madeline put yourselves at risk. And look what happened. Now you want to take on more trouble. I presume this problem has some connection with the robbery."

"Yes."

"But you don't know the connection."

"No. All I know is that tramp started it by doing something he shouldn't have."

Carol asked a question the answer to which she already knew.

"Why are you telling me about this?"

"I told him that you and Dad might be able to help him. He said no before but now he's agreed."

"If this problem is as desperately big as this man seems to think, what could we do?"

225

"I don't know, but I told him he could talk to you. You might have some advice for him."

She felt a retreat was necessary and if she reduced the scale of her parents' aid they might be more likely to give their help. She was also vaguely, almost unconsciously aware that by appealing now to her mother in her father's absence, her mother might see this as a gesture of respect, an attempt at mollifying her that was perceptible without being overt, and denigrating to both of them. They knew on this other level that Gwen was telling her she was capable by herself of coping with the matter. Carol knew her daughter was reaching for her, that to discuss this problem was dealing with theirs.

"You know, Gwen, what you're saying sounds fantastic. A man with a big problem we know nothing about. A murder. People's lives in danger. You're asking your father and me to do a lot. Especially after what's happened."

Carol wouldn't say yes quickly, because of pride, and she had to protect herself in case she had to pull out fast. Gwen caught the implication of assent. She could hardly keep from smiling. But she knew this was the last thing she should do.

"I know, Mom. I'm so sorry. We didn't know what was going to happen. But I don't feel good about doing nothing for those people. I'm responsible for what happened."

"Only in a roundabout way."

Carol was saying she was ready to forgive. Gwen knew it. She still had to be careful. She couldn't show she assumed consent. Her mother helped her.

"I suppose you have to phone this guy pretty soon."

"Yes."

"Tell him we can talk about this problem. But make no promises. Only talk. And in a public place."

"Oh Mom, thanks."

Gwen leaped up and ran over and hugged her, head nestling in her hair. Carol pursed her lips. She had given enough tonight. She felt Gwen's backbone through her cotton blouse, the rippling curve bending towards her. Carol acknowledged kinship of a deeper kind.

A meeting was arranged for early the next evening in the same park Warts had been released. Because of a court appearance, Carol couldn't meet Speaker any sooner. He wasn't hopeful. Once Gwen's parents knew the scope of the problem, they would back away from it. Alone is alone, and especially against power. And what to do about Sylvia's problem of putting up four men? Warts was in no condition to look for a place. Lynch had to keep out of sight. Al was useless. That left him. What could he say to Sylvia now after a man had broken into her house, shot her dog and threatened her? He felt that he more than anyone, even Lynch, was responsible for endangering her. He was supposed to be able to think. And he had come up with nothing.

After the call, Speaker went to see Sylvia. She was in the kitchen baking cookies. A couple of racks of them were cooling on the counter. More were in the oven. Speaker couldn't identify the smell. Sylvia was cleaning a large white earthenware mixing bowl in the sink. She turned to reach behind her to pick up a wooden ladle and saw him. There was a busy intensity to her look, about cooking, the men in her house, or the man with the gun or something else, he couldn't tell. It was hard to gauge her mood by looking at her. She had a tough cheerfulness that concealed her feelings, even from herself. She was always telling herself that her life could be worse, she was lucky to own a house and have good health. This self-indoctrination didn't always work and she would often descend into an indifference about everything. But her cheery look remained. It was difficult at these times guessing exactly what response she would give to a simple question, even a straightforward statement.

"Eat," she said, her mouth busy with the remains of a cookie. "Kiwi squash."

Speaker went over to the racks of skillet-sized cookies and took one. Though still hot it was tasty, had that delightfully indefinite flavour all of her cooking had from offbeat combinations of ingredients. He leaned against the counter and tried to make some headway with it and waited. She never seemed to sit or stand still except when she talked, and she liked talking instead of merely reacting to what she heard. She wanted it, like baking and gardening, to be a happy exercise. When talking led to action this was fine. What irritated her was talking for the sake of it. She almost threw the last spoon into a drawer, and swung her other arm up in an arc with exactly the amount of effort needed to place the mixing bowl into its spot on a cupboard shelf above the counter. As she walked to the table, taking her time, she made a little waving motion with her left hand for him to follow her. Her right hand held a cookie by its huge circumference.

"What's the good of making them if you don't eat them?" she said as she sat down as if challenging the chair to hold her. "I know what you're going to say," and her tone meant don't interrupt, "but I don't blame you for what happened. You're all still welcome to stay till the danger is over. Think about it that way. And I got so much food I give it away."

"I've been talking to Warts and Al. We've got a few dollars and would feel better if you'd take them, please."

"Keep it," she said with a flick of her cookie-holding hand, a queen pardoning quarrelling aristocrats whose crime consisted of killing each other for love of her. "I got enough from investments. Leonard and me figured things out pretty good. And I got no debts."

Gwen was sitting next to her mother and smiling as Carol drove to the meeting. It was four forty-five. They were to meet Speaker at five. Carol took her eyes off traffic for a moment to look at Gwen.

"What's his name?"

"Speaker."

"Is that his surname, his Christian name or a pseudonym?"

"I guess it's a nickname."

"I'm going to meet someone named Speaker to discuss a problem I know nothing about."

Gwen was looking at scenery, let her mother get in this bit of mock-plaintive, self-abasing trust as the car left the commuter road that cut through the park and led to the North Shore bridge, entering one that wound around its perimeter, enclosing a combination of forest, public gardens, picnic grounds, playgrounds and beaches. Carol drove past pigeon-stained statues, a yacht club, its weathered wooden clubhouse on pilings, further on a group of totem poles, a lighthouse, a beachfront swimming pool filled with nothing but sand, then turned off the perimeter road onto one that bisected the park, passing through the forest that still occupied much of the interior.

From late summer sunshine they entered the subdued light of an avenue of tall fir and red cedar, interspersed with some hemlock and spruce. This was one of the few areas in the park where the trees hadn't been thinned or topped. A couple of dead giants, bonewhite and almost branchless, towered among the other trees. Underbrush crowded the roadside, and in the upper reaches of trees on the western side shafts of oblique, warm light would fall, deepening into slanting columns of luminous citron and brass in which insects like dust motes would flicker, dancing a dance of one day. Inky green and lemon-splashed massings of branches, deep-furrowed russet fir bark and thewed twistings of cedar trunks, the soaring phalanxes, and light draining away, tilting further west into distilled intensities like a glorious accolade to a forgotten land waiting for the dark, the hand-obliterating blackness that would leave nothing but treetop glimpses of eternal blue, the star-set voyages.

Carol parked on the western side of the road, where there was a path to the only lake in the park. She and Gwen got out. A few cars passed but nobody else had parked on the roadside. There had been the usual collapse of interest after Labour Day. They walked over to the path entrance, a green trash drum sitting empty in front of it. A wooden sign with the name of the lake incised into it was nailed to a tree. They started down a path of well-trodden pea gravel and grey dust. Alongside it a clear creek trickled over a bed of slippery soft mud and water smooth pebbles. At first Gwen thought it sounded like the kitchen sink emptying. But more musical, she decided after listening again. The path ran straight for thirty yards through bushes and a sporadic grove of young fir, branching into left and right forks in front of a mass of bullrushes at the edge of the lake, obstructing the view of it. The path went around it, splitting into others along the way. The left fork was marshy, bounded on both sides by black mud and rotting skunk cabbage and tangled alders, through which glimpses of open water could be seen. The air smelled of ditchwater and mouldy decay. Occasionally the entire lake was visible, two hundred yards across, large sections covered with pink or white lotus with a flaring diadem of yellow inside. The right fork, the one they took, was firmer, winding past thinning rushes until the whole lake could easily be seen, with sections clear of lotus on the near side, and occupied usually by mallards and wood ducks used to park visitors feeding them breadcrumbs. There were log benches here and it was to one of these they hurried.

Speaker was there, crouching by the lakeside in front of the bench where they were to meet, a quarter of the way around from the entrance path. He was very still, surrounded by the small, shy wood ducks, the drakes feathered in glossy green and satin white, mottled brown and lustrous blue. They ignored him and picked at the gravel. As Gwen and her mother were approaching, the ducks waddled into the water and paddled away into a formation of mallards. The mallards scattered them with a few lunges of their beaks. Speaker turned and straightened up. In a white blouse, beige jacket and slacks and open-toed sandals, Carol walked ahead of Gwen and quickly up to him and extended her hand.

"I'm Carol, Gwen's mother."

"Glad you could make it," Speaker said, taking her hand.

"Let's get started," Carol said, going to the bench and sitting down.

Gwen, playing at obedience, sat next to her. Speaker sat on the opposite side from Gwen, a little apart and uncertain with his hands, as if they were undecided thoughts. Carol waited, a polite smile fixed in place. She didn't feel like smiling. I don't believe I'm here. I really don't. Who is this guy? He doesn't look weird. But how do you know? I'm here with my daughter and no protection. There's no one around. How fast can I run? Will I be dragging her or will she be hauling me? I'm smart. I'm really smart.

"This is what I know," Speaker said, making her start but so slightly the others didn't notice. "The tramp Gwen and Madeline were trying to help, while robbing suites in your building saw someone rape and kill a child. He ran away with a briefcase. Left it in your apartment. I went there with him and looked at the contents. Among other stuff were two notebooks, one with names and phone numbers of pedophiles in this city. In the other were comments on prostituted girls and the names and numbers of pimps. There was also a flash drive. I looked at it on a library computer, and it contains what looks like detailed coded information on a global pedophile network. The code is in one of the books and I've deciphered some of it. On Saturday night a hit man thought he killed the tramp. It was somebody else. He realized his mistake because the night before last he broke into the house where we're staying. I told him Lynch, the man we're talking about, wasn't there. I gave him the briefcase. He thought nothing was missing. I still have the notebooks and flash drive and know the name of their owner."

"I assume it's in the notebooks," Carol said.

"No, only his handwritten initials. The comments on girls he used are in the same handwriting. Those initials are stamped under the strap of the briefcase. His full name is printed on papers inside and his signature is on several documents. Do you want to know his name?"

Carol nodded. "Go ahead."

"Cobbie Kind."

Carol made a slight sideways motion with her head and pursed her lips. She looked out at the lake. The clear section near where they sat was empty of ducks now and the sun was lost in the highest branches on the western side. The shiny darkness of the water was dimming, becoming a black circle. It could have been a thousand feet deep. The still clusters of lotus flowers on their flat pads were floating meadows of serrated bowls lit inside with votive candles, glowing faint pink or soft yellow. But they were going out slowly, feebly. There was a faint quacking out in the middle of the lake. A shadowy quiet settled on everything. She turned back to Speaker but didn't look directly at him. Her careful delivery, her reasoned analysis, punctuated the cooling air.

"I assume that Mr. Lynch is not anxious to testify. With his character and probably lengthy record of arrests, plea bargaining or a grant of immunity from prosecution in return for his testimony would be unlikely, anyway. A competent defence attorney would shred his credibility in minutes. So there's no chance of a prosecution for the homicide he's supposed to have witnessed. That leaves the notebooks and flash drive. The initials could represent any number of names. Without proof the notebooks and the drive belong to that person, the response could be anything from outright denial to a counter charge of defamation of character. Some handwriting expert would say there was only a superficial misleading similarity between the initials and the comments and the signatures on the documents. If you had the briefcase, you wouldn't be in a stronger position. You'd have to prove that the notebooks and drive belong to it. And explain how it came into your possession, exposing Mr. Lynch as a thief. Turn in the notebooks and drive and you'd have the same problem. What you've got is the beginning of an investigation, if you can find some organization or determined individual with enough patience and resources to take it on. People who wouldn't be scared off by power and money. Big money buys legal protection against almost anything. And you'd have to find a chink in the armour. I can't see one."

Gwen looked around as she listened. To her right as she faced the water the path was obscured by bushes and alder boughs. To her left the bushes were much smaller and she could see the whole of the distance they had walked from where the path forked. She let her eyes rest on that curve and on the hedge of lakeside plants. The tiny pink blossom clusters of the hardhack, like cotton candy, had mostly turned brown. The purple berries of the trailing salal were shrivelling among laurel-shaped leaves. A grey squirrel scampered along the top back log of the bench seventy feet away and stopped halfway across, its fuzzy plume of a tail almost vertical. Motionless, it stared at something for a few moments before twitching its tail and disappearing in a dive down the back of the bench. Gwen smiled, then saw. Where the entrance forked a man stood behind some bushes, wearing what looked like a black suit. She couldn't tell for sure. But he didn't appear to be dressed for visiting a park. He seemed to be staring into the rushes. Her mother's voice stopped abruptly.

"Mom, there's a man over there. Where we came from."

The ninety-five yards separating them seemed miles and nothing, and the forest a hideaway or a trap. They stared at the man. He turned and without looking in their direction walked up the path. Gwen saw something dark between trees further up the path.

"Do you recognize him?" Carol asked Speaker.

"He's the guy who broke in."

"My car is parked up there. I left my phone in it."

"I left mine at the apartment," Gwen said. "I knew you'd have yours."

"We could go around to get it," Speaker said, "but he'd probably be waiting nearby. He's armed, so we'll have to walk out of the park."

Speaker fought his nervousness, trying to appear calm for the sake of the others. Carol hid her fear for Gwen's sake. Gwen thought she could run faster and hide better than them. Hadn't she and Madeline fooled everyone on the school camping trip last year when they'd played hide and seek in the forest? They'd kept still, shaking with suppressed giggles. Girls trod by mere inches away. But fat Jenny Buller-Haynes and half-blind Tansy Parkinson didn't have guns.

"I think I can still see that guy."

"He's waiting for us to move," Speaker said. "There are two other ways out of here. The path to our right branches off into one that's longer and goes through the forest and comes out onto the main park drive near the beaches. It's a lot of walking. The other way is much shorter, behind us along the creek that runs out of here and down to the harbour and the seawall. At this hour there'll be plenty of people. Either way along the seawall takes us to the park entrance and safely out."

"That's obviously the way," Carol said, looking where the man had stood. Anxious to start, she cursed herself for having agreed to the meeting. Getting involved in something that others were far better equipped to handle was idiotic. She thought of them hurrying through twilight forest. The path behind them was narrow, twisting into grey shadow.

Gwen no longer saw anything between the branches. The lake seemed only a clogged pool with some stupid ducks. The bushes appeared higher, the trees closer together. She wanted to say she was sorry. Another mistake. Bigger. She scuffed a sneaker on the gravel.

"We'll go to the right," Speaker said. "Cut through bushes and get over to the seawall path."

They stood up and Carol and Gwen followed him, holding hands. Thirty feet along the path Speaker stepped into the forest. He brushed by trees and hopped over small depressions half-filled with stagnant rainwater and needles like scatterings of flattened rusty nails. He stopped to let them catch up. Carol had to pull her jacket through tangled brush and low branches. Dry twigs snapped like firecrackers when they stepped on them. Their shoes sank into mushy soil and almost came off when they pulled them out. When they got to the seawall path, they were twenty yards from the lake. He looked back and ahead before motioning with his hand for them to follow. They began to walk down a slope. Along this path flowed a creek carrying lake water to the harbour. It was the counterpart to the other creek and meandered around mossy boulders, clumps of fern, skunk cabbage and straggly grass. Almost touching the water were bowed branches of vine maple that caught noontime light in baskets but now sagged into leafy hammocks. There was no gravel on this path, under the close canopy still not completely dry even at the end of summer. The air smelled of creek mud and humus and twilight dampness. They crossed a small bridge. Unpainted planks echoed their steps as dull tappings from under the earth. Some trees leaned out over the path, seemed natural places for an ambush, but nothing happened as they passed several of them. The path levelled out with the creek and mingled with its black mud, getting soft in places. Towards the end there was another, smaller wooden bridge, and the two concrete pillars of an overpass a few feet beyond. Fifty feet above, it was part of a connecting road that turned off the main park drive and was little used except by hikers.

Approaching the pillars, they could hear the low gurgling of a small waterfall close to the other side of the bridge. Gwen saw it first, a bit of black sticking out from behind a pillar. She pulled at her mother's hand. They were less than thirty feet away in the fast-encroaching twilight. Gwen clapped her hands twice, hoping Speaker could hear her. She and Madeline did that in their forest games when they had to communicate at a distance. Carol looked at her and they stopped and turned and ran back up the path. Holding hands again, they headed towards the lake. With Gwen slightly ahead, they rushed through a forest they didn't recognize. Statues of bark leaned out, branches poked them in the side and scratched their faces. The path was slick in the steepest places and they slid back. Straying into the creek, they felt watery mud soaking their feet and holding, miring them there. Pulling free and more running, blindly now, Carol caught a sandal on a plank end above ground level at the bridge they had crossed two minutes ago. She tripped and fell onto her knees and rolled against the railing. Gwen felt her mother's hand slip out of hers, heard the sharp syllable of pain live and die in its profound second. When she turned she saw her mother holding a knee and biting her lip. Gwen's beautifully abstract idea of a pure flight to safety was soured by exasperation. Those floppy sandals were so stupid. Did she have to wear them? Gwen crouched beside her.

"You all right, Mom?"

"I twisted my knee."

Carol straightened her right leg slowly, groaned and put an arm on the railing to lift herself. Gwen helped and put her mother's right arm on her left shoulder and they crossed the bridge. Carol grunted as they struggled up the path. A few minutes later Gwen saw the lakeside bench through a gap between two hemlocks. She pulled at her mother, got to the bench and eased her down onto it. Her mother leaned back against it. Her voice sounded lame now, too.

"I don't—know—if—I—can."

Gwen knew she was going to say this. Exasperation with her mother came over her again. She wanted to say, I knew you were going to screw up. The anger shaded into pity when she saw disappointment and fear in her mother's eyes. It became instinct, a red flash through her blocking out everything else. She knew she would die for her. Gwen was squatting, resting as she wondered what to do. Her mother couldn't be left behind. And besides that man, there were coyotes in the park. She didn't know if they would attack a helpless person but she would never take that chance. They would go slowly and hide when necessary. She looked around, it was getting dark, the forest was big. There was only one man. But he seemed to be behind every tree. She stood up.

"We've got to go, Mom."

"Help me up."

Gwen took the path to the right, the one with lots of trees and thick underbrush on both sides of it as it curved around the lake. Carol bent her right knee as Gwen, almost the same height, draped her mother's arms over her shoulder and took her weight. She glanced behind and ahead but saw nobody in either direction as the path became a hazy green tunnel of escaping light. Eighty yards along, a path branched off and seemed to go deeper into the forest. Gwen decided to keep going. A further forty yards and a second exit path appeared. It went uphill and through a sparse stand of second growth and some low bushes. It looked as if it might lead quickly out of the park. Gwen knew they would soon complete the circuit of the lake and thought this path was probably their last and best chance. The uphill walk made Carol wince every time she had to put pressure on her right leg but she said nothing. As Gwen heard these sounds squeezed out of her mother, she made herself concentrate on the distance in front of them. The path levelled off after they passed the stand of second growth. It joined a paved one leading southeast out of the forest. Gwen could see an expanse of lawn through a young grove of grand fir but saw someone two hundred yards away at the end of the path. Fading light made seeing difficult. They had passed an opening in the bushes that appeared to be a rough trail. It went to the left and eastwards, towards the road where their car was parked. Gwen decided to avoid the figure up ahead. She turned her mother around and they headed back to the opening. The first few yards were strewn with a mass of fallen rotting trees, gigantic stumps, clumps of fern and nurse logs. Beginning to think the trail had died, Gwen spotted it on the other side of a pile of dead brush lying like a fallen broom. They used their free hands to sweep aside low branches, twigs, ferns and brush. Sometimes they held onto them for balance on the bumpy forest floor or when they climbed over decayed logs that crumpled under their feet. Chunks broke off in their hands, scattering grey wood lice and releasing the smell of dry bark and soft papery wood.

The trail eventually ran down an eroded slope and widened past an empty paddock, a stable, a shack and some horse vans. There were no cars or trucks around. From the shack an unpaved road led to the east. Gwen almost shouted when she saw it. They walked past the paddock. They could hear mosquitoes flying around and preparing to land. When a horse's hoof banged against a stable door Gwen jumped. But an edgy silence returned, with the zizzing sound of mosquitoes. Full of potholes and less than forty yards long, the gravel road ran up a slight incline directly into the park drive. Gwen could hear at least one car. Tugging at her mother as they neared the exit she could see a green trash drum, the bright red stub of a fire hydrant and the sidewalk, only on their side of the drive, and incised wooden signs on the other. Their car would be to the north. The park entrance would be south. That would be the safer way to go. If they could get near the entrance, or latch onto people before, they would be all right. When Gwen stopped to peek out at the drive, her mother slumped onto the grassy margin of the forest, four yards from the drive. Feeling her mother's hand slip away, she looked down at her.

"We can't stop now, Mom."

"I need a rest."

"We've got to get out of here."

"Dammit, this knee hurts. Like somebody pulling my leg apart."

"We've got to go, Mom."

"I thought only mothers nagged."

"All right. We'll wait till you feel like moving."

Gwen sat on the grass. She looked up and down the drive, picked some red clover, smelled it and tore it apart. She tossed the bits into the air. She looked sideways at her mother, who had begun laughing.

"Haven't you figured it out yet?"

"What?"

"Your friend, the ponytail guy. He's in no danger."

"Sure he is. He could be hurt or dead."

"Oh, God. Save me from smart kids. Look. He's waiting there for us. That guy appears. And we run straight into a trap. We get away. No shots. Nobody follows. And we've got the speed of a couple of caterpillars."

"We got away because the guy went after him for the notebooks."

"That's the smart part. He's sold out. Part of the bargain is he's got to scare us off. He tells me enough to convince me that nothing can be done. He picked that trail. He said there were two ways out of there besides the way we came in. We found two others. Why didn't he mention them?"

"Maybe he didn't know, or forgot because he had to think in a hurry. He picked the best trail. That guy guessed right. I saw him waiting at the overpass."

"You were supposed to. We were supposed to run. So scared we'd never figure it out. And forget the whole thing. No blood. Cost nothing. Except your friend. I'll bet chicken feed grinds in his mill."

Gwen tore out some grass by her thigh.

"I don't believe it."

"Honey, we can stroll out of here any time we want. At least I'll try to."

"He wouldn't do this for money. He saved Maddy and me from a bunch of guys. I didn't tell you and Dad. Didn't want to upset you."

"So he's not a pedophile. That's something to be grateful for. But to put it crudely, he looks hard up for cash. A little would help pad his welfare. He is on welfare, isn't he? Doesn't look as if he's had a job in a while. Probably never had a steady job. Too noble to sweat."

"You're saying these things about him because you want me to see him the way you do. You think I agree with everything he says? But I respect him. There's not only people like you and Dad that are good, there's people like him."

Carol appreciated being paired with her husband. That competition with Roger for their daughter's respect and love was deadening. They were at least on an equal footing in Gwen's estimation of their values. Flexing her knee, Carol looked up in pain into the drooping boughs of a hemlock. Closing her eyes, she leaned back against the trunk as Gwen picked at the grass.

A man cycled towards them. Coming down the drive from the north, he was dressed all in white except for broad fire engine red suspenders and a flat-brimmed straw hat. There were clips around his ankles. Grinning, he coasted up to them, applied the hand brakes and put a foot on the sidewalk. His body was wiry and appeared tensely fragile.

"You ladies all right?" A thin voice with a vibrating edginess, to some ears it could sound impatient.

"Yeah," Gwen said, noting the man's face was very pink. She thought it made him look sick. She wasn't surprised at her calmness, put it down to being tired. To her the old man was irrelevant. Wouldn't understand, probably senile. Might get too excited, have a heart attack. And suppose her mother was right? No, couldn't be. Thinking like that because of her knee. If the old guy had a heart attack, she could pedal out. Put her mother on the handlebars. She almost giggled.

"Ride through here every morning. Seawall, too. Catch the sunrise. Take a spin in the evening sometimes. In the winter I walk. Not the whole way. Enough to get the joints warmed up. Getting dark earlier. Bit of a chill tonight. First night I noticed it."

As he spoke a red convertible full of laughter spilling out of its open top rushed past. In its wake the breeze whipped up a few maple leaves into handstands and cartwheels and flipped over a newspaper page on the road. A white van with dark windows raced by. Gwen noticed that the arc lights were beginning to kindle.

"You ladies from out here?"

"My mother and I are. My father is from back East."

"I hail from there. Wouldn't go back. Had my fill of snow and cold. Daughter lives there. Comes out every summer. With the husband and grandson. Wife died eleven years ago."

"Could you tell me the quickest way out of the park?"

"You take this road, same way I'm going, down to where the roses are. There's a big rose garden. You go up a hill that's part of the garden. And down and over a stone bridge. Or you can stay on this road and it'll take you right into traffic. Either way is ten minutes. I guess you're looking to get out now it's dark. I've got to get going. Got a meal waiting for me. In my apartment building, next to the park. Everybody takes a turn making a meal for the others. Put on a feed and lots of dinners in return. There's only fifteen suites. Built in the late Twenties, before the War. Good timber. Wide staircases. Everybody's always worried about fire. Keep the sand buckets and hoses handy. Tonight Lucilla's cooking. She's from Chile. I love foreign food. Doctor said I'm eating too many hot peppers. Said they'll burn my stomach lining, give me gastric ulcers. A lot he knows."

Gwen looked at her mother. Her eyes still closed, Carol was dozing.

"My girlfriend goes by here every day. She's eighteen. I call her my girlfriend. She takes care of the ponies on the pony rides. Takes them around the trails for exercise. Got a pigtail. Talks to me during the summer. Going back to school next week. She's going to be a kindergarten teacher. You're welcome to all those kids, I said. I had one daughter and that was enough.

Kindergarten isn't too bad. Not like high school. All those drugs and that sexing around. I think sex should be part of marriage. Guess I'm considered old-fashioned. But I'm not bothered in the least by what anybody else may think and I never have been and I'm ninety-eight."

He stopped as if expecting astonishment and congratulations, or perhaps he was out of breath. His pink face was fading into the grey twilight. The nearest arc light, twenty yards away, cast a yellow circle over asphalt and concrete and gave roadside bushes and trees a wash of lemon, with tinsel glimmerings from the rising moon, and between these interwoven lights darker checks of green. Along the empty drive the muted grey of evening deepened.

"School started this week," Gwen said.

"Ninety-eight," he repeated, "and still learning about people. Best friend cheated me last year. Told him confidentially in my office downtown about this new idea a client had for industrial scrubbers. To remove pollutants from the smoke coming out of smokestacks. Explained everything to him. Showed him the plans and punched it up on the computer monitor for him so he'd see it from all angles. My client didn't have a patent. That's my job, protecting and selling new concepts. The guy stole the idea. Cost my client loads of money. And me my commission. That doesn't bother me much. Cheating gets me, though. And not protecting the interests of my client. My friend is a lawyer. One of the downtown types. You can't trust any of them."

Carol opened her eyes, looked up at him.

"Thanks for the directions," Gwen said, glancing at her mother.

"No trouble. Goodbye."

"Bye." Gwen watched him pedal away, a hunched figure getting smaller and smaller.

She got up and walked into the road. Columns of fir alongside it stretched northwards like twin ranks of an honour guard. To the south she could see sloping lawn. She went over to her mother, back still against the trunk of the hemlock, legs straight out in front of her.

"We better get started, Mom."

Carol held out her left hand, and with the right braced against the trunk pushed and was lifted to her feet. She steadied herself and put her arm over Gwen's shoulder. They stepped along the sidewalk, Carol probing with her right leg to see how much pain the knee would give now. She winced and they stopped, waited for the pain to subside. After a minute they were going downhill. The forest ended, replaced by a scattering of maples and oaks on sloping lawn bordering the drive. They saw a rose garden. Beds occupied both sides of the drive, an arranged geometry of circles, ellipses, rectangles and squares sliced into the lawn and filled with bushes. To Gwen some plants looked more like weeds, with small flowers clustered in bunches on tangled vines. But most conformed to the conventional idea of a rose and shone in the fading light as glimmering pink, yellow sheen, tinted orange, violet silk, voluptuous red.

Immediately before the rose garden the sidewalk curved westwards as part of a minor road leading to some wooden garages and toolsheds used by park work crews. The buildings were closed, dark. They crossed, Gwen helping her mother over the curb and onto close-cropped lawn that surrounded the beds. The left side of the drive was one hill covered with them. The right descended into a level area, the beds bounded on the far west side by a stretch of lawn with an occasional oak. Forest loomed behind that. Gwen looked around for people, thought she glimpsed someone peering over the hill for a few seconds. Laughter came from somewhere and traffic noise was more noticeable. She knew they should hurry. But they were moving slowly, anyway, so as they passed each bed Gwen looked down, enjoyed the colours and shapes and occasionally sniffed a wisp of fragrance brought up by a current of evening air, making her think she was dreaming. It would have been a drain on her mother's stamina to draw her attention to the roses. Gwen promised herself they would return together. To the right a concrete walkway went east and west. An arbour, an attenuated latticework trellis, covered the walk in a floral arch of white roses from the drive to a crossing walk going north and south. The arbour was too much. She must lead her mother through it. The crossing walk would take them to the park entrance. When they got to the arbour, she turned her mother gently. They began walking past walls of roses giving off their perfume after a warm day. Glossy white corsages flanked them, over their heads more roses, including fragile-looking ones with a few twisted petals of a violet-tinged white. The arch appeared to glow in the greying light as Gwen and her mother with halting steps entered this extended bouquet of late summer cresting over them with woven stem and leaf, a creamy froth of petals, twilight rose odour blooming under a white veil.

"Beautiful," Carol murmured.

The sound was soft. The rose garden was so quiet Gwen heard. It came from the park drive, the sound of car brakes. She turned and looked back through the end of the arbour. Someone in a car appeared to be staring at them but she wasn't certain because the light was too grey to see clearly, the sky losing that faded, almost white blue that will deepen into the indigo of the night. All sounds seemed to have stopped, except for her breathing and the soft falling of their shoes on petals and concrete. The western end of the arbour was a few feet away. Her mother's injured knee robbed them of a fair chance. But Gwen accepted she had gotten them into this and should get them out. She guessed he was waiting for more darkness. That gave her time. She decided not to say anything yet. Hadn't that guy with the bike mentioned a bridge over the hill? But it was on the other side of the drive. The walkway ahead probably led to it. She looked back again, turning her head slightly so as not to give herself away. The car was gone. He would be waiting somewhere in the dark. She saw the reason for his going. A party of visitors—canes, walkers, white slouch hats, orthopedic shoes—was touring the garden, mumbling like bees and bending over to sniff the roses. Some were making for the benches. She sat her mother down against the trellis and went to speak to them.

A woman with a face like a dried fig looked up at her from a bush she was leaning over, not too far. Gwen smiled, part of being kind to the aged and the ill.

"Could you help me, please? I'm looking for the quickest way out of the park."

"Don't ask Harriet, dear, she's potty."

A second woman edged around the other. With planted steps in corrective white shoes, she came over to Gwen. White face powder, purple lipstick smeared over the edges of her lips, she wore a white angora sweater and pleated skirt too large for her sagging frame. Her batwing glasses seemed from a Halloween costume.

"The way out is the way we came. You go under a bridge. Cross before. Be careful. Drivers will run over you, leave you like dirt in the road. You go down a hill. Walk past the yacht club and that's it."

"Thank you. My mother and I have been trying to get out of here."

"Pretty," the first woman said, her voice the rustling of tissue paper. She stroked with one finger the large petal of a pink rose as if it were the ear of a cat.

"She says that every time we come here," the other woman said. "The only one she ever notices. Paddy's Folly. Nothing special about it, is there? Hybrid stuff."

"I don't know anything about roses," Gwen said.

"This is pretty. Got no character. Now, those old English roses. Full of petals. Like puff pastry. The whites and reds are natural colours. Smell wonderful. Wear one, you don't want perfume."

"If you don't like this kind, why do you come?"

"These are my friends and they like to get out. I come along but there's nothing to see."

"Cynical Sue," a cawing male voice said with arrogance to spare. Gwen looked and saw a bony man sitting on a bench. He wore a white sweater and pants and a white slouch hat pushed back on his forehead. His legs were crossed, his big toe swinging a loose plimsoll up and down. He swung it abruptly. He was sitting between two women who looked as if they had spent their lives making preserves. He seemed a man who had always been successful with woman.

"Shut up, Archie," the woman said in a sharper tone. "You wouldn't know what to do with yourself if we didn't look after you."

"Look after me? So it's love, is it, and I thought it was only my body you wanted."

"If you don't behave, you won't be asked along next time."

"Oh, pardon me," the man said mockingly but almost in a whisper.

The woman smiled at Gwen.

"He likes to show off."

"Oh," Gwen said. She was reacting to the first woman, who kept tugging at a sleeve of her jean jacket. Square false teeth between slack lips, blue eyes round and shiny with the need to tell something. Others from the group began to gather around them, staring. Gwen attempted to pull free but the fingers held on fiercely. For a moment she believed they were forest creatures, intending to take her into its dark depths. "Pretty," the woman cooed. Gwen tore her arm free. The woman fell over, her crooked fingers bleached bat claws. She looked up at Gwen, who was suddenly stung with pity for her helplessness. Too weak to get up, the woman lay on the grass, fingers still outstretched. She looked like a plaster garden gnome that had fallen over. Compassion mingled with disgust. These mumbling arthritics moved with every bit of their concentrated energy. They were rotting away, shrivelling in a moonlit landscape losing its boundaries, drowning the roses in darkness. What if the way out were only another way of being lost? She wanted to run.

The man on the bench laughed.

"Let her go."

The gathering circle fell back and Gwen hurried over to her mother.

"I know the way, Mom. It's not far."

Eyes closed, Carol sat slumped against the arbour. Feeling the thorns as well as the roses, she was too tired to care. She opened her eyes at the words. Anticipating hanging onto Gwen in the painful walk ahead, she grimaced. She had been dozing, dreaming in fragments. Her husband proposed to her again and she asked why. He said he hadn't been a good enough husband and wanted to start over. She had accused him of infidelity and he denied it. She demanded proof of his love. What proof? he asked. Gwen's head, she answered. Tell the axeman to sever her fair neck with his keenest edge. She had said something like that. Never, he shouted, suddenly dressed like an Elizabethan nobleman, black velvet doublet and hose and white pleated ruff, she a queen in a gown of shiny blood-red silk with huge puffed sleeves and billowing skirt and over her breast a lion rampant worked in gold thread with a fiery tongue coiling around her left nipple, tickling it. Moving to put her arm over Gwen's shoulder, she found the lion's tongue was a thorn that had pierced her jacket.

They headed over the lawn towards the crossing walkway, Gwen avoiding the people clustered around the benches but glancing in that direction. She couldn't see the woman who had clutched her sleeve. The other woman seemed to have gone, too. And the man on the bench. In the grey air floated shapes of white clothes, glowing as in some old photographs in which anything white radiates brightness. The faces had vanished. The shapes began leaving. Jackets, pants, dresses and shoes appeared to move on their own, as if the people long ago disappeared, returning in the only light they could be seen.

Gwen and her mother made their way southwards out of the garden. The arc lights were spread far apart. The evening was almost gone. They could hear city and commuter bridge traffic. There was nobody on the crossing walk. It ended further south on that section of the drive they left. An occasional oak provided the only cover. Gwen helped her mother off the walk and onto the drive. Two minutes later they reached a stop sign at the bottom of a slope where the road levelled out and went in two directions. The right fork of the drive merged with the northbound traffic on the main road, which led to the commuter bridge. The perimeter park drive fed into the southbound traffic on this road, which went past a lagoon. Beyond it she could see the lights of apartment buildings. The left fork and a single-lane road bringing in traffic from the park entrance merged under a stone bridge for pedestrians. Its archway offered concealment, and the way out was on the other side. She hurried towards the bridge.

"Please remember my knee," Carol muttered.

"Sorry, Mom. We've got to hurry."

"For what?"

The pedestrian bridge was wide and the stone had weathered to a pale grey, its sides and the curving railing and thick balusters flanked by cypress and Pacific yew and covered with ivy that dangled below the top of the archway, cut into it like a keyhole. A car came around the curve of the entrance drive and disappeared into it. Gwen saw a sidewalk inside with a railing but the walk was on the entrance side of the drive. Once they were on the sidewalk she halted, staring into a darkness that made the night brighter, with crescent moon and arc lights and old-fashioned streetlights with single globes topped by a cast-iron finial on the broad railings of the bridge. She stepped into the gloom, holding her mother's hand tighter, other hand on the cold steel railing.

"Careful, Mom. It's dark."

"I can see that."

Their words echoed off the walls, sounding hollow. Decades of traffic had left traces of tread, leaked crankcase oil and flakes of rust on the asphalt underneath, and exhaust had darkened the passage, and all this had accumulated into its own memorial, mingling with damp winters to produce an odour of stale travel.

"Only a little way now, Mom."

"Why don't they put lights in here?"

"Probably because nobody walks through here after dark."

"That's comforting to know."

"That's why we're taking this way. Dark and lonely."

"Shut up, Gwen. At least you can run from muggers."

"I wouldn't leave you, Mom."

Gwen could see the end of the archway in faint outline. A cool gust of night wind blew through, bringing with it the sooty smell of city pollution. The wind scattered leaves on the walk and road, making a sound like insects scratching. Gwen's eyes began to burn. She felt grit or cinders in them. She took her hand off the railing and rubbed her eyes. When she looked ahead again there was the black shape of someone standing outside. She pulled her mother to her. "There's somebody there," she whispered. They waited.

"Come on out, I'm a police officer." The voice sounded official and somewhat impatient.

"Thank God," Carol said. "I thought we were going to be mugged."

"Wait, Mom."

"Don't be so damn silly."

"Shine a flashlight on your uniform," Gwen said out loud.

There was no response.

"The park detachment wear uniforms and ride horses," she whispered. "Even if it was a city patrol car, the guy would be in uniform."

They were too far back in the archway for him to get a clear shot. He would have to come in after them. And Gwen knew he wouldn't because of her. Even uninjured, her mother couldn't escape. But Gwen knew she could outrun him. She understood now why he hadn't gone after them in the park. He wanted to be sure he got both of them. She would never leave her mother behind. He didn't know that. She placed her mother's weight against the wall, scoured the walk with both hands, found something and put it in her pocket. As she straightened up, a van came into the archway blaring rock music, the bass shaking the air like sound blasts from artillery fire. She waved but it went on its way. She followed the slow sweep of the headlights to see. He was not there.

"Why doesn't he come after us?" Carol whispered.

Gwen leaned close to her but glanced around. In the hollow darkness her voice sounded like gas escaping from a cylinder.

"He's gone to the other end, thinks we're going to go back. We're going out this end. We've got to get to the seawall walk. It's not far away. Hold on tight."

Gwen knew their situation was almost hopeless but made herself believe. She didn't look back when they came out. She hauled her mother up and over a small rise on the south side of the drive. She dragged her like a large parcel, one hand around her waist, the other clutching a shoulder. There were cries and groans and then one of the groans sounded like a surprise. She kept going, reaching the beginning of the seawall walk, where it ran along the inside curve of a small inner harbour and by the yacht club. It was broad, with a stone railing and balusters like those on the bridge. On the other side the water shone, a velvet blackness among moored excursion boats and private yachts. She heard something hit the asphalt in front with a whining ping. There was another one. Then another groan of surprise, and it seemed disappointment too, and she felt her hand getting wet from her mother's jacket. She was pulling her mother now and tiring. Grunting, she heaved her against the railing, felt her mother's head go slack as if asleep.

"Oh God, Mom, come on."

Gwen was crying as she spoke. Her mother wasn't moving. She would have to carry her and she couldn't any more. She stood holding her up against the railing and embracing her limp arms and body. They were ninety feet from street traffic.

Two cyclists wheeled up. And two more. Small headlights shone on Gwen and her mother. One of the cyclists phoned for help. Another came over. An intruder now. "What happened? Your mother hurt?" Gwen gently put her mother's weight against him and reached into her jacket pocket. She took out what she had picked up in the archway. She ran into the middle of the walk. Hardly able to see through her tears, she threw a rock as hard as she could in the direction of the bridge.

Carol had died when they reached the seawall. Gwen knew. Roger was told the next day by the coroner's office that one bullet had fractured Carol's left collarbone, glancing off it before traversing her neck and lodging in the brain stem, the other had entered mid-back to the left of her spinal cord, fractured a rib, exiting through the lower right abdomen and causing severe internal hemorrhaging. The coroner's office also informed him that Carol's right knee had suffered ligament damage.

Gwen watched as the body, covered by a white sheet, was carried by paramedics to the ambulance. They slid the stretcher inside and closed the door. She felt alone and needed her father. A patrol car arrived and a policewoman had taken her name and father's phone number. Roger had been notified and was on his way from the suburbs. He promised to be at the apartment in an hour. It was eight forty-seven. The crowd of onlookers was dispersing.

They sat in the patrol car and the policewoman asked if Gwen was hungry or thirsty and if she felt like talking about what happened. Gwen decided to say a man stalked them. He chased them under the bridge and shot her mother as they ran away. Why were they in the park so late? She said they had gone out for an evening drive and decided to get out and look at the lake. That was where they first saw him. They had been able to hide from him for an hour. But as they were walking towards the bridge they saw the man again and tried to get away by hiding under it. But the man had seen them and they had run out, over to the seawall. As they were running away, the man shot at them and hit her mother.

Gwen thought she should leave Speaker out. He might be dead, his body lying in the creek beside the seawall trail. If he was dead, she would talk to her father about what her mother discussed with Speaker. If Speaker escaped, she would talk with him. They would decide how much to tell her father and when. She would phone Sylvia and find out if Speaker was there or if she had heard anything about him. But Gwen didn't know Sylvia's telephone number or last name. She and Madeline would go over and see if Speaker was all right. Thinking of Madeline made her feel better, and want to cry. Gwen went over the possibilities to keep herself from thinking about what had happened. She felt guilty about involving her mother in Speaker's problem and responsible for her death. The feeling wasn't logical but it was there. And it all began the day they decided to help that tramp. Their decision had ended in disaster. Gwen hated him.

Chapter 15

Roger was at the apartment when Gwen arrived with the policewoman and another officer. She ran to him. They embraced and she cried as he held back tears. "You all right, Gwen?" "Mom's dead." She was five feet, eight inches. But he had to reach down to stroke her hair. His hand touched it as if he could hurt her. He hadn't taken off his overcoat. She buried her head in its black wool. The fibres smelled of cool night air. The officers told Roger what they knew, including what Gwen had said. They asked questions and said Gwen should let them know if she remembered anything else. She hadn't seen the man clearly enough to recognize him from a photograph, she had told the policewoman in the patrol car. There would be an inquest. Roger would be notified of the date. Then they were alone, sitting on the chesterfield, her head resting against his dress shirt. The overcoat and suit jacket lay in a heap on the loveseat. Gwen's jacket lay beside her, the sleeves turned inside out. Roger had downed two stiff drinks of whisky. After a glass of milk and half a granola bar, Gwen had fallen asleep.

"How does it happen?" Roger said in a low voice, his left arm around Gwen's shoulder, the fingers of his right hand picking at the thick woollen and polyester weave on the armrest as if the answer were hidden in the interplay of the fabric. "You wake up one morning and that day is going to change your life. You don't know it yet. You brush your teeth, you shower, shave and dress and eat. You're not expecting anything different, and wham."

Dreaming, Gwen saw the shadow of a man along the grass on the hill beside the bridge. Her mother was standing by the seawall railing in a bloodstained jacket and slacks. She tried to run to her mother, pulling on her legs but they wouldn't lift. She started, jerking herself awake. Roger patted her shoulder.

Gwen lay her head on the side of his chest again and fell asleep. Speaker was strolling out of the park with a wad of bills in his hand. As he counted them, he was grinning. She followed him.

"Why?"

"I have to make money."

"You tricked us."

"It was fun."

"My mother's dead."

Speaker kept counting the money. She grabbed it but the bills were hot and sticky. When she looked again they were limp, dissolving into blood. They dripped in stringy blobs from her hands. She saw her mother's face below the surface of the lake. It was streaked with blood. She ran after him, holding out a bleeding lump of flesh.

"Take it back."

"It's yours now."

Sylvia was rubbing furniture polish into the glossy walnut finish of the coffee table in her front parlour when she heard the banging on the back door. Al was pretending to be asleep, watching her with half-closed eyelids. Recovering from his walk in the park, Warts was sleeping in the sewing room. Lynch was sitting on his basement cot, finishing a chewy slab of red bean and hazelnut pie ("the secret, a little cocoa") Sylvia made earlier that evening. It was almost ten o'clock. Shaking and chiding herself for that, she turned on the porch light and pulled aside the curtains in the glass panel of the door. Lips drawn back against his teeth, Speaker was breathing heavily. She unlocked and opened the door. Before she could say anything, Speaker slammed and locked the door and leaned against it.

"Can only stay a few minutes," he gasped between breaths. "Had to run part of the way. Need something, please. Before I talk."

Sylvia took out of the refrigerator an apple, banana, beans and rice casserole ("the bananas have to be very ripe") baked earlier. She had fried some pork chops but Lynch had finished them. She brought him a big slice, along with a glass with milk, before going to the stove to make herself tea. He choked on his first swallow of milk. The rest went quickly. "Thanks," he said, coughing, when he finished. After putting the kettle on to boil and getting the teapot ready, she returned and sat down.

"I met Gwen and her mother," he said, speaking more easily but still agitated, "to talk about those notebooks, find out what could be done. Couldn't let it go. I was followed. Or they were. Maybe Gwen was seen here the other night. I don't know. Her mother said nothing could be done unless we got someone to start investigating. Gwen saw this guy, the same one who broke in here, at the lake where we met. I tried to get us out of there but he was waiting on a trail. Gwen saw him first, clapped twice. They ran back. I dove into bushes, climbed the bank to a road and ran, found another trail and a smaller one leading off it. Came out at one of the beaches, near a playground and a golf course. There were people around. I was careful getting out, took a bus over to Main. I've got her apartment number. I'm afraid of what I'll hear."

"Wait a second." Sylvia hurried over to a whistling kettle. She made the tea and brought everything except the spoons. She remembered, got them and sat down. "You've got to hear it, no matter what it is."

He took a slip of paper from his jeans pocket, went into the front parlour and phoned.

"Is Gwen there?"

"Who is this?"

"I'm a friend of Gwen's. I met her and her mother today to discuss something."

"Gwen's mother is dead." Roger's voice was shaky as he said this.

"I'm sorry. Is Gwen all right?"

"Gwen is sleeping. Who are you?"

"My name is Speaker. Please tell her I phoned."

"Shouldn't you be speaking to the police instead of calling here?"

"It's complicated. Gwen will explain. She may not want to speak to me. Tell her I understand and I'm sorry about her mother."

"My wife was murdered tonight. If you don't want to talk to the police, tell me."

"That's up to Gwen."

"What kind of goddam mess is this?"

"I know you're upset. But you've got to understand. Somebody else was murdered before your wife. Because of what we talked about."

"Maybe we'd better meet."

"Sure. But Gwen has to agree."

"I'll talk to her tomorrow. Give me your number so she can reach you if she wants."

Speaker returned to the kitchen. Sylvia was cleaning the counter. He sat down, folded his arms on top of the table and rested his head on them. He spoke into the dark space they formed. His voice sounded tired.

"Her mother was murdered. Gwen's father told me."

"Oh. That's terrible. Poor little girl. So where are you running to?"

"Nowhere, I guess. But I can't stay here. Be too dangerous for you. That guy is going to come here looking for me."

"It's dangerous here now, isn't it? How's your running away going to help?"

"The notebooks make me dangerous to you or anybody else around me. I'd be drawing danger away."

"That guy might think Lynch's here and has the notebooks. Isn't that dangerous for me?"

Speaker raised his head. Sylvia could see his eyes were bleary. The guy was always wanting to think pretty. And while he was thinking pretty, he forgot about people.

"I tricked the guy who broke in here. He wants me for revenge. He knows Lynch would've sold him the notebooks. Lynch would've been easy. Buy the notebooks and kill him. But this guy and his boss know I'm more dangerous. I'm not after money."

Sylvia put down her dishcloth, came over and sat down.

"After that girl losing her mother, you better be after something. I'm putting up with you and your pals and a killer breaking in here. I don't even have my dog. And you're talking about running away."

Mentioning Rowser made her blink. She bit her lower lip.

"I wasn't running away. But it could look like that."

"Forget what it looks like. What the hell would I do with Al? And the others? You can't drop people here and forget them."

"All right. Better sleep in shifts. I'll stay up till seven. Maybe Warts could help starting tomorrow."

"Sure, but not the other two. Don't want to be robbed while I'm sleeping. Or waked up by a nut tearing around screaming about women coming after him. I'll be up at eight."

Sylvia went upstairs at eleven. She planned to get up an hour earlier so Speaker could turn in before seven. After she left, he got up and pulled aside the window curtains. The broken pane had been replaced that day by a retired glazier Sylvia knew through her husband. Beyond a wan yellow semicircle provided by a light bulb over the porch, everything was deep darkness. Speaker could hardly see her garage. Back alley? Should be called the black alley. He went to the front window and outside another dim bulb was doing the same dismal job. Beside the stairs ten tigers could have been chewing on fresh kills.

"Watching out, are ya?"

Speaker jumped. He recognized the voice but couldn't stop his reaction in time. He turned and in the darkness saw Lynch's outline in the hallway. The kitchen light was behind him. He smelled of fried pork grease.

"Come up for a breather. Can't stay down there all the time."

"Keep me company, I'm staying up all night. Let's have some tea."

Speaker made the tea quickly, not as strong as Sylvia's. They sat in the kitchen and drank it from mugs, Speaker thinking it a liberty to use the good cups Sylvia customarily set out before her guests.

"Nuthin' here to drink, I guess," Lynch said, warming his hands on the mug. There were grease smears on his shirt.

"You know Sylvia doesn't drink."

"Yeah."

"Gwen's mother was murdered tonight."

"Yeah?"

Lynch knew. As he had already known about the break-in and the kidnapping of Warts before Speaker told him. Without boots he had crept up the basement steps and listened from behind the door. And tonight he had listened to Speaker's conversation with Sylvia.

"I met them to discuss the notebooks. That guy who's after you showed up. We scattered and I phoned Gwen's apartment later to find out if they'd gotten away. Gwen's father told me."

"Yeah?"

"I've got to find out if Gwen wants to go any further with this."

"Yeah?"

"All that liquor has washed out your last few brain cells. You're a one-word robot."

"Listnin'."

Lynch looked into the mug. Don't even know how to make a cup of tea. Always acting sperior, thinking he's better 'n erybody else, smartyass bastard. Now he's got shit all over hisself. Tried to help him make some money out of this. He's got to fuck up. Sipping the fuckin' tea. Fat arse of a Sylvia falling for his shit, too. We'll get fucked 'cause of this prick. Not me.

"We'll get out of this but it'll be rough for a while. You all right in the basement?"

"Yeah."

"I could talk to Sylvia about letting you share that room Warts is in."

"Nah, forget it."

"You feel safer down there."

"Yeah, that's it. I slept some tonight. I'll watch out front while you're watching here. Or vysy versy."

Lynch left. Speaker took the mugs to the sink and washed them. When he sat down he put his arms on the table and laid his head on them and fell asleep immediately. Sylvia woke up at seven, washed and dressed in a hurry and went downstairs. She yawned as she came into the kitchen. Speaker was sleeping, head on the table. His right arm was dangling in mid-air, dragging his shoulder after it.

"I'm here. Go into the front room and get some comfortable sleep."

Speaker lifted his head and blinked at the early morning light. He looked at his dangling arm and pulled it up.

"I'm a great watchman. Passed out as soon as I sat down again after Lynch left."

"Did he come up?" Sylvia put the kettle on to boil.

"We talked for a while. Said he'd keep an eye on the front of the house."

From the refrigerator Sylvia took out a butter dish and a loaf of oat bread she had baked the day before. She cut two slices, dropped them into toaster slots, pushing the lever down before turning to Speaker.

"I didn't see him when I looked into the front room. Guess he's in the basement."

From a cupboard under the counter she took out an unopened jar of orange marmalade and a large tin of cinnamon. She saw him looking at her preparations.

"I'm making my sharp toast. Wakes me up. Make you some later. If you want."

"Sure. I'll get a couple of more hours."

Speaker stretched and yawned and went into the downstairs bathroom before heading for the sofa. Sylvia was scooping marmalade onto cinnamon-sprinkled, buttered slices of hot toast when he rushed back.

"He stole the notebooks and flash drive. I put them under the sofa cushions, between the back and springs. When I went to lie down, I saw a cushion half off the sofa. Put my hand down but I knew they were gone."

"Why'd he take them?"

"Wants to sell them."

"How's he going to do that?"

"He must have a contact. Maybe whoever helped with the robberies."

"He could get killed."

"I warned him. Thinks he's going to get rich off the bodies of young girls."

"That's Lynch. Gets a thrill out of making dirty money."

"What am I going to tell Gwen if she wants to go further with this?"

"It's not your fault. He suckered you."

"It is my fault. I've known him for years. Even analyzed his criminal bent to him. Now he makes a fool out of me."

Sylvia bit into her toast. She pointed to the chair opposite and pushed her untouched cup of tea towards him. Speaker sat down. Mouth full, she got up to get herself another cup.

Doughnuts answered when Lynch telephoned the garage at eight, using a booth four blocks away.

"Ya get much for that stuff?"

Lynch waited but not for an answer.

"Got something ya want. This time I get paid or I give 'em to somebody that'd be intrested."

"What ya got?"

"Ya know. Somebody ya know does, anaways."

"How do I know ya got 'em?"

"I got 'em. Talk to your friends. Call ya tonight. No sucker stuff. Ya got me once already."

"Call at eight."

Lynch's last meal had been dinner yesterday. Sylvia's pork chops were tasty, and handy as casserole scoopers. Thinking of the pork chops made him thirsty. He would head down to Main and try to bum a drink off somebody. He knew all the places to look. Ten minutes later he was stepping over bricks littering the concrete foundation of a building that had been an apartment block with a ground-floor grocery. Demolished ten months ago, the ninety-three-year-old structure was to have been replaced by condominiums but the developer had gone bankrupt, and this space was now a convenient drinking venue for winos that panhandled around the liquor store in the next block. Lynch knew many of them, had shared a bottle with some. He knew the mean ones, who went into a rage after a few drinks and swung at whatever they could hit. He sought out those who lapsed into a comatose state, allowing him to finish the bottle. There were periods when he couldn't drink. The taste of alcohol would make him sick. These would last for weeks, sometimes longer. They always began with him unable to move when he woke up. He would take hours to focus his thoughts or move his legs with any control. At these times he kept telling himself he would recover. And each time he had.

Lynch saw a man in the far corner. He was sitting on concrete and leaning against a pile of brick rubble iced with oozed bits of once creamy mortar. Thickset and needing a shave, he was wearing a heavy woollen plaid jacket and cap, a work shirt, drill pants with the cuffs rolled up, scuffed boots, and was holding a bottle of wine wrapped in a brown paper bag. The neck of the bottle stuck out of the bag and the top was off. He swung the bottle up and tilted it to his open mouth, the two necks forming an arching line and the dark fluid bobbing in spasms as his Adam's apple jerked up and down with his swallows, his lips like flabby suckers gluing themselves to the other mouth and his tongue rasping the rim at each swallow. A sucking noise came intermittently and when he took the bottle away saliva made pink by wine dribbled down his chin, trembling in drops before falling off. He rested the bottle against an inside thigh of his crossed legs and shook it in a jagged rhythm, his dull eyes staring at nothing.

Lynch grinned, putting his hands into his trench coat pockets as he got closer. He was promoting an easygoing air of chumminess, as if being there gave him the happy opportunity to renew an acquaintance. He knew Bill Kaminovsky. Kaminovsky had been raised on the prairies. Until a few years ago he was a pipefitter at West Coast Plumbing and Heating. There had been too many sick days and arguments with the boss, and finally he had knocked him down before walking out. His wife had left a year before that to live with a fisherman. She had taken their daughter. The only thing Lynch knew about him was his Christian name. That was all he needed.

"Hey, Bill?"

"Ha?"

"How ya doing?"

"Dookay."

"Looks it. Finishing her good?"

"Ha?"

"Bottle's almost gone."

"Yoo. . . ."

The beginning of an invitation or a curse, Lynch didn't know. He knew that Kaminovsky wasn't sure either. Lynch had seen the neck of the other bottle sticking out of Kaminovsky's coat pocket. He sat on that side. He picked his nose, said nothing for a while, kicked at a piece of brick. He watched the traffic on Main. He glanced around casually to see that they were alone.

"Winter comin' on. Smell it. Wind blowing cold rain at ya in sheets so's ya could drown in it. Not much snow out here. I seen the country. Some places snow's so deep ya can't find your ass. I bin cold, too. Frostbite. Lost a toe. Course there's erythin' comin' at ya out of that North 'Lantic."

"Ha?"

"Ya, Bill? Ya bin cold?"

"Mileschool. Daark. Snosewhitenumrub. Yureersnuffscarfs. Mittoo."

"Right, Bill, that mittoo helps. I could've lost my whole foot without it."

Kaminovsky tilted the bottle, drained what was left in two gulps and tossed it away. Because of the bag, the bottle made muffled clinkings landing among a pile of bricks. He reached for the other one but Lynch had taken it when he threw the empty away. He grabbed at his empty pocket. He stared, trying to figure out what happened.

"Ha?"

Lynch looked up at the sky.

"Them prairies is beautiful, though. 'Specially when them grounddogs is out chirping. 'Boggin' on that permit frost must be something, huh, Bill?"

"Yoo. . . ."

Kaminovsky jerked the empty pocket at him. He put his hand inside, poked around with his index finger. It looked like a gun. His hand came out and reached, seizing Lynch by his coat lapels.

"What're ya doing?" Lynch croaked between shakes of Kaminovsky's massive hand. "You 'cusin' me of something? I done nuthin'. Search me if ya want."

Kaminovsky scrambled to his feet, holding onto Lynch's trench coat and dragging him up. Lynch tiptoe, he rummaged in the pockets with his other hand. He let go and both hands dived into every pocket Lynch had. Spinning him around and probing with stiff fingers and punching randomly with heavy-knuckled fists, Kaminovsky appeared to have sobered up quickly.

"Trying to kill me? Lemme go."

The fists stopped and Lynch slumped to the concrete slab. His ribs and arms were aching. Kaminovsky squatted, threw aside the bricks around him. One hit Lynch in the elbow, numbing it. Kaminovsky straightened up and stared at him, trying to focus, and lurched away across the broken brick and cracked concrete slab. He caught his shoe in a jutting edge of concrete and fell like a tree. His head smacked against the concrete, bouncing once and making the hollow sound of a dry gourd. He got up and headed in the direction of the liquor store. His right temple was scraped and swelling. From bleeding lips a rivulet of blood made its way down through cement dust on his chin.

Lynch watched him go. He checked to see if anybody was looking. He scuttled over in a half-crouch to a pile of bricks several feet away. He had gently tossed the bottle in its paper bag there in the few seconds he had. The empty one hitting the bricks had covered the duller sound of the full one. When he picked it up he knew it wasn't broken. He shoved it into his trench coat pocket without taking a drink. Kaminovsky would be returning, another reason he had for leaving fast.

Lynch hesitated. Maybe a nip on the way. He pulled out the bag and began to unscrew the bottle cap. From somewhere overhead came a man's voice. He looked up and saw the man standing almost directly above, his feet balanced on the edge of the cornice of a hotel beside the demolished building. He stretched his arms in a curve towards the sky. A woman swayed alongside him as he spoke.

"I know the answer and it's real. I am technically there."

He fell. Lynch scrambled to get out of the way. The body crashed into the brick heaps and cracked concrete like a sack of cement, raising dust. A glass pipe shattered in front of Lynch. The woman was screaming now. He jammed the bottle into his pocket and scurried away. Fuckin' crackheads. All them loopy-eyed dopers and junkies. Sticking ya up or snortin', sniffin', smokin' or stickin' theirselfs. Never tried none of that shit. Fucks up your brain so's ya can't 'spress nuthin' right.

Lynch hurried north along Main to the light at the end of the block. He crossed the street and went around to the alley, behind restaurants, junk shops, a porno theatre and hotels with pubs. A dozen quick yards to Binner's dumpster and he banged a fist on the side. Binner didn't drink and would let him stay until it was time to call Doughnuts.

"Announce yourself, please."

"Open up, it's me."

The dumpster lid didn't open. Lynch waited. Fist raised, he was about to bang again. The lid lifted enough for a pair of eyes to peer out at him. Binner didn't sound as relaxed as usual.

"Hello, my friend."

"Told ya it was me."

"Sorry, but I get a bit anxious on collection day. I don't like being seen."

"Them garbage guys never empty yours. None of 'em here now, anaways."

"Apparently not. I get confused by earth schedules. Daily, weekly, monthly, yearly, biannually, biennially, centennially, millennially. What don't they mean? Star time is different. In my realm multiple seconds collapse in on themselves or expand infinitely. Time has no definite, always-existing limits. This is a superimposed notion having to do with human work. Eternity is a second that never ends. An awesome now with all of its future here: going and coming are actually only atomic oscillations in the one second that is all seconds. Incidentally, why is a second called a second? Because the first has already gone when you think about it."

"Listen, Binner, I got to stay for a bit, till I got some 'portant business to do."

"Certainly. I have no food as yet, but something will come along."

"Don't need no grub. Got a bottle."

"No alcohol for me. Interferes with the messages."

Binner lifted the lid and let it rest against the brick wall behind it. He helped Lynch inside. Lynch stepped on flattened boxes and bundles of paper and sat down in a corner. He avoided Binner's corner, called the "receptor." Binner received all extraterrestrial messages in this spot. Anybody who occupied it would not be welcome any more. He had seen Binner react after

262

a wino passed out there. When he came to, Binner stood over him. A recitation from the Book of Laws followed. This was an invisible collection of statutes applicable to all parts of the universe and enforceable everywhere. Binner had memorized it. As he delivered the fourth law the wino toppled off the side of the dumpster.

Binner lowered the lid. Lynch took out the bottle and spun off the cap. Lips and glass mouth met, he took a quick swig before sucking more drink down. The cheap wine hit fast, surging through him. Head lowered in the darkness, he heard but wasn't listening.

"This is unusual. I'm being congratulated for something I didn't do. Haven't issued any new regulations on the marriage of people of different levels of intelligence. Forgot, actually. But what's happened is that the petition against changes has acquired so much momentum that any new laws would have been difficult to enforce. Not impossible. No, my subjects obey my laws. But now I'm being congratulated for having the foresight to ignore the proposal for changes. Existing regulations are perfectly workable, anyway. The beauty quotient helps the women, except for the morons. And when an exceptionally intelligent man marries one, the resulting mess is a lesson to almost everyone. Exceptionally intelligent woman apparently don't need a lesson. Should I raise the beauty quotient? Or perhaps I should suggest that. It was created for women. And they won't get carried away as they do here. Where morons have defined the standards of female beauty. Vacant eyes trying vainly to convey something beyond mere sentience. Slack mouths with a suggestion of the rut. Breasts shoved forward for inspection. Rumps thrust at the gawker, the potential inseminator. No wonder they proliferate. The act itself becomes a kind of puerile secret forbidden except to those who obey either set of two moral codes that contradict each other. Marriage. No marriage. Children. No children. Fidelity. No fidelity. Equality. No equality. They spend so much time being fascinated by the act that they subsume all questions under it. Nothing beyond it is significant, no matter what they say. What would be sublime to them? A heap of naked bodies exhausting themselves like a tangle of snakes, I imagine. Later they would be snoring. It must be difficult to be intelligent in this place. One would expect mass trials and midnight lynchings of the brainy. But there wouldn't be mass trials. Not enough of the intellectual type. Always be rare here. No need for regulations. A mutual repulsion already exists. Not many are immune to it. Some of the more devious intelligent get revenge by promoting doctrines enabling them to lead the idiots, politically, economically, socially and morally. More disaster. Biology versus intellect, the battle of the beds.

"Yes, I was thinking about the regulations now. As you called. I heard about the movement against change. The proposal for amendments was simply wrong. I will never alter any laws or regulations unless they require it. I could see that these didn't. Thank you. A wise ruler knows when to say nothing and when the status quo is right."

Lynch had passed out. Regaining consciousness, he forgot where he was. He crawled around the dumpster. "Can't see. I'm dead." He bumped into a wall. "Hey, dig me up." Binner lifted the lid as Lynch stood up. Night lights dissipated some of the gloom inside the dumpster. He slumped down. "Sure I was a goner. Or in one of them coffings." Binner sat down, crossed his legs and folded his arms. "You're no deader than anyone else."

"Where's the bottle?" Lynch groped around and found the uncapped bottle. It had slipped off his lap when he began crawling and the remaining wine had spilled out. He threw the empty and it shattered against a wall.

"I do not tolerate violent behaviour in my apartments," Binner said.

"Your 'partmints? This here's a big garbage can. Fuckin' crazy bastard. Sending messages fuckin' nowheres. Speaking to the air. A ruler of shit, that's what ya are. Ready for the booby hatch."

Binner said nothing, stared ahead as Lynch stumbled over dark lumps of boxes and cartons to the side of the dumpster. He pulled himself up and rolled over the top of the thick steel edge, lowered himself slowly and hurried to the end of the alley. He checked a wall clock in the lobby of a small hotel a half block off Main. It was twenty minutes to eight. He walked to the Fountain, a hotel pub on the southeast corner of Main. He sat at a round wooden table and signalled for a glass of beer. The waiter brought the usual lager the pubs in the area served, thin, pale and soapy tasting. Lynch told the waiter to bring him a package of pretzels. They were stale and too salty but he was hungry and ate them quickly, gulping the beer as the salt took effect. It was time to call Doughnuts.

Lynch went to a wall telephone near the lobby, in the hallway between a pair of swinging doors to the pub and the reception desk. On his way out he passed a dozen people at the tables. Their mumbling blended with the muted sound of a football game on a television screen on the wall at the far end of the room. The hallway was empty. He stood on a strip of worn red carpet and put coins into the telephone and punched in the garage number. Doughnuts answered. His voice had a forced cheeriness.

"Yeah?"

"'Bout what we talked 'bout. Ya got a answer?"

"Hundred. That's a few bottles. Ya could rent a room. Have a good time."

"I want a thousand. My price or nuthin'."

"You're looking at nuthin'. Cold winter comin', I hear."

"Not cold for me. Somebody'll gimme money."

There was no answer. He heard muffled conversation at the other end and figured Doughnuts put his hand over the mouthpiece. A middle-aged couple passed by on their way to the pub. They smelled of cigarette smoke. The man had a hand on her rump and was squeezing it. Lynch thought of warm sheets and the silky soft inside of a woman's thigh. They seemed parts of a dream, things he heard about once.

"Could talk about this," Doughnuts said.

"No talking. I'll go to them 'vestigations shows on TV or papers that does scandals."

"The money could be upped, but we got to see the goods."

"How fuckin' loosebrained ya think I am? Two people's dead. Gimme the money. Or I go somewheres else."

"All right." Doughnuts' cheeriness was gone.

"Courthouse steps, noon tomorrow. Put them bills in something like a envylope so's I can see. No phony shit. I passed lots of that."

Lynch hung up, hands shaking, knees feeling weak. He went into the pub and drank another glass of beer, felt a gnawing in his stomach and ate a bag of smoked almonds. He grinned, remembering where he had stashed the notebooks and flash drive. The grin vanished when he thought about the tall man and Doughnuts and Zimmo. They would follow Lynch after the payoff and try to kill him on a side street or in an alley, or snatch him and take him away somewhere quiet and kill him slowly and dump his disfigured body into the bushes along a dirt road. They might burn him with cigarette ends before strangling him with piano wire or chop a couple of fingers off before blowing a hole through his skull. Cruelty was part of the business, a warning to others. We're worse if you make trouble for us. You start something, we finish it. The longer we take the worse we look, the more we have to hurt you, and so the longer we take when we get you. Your only escape is your death. And we will pick that day.

He heard a crowd's faint cheering coming from the television. The game had ended. His teeth crunched the last almond. It had no taste. The swill of beer and rubble of pretzels and nuts in his stomach made him queasy and he belched a few times. The waiter came around again. Lynch didn't want anything. As the waiter reached for his glass he got up and walked out into the late evening. Rain was beginning to fall in large drops. The light traffic had thinned even more and he could hear drops hit the dusty sidewalk as he walked along Main. The wet spots increased until polka dots covered the concrete. Dots merged into solid patches and they gradually became a seamless dark wetness of road and sidewalk. A wind had come up, smelled of dust and cool rain. The air felt chilly, his skin cold.

Fuckin' rain. Still shaking. Got to be nerves. Sylvia's place be good. Out of the rain. Speaker. What a shit. Telling me erything 'bout that stuff and 'specting me to leave it. To the 'thorities that'll do fuck all. Thousand's enough. More and they hunt ya for the money. This way they get the stuff cheap and forget me. Shit. Fuckin' gut. Fuckin' goddam nuts. Enough to get a room and grub till something comes along. Too old to walk the fuckin' streets like them goofs and winos. Get sick bad. Not a basement dog. Help the dirty bum. Helps hisself.

Lynch had been heading north. He was close to the viaduct arching over Main and connecting the downtown business core and the prosperous west end with the east end. Below the overpass at its eastern terminus was an opening like a shallow cave with concrete above and a dirt terrace below. The terrace filled the space between the sidewalk on Main and the downward slope of the arch. Along the south side of the viaduct at the east end there was an incline between it and a road running parallel and merging a block away. The incline was covered in bushes. Transients and the homeless had used both open and covered areas for years as sleeping places and had been periodically cleared out by the police. That night people were huddled together in coats or blankets and sleeping under the arch. In the bushes Lynch could make out the top of a makeshift shelter put together from the sides of cardboard boxes. It looked like a small hut.

The rain swept by in gusts now and splattered concrete and asphalt. It fell so fast that gutters overflowed. The road became a shallow lake lit up by the rain-clogged shafts of headlights. Tires left tread wakes. The wind bowed cables and wires, swung hanging stoplights like lanterns. Under the pods of arc lights the glistening mass flung down looked as if light had liquefied. New drops landed on the road like splashings of thousands of crystal fish.

Lynch's trench coat and pants were drenched, boots soggy, socks waterlogged mashings of squish at each step. His hair seemed a piece of shiny plastic melted onto his scalp. Shaking rain off his face, he stared at the cardboard shelter. He scurried down the road flanking the incline, stepped across the sidewalk and up over a low wall bordering the bushes. The slippery earth gave way under his boots. Bushes sprayed him as he squeezed past them. He could see rags over the top corners of the hut, one a red handkerchief with white polka dots, another a faded piece of denim. Like the cardboard, they had been soaked to a deeper shade. The structure was much larger than it appeared from the street, about five feet high and wide and ten feet long. Thin plywood scraps shoved into the ground reinforced a couple of the sides. On the upward side of the incline, facing the viaduct, the entrance consisted of box flaps held together by string threaded through holes in them. The ends were inside. He leaned over. A dissolving mask of water ran off his face in streams.

"Cops comin'," he shouted.

"What?" a sleepy male voice said.

"Screws. Bulls. The heat. The fuzz. Comin' to bust ya."

The flaps loosened and fell outwards and a man of about thirty poked his head out, and with it came the smell of long-unwashed flesh.

"What ya want?"

"Cops clearing out the place. Get ya on a vag charge. Toss your ass in the can. From out of town?"

"Back East."

"They don't like furriners. They're on Main clearing erybody under the bridge. Go down this street, head up north. Get to a mission. Find a bin."

The head disappeared, the man emerging a few seconds later with a knapsack into which he was stuffing a blanket and a tin cup. He shoved smaller items into one of the side pockets before hoisting it over his shoulder by a strap and striding off in the rain.

Lynch watched him go but not for long before entering the shelter. It was warm inside from body heat, and the man had left some dry rags. He took off his trench coat and pants and wrung them outside and ducked back in and threw them into a corner. Wiping himself dry with rags, he used them as blankets when he lay down. He yawned as he shivered. Not much water had leaked into the shelter and now his own body heat raised the temperature. Before falling asleep, he pulled the flaps shut. He slept for four hours, woke up and went outside to pee. The rain had stopped and a few stars were glittering between clumps of cotton-fluff cloud shredding across a blue night sky. Shivering, he hurried back inside. He woke again three hours later, feeling hairs brush across his cheek. Opening his eyes, he saw the bulging outline of something in front of his face. He reached out and felt the sleek-haired hump of a rat. A squeal and teeth bit into one of his fingers. He yelled and stood up, his head butting the rain-softened roof. It gave way and his head poked through, up into the night. Tearing the roof open pulled the shelter apart, soggy cardboard tearing like wet bread, Lynch carrying it now on his shoulders. A tail whipped against his bare ankles as the rat sought a way out. Lynch had heard of frenzied rats climbing up inside pant legs and tearing genitals apart. Feeling more vulnerable naked, he kept lifting his feet, stamping on the cardboard base of the shelter. It slipped on the wet incline and his feet went out from under him. He landed on his buttocks. The base tobogganed down between the bushes with Lynch sitting on it, his head sticking out of the roof like a Puritan's in the stocks. Everything shot off the low wall and out onto the sidewalk. Caught between sides and roof in this suit of penitent's armour topped by an errant head was a whirling, lunging shape. White polka dots bulged and swirled, frantic teeth scissoring through the red handkerchief, a head popping out followed by front legs. The rat skittered away along the sidewalk, leaping over the wall and disappearing among bushes that tangled and tore away the flag of distress.

A sprawled, dazed Lynch pulled pieces of cardboard from his bare shoulders and arms. He put his hands on the sidewalk for support and got up. He looked at his bitten finger, saw the bite was superficial. Kicking away a piece of cardboard clinging to his foot, he looked around and saw his clothes. They were wet but he put them on. He felt stiff, as much from dampness as the fall. He had to find a warm place to spend the last few hours before dawn. He decided on The Hot Plate, an all-night restaurant on Broadway five blocks south. He had money wrapped in a rag in his pants pocket. He felt for the lump to be sure. He swung his arms to get warm. Reminding himself with each passing block that he had not sneezed once, he felt better.

Part of a local chain, The Hot Plate was on the northeast corner of Main and Broadway. All four were rectangles of brick and plate glass with fluorescent lighting and booths with plastic tables between poppy red high-backed vinyl bench seats. The name in flaming letters decorated a round sign painted to look like a plate. Food was self-serve, cafeteria style. At four in the morning the place was usually almost empty, the only customers cab drivers, insomniacs on the long trip to dawn, neurotics going through various stages of mental aberration and lovers who thought the world too gaudy by daylight.

Lynch left wet tracks on the grey linoleum tiles as he headed for the washroom. A member of the staff, a junior employee of twenty-two whose dream was to own a chain like this, scrutinized the soggy tramp as he slopped to the rear, looking like a rare and not very sociable species that had climbed out of an aquarium. Lynch kicked the door open with his boot and looked inside. He would be alone. He stripped, wiped his body with wads of toilet paper. After using the hot-air hand dryer to dry his hair, he swivelled the metal outlets of both dryers so they were pointing up and put his shirt on one and pants on the other, going back and forth and pushing the start buttons when the machines stopped. After drying socks and long johns, he dressed and put a boot on each machine. He had been in the washroom for twenty-five minutes when the junior employee, who had been busy, came in to check.

"What are you doing, sir?"

"Getting dry."

"You're not supposed to put shoes on the dryers, sir."

"Them boots gonna be dry in a second."

"Those machines are meant only for drying hands."

"They work good on clothes, too."

The junior employee wanted to remove the boots but their smell, intensified by the heat from the dryers, was too much.

"Remove them now or I'll have to send for the police."

Lynch took the boots off the dryers and put them on, crouched and laced them up as the junior employee waited in his white uniform. Lynch straightened himself with a groan and went to a urinal.

"Got to piss. You gonna watch?"

The junior employee walked out of the washroom. After filling his pockets with toilet paper, Lynch came out, went to the counter and picked up a tray from a stack. He put a piece of pie from a shelf in the dessert section on it. The sign said it was apple pie. It looked like partly coagulated tan glue between pieces of worn leather. Lynch went to the end, where several pots of coffee had been brewing for hours. He poured himself a cup of Arabica Zoom. The notice underneath said it would keep you awake until dawn. The bored middle-aged cashier bulged in her uniform. She told him the price was $9.24.

"For this junk?"

"That's what I said."

"Keep the pie. I'll take that coffee."

"That'll be $3.25."

"For the coffee? That's 'spensive for poor people."

"That's the price. I didn't set it."

"Some rich bastard did."

"Do you want the coffee?"

From his pants pocket Lynch took out the rag in which he'd wrapped his money. He pulled out a damp crumpled bill and smoothed it flat with thumb and forefinger. The cashier had been smelling him for too long already and pointed to the counter. He placed the bill there.

"That's a five I'm giving ya."

She punched in his purchase and with two fingers picked up the bill and put it into the cash drawer. She took out his change, holding it up in front of him as she counted before putting it on the counter.

"That all I get?"

"That's your change," she said in a tone that announced the end of the conversation.

Lynch put the coins into the lump, squeezing it before jamming it into his pocket. He picked up his tray and looked around. Pointing to a newspaper, two cabbies were talking at one table. A young couple argued in whispers at another. An absent-eyed worker going on shift or off shift was trying to wake up or stay awake. Solitary figures sat hunched over private miseries. Lynch still felt cold. The restaurant was not warm, the temperature deliberately kept below what would have been comfortable. The aim was to keep customers from using the place as a cheap hotel.

Lynch picked a booth near the kitchen, hoping it would be warmer at the back. He slid between the table and bench seat and sipped the coffee. Bitter but hot, it warmed him and he sipped some more. Sounds of pans bumping and knives and forks crashing into stainless steel sinks came from the kitchen. He pulled a wad of napkins from a dispenser and shoved them into his coat pocket and looked at the wall clock behind the counter. It was four fifty-eight. The cabbies were flipping a coin and the one who flipped laughed. The couple left, she following and speaking in a sharp voice but he wasn't listening. Two girls came in, one blonde and one black haired. They carried jackets over their arms and wore tops and short skirts and four-inch heels. They were skinny, their legs long sticks with calf muscles like a knot in chopped firewood when the split follows the grain around it. Each paid from her handbag for a coffee and a piece of chocolate cake. When they sat down Lynch could see the blonde wore blue eyeshadow and scarlet lipstick, the black-haired one violet eyeshadow and purple lipstick. They had small faces and pouty lips and doll noses. They looked around between bites and sips and spoke in bored monosyllables.

Melindee, Sabinee. Mamma Mike's, the wine with sparkles dancing in the glass, and a golden tongue down your throat. Riding towards dawn, tiring into the snoring sunrise, silk beds drowning, red billows of pillows. A hot box, the journals needing oil to ride you the distance. Lynch among the millionaires of dreams sprawled in icy boxcars tilting, swaying coupling by coupling across the frostbitten prairies, past the rippling of white waves caught at mid-crest, the stiff earth shrunk drybrown and hard as petrified wood in stingcold darkness. Mountains split for rough pine and larch, and the fir forests of the coast gentle down where they said winters were damp. Red cedar smoked sockeye the taste of her. Spruce up those ragged branches, bark grey coins coming off like a skin disease. You paid, you put your pants on. The doctor said, you bums should watch out. The brakeman's voice was breathing snow at night in a freight yard. Warning him. He couldn't hear, his fingers frozen to the handrail of a boxcar. Uncoupled, shunted down along the starlit rails. The jolt of separation, the slide away.

Lynch felt a push on his shoulder, opened his eyes and raised his head from the table. The junior employee was staring down at him.

"You were sleeping, sir."

"So what?"

"Find somewhere else to sleep. This is not a hotel. You must eat or drink something. You've been here for three hours."

The junior employee leaned over Lynch and kept staring pointedly at him. Lynch picked up his cup and ostentatiously took a sip from it. He looked through the plate glass window at the early morning. The sky was pencilled in broad cloudstrokes hastened along by a high wind, and behind the wooden houses and squat stucco apartment blocks lining the horizon of the old east end a yellow glow was slowly absorbing the faded blue.

"That cup is empty, sir."

"No it ain't neither."

"If you don't leave, I'll be forced to call the police."

"I'll show 'em the cup."

"If I give you a free coffee in a paper cup, will you leave?"

"I'm sitting here and finishing this coffee. I don't like being thrown out. You're 'scriminating 'gainst me. I want the manager."

"I'm the temporary manager."

"Where's the real one?"

"He's off sick. I'm taking his place."

It was nearly eight o'clock. There were more people in the restaurant. Almost all were listening. Seeing the junior employee was embarrassed by this, Lynch lowered his voice.

"Gimme a pie and I'll go. If ya don't, I'll be sick and throw up lots real easy."

After pondering this, the junior employee decided that because Lynch was an unknown quantity, might do something that would jeopardize his future career with this chain, or hinder him in another avenue of corporate advancement, he should get rid of him the easiest way possible. He looked into Lynch's cup.

"I'm sorry, I see you still have most of your coffee. This restaurant will be glad to give you free your choice of a dessert. Please come with me."

"Better be a whole pie," Lynch said loudly. He got up and followed him to the steelshiny swinging doors of the kitchen.

As a signal for Lynch to wait, he put up a hand and pushed one of the doors open and went inside. He returned with a white pie box and handed it to him.

"What kind?"

"I don't know," was the whispered reply.

"Better not be rhubarb."

"We don't sell rhubarb pie."

"There's enough that's sour 'round here."

Lynch glanced towards the booths. Nobody was looking directly at him. Most customers were staring at tabloid headlines and pictures, dissecting elastic pancakes coated with "maple flavour" house syrup from a squeeze bottle with a pointed spout, or using a blunt-ended knife to scoop ketchup out of a plastic mini-tub for bloodshot eyes on their assembly line eggs. There were glances as he passed by on his smelly progress, noses sniffing fumes of fetid dumpster garbage, spilled cheap wine solvent reek, pee stains. He made a strutting exit.

The pie box under his trench coat, Lynch shoved the door open with his boot. He strolled across the half-filled parking lot. He felt better than he had last night. His clothes were dry. He hadn't sneezed during or after the rain. His sleep in the shelter and the restaurant was more than he usually got in twenty-four hours. It didn't look as if there would be more rain. He had plenty of time to eat the pie, over two hours, before he took a bus downtown and collected the money. First he would pick up the notebooks and flash drive. That would be easy. He headed north along Main to hide in skid row. Speaker might be looking for him. He passed the small park in front of the railway station. Even Speaker could find him in those places. He walked by the viaduct. Most of the transients and homeless had left the terrace. Pieces of cardboard he had flung away littered the side street.

In the next block he saw the Black Cat porno theatre. He could stay warm in there and eat the pie. But the admission was too much. He would pass up *Coed Lust* and *Brides in Heat*. Crap, anaways. He had taken refuge in there from the snow once and fallen asleep to fake moans and woken up to see on the large screen a ten-foot half-erect penis being squirmed by hand like a reluctant python into a slack vagina as big as a manhole cover. This was accompanied by a slurred soundtrack of a herd of rutting saxophones. The floor shook and Lynch looked around. A few seats away in the semi-darkness another customer had a flailing hand inside his unzipped pants and was jerking around in his seat. The same thrashing and heaving were occurring elsewhere in the sparsely-occupied theatre. He left and hurried through blowing snow obliterating the empty pre-Christmas streets.

Lynch walked around to the alley behind the porno theatre. He was on the edge of Chinatown and four blocks from skid row and would use alleyways to get there in case Speaker was looking for him. Doughnuts and

Zimmo might be searching, too. Binner's dumpster lid was down. The rear exit door of the theatre opened as Lynch passed and an early customer hurried out. Luck. Never turn down a chance. He instinctively grabbed the door before it closed. He edged up a dim passage leading to the seating area. There were only two customers in the stiff-backed wooden chairs, a man who was sleeping and another who was staring hard. He crept halfway to the rear, to a staircase built against the side wall. It led to a balcony and no one was up there. The projector beam flickered in the dimness and there was a slight whirring noise. On the soundtrack was the usual clamorous attenuation of unintentional hilarity from trombones and sex-starved saxophones to accompany the double-underlined innuendoes of the dialogue. The balcony seats were attached in rows and had plush-covered foam cushions. He sat down and settled back, put his feet up on the armrests of seats in front and closed his eyes. Within a minute there was a voice too near to be on the soundtrack.

"You have a ticket?"

"Huh? I lost it."

"Come with me."

The man led him down the stairs and around the main seating area to a makeshift lobby behind a floor-length set of heavy drapes. He pushed open a swinging door at the back of the lobby. This was the main entrance, a short vestibule with a door to the street and on one side a booth with a small window. Behind the window, with a slotted metal disc for speaking and an opening at the bottom for passing money, sat a woman knitting. She held a ball of wool, and from the knitting needles in her wrinkled hands dangled the toe of a sock. The man spoke to her in Cantonese. She looked at Lynch.

"I no remember you."

"You watch, you pay," the man said.

"I paid."

The woman shook her head.

"You can pay now," the man said.

"For this shit? I want my money back. Showing nuthin' 'cept old stuff. Them broads probly in 'tiremint homes now, 'less their insides fell out. Tell ya what. I'll forget erything and ya can even keep my pet snake. It's in this box. I got to tell ya, ya can only feed it them little mice or it gets mean."

He had taken the pie box from inside his trench coat. The man backed away. The woman pointed a knitting needle at Lynch like a sword. He moved towards the street door backwards, bumping into a customer who had his coat collar up and head staring down. Lynch turned.

"Ya won't be choking the chicken looking at this shit. I can get ya a girlie magazine, no pages missin'."

The man's head turned, his feet swivelled around and he walked out. Lynch followed quickly before the theatre manager could do anything. Outside, safe. He grinned. Pie safe too.

The smell rose in the warmer air, crust and sweetened fruit. Lynch guessed apple as he hurried around to the alley. He passed the back of restaurants and markets, banks and small office buildings, and a couple of old apartment buildings made of wood, their sagging porches rising in tiers of railings, and a narrow stairway zigzagging up from floor to floor. After Chinatown, skid row with addicts and winos and dark pubs. He was only a few blocks from the garage and Sylvia's house. There was a vacant lot filled with trash, where he could hide. And the nearby waterfront was a maze of warehouses, stevedoring companies, railway tracks and wharves. The courthouse was fifteen minutes away by bus. He would have time to eat and rest before leaving. And time to pick up the notebooks and flash drive.

Lynch felt tired when he got to the vacant lot beside the Nanton Hotel on Water Street. He went into the Nanton pub for a beer to prepare for the pie. He took off his trench coat and wrapped the box inside and put them on a chair. The small room had few lights, its wood panelling a flat maroon. Under square wooden tables scuffed ash white linoleum showed dirt swirls from a quick mopping. Behind the bar a television screen was blank. The skinny waiter wore a floppy white shirt and had boils on his neck. Sparse hair thinned from his temples, leaving a tongue of it above his forehead. He put down a glass of washy straw-coloured lager with an enormous head spilling over the brim. Lynch tossed money onto the waiter's platter.

"Buyin'?" the waiter said in a low voice. "Uppers. Downers. Doing anything? Snort? Crack? Meth?"

"See this coat? There's a pie in it. I'm going to eat the fucker once I get out of here. After drinking this shit."

Lynch finished his beer in four swallows and hurried over to the vacant lot. As with others around skid row, this one had become a dumping ground for junk: bald tires, torn mattresses with stains like giant amoebas and ragged holes in the padding, mattress coils, wooden crates missing slats, pallets missing boards, rusty coffee cans, jumbled wire, splintered planks, stacks of newspapers and magazines that rain and heat had fused into solid masses of pulp, bent and pitted spoons, used syringes, plastic bleach jugs and empty wine bottles. Grass and weeds sprouted around the trash. City garbage crews would clean up the lots periodically but within days the junk would reappear like species of native flora. The yellowed squares, triangles, rectangles and circles of dead grass it left became a temporary and useless lesson in civic geometry.

Lynch sat on a mattress behind boxes and tires, out of sight from the street. He unwrapped the trench coat and opened the box, dug his fingers into thick crust. They came out sopping with a snail grey slick goo stuck to shards of crust. Into his mouth the sticky fingers slopped. Apple, nah, peaches, nah, pear. Don't make no pear pies. It was sugary and the taste was an indeterminate, artificial additive between cinnamon and allspice and cloves and nutmeg and mace. He dug again and crammed more of it into his mouth before breaking off a slab of crust and chewing on it. Underneath it was slimy undercooked dough and on top large flakes as sharp as dried glue. He kept shovelling out chunks dripping with what looked like partially congealed saliva until he had almost finished off the pie. He hadn't eaten since those bags of pretzels and almonds. The mixture of beer and pie grew a gassy, elasticized ball in his stomach that cramped. He bent over in pain, dropping the open box onto long grass. The aluminum foil plate spilled out, getting the quick attention of flies. He slid off the mattress and against the side of a truck tire. Spasms flowed downwards through his bowels, demanding exit. He groaned. Crouching, he pulled his pants away from his buttocks in time. The flow blurted out the way water stutters at first from a hose that has been lying around for a while. Another site competed for the flies' attention. He pulled up his pants and fell against the tire. But the cramps returned and he had to squat again. Gastrointestinal writhings from fragments of crust being churned into sludge, contraction on contraction, heaved in all directions. Saliva was dribbling off his lips, his mouth gaping like a fish.

Someone was crossing the vacant lot. He saw Waste searching among the trash. With a practiced hand, the scavenger scooped up three beer cans. He slipped them into his garbage bag. Lynch managed to pull up his pants before being seen.

"That is the surprise of the morning," Waste said, and put down his bag.

"I was having some grub. Too bad ya didn't come sooner, I would've give ya some."

"No matter of mine."

As Waste began to walk towards him, Lynch moved away from the stained tire and corrosive stench and oily yellow puddle seeping into the grass. He realized he no longer had enough money for bus fare to the courthouse. He felt too weak now to walk there. He had to pick up the stuff, too.

"I'm meeting this guy. Could ya gimme some money for the bus?"

"That's not the bottle of wine?"

"I'm really meeting a guy, like I said."

"That's the trust I would have."

Waste put his hand into a voluminous pocket of his baggy black pants and took out a handful of what Lynch thought were coins. He went over and looked. They were almost lost among slugs and buttons, tags and keys. Picking from the outstretched hand the quarters and dimes, he took more than enough for bus fare.

"Be seeing ya, Waste."

"That is where the diggings are."

Lynch felt aftershocks of cramping squeeze his bowels as he left the vacant lot. But the spasms passed and he continued east, over to Alexander. He walked slowly now and kept close to the buildings. It was less than a block and half to the garage and two more to Sylvia's. Lynch turned a corner and went half a block before slipping into the alley behind the garage. Fifty feet in he stopped and glanced around. He squatted and pulled a plastic bread bag from under a loose piece of asphalt between a telephone pole and the rear wall of a machine shop. Scuttling away, he shoved the bag into his trench coat pocket. Erybody's heard of them guys. No snoopers come near. Safest place in town.

He checked the time on a clock in a café near Main and Alexander. Ten fifty-two. Time to head for the courthouse. He boarded a bus that would stop within a block of it. It would take fifteen minutes, which left him time to check for any traps before the exchange. The bus jerked away from the curb and nudged into traffic as Lynch took a seat behind the rear doors. There were three other passengers. He closed his eyes and let himself feel the forward motion. Somebody was finally taking him somewhere, he didn't have to walk. Movement itself was accomplishment, that sense of space-time tunnelling in one direction. The footbound ignored stoplights or stood in a stupor or limped to nowhere or raged at nobody or blinked away the day. All were stopped there among shabby hotels of faded brick sides and narrow fronts, apartment blocks with dim anonymous hallways, pawnshops with guitars and hunting knives behind barred windows, dusty stores peddling souvenir postcards and miniature totem poles and paperweight carvings of seal pups in local jade. A bus passed every few minutes but couldn't take one of them from those streets. Lynch was taking the cheapest way out of a large vacant lot full of debris. The driver honked at somebody staggering in the middle of the road, jaywalking across the mid-morning traffic.

Lynch stepped off the bus two blocks from the courthouse. It was eleven ten on a wall clock in a jewellery store. The bus had been a little slow. He would walk around the courthouse from a block away. Moving in closer until the appointed time, Lynch would watch for the tall man. Doughnuts or Zimmo should be alone and make the exchange. Anything else meant a trap.

The courthouse was a stale neoclassical square of grey granite with derby dome and columned entrances below pediments on two opposite sides. In front of the main one, broad stairs led down to a pair of stone lions sitting in eroded majesty on pillars. A concrete walkway bisected the large lawn there, encircling a fountain before it ended at the street. A shorter flight of stairs at the other entrance went directly down to the street. Across the street terraced lawns and gardens surrounded a complex of newer government buildings, including law courts. There were restaurants and other private businesses in the complex. In fine weather noontime crowds gathered on the lawn or sat on benches scattered around. Some would stroll across to the old courthouse, both entrances sometimes congested by lunch-hour demonstrations and protests. Lynch had chosen the place and time as insurance against any plan to murder him. As he circled he saw nothing unusual. On the lawn in front of the main entrance people were assembling for a demonstration. Two of the demonstrators unwound a long white banner with "Save the Trees" in fir green letters formed by painted conifers. Another tested a bullhorn. Others set piles of leaflets and petition sheets on a plywood table. Several burly men in woollen plaid jackets and caps stood on the street and looked.

Seeing nothing suspicious and figuring he had time, Lynch lay down on the lawn near the main entrance and closed his eyes. Tired, he fell asleep. The noise of the noontime crowd woke him. He rushed over to the stairs, pushing past shouting demonstrators, but didn't see either Doughnuts or Zimmo. He hurried around to check the other entrance. Holding up his placard on a stick, a lone demonstrator stood on the stairs among the sitters. "Butter" was painted in wide yellow brushstrokes on white, and printed underneath in black was "margarine" with an X through it. The demonstrator wore an Indian yellow jacket over a shirt with lemon checks, buff workboots, baggy blue jeans and sported a cadmium yellow peaked cap.

"But-ter is good for you," he said in a spare rural accent, stressing each syllable. "But-ter is the cow's gift, the grass munchable. They won't tell you, the margareene people. They won't tell you they're hardening your brain cells with hydro-genated oil. Your old thinker gets like a rubber ball. Try cogitating with that. Millions have been rubberized. You are being rubberized if you are eating margareene, bee-lieve that."

Somebody threw a crumpled napkin with a mustard stain on it in the demonstrator's direction. "There goes a brain now." A few sitting on the stairs or leaning against the railings laughed. Most ignored the demonstrator and the joker.

"But-ter is the health of the dairy cow spread before you. It is sun-distilled energy. Don't bee-lieve margareene pro-ducers. Save your precious brain."

"Yeah, serve it with butter."

"What about your heart?" a woman said. "Butterfat contributes to arteriosclerosis and atherosclerosis, doesn't it?"

"That is a lie," the stout demonstrator said, turning towards her. "But-terfat is good for you. Helps you get your vitamins and minerals. But-ter is the colour of the sun. Margareene is dyed yel-low. It is an impos-ter. Hydrogenated oil is the assassin of your heart and arteries. God would not create the natural but-ter if it would hurt you. This gentleman here has probably eaten a lot of it in his lifetime and been much the bet-ter for that reason. Isn't that so, sir?"

Lynch stood four steps below the demonstrator and near the right railing. Looking among the leaners and sitters for Doughnuts and Zimmo, he heard the words being directed at him but ignored them. And then he saw the tall man making his way through the sidewalk crowd towards the stairs. He was carrying a brown envelope. There would be no money in it. Lynch looked for a way to escape. He turned to face the demonstrator, who still waited for an answer.

"I know that guy," Lynch yelled, pointing at the tall man and jabbing his finger at him. "He's one of them margeens. They hates butter people. He'll 'sassinate ya."

His foot on the bottom step, the tall man grinned and shook his head, as if to say Lynch was crazy. But he knew he couldn't touch him now. Lynch hurried down the stairs. He pointed as he passed him.

"He don't like me warning ya. Got a gun, start shooting."

Lynch dodged into the sidewalk crowd. Space appeared around the tall man as people scrambled to get to the railings. The demonstrator held his placard directly in front of him as he sidled across the top step. In the centre of a widening circle the tall man froze. A block from the courthouse Lynch caught the first bus heading east. Because he had taken more than he needed from Waste, he had money to make a call. Fifteen minutes later he was in a hotel lobby, his hands shaking. Speaker answered Sylvia's telephone.

"Don't say nuthin', Speaker. Nearly got it today. I got to come over right now. I'm bringing that stuff."

"I'll ask Sylvia."

Speaker came on the line again.

"All right."

Lynch made a wide detour around the garage. He glanced at passing cars and used alleys. Everything was simpler now. Grub, place to flop. No more 'scaping. Speaker be glad 'bout them books and that plastic shit. Sylvia won't gimme a hard time. Lynch opened the gate and thudded up the stairs on sore feet, his boots cans of cement. Before he knocked, Speaker opened the door. Motioning him inside, he shut the door as soon as Lynch entered, went to the parlour window and peered around a drape. Lynch yanked the bread bag out of his trench coat pocket, threw it on the coffee table. He trudged along the hallway, stopped to peek into the kitchen. Sylvia was not there. The cot waited downstairs. His tired legs took the jarring descent into the basement. His boots seemed magnets sucked to and torn from each step.

Chapter 16

In the kitchen later Sylvia and Speaker sat drinking tea as they looked at the bread bag. The telephone rang and Speaker answered. It was Roger Chalmers. He sounded tired.

"I don't have much time. Gwen woke up an hour ago. I told her what you said. She wants to see you after the funeral. It's on Thursday. She thinks I should be in on this. I don't want to frustrate her. Hope I'm right."

Speaker returned from the front parlour and repeated everything to Sylvia. She took out a handkerchief with her husband's initials on it and wiped her eyes before taking another sip of tea.

"Poor little girl."

Half-awake, Gwen glanced over and saw on the dresser a framed photograph of her parents standing beside her at the beach. They flanked their four-year-old daughter as she held onto a beach ball. In tiny halter top and shorts she was laughing, child hands squeezing the pink ball. In his bathing suit Roger grinned, feet splayed and hands on hips. Wearing a bikini, Carol had raised a hand to shield her eyes from the sun. A visor of shadow covered them. It seemed as if her mother was waving to her now and that smile held new knowledge. Carol's eyes appeared to stare at Gwen. Gwen felt the pull. An annihilation of will blotted out all ways of knowing that she knew, threatening the small but important comfort of conscious denial. Never ready to let go because never so inhuman in the ultimate sense, the mind must still hold onto the sought world as Gwen had clung to the beach ball on that blazingly bright day that faded ten years ago. The eyes dimmed, flared darkly for another moment, and nothing. She felt the loss as something she could hold onto, like seeing in the dark. Mother and daughter, space and interspace, nowhere and place, overwhelmed her with a sweet pain that floated through her and Gwen moaned, fell asleep again.

Hearing her moan, Roger opened Gwen's bedroom door. He heard her heavy breathing, saw her closed eyes and shut it. Awake since dawn, he had been making arrangements for his wife's funeral. A grim sense of accomplishment helped him cope with his shock. He phoned Mary. She and Madeline would be coming over in the afternoon. He called the office, cancelling his appointments and other business until after the funeral. He had never done anything like this before. He was in Europe when his parents died, so his brother had handled the arrangements for both of his parents' funerals. He had loved his wife despite their differences over Gwen. Carol gave him what he wanted as a young man, stability and a safe marriage. He remembered the first time he saw her, in her father's law office downtown. She was two years out of law school when he went there because he suspected an employee of embezzling company funds. He had been sitting in Bill McCready's office when she came in and reminded her father there was an important family anniversary party that night. He shouldn't stay too long at the office. Carol hadn't looked at him. He noticed her soft blonde hair and her delicate complexion of cream and pale pink. He looked at her legs and thighs as she left. Months later she admitted noticing him in the outer office and going in to speak with her father so Roger would look at her. The first couple of dates were awkward, filled with aimless talk. But they felt comfortable with each other. Each felt apprehensive about marital politics. Sex didn't bring them closer. It simply and decisively ended one set of guesses with another. But neither of them was selfish enough to be irritated or made vengeful by any inconsistency of response or lapse of tenderness.

After Gwen was born, Carol believed but never said outright that their daughter drained some of her husband's passion away from her. Roger began to feel guilty about loving Gwen so much. He sensed his wife's annoyance but hadn't known what to do. And masking his feeling for Gwen would have been dishonest. He didn't feel ashamed of it. But he didn't know how to handle his wife's frustration. Never discussed, it became a taboo subject. She would occasionally joke about him coddling his daughter but they both knew she meant something else. Her joking stopped after the burglary and he had little time for a new accommodation. He believed they would have reconciled. In an irrational state of forlorn expectancy, he went through the day. It seemed as if Carol were still there and he could make good his lapses and deficiencies. None of this made sense but he wanted to think it did. And he still had Gwen. He knew that better than anything.

At two o'clock the intercom buzzed. Gwen was waking up. Roger looked in on her and she opened her eyes and gave him that almost smile that says, I'm doing the best I can. He told her who was coming up. She smiled and nodded. There was a knock at the door. He wondered what Mary would say. Nothing too embarrassing, hopefully. Framed in the doorway, she wore a black jacket and skirt topped off with a white derby hat with a black band. Her eyes were red and eyelids puffy. Madeline wore her school uniform. Pale, she looked uncertain. After Mary's condolences, he told them Gwen was getting ready. They followed him into the living room and sat on the loveseat. He took the chesterfield and waited, jaw set.

"I can't believe it, Rog," Mary said, sitting on the edge of the cushion, her feet together. "How can people survive in this city? All these killers and perverts running around. Why did she go to that park?"

"I only know some of it. I'll let Gwen tell you when she's ready."

"I tried to get something out of this one but she's waiting for Gwen to say something. How is the poor darling?"

"You know Gwen. Remarkable. It's quite a blow. She's fighting her way out of it. She feels responsible."

"How could she be responsible?" The tone of Mary's remark made it an open question.

"Yes, how could she be?" Madeline said, and Mary looked at her.

Roger was glad she said this. Mary made a strategic retreat.

"Who's taking care of the funeral?"

"Minton Brothers."

"Oh yes, they're good. Mabel Anson's funeral was there two years ago.

Beautiful chapel. Done in mauve and soft apricot. And they don't crucify you with the organ. Service will be at St. George's, I suppose. Reverend Hopton. Said some touching things about Mabel. She was married there in the Fifties. He wasn't there then, of course. Guess her daughter had to fill him in about her."

Roger clenched his teeth. How the woman drivelled on, dressed like an airline stewardess on her last flight. They heard Gwen's bedroom door open. She appeared in the hallway. She had on a pink quilted dressing gown that went down to her feet. She wore floppy white slippers. She had brushed out her hair but hadn't combed it. Her face drawn, lips barely pink, she went over and sat beside her father.

"How are you, dear?" Mary asked.

Gwen shook her head and sighed.

"It'll take time. Must've been terrible. I was telling your father there are too many of these killers and perverts around. Something's got to be done."

Gwen turned to her father, her voice a little hoarse.

"Did you phone?"

He nodded.

"I'll arrange something after Thursday."

Gwen looked at Madeline, who tried to smile. Gwen's lips began trembling. Two slow tears rolled down her cheeks. She leaned her head against the back of the chesterfield and sobbed. Madeline put her head down and sniffled, hands in her lap. Roger had to look away. He put his hand against his forehead.

"I really did love Carol," Mary said, as if someone said that she hadn't. "Even though at school and university she was smarter than me, I didn't envy her. She was prettier, in her own way. But I wasn't jealous. We were still best friends. Never tried to steal boyfriends from each other. And always honest with each other. That's important in a friendship."

Madeline raised her head slightly and glanced sideways.

"Please, Mom."

"I've got to make a call," Roger said and went into the master bedroom. Mary wondered about the call. Was it to the person Gwen had referred? Roger had told her the bare facts when he phoned. She guessed everybody knew more.

When he returned, it was decided that Madeline would stay with Gwen until the funeral was over. They had been talking while he was away, suggested the arrangement and vetoed his idea that Gwen should stay at Nita's for a few days. He secretly felt relieved. Gwen would be closer. He needed not to be alone now. Relatives and friends were flying and driving in and many had phoned and some would be coming over to the apartment. He also planned to see Speaker while Gwen was recovering. This arrangement suited Mary because her sister and brother-in-law were in town and staying at her apartment. She offered to help with the reception. Roger knew his and Carol's relatives would not be needing any help. But he gave Mary phone numbers to keep her out of the way.

"Don't forget, Gwen dear," Mary said as she was leaving, "your mother is in a better place. We should envy her peace of mind. We have all the trouble. She has none now."

She stood in the doorway. Roger had quickly opened the door. Gwen and Madeline had kissed her and were standing nearby. On her way out Mary swivelled around.

"Too bad your mother didn't have her phone with her or you didn't take yours. You could've called the police right there by that lake. Could've saved her life. I never go anywhere without mine."

"The call wouldn't have been relayed to the park detachment. They're off duty by then. A patrol car from the city would have taken a while to get there. We couldn't wait around like the trees. He was after us."

"All the same, they would have known where you were. Seeing them would've frightened him off."

"Didn't you hear, Mom?" Madeline said. "They couldn't stay in one place. So how would the police know where they would be when the patrol car arrived? There's lots of forest and lots of trails and it's getting dark and you're playing hide and seek with a killer. Of course, they could've drawn a map of their escape route, written a description of the guy, tied both to a duck's leg and flown them out."

"There's no need to be sarcastic, Madeline."

"If someone is after you, it takes more than the latest technology to stop him."

"I'll take you to your car," Roger said, shaking his head behind Mary's back.

"Thanks, Rog," she said, her smile intended to be a show of shared grief. "I know we've disagreed on this pervert thing. I'm glad you're finally coming around. Never know who's in these underground parking lots. Last month a woman was murdered downtown in one of them. The murderer had been paroled after several rapes. These courts, you know."

"I've escorted you before," Roger said, but Mary ignored his remark and the fact that they were going to the visitors' parking lot outside and in broad daylight.

"Goodbye, girls. I'll call."

When he returned, Roger phoned Speaker again in the master bedroom. He was feeling a need to know more about the death of his wife.

"Don't forget, Mr. Chalmers, you'll be exposing yourself and probably in a couple of ways."

"I know, but this thing is bothering me."

"We'd better not meet where I'm staying. Too risky for everybody. And I don't want to lead anybody to your apartment. What about the public library, main branch?"

"Fine. I could be there tomorrow at four."

"Let's meet at the information desk, second floor. I have a ponytail and I'll be wearing a denim jacket."

After hanging up, Roger began to worry about Gwen's safety. If that guy could lead somebody to the apartment, he could too. She could be kidnapped and held to buy his silence. And what would happen to her afterwards? The police could do little. They'd want to know more. He didn't have much to tell. How much would he learn from the meeting? Should he tell them? He thought about hiring a private detective. An irritation began to grow in him. Why had this happened? Possibility fell like a meteor. You saw a shooting star or a hunk of rock hurtling out of the sky. You didn't know where to walk.

You walked. You buried the dead.

They sat on the floor in Gwen's bedroom, leaning against the bed. She had told Madeline what happened in the park and what Speaker said at the lake about the notebooks and flash drive. They sat in silence for a while. Gwen broke it, her voice still with a trace of hoarseness.

"Mom's gone, Maddy. I can't get that out of my head."

"I know, Gwenner. I saw it in your face when you came in. It's not your fault. You didn't know."

"I keep making mistakes. And they keep getting bigger."

"We made them. I'm responsible too."

"But I'm the one who pushes and gets us into more trouble."

"You're pushing for something good. It's not your fault other people want something bad to happen."

"What if only bad things happen? What if we can't do anything?"

"You aren't a pessimist. Don't try to be one."

"I know. But it's so hard to think I'll ever be over this. The funeral is going to be horrible. I have to face all those relatives."

"Oh, and my mother at the reception. Doing the buffet line. Her so sad so soon routine. This ham's lovely, isn't it?"

Gwen giggled and Madeline hugged her.

The next afternoon Roger and Speaker sat across from each other at an otherwise empty table in the public library's main branch. The second floor housed the science and technology collection and was one of the less frequented sections. Speaker took the bread bag out of his pocket and pushed it across the table. Roger stared at it.

"What's this?"

"What killed your wife. Names and phone numbers of pedophiles, specifically men who rape young girls. There's also a flash drive. I had a look at it on a library computer. As I told your wife, it contains coded information about a worldwide network of pedophiles. The code is in one of the books. It's complicated but I managed to figure some of it out."

Roger opened the bread bag, glanced at the flash drive and took out the notebooks. He glanced through them, flipping the pages. He looked more closely at the names. He recognized the name of a longtime friend.

"How did you get them?"

"A tramp stole a briefcase in your building. They were in it, with the flash drive. He saw a man rape a girl so badly he killed her. The tramp was seen but got away. He's being hunted and was almost killed a couple of times. There are other facts but they don't matter. I got the notebooks and drive. Gwen found out about them."

"How?"

"After the robberies she and Madeline came looking for the tramp. When they found him, he said too much. Gwen insisted on helping. I said no but she won out."

"That's her."

"She involved your wife and we met to discuss what to do. Your wife told me there wasn't much we could do without some powerful help. That's when the guy showed up. The one after the tramp."

"Anything else?"

"The man who raped and killed the girl is Cobbie Kind. His initials are in the notebooks."

Roger's eyebrows went up.

"So he's behind the murder of my wife."

"And the murder of somebody else."

Roger found the initials, stared at them before looking at Speaker.

"I know one of these men. I've never liked what Kind stood for. Now I find out he's a pedophile. He's got a lot of friends and lots of legal help. Got the public ear, too. I'll talk with some people. Awkward right now. Busy this week. How much danger are we in? Is there much chance of the killer going after Gwen?"

"There's more chance of something happening where I'm living, but there's a group of us and we're keeping watch around the clock."

"I don't want to risk my daughter."

"There's no way to do this without risk."

"I've lost my wife. I won't lose my daughter."

"Look, Mr. Chalmers, I'll understand if it's too much for you. I wonder what I'm doing in this? Am I supposed to be a moral watchdog for a society that thinks I'm a loafer and a sponger who hides behind ideas? I've got no money, no possessions, no family, no future. This is about men killing girls and whether we're going to do something about it."

"Give me time. How did you get your name?"

"Talked a lot in espresso bars, cafés. And at meetings, protest demonstrations, rallies. Somebody hollered out once, 'Hey, you, Speaker, give us that again.' Later somebody else said, 'Let's hear what Speaker has to say.' At the next meeting people called me that. Pretty soon everybody did."

Roger looked, trying not to stare. Twenty years younger, Speaker had a narrow frame and the lean flesh of an ascetic. There seemed space around him, a refusal to be approached as a private person. Even his name fostered this idea of a remote figure. Roger didn't like being told his moral duty by a nonentity in threadbare denim. He noticed Speaker's intense eyes and the ponytail. He remembered the radicals at university. He had avoided all involvement in campus politics to finish his course in the faculty of commerce and never regretted this, but wondered sometimes over the years if an opportunity had been too casually thrown away and could have offered something. It was in the face of a girl he had seen at a campus rally. What the rally was for he had forgotten. Yet her blushwarm face on that one golden, leaf-bannered autumn day as she shouted from a platform at the crowd on the common stayed with him. It returned occasionally like the memory of some long-ago lover. He had wanted to stay and listen, talk to her afterwards. But he had a class, walked with backward glances out of the range of her softly insistent voice pleading for justice. Lost somewhere inside were the awkward gatherings of her flung soft fists, the pale mouth petalled, open in delighted conviction.

Speaker was looking at the stocked aisles of bookshelves stretching along the second floor under fluorescent lighting. Quiet knowledge. Thousands of intellects waiting to be used. Additions to human understanding, verified and offered at public expense to anyone who wanted them. Public education was on those shelves, not in schools of force-fed recalcitrance and lackadaisical teaching. Here was the freedom prated about by politicians, academics, television commentators and columnists on the op-ed page. But it waited quietly, no one pushed it. There was a sense of chance about this kind of knowledge. You had to come here. You had to want this. You only eschewed ignorance. No one could ever succeed again in convincing you of anything cheap and self-serving, the propaganda of the deliberately and dangerously obtuse. You recognized almost instinctively now those who used what little they knew to misinform and twist other minds into obedient anger. Such warfare always preceded the first artillery shell and first officially sanctioned murder for wanting the truth. All the electronic hardware and software that had made the world modern or postmodern or whatever it had become made the job of the professional truth-sayers, those sellers of facts and inspired or pseudo-scientific opinion, not harder but easier. The individual bit of knowledge was no longer as important as the technological context. Belief was in systems engineering now, in the glittering velocity of data accumulation, transfer, sorting and incorporation. The mass respected speed itself and the appearance of competence. Appearance was the key, the look of anything being almost a guarantee of its acceptance or rejection. Anybody knowing how to manipulate appearance could make hatred and ignorance respectable. Most people, desperate to be reassured, eagerly make themselves believe something barely plausible, or even quite implausible, if the appearance and tone of the delivery are right. One type of mind fills a library and another takes what is useful to it to deny what those books mean. Or are both types one doing different jobs and is the job the morality? Is doing a job more important than what it is? We're always close to disaster, information racing ahead of understanding, and most fill the gap with a special reading of what's true and what's good. They do a job without knowing why or what they're doing. And when your job is lying for someone, you use your knowledge to come up with the best lies you can.

Roger was flipping through the notebooks again. Speaker knew Roger thought he was peculiar. But that wasn't unusual. People like him thought Speaker peculiar if they were feeling charitable, and a destructive social parasite or worse if they weren't. Have some trouble turning on his own class. His next phone call would be interesting, to find out if his were inventive exculpations. Something about keeping Gwen from being permanently traumatized. Must protect his own, single parent now. What else could you expect from somebody in real estate? Property as the criterion of human values, the final arbiter determining class and economic power. Brick, concrete, steel, timber, glass: how comfortably real is real estate? Real enough to cover everything.

Roger put the notebooks down. Could she like this guy? No. Too sensible. Junior-grade hero worship. Girls go through a romantic phase. Hormones. Amazing the guys they like. Next year she won't even remember him. Probably even deny it, or laugh at herself.

"Interesting ways people get nicknames," Roger said. "I should have these to refer to, and show if necessary."

Speaker leaned forward and put his elbows on the table.

"Would be better if we each had one. Less chance of losing the evidence."

"Since this is stolen property, we're talking legal niceties, anyway."

"Let's share the guilt."

"Do you want my help or not?"

"You're emotionally upset and I won't upset you any further. I'm speaking for a group of people with no power. I need to know how exposed we are. We don't have a gun and can't afford to buy some other kind of protection."

"Even if I can, that doesn't mean I feel any safer. If you insist on keeping one, I'll take the one with names and phone numbers."

Roger put the other notebook into the bread bag and shoved it towards Speaker, who slipped it into his jacket pocket.

"Say hello to Gwen for me and Sylvia."

"Who?"

"She owns the house I'm staying at."

"Oh."

Speaker was irritated by Roger's suddenly pleasant tone. It seemed to hint at lusty fornication among the peasantry.

"I'm staying there temporarily with three other men because a fire burnt down the house next door, where we'd been living. Gwen's been to her house."

Each word carefully enunciated.

Roger stood up and put the notebook into his coat pocket. Speaker lowered his voice.

"Watch yourself, in case I was followed. Don't think I was, but can't be certain."

Shaking his head, Speaker watched him walk away. The morals of the poor are the property of the rich.

Chapter 17

At the garage the telephone began ringing. Alone, Doughnuts straightened up from under the hood of a car in one of the bays and went to the workbench. He scooped up two fingers of lanolin hand cleaner from an open can and snatched a grey towel and slung it over his shoulder. As he hurried into the office he rubbed the white cream into his fingers and wiped the watery sheen of grease off with the towel. He tossed the smeared rag onto the counter and grabbed the receiver, bringing the cloyingly sweet lanolin smell to his nose.

"Mott's."

"Didn't make contact," a flat voice said. "Watch the house."

"Why?"

"Watch the house."

"That was shit he gave me about going to the papers or those shows. Can't do a fucking thing."

"Somebody else can. Watch the house."

"He's stuck. He'll get drunk and use it for asswipe and save us trouble."

"Watch the house."

In a century-old mansion on Belvoir Drive behind spearhead spokes of a wrought-iron railing and the latest electronic security system augmented by guard dogs the telephone rang in the study of Cobbie Kind and his pink tuberous fingers lifted the receiver.

"Yes?" the heavy voice said.

"Contact was not made. I've got somebody watching."

"That's not what I wanted."

"If you're not satisfied, I'll return my fee minus expenses."

"You quit when I tell you. I didn't pay for unfinished business."

The study was at the rear of the house, its leaded windows overlooking two acres of lawn bounded by a laurel hedge inside the railing. Dominating the lawn were four atlas cedars, planted by the original owner, a timber baron. On this Tuesday afternoon two women sat in lawn chairs near one of the cedars. Sarah Edelbacher was president of Ever For Children, Cobbie Kind's international organization promoting the welfare of children. Forty-one, she was tall and lanky, with wavy dark hair that fell past her shoulders. In an oval face with small features only her deep blue eyes were notable. She had a habit of flexing her right foot as she spoke. Her voice was low and determined, never shrill or harsh. She was talking with Wissie Kind, Cobbie Kind's wife of thirty-six years. Fifty-seven, Wissie was short, with light, frizzy hair she had trouble managing. Her body was spare, not quite skinny. Her grey eyes had the depth of faded wall paint, her mouth and voice were both tight. She tended the wear the sort of outfit she had on this day, a belted light green wool dress and beige shoes. Sarah Edelbacher usually wore a business suit and a frilly blouse, the suit either blue or grey. She was wearing an aquamarine suit and a blouse the colour of clotted cream.

They met towards the middle of the week to discuss organization business. Kind had delegated the financial end of EFC to his wife when it was founded seven years ago. Family members were active in Kind enterprises. Their son-in-law headed the legal staff of the umbrella organization that oversaw Kind's media holdings. Their daughter worked in the public relations department. The Kinds had needed an unimpeachable high-profile figurehead for president of EFC. And they found one.

A professor of religious studies at Pacific Christian University, Sarah Edelbacher had been involved in anti-pornography campaigns and was among the first to join Ever For Children. She and her husband, a physician, had been trying to conceive for years since the two miscarriages early in their marriage. She was currently involved in a fertility program. While the Kinds ran the organization she spoke to women's groups and appeared before government committees on children's television, child pornography and media censorship. She avoided the strident tone Cobbie Kind's media used to denounce pedophiles but didn't disagree with the call for draconian laws. Any measures making society safer for the young were appropriate. She thought herself intellectually superior to the Kinds but recognized his business and public relations acumen and Wissie's stubborn determination to get things done. She also vaguely disliked Wissie's fondness for talking about her daughter. But the organization was foremost. Sarah Edelbacher felt proud that in seven years it had grown to fifty thousand members in the city and four million across the continent. She had as much television and print exposure as she needed to disseminate her ideas and she ignored critics who said she was a mouthpiece and a decoration behind which Cobbie Kind expanded and consolidated his media holdings, seeking influence for more than proposed reforms in the criminal justice system. Those critics saw him as a demagogic threat to free speech hiding behind abused children. This couldn't be true. A generous man, he spent his own money helping to keep the organization going. The mandatory castration of pedophiles and execution of those guilty of more than one offence seemed extreme but would safeguard children. She saw herself as a realist fighting despicable men who preyed on the innocent. Only somebody with Cobbie Kind's power and influence could bring about the admittedly drastic but necessary changes that would forever protect children from the perverted. She never considered criticism of him as anything more than either shortsighted or malicious. Cobbie Kind wasn't a hero. She shunned his magazines, newspapers and his television network, except for articles or programs on the cause. Everything else was trash. When some of her friends had asked her why she so completely identified herself with his cause, she answered, "miracles can come in strange forms."

Cobbie Kind gazed out at the women as he sat in his red leather armchair. They were facing each other and at right angles to his line of sight. Sarah Edelbacher had crossed her legs, right foot slowly moving up and down the black leather shoe dangling from her toes. Wissie leaned forward, tilting her head. Both women suddenly laughed. He got up and opened the double French doors leading out to the lawn. He walked down the three concrete steps onto the gravel path cutting through the flower beds adjacent to the house and ending down at the back gate. The pea gravel crunched under his loafers. Several yards from the women, he strolled over the grass. It had been mowed that morning. The cut blades bent with the dry sound of rustling paper. His footprints stayed a moment before the grass stood at attention once more, like an army that had only pretended defeat. The women's voices were clearer but Sarah Edelbacher's was muted. When he got to within a few feet, both women looked.

"I was telling Sarah about our honeymoon," Wissie said, smiling. "Touring Africa and India. And Thailand and the Philippines. How you used to give candies and food to those poor children in the cities. They used to gather around and you'd hand out those little packages. We didn't have much, but you managed to save enough to buy something for them. I told her that's when I knew I'd married the right man." She turned to face Sarah Edelbacher. "We didn't go to Hawaii or Mexico for our honeymoon, like all our friends. Cobbie said he wanted to see the third world, the underdeveloped countries. So when he was rich one day he wouldn't forget to help the children. 'Would I mind going?' he said. 'Of course not,' I said." She looked at her husband. "I told her about when those little Filipina girls asked if you'd take some candy to their mother and you looked so shocked. You couldn't even speak. I had to say no. It was so funny. Poor things." Wissie turned again. "That trip made me see what misery there is in the world. The children are the ones that suffer."

"Women and children have always borne the brunt in a man-dominated world," Sarah Edelbacher said. "Men have had the power. And hardly ever used it wisely. Most men, anyway."

She had slipped her shoe on when Cobbie Kind arrived. She had self-consciously added the qualifier, condemning herself but giving in as she usually did to her awareness that he liked to know he was an exception. She felt cheap about being a flatterer. But this was labour, wasn't it, she told herself so many times, perhaps too many, that justified putting up with little degradations.

Wissie studied her husband for a few moments.

"Feeling all right?"

"Fine."

"You look tired."

Sarah Edelbacher could feel the nearness of Cobbie Kind as he approached through the grey September afternoon. She felt violated in a small but strange way, as if the presence of this looming figure was the prelude to some negation of her. Something fundamental in her was revolted by him whenever he got close. She told herself his bulky body and huge pink head upset her but she didn't believe this. It was something she had never been able to explain. At those moments she tightened within herself and would use her intellectual superiority to dismiss the feeling. And why should a man who represented some of the worst aspects of popular culture be a tangible threat to her? He was only a useful tool to achieve her ends. She must never allow his brute masculine power to be anything but that, not that she wanted to be a lion tamer with a whip. She disliked both the imperialistic paternalism and hint of bestial sadism in that analogy. She never sought control in any relationship, felt it was a confession of weakness. But she was determined not to be controlled. Still, whenever he got near she felt uneasy. He seemed to be challenging her very self.

He stood almost behind her now. The back of her neck seemed exposed. For a moment she believed he was going to touch her. One of those thick-fingered hands with slabby palms was going to land on her neck and squeeze, thumb on one side and index finger on the other. She shuddered.

"Are you cold, Sarah?"

She was surprised and annoyed that Wissie noticed. But Wissie noticed more than she let on, especially little things.

"A bit. It's almost fall now."

"My second favourite time of year. Spring has to be the first. Don't you think? All that blossoming and those baby birds."

A lot of Wissie's questions were rhetorical. The woman often sounded like a birthday card.

"At this time we remember our younger days, the falling chestnuts and the playing fields. It's sad but we're richer for the memories. Piled like golden leaves. Don't you think?"

Sarah Edelbacher nodded. She was going to laugh. Concentrate on something serious. Behind. Why did he do that? Deliberate. Had to be. Those hands. Pink head. Grotesque baby. Get up, make an excuse. Remember something. An urgent appointment. Breathe slowly.

The looming shape moved a few steps nearer to Wissie, who put up her hand and slipped it into one of his half-cupped palms. He stood with his massive shoulders slightly forward in his mustard cardigan and pale blue dress shirt. His slacks rooted him to the lawn, like tree trunks with the bark stripped. He looked down at her with a quizzical half-grin and white eyebrows arched, seeming more like her child than her husband. Staring up at him with eyes as round as she could make them and a maternal smile that promised eternal forgiveness, Wissie began squeezing his hand slowly. Fastened onto the ball of his thumb, her fingers pumped rhythmically. After every few squeezes, they pulled on the shaft of his thumb.

On each of the several occasions she had seen this, Sarah Edelbacher felt uncomfortable. She would make herself think about organization business or something academic. This failed today and she looked up into the thick branches of the atlas cedar. The clusters of needles fringed the twisting boughs like prickles or thorns. A granitic muscular tree, its grey scaly trunk looked chipped out of stone, boughs like thewed thighs and muscle-knotted calves wrested free from earth. The hand-kneading usually took four or five minutes. When it was over this time, she decided she didn't care for atlas cedars.

"I was telling Sarah that we're going on a long vacation and we'll be leaving her in complete control," Wissie said. "She's excited. Wants to try some new ideas and make a few changes. She'll be telling us first, of course."

"Where are you planning to go?"

"Cobbie wants to retrace our honeymoon. Take exactly the same route. Be thirty-six years since. Isn't that a bit wonderful?"

"You must be excited."

"I am. Cobbie wants to leave right after straightening out his affairs. We're going to take longer this time. We owe it to ourselves, especially him, don't you think?"

"When are you leaving?"

"Next month. November at the latest."

"I'd better look at my schedule. I should be going. Lots of academic paperwork to get out of the way. Registration. New classes."

She stood up quickly. She picked up the briefcase she had propped against a leg of the lawn chair. With both hands she held the briefcase packed with papers and books against the front of her thighs, hesitating a moment. She looked awkward, an embarrassed schoolgirl who had come for a donation and gotten a promise instead.

"I don't know how you cope with all the work you do," Wissie said.

"The importance of it keeps me going."

"That's good for us and for the children. Cobbie will show you out."

"Don't bother. Please. I know the way. See you next week."

After Sarah Edelbacher had disappeared around the side of the house, Cobbie Kind sat in her chair. He put his elbows on the armrests and leaned back against the wooden slats, feeling the warmth of the departed woman seep into his buttocks and thighs. The first time he saw her he noticed the small swellings of her narrow rump. They barely creased her slacks on that hot, sticky day. Like a young girl's. He closed his eyes. His lips compressed slowly, methodically. Concerned, Wissie frowned.

"Tired, dear?"

"Hm hm."

"I think Sarah will do a good job while we're away. I told her to begin profiling convicted pedophiles in the newsletter. Two every month, pictures and descriptions. Past offences and whereabouts. Put it all on our website. We'll have international coverage that way. They won't be able to hide in other parts of the world."

"It's a stupid idea. Forget it."

"Why is it stupid?"

"We may be infringing on their rights in some jurisdictions. Open ourselves up to lawsuits. Bad publicity. That international stuff is for Interpol."

"I'd better tell her."

"Tell her to stick to what we do. Helping children. Got enough shysters after us already. We're not the police."

"You're right. Will you be here for the October rally?"

"Can't say."

"What about the Halloween party?"

"Iffy."

"People ask for you at these functions. You've been missing a lot of them lately. They wonder where you are. I don't know what to say."

"Busy."

"I know. But it looks better when you're there."

"Can't run things in a dozen cities and be at parties, too. That's why she's there."

"But this is our home city and people might think that you believe you're too important to show up any more. I tell them you're busy but I see their faces. And they give a lot. Sarah sees to that."

"Don't think about it, Wissie-Wissie."

The repetition of her name was a signal he was becoming upset. Neither could remember when it started. Wissie would retreat at this point. Say nothing or pick a safe subject.

"I'm getting so excited about the trip."

"Be excited," he said as if it were a benediction.

As instructed, a couple of minutes later his personal secretary came out with a phone. He began making calls as if his wife had disappeared. Wissie got up and left without a word. His eyes were still closed. He expected her to be gone when he opened them. She knew that and loved him the way in another century she would have loved a deity. She was the head priestess of the cult, and anyone who challenged it should beware. She liked Sarah Edelbacher because she recognized in her the punctilious academic who would never threaten her position, content with polemics rather than power. She would always take orders and didn't have the urge to subsume the organization within her personality. And besides, she could never threaten their marriage because Cobbie Kind didn't seem interested in other women. Sex between Wissie and him had staled decades earlier but she hadn't minded much. The hand massaging was enough to let her know he needed her in some way. Sex had never been very important to her. Liking it was tantamount to being enslaved by it, like those horrible pedophiles her husband campaigned against. Wasn't sex really only for making children? Wasn't seeking the pleasure of it actually a trap that caused adultery and divorce? Wissie had been astonished when a friend confided to her once that she and her husband made love for six hours and she had climaxed seven times. With Cobbie it had been a couple of minutes every month or so at the beginning, and then the decline set in. Wissie couldn't remember the last time. She had never had a climax, wasn't sure what it was. And some of the sexual practices her friend described had shocked her. She felt that there was a vast sexual circus going on around her: half-naked women shot out of cannons and flying through the air to be enmeshed in nets, lions roaring, painted clowns making rude noises and barkers with black mustaches winking slyly at her. It was all temptation. Society was being tempted and most of it had succumbed. A few had to remain strong, like Cobbie and her. They had to show weaker people that sex could make them do terrible things. Weren't children the closest of us to being like angels? And weren't they sexless? Sex corrupted people if it wasn't used only to make more children. Wissie was convinced that sex for pleasure created rapists and pedophiles. Why weren't people stronger? Resisting the corruption inherent in misused sex was a strength, like resisting drugs or alcohol. She adored her husband for being the strongest person she knew. He was the kindest, too. Remembering him surrounded on their honeymoon by those unfortunate children could still bring tears to her eyes. Over the years he had sponsored and attended innumerable functions and events promoting the welfare of children. This took him away from his business affairs. She wondered where he got all his energy. It must be the energy of the good, she decided long ago. Why shouldn't helping others let you do more? And wasn't that logical? He had posed for photographers and in front of television cameras with a girl sitting in the crook of each arm as he stood like a giant. Wissie thought herself fortunate. If he was angry with her at times, that was because of so much pressure from work and his cause against perverts. He needed relief and she was glad to provide it by being the target of his rages. He had never hit her, only yelled. Sometimes she had been afraid. Cobbie was trying to do too much for others and had to release the pressure. The outbursts weren't more than a few minutes at most, anyway. Later he would be sorry and invite her to walk with him in the garden or on the scenic path at their country estate. With a deep snorting sound he would laugh about his rages. She would take one of those huge hands and squeeze it as they walked. At those moments Wissie thought herself too lucky. Surely this was a dream and she would wake up married to an ordinary man. That notion would make her shiver at her good fortune.

Chapter 18

In the chapel at Minton Brothers funeral home on Thursday morning at eleven a line of mourners passed the open casket of Carol Chalmers. It lay at one end of the room on a trestle table draped in purple velvet in the middle of a dais crowded with wreaths on tripods. Roger, Gwen, Mary and Madeline had already viewed the body. They sat nearby, in the first pew to the right: husband, daughter, daughter's friend and friend's mother. Roger hadn't wanted an open casket but his wife's relatives did. Believing that she would not have wanted this grotesquerie but not wishing to alienate her relations, he had reluctantly agreed to it. Her older sister Nan said, "people should have a last look to remember how beautiful she was." A chiropractor, Nan was a large woman in her mid-fifties. Her brother-in-law called her "a mighty masseuse with a message." She laughed at this. Her maxim was: "Everything is in the bones getting a fair shake." "You're too tense," she told him once. "A few minutes with some of your vertebrae and joints and I'd fix you." Her husband Ron owned a collision repair shop and had to put up with family jokes about who straightened more bodies. Nan's first husband was a general practitioner who left her for a young nurse. There had been jokes about who was the better therapist, but she heard none of that. She and her husband sat in the pew behind the immediate family, along with Beverley, who was Carol's younger sister, Nita, and Beverley's husband Ben. In several pews behind sat Carol's other relatives. Less numerous, Roger's relations sat across the aisle. They had come from across the continent. And on both sides sat many family friends. Respectful coughing, syllables from low voices, a child's question, creaking pews, softly attenuated organ tones. Gwen and Madeline looked ahead except once. They glanced at each other, staring as if they were strangers.

After the line had passed the casket and everyone sat for several minutes, two gloved attendants came in wheeling a trolley. They closed the lid of the bronze-coloured steel coffin and slid it off onto the trolley and wheeled it to a side entrance, opening the doors there. The six pallbearers got up from the first pew to the left and went to the doors. They lifted the handrails and carried the coffin to the hearse for the journey to the church. As soon as the pallbearers disappeared, the rest of the mourners stood up and began filing out into the soft grey morning. Introductions of the never met after re-introductions of those long separated. Smiled words and soft condolences as the hearse left the parking lot.

Saint George's Anglican Church was on the edge of the business district and the oldest church still in use in the city. The stone walls had been blackened by pollution but inside the white plaster and the old beams in the rafters belied its location and the present century. Stained glass in the narrow Gothic windows kept out the sight if not all of the noise of the commotion outside. Carol had worshipped there with her parents and taken communion. After leaving law school she had been a nominal Christian. She didn't know whether she believed or not any more but still liked the idea of belief. It was traditional and comforting. She didn't lock the idea of God out of her mind but would have been almost ashamed to admit she was an absolute believer. But she felt the need to hold onto faith in some way. She left her belief at that, going there with her husband and daughter at Christmas and Easter. She liked the service and hymns and the thrilling sense of communion she felt with fellow worshippers. The big holidays brought it out, redemptive in the seasons, snow to blossom, cold to spring wind, and the blood had its own undeniable way. And it was to Saint George's they were bringing Carol Chalmers for her last public and ceremonial farewell to those doubts. And this time she would have no decision to make as she lay before the altar and under the morning light.

Saint George's was barely two miles west of the chapel but the journey took more than twenty minutes through downtown traffic. The four rode together in the same black funeral home car. Gwen wanted Madeline to be near her. Mary was conscious of the prominence this gave her as Madeline's mother. She didn't think Roger appreciated her presence, but wouldn't Carol have wanted her oldest and best friend to ride with him?

Gwen looked in the outside rear view mirror on the driver's side door and saw a line of cars following them. She turned and glanced behind her to get a better look. Four blocks long, a quiet procession made its way among the traffic. The line of headlights made it appear like a large yellow-spotted caterpillar crawling into the downtown core. People on the street stared as the procession passed and drivers pulled over to give the funeral cars the central lane. So many watching them. They were busy the night she died. Now she was up ahead and even strangers were paying attention. Why did people care now? Why was all this stuff going on today? Maybe this was all they could do. Show they're sorry she's dead. She'd never see her again. It hurt whether or not she cried. Sitting beside her, Madeline touched Gwen's hand. It was slight, enough. Gwen didn't look at her.

Roger wanted the funeral over, for himself but mostly for Gwen. He looked at her occasionally. She was sitting near the driver's side window. He was sitting between Madeline and Mary, who wore a pink jacket and skirt. That woman would choose pink for her best friend's funeral. Surprising Madeline turned out the way she did. Not like that jackass father of hers either. Must be a throwback to somebody intelligent in one of the families. That corner. Grizzard's. Used to meet there for lunch. Roast beef sandwiches and beer. She liked a dill and hot mustard. Walked over to her father's office afterwards. Took hours. Grabbed her when she slipped on the ice that time at Christmas. Leaning, soft under the coat. Warm breath. Snowflakes falling on her hair. Wanted to kiss her in front of everyone. Put her arm through, elbows locked together. Walked into the office that way. Her father shook his head. Not a bad guy.

At Saint George's the hearse parked in front of the gates in a reserved space on the street and the pallbearers got out of their car and slowly and somewhat awkwardly carried the casket up the steps and into the church doorway, where a draped trolley was waiting. The Reverend Michael James Hopton stood in surplice beside it. The cars containing the immediate family parked in other reserved places. The rest did the best they could in the tangle of nearby alleys and new construction, no parking zones and meters. Gwen and her father and Madeline and her mother walked behind the casket and sat in the first row of pews, to the right of the pulpit. Time was allowed for the rest of the mourners to be seated, scuffing and coughing against the muffled traffic outside, before the Reverend Hopton began the service. Gwen didn't listen and neither did her father or Madeline. Mary thought the service quite beautiful and thoughtful. She liked the reference the minister made to Carol's long-standing friendships. He seemed to glance her way when he said this. She thought him rather young to be the minister of such an old and important church as Saint George's but admired his elocution and manners. She appraised his height, wavy hair, long fingers and his sermon on true belief. Catching herself looking into his eyes on several occasions, she felt moved by true belief. Regular attendance might be a good idea. A needed spiritual lift. The world could use one. That would put an end to the depravity going on. What was wrong with sitting in a church and listening to an uplifting sermon? Carol's funeral was going to change her life. Those eyes appeared to gaze at her again. Her body tensed and relaxed in an ooze of pleasure.

As the minister spoke, Gwen remembered all the times she had attended Christmas Eve service at Saint George's with her parents. The ranks of white candles and the big tree looked so beautiful arrayed near the altar, and there was the singing of the carols. The congregation packed into the church stood and sang together. She would look at her mother's flushed face and her mother would glance back, both still singing. Her father's loose baritone would make them laugh. One year it was snowing, which she had thought perfect. Why had she been so happy those nights? She believed the answer had to do with what everyone felt towards each other. You were more yourself by forgetting about yourself. Singing in the old church on Christmas Eve as if you were singing to everyone in the world about something wonderful. Looking towards the casket, she vowed she would always return and sing the carols.

After the service the minister spoke to Gwen and the others outside the church. He vaguely remembered Carol's attendance. He said that was probably because he had replaced the Reverend Mallock two years ago. Roger admitted he and his family attended only the Christmas Eve and Easter Sunday services. "A lot of people do," the minister said. He smiled at Gwen. "I think I remember you." Her smile and nod, the barest response.

Mary edged in front of Madeline.

"I thought your sermon was beautiful. What you said about Carol. Even though you didn't know her. I mean, personally. She was my best friend. We met in school. Many years ago. Well, years ago. And we've been—were friends ever since. Our daughters are carrying on the tradition. I'm afraid that, like Roger and Carol, I've only attended here on and off over the years. You know, the big stuff. Christmas and Easter. I'll be attending more now."

The minister smiled politely and nodded.

"You're responsible. You said things so well. It made me think about my life. We should all be stimulated to think spiritually."

Madeline gave Gwen an agonized look and Gwen had to grin and Roger looked up as if he expected a downpour.

"Maybe some of these perverts would stop. Though they're born that way. I believe the best thing to do is fix them. You know, surgically."

"Mother," Madeline groaned.

"My daughter thinks I'm being extreme but I think I'm quite rational. A castrated or dead pervert won't ever harm a child."

"I guess it's time we were going," Roger said and moved towards their car, parked on the street flanking the nave.

"I'll be going with you," the minister said.

Mary smiled and Madeline frowned. The small party crossed the worn flagstones and turned west out of the gate and walked down the slightly descending street. Car doors slammed in a chaotic rhythm as other mourners prepared to leave in cars jammed along streets bordering the west and south sides of the church. Some cars were parked illegally in the alley on the east side and a driver was talking to a motorcycle policeman. The north end of the church was next to an office tower.

The minister sat in the front, directly ahead of Mary. She smelled aftershave, told herself to look for a wedding ring. He looked to be almost her age. Maybe a little younger. What a good influence a man like that would be on Madeline. How much do they make? What would being his wife be like? Charity drives. Tea parties on the lawn. Community visits. The old and the sick. Hospitals. That wouldn't be hard. Need a change for the better. Would be different. Carol would be surprised. Forget it. Where did you meet your husband? My best friend's funeral. He was the minister, read the burial service. Final words over Carol's grave. He's turning to—? Talking to Roger. Bucket seat. Hand. Wouldn't have worked. Probably doesn't believe in capital punishment, anyway.

The hearse slowly led the line of cars through the black iron gates of the main entrance of Ocean Shores, a cemetery in the west end and at least two miles from any body of water larger than a pond. But as someone once said at a funeral there, the residents weren't going sailing. Again the sound of opening and closing doors and the mourners followed the pallbearers and casket over lawn and around bronze plaques to the graveside. Over the narrow rectangle of the grave was a green canvas canopy on aluminum poles. Alongside were stacked rolls of freshly sliced turf. The weather was mild, the sky overcast, puffs of wind ruffling jackets and dresses. More than seventy people gathered under or around the canopy. The casket had been placed on planks laid over the hole. The two broad grey straps underneath would be used to lower it after the mourners had gone. The minister spoke and Gwen heard the words but didn't listen. She stood beside her father, who had his arm around her shoulders. Mary sniffled once and Nan had to put her hand to her trembling lips and Beverley and Nita had their arms around each other.

The burial service was quick. Several people threw sand on the casket. Glad everything was over, Gwen turned and headed back across the lawn. She looked at a hedge of cypresses with spans of lemon-tinged needles fringed like doilies. They fronted the cemetery fence and sounds of small birds were coming from them. A couple of crows strutted between the plaques searching among debris left by mourners. Nothing seemed related, a bunch of objects, things moving among other things. Her mother had taken reality with her. The further she got from the graveside, the quicker she walked. She would wander forever. She heard somebody running, turned and saw Madeline, hair a silk banner in the wind.

"I can't stand her. I wish there was a mother exchange."

Gwen laughed. She couldn't see through her tears.

Madeline flicked hair away from her face when she stopped running.

"Where were you going?"

"Forever."

"Why?"

"My mom's there."

"You have to wait."

"I know."

They heard shouting as a pink blur rushed up to them. Mary caught her breath as she gasped out her words.

"What are you doing? Everybody's leaving for the reception. Your father's waiting at the car, Gwen. Really, Madeline."

"Yes, I am."

"What?"

"I'm really Madeline."

"Oh, come on."

The reception was held at Nan's half-timbered Tudor-style house in a middle-class neighbourhood in the west end. Bought eight years ago, it had been renovated. Walls had been removed to make an extended dining room, renamed the banqueting hall. The house had been loaded with medieval paraphernalia. Ron's handiwork was everywhere. Shields emblazoned with heraldic arms hung on downstairs walls and suits of armour lined the entrance hall and even upstairs hallways. Wrought iron worked into candlesticks decorated tables, and chandeliers of chains and hoops with welded candle sockets hung from most ceilings. Pictures of knights saving Pre-Raphaelite damsels filled stairway and bedroom walls. Costume parties featured medieval themes, "thees" and "thous" studding the speech of the hosts. Nan's small breasts in the cleavage of her doubleknit gown tried at buxom maidenhood. Milord and milady and their honoured guests feasted from trenchers heaped with joints of boar or ox roasted on a spit. Homebrewed ale and claret served as libations on these occasions. Ron had even made broadswords once and staged a series of fights. But a drunken guest was cut for several stitches by his enraged wife, who insisted on being his opponent despite Ron's objection ladies never fought with broadswords.

"Knights are supposed to be faithful to their ladies," she roared. "He was fooling around in a bedroom and I caught him. I demand satisfaction. Get out of the way." After wounding her husband on the forearm, she had cried. Both said they were sorry, which brought tears or grins from the other guests. Nan put a tourniquet on the slash. One of the less inebriated guests managed to drive the husband to the emergency ward.

On this day there were several tables of food on the back lawn and one of drinks. Mourners broke into groups. The mood was low-key, like a party after something embarrassing has happened. Nan came over to Roger as soon as she could.

"I haven't had a chance to speak to you, Roger. How's Gwen doing?"

"Pretty well."

"That's good. How about you?"

"Managing."

"Terrible, wasn't it? Was it a mugging?"

"No."

"Oh, something else? Anything to do with narcotics? Did Carol get in the way of a drug deal gone bad? Not an attempted rape? A pervert? Homicidal maniac? Not a cult, was it?"

"I really don't know that much, Nan. I should see how Gwen is doing."

"Why don't you while I see to some of the other guests. I'll talk to you later."

Roger searched for Gwen, saw her and Madeline talking with Ron. They were standing below a metal shield emblazoned with a coat of arms and hanging over the fireplace in the banqueting hall. A silver stripe ran diagonally from upper left to lower right across the shield. Left of the stripe and against maroon a silver gauntlet held a raised silver broadsword. To the right against maroon and in silver a crescent moon hung over a stag.

"On a field gules a stag argent couchant regardant," Ron said as Roger was heading for them. "That's heraldry. I had this researched by a genealogist. Traced my lineage way back to the fourteenth century, to John Bryde, Lord Newbury. One of his sons, the Black Percy, went to Ireland later and founded the Brydes of Armagh. Built a fabulous castle. I'm also related to Henri Rougemont, the fourth Duc d'Orleans, through a common ancestor."

"If your ancestor was common he couldn't be related to the Duc," Madeline said, trying her best not to smile but conceding a slight grin.

"Was it the old or the new Orleans?" Gwen said.

"Unbelievers, huh?"

"Here's another one," Roger said, joining them.

Roger had barely managed to conceal his contempt for what he saw as his in-laws' aping of medieval life and customs. This had irked Ron. And now the girls were treating him as a lowly body and fender man with aristocratic pretensions. Carol's funeral reception was not the right place to pick a fight. But he had been drinking. His face was flushed, chin lifted, and he had clasped his hands behind him. Much shorter than Roger, Ron stretched himself to his full height.

"Gwen doesn't know much history."

"She knows truth from fiction."

"You think ancestors are a joke. What's wrong with wanting to know who you're related to?"

"It doesn't interest me at all."

"You think all this here, all we've done, is nothing but a big laugh. We're a couple of clowns. Right? Right?"

Ron's voice had steadily risen. Even on tiptoe, he had to look up at the large man facing him. He wanted to punch him, gripped his hands tighter behind his back to keep from smashing that slimy grin into a mouthful of loose and bloody teeth. Without knowing why, he began speaking about his coat of arms in a by now bellowing voice. As he shouted, guests came from other parts of the house. Those in the garden could hear and hurried to the banqueting hall. They stood inside or crowded near the entrances.

"I had this goddam thing reproduced from the original in a castle in Ireland. Dates from the late fucking fifteenth century, when William, second

Baron Bryde, later Viscount Gough and after Earl of Marchers, captured the cocksucking castle from the Irish. He chose the gauntlet and broadsword to show his power. The stag and crescent show his love of hunting, even at night. He fought the Irish into the sixteenth century, until he controlled all of Armagh. People shit themselves when they saw his arms. They meant death to enemies. No mercy since Percy. Hacked their heads off with that broadsword. Punched their fucking skulls in with that gauntlet. Not a man in Armagh didn't clutch his balls when he heard the name Bryde."

"Some brides can make you do that," Roger said under his breath.

Ron O'Bridey turned and faced the gathering. He jabbed a forefinger into his chest.

"I got the papers. Documents. Researched. Paid for. That I'm an Armagh Bryde."

"A mail-order bride," Roger said out loud.

Nan elbowed her way past some onlookers and grabbed her husband by the arm. Face as red as a pepper, she spoke with jaws rigid.

"Too much to drink. Come on."

She pulled him into the entrance hall and towards the staircase. Stiff-legged and tottering, he went. She gave him a push in the back. He grabbed at the railing and missed the first time. She watched for a few moments as he yanked himself upstairs to the rhythm of his muttering.

"Noble blood. Crusaders and conquerors. You peasants. Wouldn't know the peerage from horse piss."

On the second floor landing he glared down at those who remained despite Nan's attempt to shoo everybody into the garden.

"Fucking bastards. I'm not you. Below the salt. I got ancestors. Aristocracy. Fucking breeding. The crème de la crème. 'Knowledge lor lawful liege lord. Grovel, you turds."

Nan rushed up the stairs. Ron put a leg over the railing, his hand on it slipped and he fell. Twisting sideways, he landed on his back. The damage to nerves and vertebrae made him an instant paraplegic, his spinal column out of reach of his wife's professional skill. She went into shock. From bad luck, according to Roger. "Too bad he didn't land on his head, at least," he said to

Mary. "She might have fixed that bone." Mary thought this unkind. They were a devoted couple.

A couple of days later Kendra phoned Gwen, said she was sorry to hear about her mother. Gwen invited her over. They sat in the living room. Madeline had gone home that morning. She would be returning the next evening.

"Maddy and I won't be doing any more pig vigils or demonstrations. Or going to animal right conferences. We're involved in something big. It got my mother killed. It's got to do with kids. Baby girls. They can't speak for themselves. Like the animals. This has to be first. It's more important."

"I understand. You guys will always be welcome back. Know what I think? What you and Maddy are doing and what Innis and I are doing are connected. Respecting animals, giving them their own lives, is part of living together with everyone and everything else in a peaceful world. If we keep going the way we are, we're not going to be here very much longer. Loving animals is giving love back to the world that created us. If we don't try to live with that world, we lose contact with it and don't realize we're killing ourselves as we kill it. I wonder about business guys, greedy-eyed and blind to everything except getting a buck, a fuck, a feed and a high. They're afraid of love and try to love money instead. Some women do this. Like stocks are sexy and the big dream is to snag yourself a sugar daddy. We have to look at things differently or we're not going to save the planet. It's got to be share or get nothing."

"Maddy and I vowed never to eat meat or fish again. We'll stick to that. But sometimes we get thoughts about certain foods. Butter and cream cheese, and maybe an omelette. Not from factory farms. Dairies where the cows are grass-fed and calves aren't taken away from the mother. And eggs from pastured hens fed organic grains. We feel guilty about it."

"I hear you. Innis and I are prepared to sacrifice our health to save animals. We know there's a chance we're not getting the absolute best nutrition. A chance. We're willing to take it but we wouldn't expect you to do the same. Listen to your bodies and if you need that food, eat it. You can be vegan again. If cultured meat is doable, we're all off the hook."

"What's happened to Dr. Todd?"

"He's toxic. Over half of his subscribers have unsubscribed. If this keeps up, he'll have nobody. The company planning to put out his line of vegan supplements has pulled out. He tried to speak last week at the animal rights conference and was booed off the stage. All the vegan You Tubers, and even the carnists, have been attacking or making fun of him. He's 'Todd the Fraud.' The woman he was with is being sued for divorce. You guys rocked. One, two, bam. By the way, a lot of guys are saying how great you and Maddy were and how hot you two look."

Gwen's face turned pale pink. Kendra smiled.

"We have a sanctuary for abused and rescued animals. Volunteers look after them when we're not around. You and Maddy should visit. Be prepared to have your hearts stolen. Every time we come home they energize us.

"We decided a few years ago not to have children. It wasn't easy and wasn't because of overpopulation, though that would've been a good excuse. We decided the animals would be our family. When we found out how many are abused, how many are injured by cars and pollution, we started our own sanctuary. We take in those rescued from the crimes committed by factory farming. We knew we'd have to sacrifice some of the time we spend on vegan activism, but we couldn't say no to so many helpless creatures. There's so many we've taken in during the two years we've had the shelter. Rescued pigs and chickens and turkeys, a lame duck, an owl with one wing, a goose that turned up one day, a heifer and more. They all get along. There's so much love you can feel it. No, it's not only gratitude because we feed and shelter them, it's goddam love, the real thing. People who visit say they've never felt anything like it. Visitors have been generous but we're always in need of funds. There's more satisfaction in a donation than people will ever get from buying a lotto ticket, a carton of cigarettes or a case of beer. You don't need a lot to get by in this life, but you need love. And I don't care how lame that sounds, it's true. Sometimes we feel we're wasting time, people won't change, they'll always want to destroy animals, that destroying things is too much a part of us to change. We know it's not going to happen overnight, if it's going to happen at all. So it's a gamble and we're gambling on hope, that our lotto ticket has the winning number. But no matter what happens, we know we will have done the right thing. You can't look into the eyes of any animal we've welcomed and not see that. If you're going to spend your life trying to do what seems impossible sometimes, the best reason is that you did it for love."

Gwen went into her bedroom and returned with a ten dollar bill.

"Here, take this. Say it's from my mom."

A few days after Carol's funeral Roger phoned Speaker and arranged to meet with him, this time accompanied at her own insistence by Gwen. They met in the main library again. Already seated, Speaker had been reading. He put aside his book and smiled up at Gwen, avoided what would be pointless condolences now. She sat beside her father on the other side of the table. Her father seated himself heavily, and she could see that he and Speaker weren't compatible. She wanted to sit on the other side. She didn't know why. Her father began gruffly, voice stiff. She had never heard him speak this way. Speaker looked at him as if he expected what he was getting.

"I asked around concerning the matter we discussed. He's never been linked to any scandal. He's chairman of more charities than anybody else in the city. Gets awards. Father of the year. Man with the biggest heart. I couldn't find anybody with anything bad to say about him. Except that maybe he rides this pedophile thing too hard. But I think like the others I spoke to that he does this for circulation and ratings. It's not personal."

"What about the notebooks and flash drive?"

"There's no link to him. I showed the notebook to a television journalist, a good newsman. Said it's a bunch of names and numbers. Could be people who all donate to the same charity. From what I told him about the other, he said without the guy's name it's not damaging. You'd have to prove the notebooks belong together and the initials and comments are his. And you'd have to do a lot of digging around the continent and the world and put everything together and connect it up with him. The journalist said he's never heard a whisper of scandal about him."

"Two people have been murdered."

"The murders could be unrelated. Lots of things happen in parks now. My wife shouldn't have gone there. Not without some kind of protection."

"The tramp who stole the notebooks was almost killed before and after he told me about them. He was almost killed again when he tried to blackmail the owner. Why would anybody bother murdering a tramp? If the notebooks are as inconsequential as you now believe?"

"Look," Roger said, putting his hands on the table, palms down, "I never told you I believed the notebooks proved anything. I was willing to dig around and see if there was anything against this guy. I haven't found anything. That's all."

Speaker stared across the table before shaking his head slightly.

"Give me the notebook."

"What are you going to do with it?"

"Why do you care? You're not involved."

"Gwen will be if you go on with this, and I have to think about her safety."

"She's your daughter, look after her. I have to think about some other people."

"Give him the notebook, Dad."

"Only if you say you won't get involved."

"I won't."

"I suppose I can trust you this time."

Surprised at the bitterness in his voice, Gwen felt the words like a stab in the belly. Face flushed, she felt hot to the roots of her hair. She stared down at the table, sick to her stomach. Speaker could see Roger Chalmers was trying to make Gwen feel guilty about her mother's death, that his concern for her safety hid something else.

"You all right, Gwen?"

She nodded. If she said one word, she would vomit. Her father was a bulky mass beside her, a burden she wished she didn't have. She knew now why she wanted to sit on the other side of the table. Her father came to get rid of Speaker, not discuss the notebooks. This had something to do with her but it wasn't protection. She was protecting him from the realization of his own inadequacy. He coddled her because he didn't want her to grow up. He was jealous of Speaker. His concern for her safety was an excuse to keep her away from Speaker. He was no different from Mary Dalrymple. She used her worry about Madeline to bind her to her, substituting her for the missing parent. Gwen understood now that she had always been a child-wife to her father, a safely idealized, playpen version of her mother. Trapped into a falsity and feeling a sudden panic, she wondered if there could be something else that would eventually show itself and shock her. That would be impossible. Her father was too normal, too ordinary. Yet his attitude towards Speaker was new to her, strange in its seemingly misplaced intensity. He was deliberately sacrificing the investigation to eliminate Speaker as a rival. She tried to push that thought away but it loomed black and obstinate in its gathering force. How could this massive man be so petty and childish to protect his fantasy? She saw his adoration, bumbling and stiff, as an embrace smothering her against his huge chest and keeping her from seeing, what? Gwen wouldn't look at her father, stared straight ahead at a shelf of books. She concentrated on the widths and colours of the spines, the fonts of the titles. She could feel her father looking and almost sense his embarrassment. Good, be ashamed about Mom.

Roger took the notebook out of his coat pocket and tossed it on the table. He stood up and walked with slow steps towards the elevator, black coat like a cloak over his buffalo shoulders. Gwen looked at Speaker, who was picking up the notebook. She grinned, Speaker frowned.

"You promised."

She kept grinning. He couldn't be that stupid.

"I've got enough trouble. Your father will get mad and he'll have a right to."

Gwen glanced at her father waiting by the elevator, his back still to them. She stood up.

"I'll phone you. Madeline and I have a few ideas."

"Help is what's needed."

"We know that."

Hands in her jacket pockets, Gwen strolled over to her father. He pressed the elevator button. She raised herself up onto her toes a couple of times. She thought about her mother. Something would be done. And she raised herself several more times before thinking that in her mother's memory she should be a little less showy. They didn't talk as they left the library.

In the street the noise of cars and people made Gwen feel nobody cared. She wanted passers-by to help find her mother's killer and rescue girls from pedophiles. What were people doing walking or driving who knows where instead of helping her? Why did people ignore the troubles of others? They waited for the light to change at the crowded intersection. Jumbled conversations of strangers. Where was everybody going? Everything was so quick. Even helping others was fast and loud. Ambulance sirens, charity drives, campaigns to feed the hungry overseas or here, crusades against whatever you didn't like, newspaper headlines, television news. Cities were getting bigger. These crowds of strangers lied and cheated, robbed and murdered. And who was responsible? Good and bad, like people, were becoming anonymous.

The light changed and they made their way through the jammed crosswalk. Heads bobbed and swayed, disappeared and reappeared in the current. In one moment this flowing anonymity changed. Gwen thought she saw the head of the tall man. She was afraid, even among all those around, perhaps because of them, their mindless purpose promising nothing but a speedy departure. She looked in that direction again but didn't see him. She didn't say anything. When they reached the other side she peered into the late afternoon crowd surrounding her. Intent faces poured past her, a slow-moving obstacle in the way. A red-faced man rubbed his beefy suited body against her as he shoved past, his briefcase bumping the back of her knee. Her father was a few paces ahead of her and she hurried to catch up. They were headed for a parking lot two blocks away. She kept glancing around. Soon the crowd wasn't a hiding place, became again a placid surfacing of heads. At the car they began talking, her father first, in an obvious attempt to re-establish their usual easy way with each other.

"What's Madeline doing today?" he asked as he got behind the wheel.

"She's with her mother," Gwen said as she sat beside him. "Be over at seven."

She was relieved her father wanted to forget what happened. Too tense for a prolonged coolness between them, she needed to concentrate on helping

Speaker. Her father knew she was going to break her word. He had to trust her and hope she wasn't going to do anything dangerous. Her silence in the library had silenced him. She was turning out to be the daughter he pretended he wanted. She scowled thinking of the schoolwork she had to do. It seemed so trivial. A waste of time. On their way to the apartment, she kept her eyes on the side view mirror.

Chapter 19

That night, as they sat cross-legged and facing each other on the floor in Gwen's bedroom, Madeline told her about Sarah Edelbacher.

"Mom knows her. She belongs to Ever For Children, and Sarah Edelbacher is the head of it. We met her at a meeting. Today Mom was getting tingly feverish about the next one."

"What's she like?"

"She sort of looks like a nun. Importantly spiritual. With religious eyes. As if she's waiting for God to show up and tell her what to do."

"She works for Cobbie Kind."

"She's always speaking for children."

"He says he's for children."

"She wouldn't put up with anybody who would hurt them. You can see when she talks about it."

"Speaker has the notebooks. She'll have to see them. We'll tell him about her. Then we'll phone her."

"She's going to think we're crazy."

"We'll go see her."

"I'll tell my mom we want to go to the next meeting and she'll get the tickets."

"We'll talk to Sarah Edelbacher. Tell her that we've got something about girls being victims. Make an appointment to see her. She's probably got an office. We'll show her the notebooks."

"Yeah. Oh, puke on it. My mom will go frazzles when she hears. She'll think I've been molested."

"Tell her you haven't been."

"She won't believe me. You don't know her."

"Got it. After we're introduced, you take your mom somewhere."

"I'll lock her in the washroom."

"Find out when the next meeting is."

"Easy. My mom knows the dates of all their stuff by heart."

Sarah Edelbacher lay naked on the bed, head on a folded pillow and her husband sleeping with his back to her. She had thrown the covers off and in shaded light from a table lamp was looking along the length of her body at the flat pouches of her breasts, the taut skin indenting her ribs. The jut of pelvic bone around her belly, the thin shanks narrowing into almost calfless legs, the slabs of feet. Dinosaur claws, schoolgirl friends had called them. She achieved a measure of respect by leading the high school volleyball team two years in a row to the championship. But the kidding hurt. Skyliner had been her nickname to her face, but she found out that behind her back she was known as Corpse. Well over six feet without shoes on and always skinny despite occasional binging, she had been awkward and shy throughout high school. Dates had been disasters. Only after joining the Christian Fellowship in her penultimate year did Sarah Edelbacher find the answer to a question she didn't know she had been asking herself. At university and the theological seminary she was a consummate organizer. Academically she had been brilliant, becoming a doctor of divinity with ease. After three years of missionary work in Madagascar she had begun her university teaching career. She was now at forty-one a full professor at Pacific Christian. Married for eleven years, she met her husband in Africa. Norman Mackinson was a pediatrician who had been there for more than half a decade fighting malnutrition and various childhood diseases. They met when she on her own initiative organized a joint project to supply water pumps to the villages in her area. His international relief agency and her church-sponsored one fell in love. They were married six weeks later and returned within a year from overseas to an academic career and a pediatric practice. Her surname sometimes caused confusion. She had joined her husband's name to hers when she married. But the hyphenated surname was so cumbersome that she eventually retained it only in legal matters and used her maiden name otherwise and he had not minded.

The marriage had been conventionally happy except for the lack of children. Early miscarriages saddened the couple but they kept trying to conceive. Adoption had been postponed in case of success. As a last resort Sarah Edelbacher enrolled in a fertility program at another university a year ago. She was fatalistic now, ready to adopt to fulfil her love for children. What's the difference? she told herself. Everyone's child is everyone else's. All children are a miracle. This would be a chance to show love for God through love of them. But her biology made her want to keep trying a little longer. In bloodsong and bone marrow the special loneliness of the barren woman ached in her. It wasn't failure the way a man can fail at something, because he isn't any good at it or simply has bad luck. It was a lack that had no reason except arcane biological ones that seemed petty and meaningless. Some women had trouble not conceiving, used pills and abortion clinics. Such natural fecundity seemed wasted on those that didn't even want it. In a battle between frustration and faith she began to think God had a purpose for her, that He was saving her for some reason. She suspected it had something to do with children. In moments of self-criticism she told herself this was a selfish wish on her part and had nothing to do with Him. But at other times she was almost certain it had. She began to work for children's charities and to become involved in anti-pornography campaigns, focusing on the victimization of the young. And when Cobbie Kind founded Ever For Children she had joined immediately. Offered the presidency, she had gladly accepted it. What was more fitting in His eyes than helping victimized children? It was a saint's work. Not that she was a saint, she was careful to add. But she would do her best. Her work had been in the main satisfying, but she felt lately that she was not succeeding. There seemed too many speaking engagements and television appearances, too many articles and fund-raising dinners. The children appeared to have been forgotten. She had begun to feel guilty about this. There had been accusations that Cobbie Kind was using EFC to counteract the image of him as a vampire who sucked the intellectual and moral blood out of print and broadcast media and left them drones that mocked all truth and honest reason. Such criticism never appeared in Kind's media, of course, and she didn't believe it. The first time she met them she believed the Kinds were sincere and generous, giving their full support to helpless children. He never refused her money or airtime. No matter what she said in speeches or articles he supported her. But when he stood close to her on the back lawn or at parties, she sensed his eyes staring at her body. She had gotten to the point of not wanting to visit the house, but told herself she was overreacting, that her imagination was agitated because of overwork. This unreasonable dread would have to be overcome. He had never gone beyond this scrutiny. But no matter how she calmed herself beforehand, Sarah Edelbacher felt uneasy during these encounters and had to face the truth. Only the man knew.

He must know what he's doing. Suppose he touches me? Suppose I'm alone? Never been able to look into his eyes. He's not like most men. How would I know? Only known Norman. I'm sure he's different. Wissie would know. But she's so adoring she would excuse anything in him. Maybe he's overactive? Wissie can't. I haven't heard. Those hands. He's big, I'm sure. Wouldn't, no. His type. On top like an ape. Suffocating. A club. A bottle of buttermilk. Slobbering out. Better sleep. Look at my legs. Hair down there. A toilet brush. Knees and elbows, that's what I am. Sharp edges. No child could live in there. Learn to die twice. God's punishment. What did I do? Bleed every month, twelve times a year. I'm wounded between my legs. Down there is all life. Warm eggs. One down. Blink. Science will save me. No, God. God knows, Norman doesn't. None of the Normans. If it's God's purpose, we'll do it. Cold. Cover. Warm me. Turn and know me.

Waiting through the darkness. Hours an if of sleep. Headlights churning, cups of coffee clinking through it. Time left in the sorrow of morning, a gathering fog at daybreak, the decades of buildings, worn staircases climbing up more slowly than the hands of dawn. The early do not know the late, their length of time. Hours of need, cold sips. Shivering in damp clothes in a dark alley at midnight.

"Why are you so interested? I've had to drag you there the few times you've gone."

Mary was speaking next morning over the phone to Madeline, who was using her most persuasive voice.

"We want to help. Might make it a school project."

"This isn't a joke?"

"I wouldn't joke about that."

"I guess you wouldn't."

"When can we go? This week?"

"The next meeting is a week from this coming Monday."

"That long?"

"Why are you so eager? Are you telling me everything?"

"Do you think we've got time to waste?"

"I guess not, if Gwen is involved."

"Thanks."

"You've disappointed me before."

"Let's not talk about that."

"Well, when you want a favour that sounds so odd coming from you, I've got to wonder. You fell asleep in your seat last time. I'll get a few things together for you to read. Last few issues of the newsletter. If you promise to look at them when you get back, I'll get some tickets for the program this Sunday. She's going to be on this one. That should hold you until the meeting."

"I forgot about the program. Thanks, Mom."

"How long are you staying there?"

"Not much longer."

"I miss you."

"You've got relatives staying."

"It's not the same. You're my daughter."

"I know."

"Don't be sarcastic. I can withdraw the favour."

"Bye."

Gwen phoned Speaker and told him about Sarah Edelbacher and the plan.

"How free an agent can she be, employed by Cobbie Kind? You don't know her."

"Madeline has good feelings about her."

"If she goes to him, you're trapped. And that's not a feeling."

"Madeline's good at this."

"I'm supposed to trust in that?"

"You can trust my feeling that you're not going to come up with anything better. Come with us."

"I'll give you one of the notebooks to show her."

"You trust me as much as you trusted my father."

"I don't trust the situation. I've got to keep something in reserve. If she's interested, we can all meet. I don't think she will be."

"The program is this Sunday."

"You'd better pick up the notebook here. If I brought it over, I might lead someone to you. Phone a day ahead, so we'll be ready. Take care of yourselves."

Later they were lying on the floor of Gwen's bedroom and staring up at the ceiling and Madeline finally broke the silence.

"You know, Gwenner, I've asked myself about him."

"Um."

"I like him. Even though we argue. Maybe because we do. He treats me like an adult. Sometimes I think it's more."

"Um."

"I don't know if it's because I don't have a father like yours, full time. Or it could be, you know."

"Um."

"There's nothing to be ashamed of if I were, you know. It's natural. Juliet was close to my age when she met Romeo. And he's not so old. I don't see any bald spots or grey. But I don't feel like I'm supposed to. It's all confused. I'll go ahead and say I'm not ashamed of liking him. I've been over the side about guys. At least two. But he's like a bunch of guys together and I can't figure out which one he is.

"What I'm saying is there are different kinds of liking and he's a new kind for me. It's not the bursting heart kind. I won't even die if I never see him again. Sometimes he's monkey-on-a-chain. I'm reaching for peanuts."

"Um."

"What can I say that won't sound stupid? It's the situation, too. Al's place, the fire, and Sylvia. Great, isn't she? I've become part of a story, complete with a monster. Wish I were like you. Supremely mistress."

"Um."

"You are the moon goddess. Huntress. But you haven't met your Endymion. You'll survive when you do. Have him on a string. I'm not a goddess. More like a wood or water nymph. Wood, I think. I'm not a good swimmer. I'm among the trees. Naked except for silky leaves stuck to certain parts and rosebuds in my hair. I like to frolic. I like that word. The wind caresses every inch of my body. Blows it clean and sweet. I walk with bare feet into the clear stream and feel the coolness flow between my toes. I'm shy except with animals, especially squirrels. They eat nuts out of my hand. I've already cracked the shells and thrown them away, so the squirrels are particularly grateful. They bring me messages about what's going on in the forest. And one day they tell me there's someone coming towards me. I'm frightened and wait, hiding behind a tree. I see somebody trying to find his way out of the forest. He doesn't even know about me yet. He won't hurt me. Somehow I'm sure. So I come out from behind the tree and offer to help. He's glad, it's different from the animals. I can see in his eyes I'm a special guide. And he's new to me. We're together until we get to the edge of the woods. Then we'll part. I know that. I'll be glad he's out of trouble. And sad I won't ever see him again. We'll each have a memory. It'll hurt in a way that never ends. Thanks, Gwenner. You'll say what you think, no matter what. That's why I like talking to you. I don't have to work it all out by myself."

"Um."

The EFC program was televised Sunday mornings at eleven o'clock on Kind's station and carried simultaneously by all the affiliates along his network. It was an hour of interviews, videos, talks and fundraising. It reflected the organization's announced purpose of promoting children's welfare, together with an ostensible and not less important corollary intention of eradicating child abuse. A studio audience of two hundred, most of them organization members, provided vocal support. When in town Sarah Edelbacher co-hosted, giving a talk and interviewing the special guest. The programming and time slot emphasized the strong religious slant. Potential guests were screened for their religious and political views. Unorthodox opinions guaranteed rejection. Sarah Edelbacher set the tone, earnest and unrelenting. The Christian faith through its churches was the best instrument for remedying child abuse. Faith in God meant one couldn't harm children. And the way to salvation led away from this sin. She wasn't fanatical or ignorant. She knew about modern psychology and rejected it as dealing with part of the person. It didn't treat men's souls, the only way they could be cured of pedophilia.

The program had quickly established itself as a ratings success, due in large part to the loyalty of EFC members to Sarah Edelbacher. She had become the embodiment of the organization after assuming the presidency. Her program appearances in the six years since its debut had made her one of the most recognizable women in North America. There were news stories about her and interviews on Kind's network. The mainstream media reported some of her speeches. Millions who had never seen the program recognized that lanky figure and those deep blue eyes in an otherwise sedately composed face. Tickets weren't easy to get for non-members, but Mary was a founding member and a lot of her friends belonged to EFC. A generous donor, praised by zealots and tolerated by moderates, she made a phone call and the two extra tickets immediately became available for the next program.

The program was simply called Ever For Children, to remind viewers of the link to Kind's organization. It was recorded at nine, two hours before it aired. On Sunday mornings a churchlike atmosphere pervaded the almost deserted station, especially in front of the studio. Woman invariably made up at least eighty per cent of the audience. The men were mostly husbands and noted for their meek behaviour and pain-anticipating faces, as if someone were waiting on the other side of those big studio doors with a long and very dull needle to probe their psyches and draw out secret guilty substances. Dress was conservative: muted colours and conventional styles for woman and dark suits for men. But the chatter in the hallway before the program was gossipy, with that restrained, eye-probing eagerness of churchgoers before they enter the sacred precincts. Gwen and Madeline watched her mother engage immediately on their arrival outside the studio. She and several friends made a circle like a flock of ducks bobbing for bread crumbs cast on the serene waters of their Sunday spirituality. "God," Madeline said, "look at my mom." They looked for Sarah Edelbacher. When the studio doors opened and the crowd began to file in they saw her. Microphone in her ear and standing near a camera at the side of the set, she was flipping hurriedly through some pages of background material. The audience dutifully found their places among the rising tiers of seats. Mary led the girls to seats in the second row, slightly right of centre, her favourite spot.

"You can see everything from here," she whispered as she leaned towards the girls. Madeline was seated between her mother and Gwen.

"It hasn't started yet," Madeline said. "You don't have to whisper."

"You know, Madeline. . . ."

But Madeline had turned to Gwen and they were talking about Sarah Edelbacher, who had given the pages to an assistant. She was chatting with members of the audience.

"Look at her eyes," Madeline said. "Blue Sarahphires."

"An ancient gaze," Gwen said.

"Abbess of the Skies." Madeline waved her arms, skimming the top of Mary's head.

"Mother Superior of the Cosmic Storm of Justice," Gwen added, though she knew Madeline was better at this.

"What are you girls talking about?" Mary said in a louder whisper.

People on the set began to move into position like pieces on a chessboard. The audience was hearing over the public address system how close it was getting to show time and slowly became quiet. The lights darkened around them and the set appeared much brighter. Lisa Dunstable, the co-host, stood in a circle of light. Behind her were softly lit enlargements of children of various races and ethnic groups. With an attitude carefully calculated between cordiality and concern and appropriately tailored in muted grey and reduced in jewellery to pearl earrings and a gold wedding band, she read from a teleprompter, speaking about the contents of that morning's program. She said the focus would be on the plight of runaways in large cities, particularly young girls who had become prostitutes. The special guest, Susan Belding, ran a shelter for runaways in the skid row area and had brought two girls who were currently living there. Lisa Dunstable said that, before their appearance, she would be interviewing social workers on the problems of runaway girls in skid row. The set became dim and the audience could see on monitors suspended over their heads a promotional spot for funds to keep the program on the air. After the spot the lights went up. On the set were four chairs arranged on a dais. The co-host spoke with her guests for the next twenty minutes. After another promotional spot, called a "chance to help," the lights went up again. The chairs were occupied by Sarah Edelbacher in a steel grey suit and white blouse, Susan Belding and two unnamed fifteen-year-old girls.

"It's Cheryl," Madeline shouted.

Her voice carried to most of the audience. It was a verbal shock wave to Sarah Edelbacher and her guests. Motionless, Mary stared ahead as the next few seconds became a torture of embarrassment before the dozens of whispering faces turned away. Sarah Edelbacher waited a few moments for the murmuring to die down before beginning. Unconscious of causing any disturbance, Madeline turned to Gwen and spoke in a low voice.

"She's the one who ran away from school two years ago."

"Ssssh," Mary whispered sharply.

Gwen remembered a girl with braces on her teeth who had disappeared after school started that year. She stared, trying to recognize her. Both girls looked in their twenties, with lifeless eyes and limp hair. Skinny, they were pale despite make-up and wore jeans and simple tops. They kept their legs crossed throughout the interview. When one began to play with her fingers Gwen recognized her. They spoke impersonally, as if the facts were things to be mentioned on cue. Both had been molested, Cheryl by her father and the other girl by her stepfather. They had been warned not to tell anybody and made to feel what happened was their fault. Cheryl finally ran away. The other girl's mother threw her out when she told her. Susan Belding said most girls who came her way told similar stories. Middle-aged and tired-looking, she had grey hair. Shelter workers were volunteers, she said, included some professionals helping in their spare time, it was overcrowded, they received no government funding and donations kept them going. Sarah Edelbacher asked how she managed to cope.

"I believe in God's love, Sarah. God loves everyone, and when you accept His love you can get through anything."

The audience applauded spontaneously.

"May the spirit of the Lord be with you, Susan, and Ever For Children has pledged to help your shelter."

More applause.

Another break followed the interview. Afterwards, Lisa Dunstable appeared on camera against a background of enlarged photographs of children. But now their faces were brightly lit. She announced next week's program would be about the malnutrition of children in South America. The studio lights came on and Gwen and Madeline popped out of their seats. They made for the dais. Too far away from them to be heard except by shouting, Mary edged along the row of seated audience members, apologizing as she tried to catch up.

Sarah Edelbacher and her interviewees were standing beside their chairs. She was chatting with Susan Belding. Madeline stepped onto the dais and hurried over. "Hi, Cheryl." Cheryl turned and looked but didn't recognize her at first. The past returned with the old identity. Her face dropped some of its years and she smiled the smile of a girl. "Madeline?" They hugged. Gwen came over and said hi. The other girl was introduced as Michelle. They talked mostly about school. Sarah Edelbacher and Susan Belding continued their discussion of the problem of funding the shelter. When Mary arrived she was too embarrassed to say anything and returned to her seat.

This was their chance. Things hadn't worked out the way they planned but they did have an excuse to be there and Madeline's mother was out of the way. Sarah Edelbacher was assuring Susan Belding that the promise made on camera would be kept. She glanced around, looking for the program director, and saw the intensity in Gwen's eyes. It wasn't hero worship. Gwen didn't look the type. Sarah Edelbacher kept looking, trying to figure out what it was. Taking this as a cue, Gwen came over.

"May I see you about something?"

"Can't my staff take care of it?"

"It's really important."

"I'm very busy." She said this because it was customary and because she wanted to know how badly Gwen needed to talk with her.

"It's urgent. You'll know why when I tell you."

She gave in to get away from her guest, and fans who gathered after every program to speak the praises and offer the adoration she never wanted. Invariably, some of the girls who came up from the audience afterwards wore tops with the slogan, "I'm an Edel Backer."

"I can give you five minutes."

"That'd be great." Gwen felt her face flush, hoped she didn't look too silly.

"Bye, Sue." Sarah Edelbacher held out her hand.

"Come on," she said to Gwen, grinning, tossing the entire length of her dark hair.

Gwen followed her off the dais, aware that dozens of people were watching them. Madeline raised her hand slightly as they passed. Proud, Gwen forgot she hadn't said a word yet about the notebook. She could barely keep up as Sarah Edelbacher, holding a sheaf of papers, loped in stiff-legged strides down a long corridor behind the set. Bypassing the elevator, she climbed the stairway. She took it two steps at a time to the third floor and held open the stairway door. Gwen was out of breath when she got there, gasped out a thank you. On both sides of the hallway glass-panelled doors with lettering on them led to suites of offices. A door was partly open and people were talking. A telephone began ringing. Somebody told a joke about somebody named Terence and several people laughed. Sarah Edelbacher lunged down the hallway to a door at the end and took out a ring with a bunch of keys attached to it. Her long fingers chose a key quickly, slipped it into the keyhole and flicked it in one motion to unlock the door. Gwen, who had hurried after her, saw no nail polish and only a wedding band.

The outer office was the usual collection of grey metal filing cabinets and black and chrome metal desk with computer and photographs of loved ones as potted plants draped their spotted fronds and tufts of swordshaped or ferny leaves on the windowsill and cabinets and desktop, some secretary's ecosmart idea of business aesthetics and filtering the air-conditioned air. In four strides Sarah Edelbacher was through it and the doorway to her inner office. She threw her papers on her desk and an invitation behind her. Gwen was off balance. It was the pace. More than on the set, here she felt that she was in another world. What she had to say and show began to seem irrelevant. Everything was speeding by too fast for a fair hearing. This was Cobbie Kind's world, where he could hide among the people he hired. Weren't they paid to believe him? Who would believe her? The inner office had the same look as the other but was larger and three of the walls were lined with bookshelves. As she sat waiting in one of the black vinyl chairs and the tall woman sat behind her desk and went through some of the papers she brought with her, Gwen noticed there was a shelf of books dealing with obstetrics. She wondered what they had to do with the program. Sarah Edelbacher dropped the papers on the desk and looked at her.

"Well?"

Gwen's mouth was dry, her stomach queasy. Her nerves were short-circuiting like pinwheel fireworks. She couldn't feel where her feet were. She checked by tapping her sneakers on the floor before looking across the desk. Sarah Edelbacher's eyes were wide and quietly waiting. Gwen saw something in them that made her wonder why she had ever hesitated. She didn't know what it was but she knew she had this woman.

"A tramp saw somebody kill a little girl. The killer is an important guy. This tramp stole two notebooks, a flash drive and other stuff from the guy. One notebook has a list of men who have sex with girls. The other has a list of men who can get girls for them, and the flash drive has a coded worldwide network of pedophiles. The guy's initials and phone number are in the notebooks. I've got one with me."

"I'll ask the obvious question. What is your name, by the way?"

"Gwen."

"Why bring it to me, Gwen?"

"You know the guy."

Sarah Edelbacher raised her eyebrows, figured that it must be somebody she barely knew at the university or in EFC.

"What makes you think that?"

Gwen's eyes were wide open and waiting. And the longer she waited, the less assured Sarah Edelbacher was. She wasn't sure what to ask next. She became uneasy, as if this girl could destroy her. The power had shifted in the room. Both knew. She wouldn't let her mind focus, afraid if it did she would know something terrible. But she knew she couldn't escape. This had to happen. It was God's will. This girl's appearance wasn't an accident. Holding her voice steady, she blew the word out of her mouth.

"Who?"

"The man you work for."

A laugh escaped in two bursts of air. Sarah Edelbacher shook her head. She looked out of her office window at the view of the North Shore mountains. Drained to a flatness, their blue faded against the grey sky. They were big dry rocks at the end of summer.

Sarah Edelbacher looked back and what she planned to say left her. Gwen took the notebook out of her jacket pocket and held it out to her. She reached for the notebook. Gwen put it in her long palm. Reading each name as if it were his, when she saw the initials she couldn't see anything. The man was standing behind her on the lawn and staring. When she spoke, it seemed she couldn't help speaking for him.

"This doesn't prove he killed anybody."

"The tramp says he saw him do it."

"Who is he?"

"A homeless guy."

"Nobody would believe him."

"That's why I came to you."

"What do you want me to do?"

Gwen didn't answer.

"I can't believe he'd have sex with children," Sarah Edelbacher said and was sorry.

"I have to take it back to the man who has the other one. If you want to see it, you'll have to meet us."

"Who knows you came to see me?"

"My girlfriend, Madeline, who's here with me. And this guy with the other notebook."

"Why haven't you let adults handle this?"

"Because that man had my mother killed."

Gwen pursed her lips tightly together and blinked. One of the sudden floods of sadness that had been washing over her since her mother died was carrying her away. She stared at a corner of the desk. The casket, the wreaths of flowers, the cemetery, the long ride out and back, returned as desolation she had to bear. Sarah Edelbacher closed the notebook and watched her stare into the somewhere she had been. She felt an impulse to hug Gwen and a stronger one to lie to her to get her out of the office. She could do neither, gathered the papers on her desk.

Dear God, it's everywhere. Child victims. The survivors. Disease of the flesh and the soul. Creation destroyed in a parody of love. The little bodies played with, torn apart. Men too sick to love a woman. Jerking spasms into the forked and hairless innocence of tiny girls. Men groaning, sweating on top of babies and not hearing the screams. Maybe excited by them. Heaving, tearing and blood and semen and the fear making urine and feces and stink. Smears from the wound, cancer of desire. Reeking death. Dear God, forgive us.

Gwen was still staring at a corner of the desk when Sarah Edelbacher spoke.

"Would it be all right if I kept this for a while? I'll get it back to you."

"I'll have to ask the guy who has the other one," Gwen said, looking up.

"Could you reach him now?"

"Yes."

"I'll leave you alone. I'll be out there."

With a nod she indicated the outer office and stood up. She came around the side of her desk, touched the back of Gwen's chair, two strides and out, the door shut quietly.

"We can trust her," Gwen kept repeating into the phone to Speaker, who was hesitating.

"Suppose you know who or his paid help take it from her? You know she's going to him, don't you? That's why she wants it. Let her copy a few pages. Don't say any more than you have."

Sarah Edelbacher did the photocopying in an office down the hall. While waiting, Gwen saw a framed photograph on the desk. It had been taken in Africa at a conference on waterborne diseases. Sarah Edelbacher had been married two months. She and her husband were sitting at a rough wooden table covered with medical and scientific papers. In the background could be glimpsed other participants at other tables. She looked as if the African sun were in her eyes. But this was impossible because they were under a tent. It was her favourite picture. There were two copies at her apartment.

After Gwen left, Sarah Edelbacher stared at the mountains for a few minutes before phoning Wissie and asking to see her husband that evening.

"He's very busy, Sarah. I'll see if he can spare some time."

Wissie returned and said she would get ten minutes, her appointment beginning precisely at eight.

At five to eight Sarah Edelbacher drove up to the mansion in a dark green all-terrain vehicle. The front gates had been opened electronically after she called Wissie from her phone. The outside lights were on, as well as a light downstairs. When she shut off the engine she could hear the guard dogs barking but knew they were in a run at the back most of the time. Her strides took her briskly across the asphalt driveway and through the late summer evening. She swung her briefcase at her side. She felt comfortable carrying it, as some people like to wear a watch or lucky charm or carry keys in their hand. Her leather-soled shoes made slight scraping noises as she climbed the concrete stairs to the front door. Wissie had been waiting and opened it. The servants had the night off, she said. As usual, the careful smile and bland look were in place. Wissie knew this had nothing directly to do with her, at least so far. They spent some moments chatting before Wissie checked her watch. At one minute to eight she led the way to the study and tapped lightly twice on the ajar oak door. After waiting a few moments, Wissie pushed the handle and stood aside.

He was hunched forward in his red leather armchair behind his honey oak desk and reading reports. The only light in the room came from a reading lamp on the desk. The bookshelves and furniture were in shadow. Drapes covered the windows. The blinds on the French doors were closed. Sarah

Edelbacher stood and waited, heard the door shut behind her. The pink dome rose like a planet from the oak horizon. The thick lips were frowning. The eyes appeared blank. Cobbie Kind didn't like last-minute meetings unless he was the one who demanded them. He made sounds between a grunt and a clearing of his throat.

It was her cue to speak. She had talked to people who had dealt with Cobbie Kind when niceties were not being observed. He hadn't asked her to sit down. But that didn't matter. She was there to clear up something. The dim lighting bothered her but she tried to forget it. She was glad her voice was naturally low and steady.

"Cobbie, I've come about something that was brought to me today by someone I don't even know. It's quite serious so I thought I'd clear it up right away."

This time she detected in the guttural rush of air an interest that seemed to threaten her. She held on to her voice.

"It's hard to begin. This has to do with a notebook with a list of men's names in it. I've seen it and your initials are there. I understand there's another notebook. It supposedly has a list of suppliers of young girls. The accusation is that you are involved in a sex ring that exploits them. It all seemed so fantastic, of course, I. . . ."

She heard the leather squeak as he shifted in his chair. The bulk of him rose and she knew he would come close. She swung the briefcase in front and held it with both hands. He didn't come directly towards her. He went over to her right side and slightly behind. She turned to face him and he moved. She could either keep turning or look at empty air. She stopped. Peppermint-scented breath licked at her ear. She felt something blunt and thick prodding at her elbow. He wanted what his wife did. Brushing down along her jacket sleeve now towards her hand. She tensed. He took a hand away from her briefcase, she letting it fall to her side. Mind numbed. She wasn't doing this. Thumb gone and she heard a zipper and felt the swollen end, rubbery soft, of his erection pushed into her palm. Too late. She retched, her drawn lips burning. Pushing against her, making a meatus of her palm, he poked in a quickening rhythm. Peppermint blew at her in gusts. He began bumping her, thigh against thigh. Fingers under her skirt grabbed a cheek of her rump, pulling at her panties. And gone, babyfat tubeworms wriggled into her, squirming her open. His bulk a sugary stink, feet splayed out, he pushed her down towards the carpet. She was off balance, tilting. He spoke with the greedy voice of a spoiled child, a child jerking uncontrollably.

"Mommy."

She pulled herself free and pivoted, with both hands swinging the briefcase around in a heavy arc that almost took her off her feet. The briefcase crashed into flesh and bone. He slumped to the floor in the dimness. She ran, twisted the doorknob as if the door would be locked. It wasn't. She raced through the quiet house, left the front door open. The night air felt cold. Reaching her vehicle she stumbled and banged her knee against a fender. She turned the ignition key and prayed. The car careened down the driveway to the gates, breaking the electronic beam that automatically opened them. As they were slowly swinging open, she thought she was going to wet herself. Finally out and speeding along the empty road, she began to shake. Dear God. Oh, my dear God.

Chapter 20

"Don't eat it if you don't want to."

Sylvia had placed a dessert dish in front of Speaker and he was staring at it, trying to figure out what the square object on it was.

"I give up. What is it?"

"Don't you trust me enough to eat it before you find out?"

"I was asking out of curiosity, not fear."

"It's made from some of the stuff you brought me last week."

Warts came into the kitchen from the front parlour, where he had been dozing. He saw the square. Sylvia glanced at him and spaded out another piece from a rectangular Pyrex plate. She put it on the dessert dish she planned to use. She looked at him again and he sat down, warily deferential since their last conversation. She placed the dish and a fork in front of him. He chopped into the square and gobbled it.

"That was delicious, uh, Sylvia, yeah, sure was."

"Want another piece?" she asked with a bit of hauteur.

This was more for Speaker than Warts. Show him.

"Uh, sure, Sylvia."

Warts held out his dish for her to deposit another square. It went quickly, too. Speaker was grinning. With two fingers he picked up a fork and swung it like a metronome.

"I think I've figured out the difference between Europeans and us. It's confidence. We'll try anything. We expect it to be better. Even when it's not, we'll try again."

"You got that from my dessert?"

"The exquisite taste of reason."

"Raisins?" Warts said. "Thought I tasted them."

"What? That's my rutabaga lemon tomato fig onion square. I toast the figs first. Use lots of lemon rind."

Warts concealed his incipient dyspepsia behind a smile, his eyes a mute plea for mercy. The telephone rang in the front parlour and Al answered. He appeared in the hallway. Whenever possible, he avoided the kitchen. That was Sylvia's territory.

"The wimman wants ya, Speaker."

It was Gwen. She had given her name and phone number to Sarah Edelbacher. She had called a couple of minutes ago, at nine o'clock. Gwen's words tumbled out.

"She's scared. He did something gross. She didn't say what. She didn't get a chance to show the copies. She doesn't know what she's going to do. I told her I'd phone you. She gave me her number."

"Phone back, tell her about the hit man. Tell her to avoid public places. If she's going to help us, we should meet soon. Tomorrow if she can."

After calling her, Gwen phoned Speaker. The three would meet next morning at ten in Sarah Edelbacher's office at the university.

She hardly slept that night. She told her husband enough to alert but not alarm him. She was having doubts about Cobbie Kind and something might happen that would affect her relationship with EFC. Turning repeatedly beside her sleeping husband, she kept trying not to think about what happened or what any of it meant. His flagrant approach, his breath an insidious violation, his trespassing fingers stinking of power and domination and her hand used to stain her with his stunted psyche. The attempted rape, that sickening voice. And the word. The thought kept coming to her that she had always known. She had denied her instinct, made herself blind to his perversion. He was urge personified as infant, regressive and yet cunningly opportunistic, arrogant enough to call for drastic measures to punish his own kind, blatant in his contradictions, and powerfully secure ensconced in contemptuous success at the expense of public taste.

She fell asleep for two hours at dawn. She dreamt of a giant naked baby with a penis dribbling semen. The baby crawled around in its puddles of semen like a pink ape but the black peas of its eyes were inhumanly human. It came to her and wanted to be picked up, extending its hammy hairless arms. She backed away and it followed, bawling. She reached for something to hit it with and realized she had picked up a clublike penis. Horrified, she dropped it. The baby-ape became Cobbie Kind in a black business suit and cried to her, pleading with her to pray for him. She raised her arms, making a halo of them around her head, and looked up and felt herself rise into the sky. As she rose through a cloud she felt its cool mist sweep over her skin. The crying and pleading died out far below.

Sarah Edelbacher's office was in the Administration Building. A rectangular block with a wide front and four floors, it was the main building at Pacific Christian, the largest on campus. Administration offices occupied the first two floors. Teaching staff used the others. Her office was on the top floor, near the end of a long hallway. A moderate-sized desk, four chairs, a wall of bookshelves and one of cupboards and two filing cabinets took up the available space. Beside the door was a noticeboard and behind the desk a plate-glass window. On the plywood counter beneath the cupboards were an electric kettle, a jar of decaffeinated instant coffee, a bottle of filtered water and two mugs. Posters for children's charities filled the back of the door. On her desk were ceramic pots with sheaves of pens, stacked papers, photographs in folding frames and a wood carving of an African child.

She arrived at her office a little after nine, having checked for mail and messages at the main office, down the hall. There had been nothing. Remembering what Gwen said, she had been careful since leaving her apartment. She looked in the rear view mirror as she drove, watching for anyone following her. Gwen and Speaker would be meeting downtown and taking a bus to the university. Madeline would not be coming. She had returned home after the television program. Her mother, miffed at what happened at the studio, refused permission.

When she and Speaker arrived, Gwen introduced the adults and saw the obvious change in Sarah Edelbacher. Lack of sleep gave a nervous edge to her behaviour. Looking at them as if they shouldn't have come, she forgot to ask them to sit down. Her voice sounded strained.

"I'm worried about this."

"You mean meeting with us?" Gwen said.

"That too. I mean the whole thing."

"Why did you phone Gwen?" Speaker said.

"What happened out there last night shocked me and I had to speak with somebody. Gwen brought the notebooks. Now I don't know. I hit the man and ran out. I don't know what he's going to do."

"What can he do?"

"Take me off the program right away. And eventually take the presidency away from me. I was elected by acclamation. I was picked for both."

"That's him. He's got to control everything he touches. He uses people and never gives them any real power. Only the illusion of it."

"I wasn't after power."

"If you were, you'd never last with him."

"Do you think he'd harm me?"

"He might. Don't be regular in anything."

"We thought you were going to help us get him," Gwen said.

"Get him. How? The program is run independently. I oversee the contents and select the guests. As president I have a free hand. I speak where and when I want. His wife looks after the business end. Membership drives, financial support."

Suddenly noticing they were standing, she asked them to sit down. She went behind her desk and sat in a high-backed wooden armchair that could tilt and swivel. She felt more comfortable. Her doubts could be aired, even if only an academic exercise.

"You're asking me to betray a trust. After all, I don't know that he's actually guilty of anything. He shocked me last night, but his behaviour was abnormal, not criminal. He may be an arrested personality, extremely neurotic."

"You're forgetting the notebooks and flash drive," Speaker said.

Gwen fidgeted in her chair as she glanced around the office. She told herself Sarah Edelbacher was used to seeing Cobbie Kind in a different light. She believed him to be a good man trying to help children. And she wasn't used to trouble.

"Is it that you're afraid?" Gwen said. "We are."

"Of course I'm afraid. But there's the question of repercussions. I can't simply begin denouncing the man. At this point I can't assume he's guilty of anything."

"He has all the legal help he needs to scuttle any investigation," Speaker said. "But you might be able to skewer him on his own ground of moral superiority. It wouldn't be easy. But it's the only way."

"You obviously assume his guilt. I can't make such a moral leap."

"He'll never be prosecuted. Wait for that and he'll enjoy baby girls for the rest of his life. I don't think he has the right. Do you?"

"Don't be rhetorical with me."

Speaker raised his eyebrows. Kind had bought her, lock, stock and doctorate but she had thought he could never own her. It was intellectual egotism, and fatal. It let her assume that because of her academic credentials she could survive untainted and uncompromised, the presumption of the educated who serve the powerful and the wealthy that the cool subtleties of reason outmatch the cruel subtleties of the heart.

Gwen stared out of the window. Sarah Edelbacher looked at her. Poor girl. Mother gone and she was trying to recover. Coping by fighting. If she couldn't, what then? Why didn't that man urge her to be more prudent? What was his interest in this, anyway? Who was he? What was he? And what a name, pretentious if not presumptuous as well. She shouldn't make a decision right away. She didn't know.

"I'll need some time. I'll have to talk with my husband."

Speaker raised his eyebrows once more and she could see a smile begin to form and disappear. She couldn't read Gwen's face. It seemed blank but something was there. She wanted to know what it was. She hadn't the right to ask. So much to think about. Decide.

"I'll call you and let you know what I've decided," she said to Gwen.

Gwen stood up and went to the door, a glum look on her face.

"We should take those photocopies," Speaker said, "in case you stay out of this. Unless you want to shred them."

Sarah Edelbacher took the copies out of her briefcase and handed them to him. He rolled them up and shoved the roll inside his jacket.

"Don't forget to vary your routine. You may have nothing to worry about."

After they left, Sarah Edelbacher stared at the posters for children's charities. The man was deeply neurotic. Bad enough, but not a child killer. And there were lots of people who would like to see Cobbie Kind mortally wounded so they would be rid of EFC. Child molesters, pornographers, atheists and promoters of weird causes would all want him disgraced. She would be helping them. She couldn't have that on her conscience. Hadn't he always been generous with time and money and supported her in every way she wanted? Why let silly fear of a neurotic persuade her he could do something much worse? And wouldn't Wissie know? Have done something? If you didn't watch out, people could make you believe anything. That poor girl was so upset she desperately wanted to find her mother's killer. So his initials were in the notebooks? His initials and name must be on lots of lists. What about that friend of hers, Speaker? Trust this stranger who has a common noun for a name? Norman would say stay out of it. She couldn't go ahead with it. Why did she go to the house yesterday? Why did she believe that girl?

The house returned. The silence of the hallways. The murky lighting. She had never liked going out there at night to dinner parties, though Norman always accompanied her. She felt uneasy. No matter how many guests there were. They spoke in low voices. Cobbie Kind didn't like noise. Wissie had told her he liked her voice because it was low and steady. Sarah Edelbacher hadn't taken this as a compliment. He would watch her at dinner, as if appraising her for something. He never said much, mostly guttural monosyllabic fragments. She would fall back on the fact that he supported her. So why should she care how he looked at her? Weren't important men likely to have idiosyncrasies? But the quiet, sparsely lit house still bothered her, even in daylight. She remembered that the garden meetings were her suggestion, not Wissie's.

To rid herself of the image of the house, she got up and went to her briefcase. It was on the counter below the cupboards. Her first class was in five minutes, nine students for a seminar that met in her office. It was crowded and they had to get extra chairs. But there wasn't a room close enough and unoccupied at that hour to suit her. A soft knock, a couple of taps. Too soon. She was so tired. Carrying a file of lecture notes, she went to the door and opened it. A man in a dark uniform and tie and peaked cap smiled at her. In his hand he held a small package. His voice had that touch of professional friendliness that passes for civility in those who know they will meet you once.

"Professor Edelbacher? I have a package for you."

She could see the EFC logo on the package, sent obviously by Cobbie or Wissie. Embarrassed by what happened. Wanted to make up for it. She put out her hand. The man took a form out of his jacket pocket.

"You have to sign for it."

"I'll get a pen."

As she turned he grabbed her from behind, pushed her into the office, shutting the door with a jab of his elbow. Both hands around her waist and one left. The hand returned, this time over her mouth, the other still around her waist. She had dropped the file she was holding. Dragging her to the desk, he twisted her around and pushed her onto it. The hand around her waist left and a steel finger jabbed into her side. He moved the gun to the front, rasping her wool skirt. He found the space above her crotch. He pressed the gun into the skirt, took it away. It slid down her skirt and under and between her legs. She squeezed them together but he jammed the cold barrel up to her lips. Fingernails scraped the soft inside of her thighs. He prodded gently with the barrel, as if telling her to relax. He pushed her down by her mouth until she was flat. Fingers pulled her panties away from her crotch. He brought the mouth of the barrel to her lips again. The prodding began once more, into the slit and slightly upwards in a back and forth motion. After the cold shock of the barrel scraping her, she felt breath on her cheek. It smelled of steak. She heard knocking on the door. Members of her seminar were in the hallway. After a few seconds, more taps.

"Professor Edelbacher?" a voice called. She had instructed them to come in and wait for her if she wasn't there. The doorknob turned, a slight pressure against it. He had locked the door. He rammed the end of the barrel up into her lips and she winced, felt the top edge of the gunsight cutting into her. She bit her tongue to fight the pain. "She never locked it before," a voice said. "I'll get the secretary to open it," another voice said. "We'll get extra chairs when you get back," a third added. She heard a pair of footsteps moving away. At least two members of the seminar were still outside the door. He jerked the gun away. The gunsight caught in her inner lips and the edge sliced her. She moaned. He yanked her head back. She was sure she was bleeding. She must keep quiet, control herself. The cut ached but she wasn't going to die from it. He shoved the gun into her side. He took his hand from her mouth and put it high behind her neck. He left her side and looked into her face, the steak breath an inch away.

"Talk nice and smile."

He took his hand from her neck and pushed her towards the door, put the gun into his jacket pocket but kept holding it. She was numb except for her legs. They seemed to be wading in knee-deep water. He had waited too long, torturing her. Another sick man. Where was he taking her? Somewhere to be murdered. She should have believed that girl. Obstinately blind to rationalize last night. Escape somewhere on the way. Into a crowd. Wait for the right time. Pretend to cooperate. He looks stupid. Should've worn sneakers.

He unlocked the door and they stepped out into the hallway. To the left was a double row of closed doors and the main office. To the right and one door away was the stairway exit. Four seminar members stood across the hall, briefcases on the floor. "I've got to go somewhere for a while," she said while trying to smile, thinking anything more and their lives would be at risk. They nodded, their curiosity not aroused by the locked door. He put a hand low on her back to direct her towards the stairway. They saw no one on the stairs. He stayed one step behind as they descended. At the ground floor exit he pushed the door open a bit and peeked out, spoke as if he had been asked for directions.

"Go on across the street, to the parking lot behind that building."

She walked quickly with those long strides, almost leaving him behind.

Despite her intentions, she found herself wanting to obey him. All of this was building its own inexorable momentum and she had become part of it, though she knew it was a mistake to facilitate his plans. Dear God, help me, she repeated like a chant under her breath, feeling, almost knowing, that somehow she wasn't going to die. They had come out at the south end of the Administration Building and taken a short walkway east to the road in front of the main entrance. Traffic had stopped for some pedestrians using a crosswalk and they joined them. Gwen and Speaker were waiting at a bus stop to the north and on the other side. Speaker had been looking that way, saw the two in the crosswalk.

"Isn't that her?"

Gwen turned. The lake path. The bridge. Fear, anger fused. An obliterating urge.

"You think she knows him?" Speaker said.

"Course not. Come on."

Gwen sifted through pedestrians as she made her way to the crosswalk, Speaker behind her and wondering what they could do. When they got there, Sarah Edelbacher and the man had crossed and were heading east on a narrow road beside the student union building. They were forty feet ahead and Gwen had to walk fast to stay near. They stepped onto the sidewalk beside the student union building and seemed to be going to the parking lot at the rear. The crowd thinned and she got closer. At twenty feet she ran, releasing herself in a headlong rush towards the man. She hurtled into him from the side, knocking him off balance. He grunted and fell to his knees. Sarah Edelbacher turned and saw her bending over a yard away in a half-crouch. She felt like crying and yelling but didn't do either.

"He's got a gun," she shouted to Gwen.

People began scattering across the lawn adjacent to the sidewalk. As he was running to catch up with Gwen, Speaker had seen her knock the man over. He waved at Sarah Edelbacher to run. He grabbed Gwen by the waist, dragged her back into the road. Sarah Edelbacher hurried towards the side entrance of the student union building. She pulled at the door handle, pulled again and disappeared inside, her shoes left on the sidewalk. Gwen was not conscious of being dragged away or of Speaker's presence. She saw only the man getting up and looking around. Dozens of people were trying to vanish. He began limping on a twisted ankle towards the parking lot. Gwen saw again the seawall walk and her mother slumped and bleeding onto the wide stone railing. A hunched thing hobbled away.

After the campus police arrived and Sarah Edelbacher, Speaker and a recovered Gwen had given statements in the student union building lounge amid the stares and whispers of the curious, each statement carefully revealing only immediate particulars and leaving out the Kinds, they were told they would be contacted if an investigation uncovered anything. Sarah Edelbacher parried questions about her attacker's motive. The other two posed as campus visitors who happened to see the man behaving suspiciously. Gwen followed them, got close and saw the bulge of the gun he was holding in his pocket and decided she would knock him down.

"I used to feel safe here," Sarah Edelbacher said as they walked to her office. Eyes darting in the direction of a sudden honk from traffic, she couldn't decide what was dangerous. She put her arm around Gwen's shoulder and hugged her. "Thank you." Gwen shook something off her nose.

"You don't have the power to fight him," Speaker said at the office after Sarah Edelbacher had phoned her husband and Gwen her father. Sarah Edelbacher was sitting behind her desk and her visitors were sitting near the bookshelves. "That guy saw us out there. He's going to tell him. Kind knows what you're capable of doing and he'll stop you, pick the time and the way."

"I've got the loyalty of the membership. And I'm president until the election next March. The next meeting is on Monday. I'm scheduled to speak. I'll use that venue to call his character into question."

"A couple of hours ago you thought he wasn't guilty. After what happened today, do you think he's going to let you expose him? You don't know who you're dealing with. No idea."

"He can't deny me my democratic rights."

"Don't forget to welcome a rebuttal."

"You wanted her to do something," Gwen said, turning her flushed face to him, "and now you're saying she can't do anything. Why don't you go live in the basement with that bum? She's almost been murdered. Know what that's like? I'm tired of men who aren't as grown up as I am."

Speaker stared out at the grey oblivion of the afternoon sky. Sarah Edelbacher felt the ache from the tear deep between her legs. But that didn't make her feel like crying. Something torn inside was hurting unbelievably. She fought it by looking at some papers on her desk. I was saved and I am safe. Gwen came over to the desk.

"My girlfriend told me you lived in Africa."

"She's going to get him at the next meeting," Gwen told Madeline later when she phoned her. "Think your mother will trust us after what happened yesterday?"

"I'll tell her we're sorry. We got excited. She'll be impressed. Will your father go?"

"I told him he was going."

"What about Speaker?" Madeline asked offhandedly.

"He doesn't think she'll be able to do much good. He left before my dad got there. I told him we'd give him a ride. He said he had to take a bus somewhere right away. Guys are such bad liars."

"My mom would probably creature crawl if she knew he was going. Is Sarah scared?"

"I think so. I got her to talk about Africa. Said I'd phone every night until the meeting. She said once was enough."

"I'm not breathing. I told you about those Sarahphires."

"What do we do till then?"

"Schoolwork. Can you believe?"

"Can you believe?"

Roger and Gwen had stayed with Sarah Edelbacher until her husband arrived. Roger saw the look in Gwen's eyes when she suggested they stay. After the Chalmers left, Sarah Edelbacher had Norman take her to the university medical clinic for a checkup, explaining enough of the why on the way, too much she thought as he almost ran off the road a couple of times. A doctor cleaned and dressed the cut, said it would hurt for a while but didn't need stitching and would heal within two weeks. She didn't say any more to her husband until they got to their apartment. Told everything, Norman reluctantly accepted her decision to speak before the members at the next meeting but said they should see a lawyer first. She admitted a lawyer would inevitably advise against the speech. Knowing that, he said, couldn't she wait until they at least heard a lawyer's advice and would know more about the pitfalls?

"They know the laws of libel and slander. That might save us from a lawsuit."

"Lawyers don't save you from lawsuits, they get you into them."

"You don't know what Kind will do."

"I'm president and I know what I'm going to do."

"Have you prayed about this?"

Still wearing their coats, they were sitting on the living room sofa. She looked into her husband's eyes.

"When that man was taking me away, I prayed to God to save me and I was saved through a brave girl whose mother that man murdered. God has pointed out the true path, I will not turn away."

She was on campus Wednesday and Friday of that week, for undergraduate classes and a faculty meeting. The Monday seminar was rescheduled for the end of term. On those two days, Norman drove her to the university and picked her up. The campus police stationed a patrol car at the Administration Building. Nothing happened, either there or at the apartment. She waited for contact from the Kind organization but there was none. The television show was not a problem that Sunday because it was to be pre-empted by special programming, a review of all the citations and awards Kind had received over the years for his work with various local and international charities. She had seen the program, which featured ceremonies and speeches of praise for Kind from dignitaries of national and global stature. The nonstop glorification had made her uncomfortable but she had been able to do her work, so what did those garnered honours and words matter? Now everything seemed a monstrous lie, a deliberate gulling of so many trusting people who gave their time and effort and money to his organization. As she wrote her speech she realized the program and many other things she had seen and heard about Kind were nothing but public relations, part of an incredible plan to create a myth of super generosity and selfless sacrifice. The picnics for handicapped children with Cobbie Kind stepping out of a limousine for quick photo ops and equally speedy departures, the glossy awards ceremonies with the same fast entrances and exits with the inevitable pack of reporters and cameras, the so-called "news stories" about the man visiting other parts of the world to found children's medical and dental clinics, the well-publicized holiday meals with him ladling slices of turkey onto the plates of impoverished children, and the fatuously simplistic editorials featured in his newspapers and the superficial pundits on his network predicting the fall of society unless it rid itself of perverts: wasn't it all a cynical manipulation of trust and wasn't he a gigantic fraud?

She had been one of the dupes, despite her education and intelligence. He had manipulated her as easily as the rest of his followers. She cried for a while one night as she lay in bed. But she tried not to let bitterness mar her speech. She would not twist people's feelings, she would appeal to reason. On Saturday afternoon Wissie phoned. Norman took the call. He took all of them now. When she heard him say the name she felt a seismic wave of electricity pass over her skin, leaving her nerves tremulous as it subsided. "You'd like to speak with her?" he said and looked over. She sighed and nodded. He passed her the phone and she clutched it to keep her hand from shaking.

"How are you, dear?"

"Fine."

"When you didn't show up for our weekly meeting, I thought something was wrong."

In the rush of events she had completely forgotten about it. She felt awkward making excuses.

"It completely slipped my mind. I've been very busy."

"As long as you're all right. That's what's important, isn't it?"

Stupid.

"There wasn't anything you wanted to bring up, was there?"

Maybe not so stupid.

"No."

"As long as nothing important is left unsaid. Nothing wrong with your voice, is there?"

"No, uh—. Yes. I've been speaking too much lately, I guess. I'm a little hoarse."

"Maybe you need a rest, Sarah. Cancel some of your speeches."

Showing concern. Using her name at the right time. Slipping in a helpful suggestion. Who could misconstrue that? There was a pause before Wissie's rigidly thin, almost mechanical voice came from a world that seemed far away.

"You should think about that, dear, because health is too important to play with. Will we see you at the meeting?"

"Yes."

"Hear one of your fine speeches, I suppose."

She didn't answer. She had given too much away already. The woman was finished, had found out what she wanted. The voice returned, more formal.

"Goodbye, until we see you."

"Bye." There was a tremor in her voice.

She handed the phone back to her husband and sat in a muddle of anxiety and self-disgust. Someone she had always had an intellectual contempt for had manoeuvred her as she wished, found out exactly what she wanted and had left her scared and uncertain to the point of wondering if she could go to the meeting and speak in front of all those members without backing out and mumbling some meaningless drivel. She was nothing to the Kinds. They had used her and he wanted her gone because of what she knew, the one thing that she could use to destroy him.

Five nights earlier, near midnight on Monday, there was a light on in Mott's garage. The office was dark, the door locked. The doors to the bays were shut. The light came from a fluorescent ceiling fixture hanging above one of the bays. At the back two men sat on the workbench and looked at a third in a chair.

"You're a real fuckup. You hit the wrong guy. You missed the young broad. We give you Lynch on the courthouse steps and he walks away. You can't even handle this Bible broad. We could've shaken the stuff out of Lynch that Sunday and put him away. But we're told to get a pro. So we bring you in. So you fuck up. Coming in here with a limp. What's that supposed to be, an excuse?"

Doughnuts lit a cigar. Zimmo eased himself down from the workbench and picked up a towel. He opened a toolbox and threw in two crescent wrenches and a ballpeen hammer. The man in the chair glanced at Zimmo before answering Doughnuts. The air smelled of cigar smoke.

"When I took on the job, I didn't know it wasn't a straight hit. There's too much to this now."

Doughnuts reached inside his coveralls and took an envelope smeared with greasy thumbprints out of his shirt pocket and tossed it on the workbench.

"Paying us off with fuck all."

"Can't help that. You called me. It was a flat fee. Extra time means more expense. We agreed on a percentage."

"You making us pay for your fuckups? It still don't work out. Somebody got a nice payoff for doing nuthin'. And we got to wipe up car shit."

The man in the chair made a slight sideways movement with his head and uncrossed his legs. It was time to go. He glanced down between his suit jacket lapels. He wouldn't need his piece. Why did he think he would?

Zimmo slammed down the toolbox lid and passed in front of the chair, wiping his hands with the towel on his way to the office. He swivelled around and an arm swung down at the man's head. There was a muffled crack and the man slumped over and onto the floor. Zimmo unwrapped the towel from around a large socket wrench.

"Didn't I tell you he'd try and fuck us around?"

Doughnuts slid off the workbench and bent over the body.

"Tie him up. Nobody fucks with us."

Doughnuts wheeled over a handtruck with a long red and a squat black cylinder. He turned the knobs on the cylinders. With his cigar he lit the oxyacetylene mix at the nozzle end of the brace of pipes extending from the cylinder hoses. He turned the adjustment screw on the pipes. A smoky lazy flickering of yellow flame flashed instantly into a pale dagger with the blowing sound of gas released under pressure. Zimmo picked up the man and dumped him into the chair, wrapped lengths of electric cord around his arms and neck, tying him to it. Doughnuts brought the hissing flame nearer to the man's face. The man's eyes opened, he squirmed against the cord, legs kicking out as the flame brought the smell of burning gas. As the tip seared his lips, he jerked his head away, his stretched screams traced to a scorched and melted blur. He was shrieking in spasms when the flame disappeared into his mouth, nozzle jammed against his teeth. His tongue roasted and shrivelled with his last few gurgles. The flame reappeared and burnt off the face. Gelatinous oozings bubbled and dried as skin peeled off in blisters, leaving hollow eye sockets. A stench like burning pork fat filled the garage, overpowering Doughnuts' cigar. In less than five minutes a blackened skull stared at nothing. The tall man had become another disposal problem. He would be found among roadside bushes outside the city limits.

Chapter 21

Madeline was cautious about mentioning the upcoming meeting to her mother. Mary had been upset when the girls ran onto the set at the end of the program. Left to sit alone and wait for Gwen to return from Sarah Edelbacher's office, she had sulked. Madeline understood her mother. Putting it all down later in the car to excusable hero worship and recognizing a former schoolmate didn't quite convince her. Too obviously bland glances from the traffic to them and a string of abruptly noncommittal "ms" and "hms" had told Madeline that. But she also knew her mother believed enough to be mollified by some good bait, and that Madeline had in Gwen's father.

"Gwen's dad would like to go to the next EFC meeting," she told her as they were washing dishes after dinner Wednesday evening. "He would?" Mary tried unsuccessfully to mask her interest with a low monotone. She had always liked Roger and especially after her divorce but her affection had not been returned, possibly because he suspected it would have become something else. And he could never bring himself to cheat on Carol. Besides, he thought Mary a silly woman with preposterous opinions. After Carol's death she had fantasized that she and Roger would become friends, perhaps more. She had started to sniffle again whenever she talked about, saw on television, attended or remembered weddings. She saw this as a good sign, a biological portent. And now Madeline's news.

As she dried a dish before putting it on a stack of them on the kitchen counter, Madeline looked at her mother. Madeline knew that she liked Gwen's father, from her bustling frustration when she talked about their disagreements. They might get married. She and Gwen would be like sisters. That would make her smile. But sisters fought sometimes and could be meanly jealous of each other. Friends didn't fight or get jealous. They were sisterly, anyway, without the complications. It was a good thing that her mother and Gwen's father didn't suit each other.

"I'll see about the tickets," Mary said as she dipped a plate into the sudsy dishwater, watching her wedding band disappear through bubbles stretching their foamy iridescence like bellowing frogs and slip down into the presuming greyness of soapy water. "Don't forget, Mom," Madeline said, knowing she wouldn't and rubbing her towel over the same dry dish. The two finished silently, each imagining a version of what would happen on Monday night. These versions elaborated, one in a romantic and the other in a heroic fantasy. Each intricacy and counterpoint of thrills finally justified by a monumental coda stretching to bright stars of its own perfection.

"Madeline's mother doesn't know anything," Gwen said that same evening to her father after she told him they were going to the next meeting. She had hinted broadly on Monday about all of them going. Roger had demurred slightly, didn't say no. He knew he would have to go. He could never refuse Gwen anything and she knew it. Now he was grinning across the kitchen table. He found outright acceptance less painful thinking that Mary knew nothing. He felt better knowing somebody else was in even less control than he was. That Mary had no idea what was going on made his grin wider. He was enjoying the to him appropriate literal meaning of those innocently meant words. Gwen resented his taking what she said as a cheap joke. Ever since the confrontation in the library between him and Speaker, she had mistrusted her father's motives. He must not be allowed to think Sarah Edelbacher was ridiculous. Gwen spelled it out, hoping this would rankle.

"I mean that her mom thinks Sarah Edelbacher is going to give one of her regular speeches."

"Do they come in grades like gas, regular and super unleaded?"

"Sure, like your humour."

She dug again into her organic granola, which in a tribute of self-denial to Sarah Edelbacher she was eating without almond milk. Her father attempted once more to get past the crunching teeth and clinking spoon.

"My humour is carefully distilled. Like fine whisky."

Gwen looked up from her bowl.

"Not for export. Strictly domestic."

Crunch, crunch. He no longer had any appetite for the scrambled eggs she had prepared for him.

On Sunday afternoon Sarah Edelbacher read her speech aloud to Norman. He was sitting on the living room sofa. She stood in front of him reading from the manuscript. When she finished she waited but he didn't say anything.

"What do you think?"

"It's good, Sarah. But shouldn't you be less forceful until he has a chance to say something?"

"I haven't made a direct accusation. I'm saying his image is all public relations. I don't believe it any more. I'm going to invite him to address next month's meeting or call a special one, and I'll resign if the members side with him. Maybe somebody, a reporter or a journalist, will look more closely at his life because of this."

"Maybe," he said, staring out of the living room window.

She sat down at the other end of the sofa. This was the first time in their marriage they didn't have complete emotional accord. They had differed before, but there had never been a fissure in their overall solidarity. An unspoken estrangement existed now. She knew he didn't want her to speak out at the meeting. The import of his cautions the past week was clear. He had been cheerful after the call from Wissie, saying it meant the Kinds wanted to avoid a fight and were prepared to talk. She had stared at him until he got up and left. She hadn't felt comfortable sleeping in the same bed with him the last few nights. It was like sleeping with a stranger. Worse, a stranger with a grievance she couldn't cope with without compromising her integrity. Forced to see each other in this new way, each accepted the inevitable result.

The telephone rang. Grateful for the interruption, Sarah Edelbacher answered. It was Gwen. Here was support, from a girl she thought too enthusiastic and told to call once. Gwen began shyly.

"Not bothering you, am I?"

"Of course not. I need the support."

Her husband got up and left.

"We'll all be there tomorrow night. Madeline, her mother, her friends, me, my father."

"I hope my speech works."

"I heard the interview you did last Sunday. Wow."

"We'll see. I'm a bit nervous."

She had wanted to say this all week. She had hoped it would be to her husband but was glad telling Gwen.

"Do you want a ride?"

"My husband will drive me. I'll see you there."

What Gwen had wanted to say was that she wished she could have the honour of arriving with President Sarah Edelbacher. She knew the woman sensed this and was appreciative of the feeling. That made her happy. After the call, she phoned Madeline.

"I'm shivering, Maddy. I really am. I've been talking with greatness. I've supped with a goddess. She's going to take him on alone. Standing right in front of all those people. She will be naked to sharp knives."

"I told you. The abbess of our hopes. The Middle Ages born again. Only this nun is armed and on horseback. A knight."

"What's on her shield, Maddy. Go."

"A parchment scroll. A quill dripping ink. Over them a cloud, and blasting through it the horn of a clarion trumpet. The unearthly music of truth."

"You say those words. Her armour has got to be white silver. So bright it's hard to look at. And her charger white. An incredible number of hands high. With hooves like pile drivers. Mane like silky water. Is there any truth like that?"

"It's the best there can be."

EFC meetings were held in Civic Stadium, built eight years earlier when Cobbie Kind campaigned through his newspaper and television station to replace mid-Forties Maritime Park. Allies on city council had been briefed about site and style by the Kind forces. Various levels of government were eventually induced to pay half the cost, the rest contributed by the Cobbie

Kind holding company in return for a nominal rental fee to help a nascent EFC and long-term broadcast rights for home and away games of the local teams. A domed stadium built on the same site as the other, it seated fifty thousand. Conventions, fairs, shows and sporting events filled the calendar, and almost from the opening the first Monday of each month was the occasion of an EFC meeting. The average attendance was ten thousand, about half local members and the rest from out of town. At the inner entrances young women greeters in pink-and-white uniforms designed by Wissie stood near bins with "Help EFC Help Abused Children" printed on them. With smiles and commendations they encouraged donations at the otherwise free affair. Membership cards had to be shown and anybody without one had to be accompanied by a member. Uniformed security guards were on hand to deal with protesters. There had been a single disruption over the years, when some university students began to march up and down the aisles. They held up placards that read "Dicktator Kind" and "Media Monster" and were ejected by the security guards after being attacked by the more radical members. Using their own signs ("Not Kind to Perverts," "If They Are Sick, You Got To Cut Their Stick"), the radicals had assaulted the young male students.

For the meetings the playing surface was covered with plywood, filled with chairs and divided into aisles. Lighting over the tiers of permanent seating was darkened to create a sense of community and to make the audience seem larger. The chairs faced the podium, a platform erected for every meeting and decorated with pastel bunting, swags, vases of flowers and pictures of Cobbie Kind with children. Every month on the wall at the rear of the platform was an enlarged photograph of an abused child recently helped by the organization. Television cameras from Kind's station recorded the proceedings, edited for that night's news on his network and used to make copies for sale to members. Meetings began at eight with a prayer for children by a local cleric and continued with speeches and talks by regular and guest speakers. The atmosphere was part born-again revivalism, part caregiver missionary social worker reformer manhunt zeal. Mothers would speak about finally having enough courage to expose a husband's molestation of his daughter, and reveal in some cases that they were molested. There would be talks on how to recognize child molesters, the sure signs that a man was perverted and coveted your daughter or son. Experts of various stripes would lecture on the dangers of being liberal on perversion and the many hidden costs of social rot from too much moral relativism. Each month the story of the anonymous child pictured on the rear wall would be told by a relative, social worker or child psychologist. Radical members wanted molested children identified and to have them speak at the meetings. Sarah Edelbacher said no. She was uneasy about exposing a psychologically frail child to the further trauma of the public arena. This was blood and gore theatrics and she must protect the children. Determined to avoid spectacles and demeaning exercises in sensationalism, she insisted that the protection of children should be the members' only concern. She also rejected proposals for members to shadow convicted child molesters and to inform their neighbours and co-workers about them, and to lobby political parties to adopt as policy the mandatory castration of molesters and the execution of repeat offenders. These ideas were being promoted by editors and commentators in Kind's media. Sarah Edelbacher maintained there was an essential difference between media hype out to capture readers and viewers and the high-minded aims of EFC. "We're about helping children," she would say. "We must show this society how valuable they are and how the injury of a child is an abominable act against God. We must answer to Him, on Him rests our redemption."

The radicals in EFC tolerated Sarah Edelbacher's leadership but didn't admire or even like her. They thought her too academic, too reserved. This five per cent wanted one of its own as president. Opportunities had never arisen because Wissie had always supported her. As secretary-treasurer of EFC and wife of Cobbie Kind, she was crucial to her survival. The radicals recognized the similarity between their ideas and those espoused by Cobbie Kind through his media. They couldn't understand why the Kinds supported her. It seemed hypocritical to sound tough on television and in newsprint and yet have a moderate spokeswoman who spent so much of her time speaking before middle-class women's groups and other mainstream organizations and appearing before endless snoreboring need-to-study-this-further government committees. Sarah Edelbacher's tone in her speeches, interviews and proposals angered the radicals. She was reasonable, she offered her views. The radicals couldn't appreciate that Cobbie Kind wanted exactly this tone. She was safe, no threat to break the law or encourage anything risky. He wanted to make headlines, not trouble. He demanded drastic remedies ridding society of all those like him. But he made sure this effort would be hamstrung from the start. In the carefully sealed criminality of his life, Kind could heap guilt on others. His rantings against molesters were tirades intended as circulation and audience boosters. Public anger against molesters was profitable, and that's all he intended it to be. His public mask of outrage was good business. And there were always those who would be caught and punished to satisfy the public, molesters who weren't members of his secret network of socially prominent pedophiles. Kind's duplicity as a self-styled sexual epicure remained secret because an elaborate network of contacts kept most of his suppliers from knowing who he was. The very few who had to know were too involved and too well paid to threaten him. The only one who wanted more had been garrotted with piano wire and been found floating tongueless in offshore waters. The example was before the others, and Cobbie Kind continued to hunt with the sharks and swim with the morally righteous.

About her husband's use of EFC Wissie's ignorance was astoundingly complete. But she knew what would bother him and whenever his stolid calm was threatened she moved quickly and ruthlessly to protect it. She did this sometimes before he had any need to tell her. To him this was her most valuable asset as a wife. To her it was unconscionable that such a great man should have to put up with the ingratitude and maliciousness of inferiors. Nothing must keep him from the good work he was doing so selflessly for a society that seemed so often not to appreciate him. When Sarah Edelbacher left that Sunday night, Wissie had heard her hectic rush out of the house and from an upstairs bedroom window seen her speed away. The phone call had been an alert. At the front door that drawn face, those remote eyes meant trouble. She had always liked the woman, admired the quiet way in which she did things and had enjoyed her speeches, with those edifying theological allusions. She was uplifting in an intelligent way, and not snobbish or threatening. She challenged readers and viewers, not to be good but to be the best they really could. Wissie had recommended her as the perfect woman to lead the new organization, but hurrying down to her husband's study she knew everything had changed. Sarah Edelbacher was an enemy to be destroyed as quickly as possible. This would not be a moral or intellectual problem but an organizational one.

He was standing in the dimly lit study as Wissie approached the open door. He was expecting her, as he always did when anything went wrong. This had happened many times. She had come to intuit his wishes and gone and done what he wanted. She thought of this as part of the spirituality that bound them to each other. She had never failed to divine his wishes. She stepped inside the doorway and saw his huge outline. He was standing in front of his desk, his back to her. His stance meant that he was upset with Sarah Edelbacher. She had to get rid of the woman at once. He didn't say anything but he did want something from his wife. She knew that, too. She walked up to him and took his thumb from behind and began the careful massaging, saying nothing because nothing had to be said. His grunts came intermittently as she varied her rhythm and stroke but that was all. She breathed softly behind him but not deliberately. The room was quiet otherwise. After finishing she left him and went to her study, on the second floor at the rear and next to her bedroom. It was a small room with a hewn stone fireplace, built-in walnut bookshelves along one wall, a couch with a couple of embroidered plush pillows, a rosewood desk with an oak captain's chair, and an upholstered armchair over by the fireplace. She did her correspondence here and made and took phone calls of a more personal nature and wrote expertly plagiarized articles that appeared in *For Children,* the EFC magazine, or abridged on its website version, and also planned the future of the organization. Sitting in the armchair and sipping a cup of now cold tea she had made for herself earlier, Wissie planned the destruction of the president. Destroying the woman wouldn't be difficult, simply a matter of using lies to get someone else to do the job. But that left the other problem of choosing a successor from among several possible candidates. Leaning back with her eyes closed she grinned, the names of destroyer and successor clear.

They were the same.

Mary was silent for most of the trip to the stadium. She had appropriated the front passenger seat, next to Roger. Gwen and Madeline looked at each other in the back seat, amazed at her silence. Gwen pointed at her father and grinned. Occasionally, Mary would glance at Roger, who like the girls had expected a series of triumphant outbursts from her at bringing them to an EFC meeting. She didn't look smug or complacent, but demure. She felt this might be her last chance to impress Roger. His going to the meeting must signify that he did have some feeling for her. Why else would he go? So she would be the type of woman Roger would appreciate, not a loudmouth or a chatterbox but a self-assured potential partner who was a sensible conversationalist. She wanted to gloat out loud about this carload of converts. But she managed to suppress her glee by compressing her lips into various tortured evasions of smirking as she looked at traffic.

As the car neared the dark Romanesque bulk of the stadium they could see a ring of white lights lining the bottom of the dome, a sort of electric fringe on the greying white tonsure bulging up into the blue evening. The parking lot was an adjacent half mile of asphalt to the left and northeast of the main entrance, and marked on it the horizontal ladders of white lines that most obey regardless of how full or empty a lot is. As usual on EFC nights there was plenty of room on this lunar vastness and Roger found a space fifty yards from the main entrance. Gwen and Madeline spilled out and ran towards it, calling to their parents to hurry. Left with Mary, Roger felt uncomfortable, but she enjoyed this opportunity to walk beside him. This was a family in the making, and what a perfect occasion for that. To him the discomfort of this evening was only beginning. He needed a drink. Gwen and Madeline tilted their faces against the cool night air as they ran. Mary walked slower than she had in years.

At "First Mondays" it was noisy, in contrast to the more intimate television program, with its churchlike atmosphere in the studio. The general meetings were boisterous, members splitting into factions over policy. The radicals were noisiest. Moderates invariably awaited the calming effect of the president's speech to feel that things were right again. Decorum at First

Mondays was in the hands of the permanent chairwoman, Maxine Horner, in her late seventies, a large and robust woman who, true to her role, stayed out of factional squabbles and kept meetings from disintegrating into rancorous infighting. Wissie picked her because she was too obedient to be a threat. Maxine Horner enjoyed her role. She was known to the more disrespectful as "Gavel Mouth" for the thunderclap quality of her voice. But few wanted to take her on when she stood at the lectern on the podium, five feet, ten inches, her broadness exaggerated by padded shoulders in her dresses and jackets, her hair gathered in a white braid draped behind her. "Od—der, od—der," she boomed out like a stentorian town crier as she called each meeting to order. In a wide arc she would bring down the massive wooden mallet she used for a gavel, smashing it against a pockmarked block of oak. As echoing blasts of cry and bashing reverberated, they brought quiet. Tonight as usual she sat upright and impassive in her chair, fifteen feet directly behind the lectern, waiting for eight o'clock. Meetings began punctually unless Wissie decided otherwise. Her position at the mercy of the founder's wife, the chairwoman listened only to her.

Wissie Kind was in her chair, behind the lectern and on the left side of the podium, near the stairs leading up to it. The chair beside hers was vacant. The minister scheduled to deliver the opening prayer had been told the regular meeting was being cancelled because the members would be dealing with an urgent matter. She had seen Maxine Horner earlier, briefing her about the change in program. She waited, hands folded in her lap, her best organizational smile in place below those careful eyes. Audience noise washed over her like a warm bath as she reviewed her plan. She let several minutes go by before glancing at her wristwatch and over at the chairwoman, her nod clicking into place. It was five minutes after eight.

Before meetings began, Sarah Edelbacher would sit in the first row of the audience, her symbolic gesture of unity with other members. Essentially shy, she also wanted to avoid the scrutiny of attention as long as possible. The radicals thought this reluctance to take a seat on the platform was a political tactic to ingratiate herself with the members. But the moderates loved her for it. As she sat with her speech inside the leather-bound notebook in her lap she had to control her nervousness, tell herself everything would be over soon, that she must do this only once and that she must keep herself together to give her effort all she had. She glanced up at the podium and away. She avoided looking at Wissie, knew Wissie would ignore her. Norman had offered to sit with her. She had told him she would be surrounded by friends and there was no need to worry. She hoped his offer was prompted by more than a sense of duty, told herself as her nervousness grew it surely was. She was more than ever grateful to the people who came up to her and said she was doing a wonderful job. As never before, she was thankful for the embraces of friends. She wondered when she would see those girls. Thinking about them made her smile.

Gwen and Madeline scrambled up the steps and through the round arch of the main entrance and the crowd noise fizzed and echoed around them. They stopped and waited.

"They're so slow," Gwen said.

"We're missing it," Madeline shouted at her mother.

Like scolded children, Mary and Roger walked a little faster and arrived.

"No, we're not," Mary said belatedly, glad they were eager, hoping her companion was also getting excited.

"Is this free?" Roger asked, his face blank.

"We accept contributions gratefully."

More gratefully than this sucker will be giving, he wanted to say. How much grateful could he afford?

Inside the entrance an open space went around the seating area like a doughnut. Several entrances around the inner ring led to the seats. Two were open for these meetings, the more used directly across from the main entrance. Beside each one stood a bin for donations. The greeters were stationed there. Ready to welcome members, they had been taught to apply pressure to extract generous donations. The security guards watched, ready to intercept unaccompanied non-members and to spot potential troublemakers. Their uniforms had also been designed by Wissie, who had chosen the colour, baby blue. As the four approached the entrance, a greeter came over to receive them with her professional smile. As the rules of her job stipulated, she wore little make-up and no jewellery. Her fingernails were clean and not painted. Her voice was friendly and yet restrained to stress the serious purpose of the occasion. The classes she attended covered everything from speech and facial expressions to walking and gestures. She recognized Mary and Madeline and saw the others were new. Her job would be easy. Mary was the one to work on and that was going to be a cinch because she was trying to impress Roger. Her professional smile became wider. Her voice caressed them.

"Welcome. Hi, Mary. You never miss a meeting. If everybody was as loyal as you, we'd have no trouble meeting our obligations. I see you've brought guests."

"They'll learn something here," Mary said, blushing as she followed the voice towards the bin.

"I'm sure they will," the young woman said, standing close to the Wissie-designed bin. It was covered in flamingo pink satin and on the top was a very thin slit for bills and cheques only. On the front, above block letters printed in deep pink ("Help EFC Help Abused Children"), was yet another inspiration of Wissie's, a melting script in gold with the promise, "This will speak for those who cannot speak for themselves." The adjacent sides featured photographs of children. Small red hearts in velvet covered all of the edges. Mary snapped open the clasp of her black patent leather purse and took out a white change purse, also patent leather. Conscious of Roger looking at her, she carefully unzipped it. She took out a twenty dollar bill, her customary donation, then added a five, more to impress him than from any obligation to pay for the others, but when she slid the bills into the slot the five jammed. She had to use both hands to flatten the worn bill and feed it through, silently cursing herself for choosing that one. The young woman knew better than to draw attention to what she was doing. Roger felt pity mixed with a little sympathy for Mary. He pulled a new ten out of his wallet and eased it into the slot, trying not to acknowledge Mary's smile. It was enough to show his support but not enough to show her up. The greeter noted that he didn't behave like any of those males she usually encountered at meetings. Most were docile husbands, mumblers in misery, apologists for men and more anti-male than the women radicals. She put him down as a one-timer. Rather than waste words, she bestowed a farewell smile before hurrying over to a prosperous-looking group of couples from out of town.

An usher, a girl wearing the same uniform as the greeters but holding a flashlight, led them down the darkened tiers of permanent seats. She was less versed in public relations. A simple job, but she did aspire to stand beside a bin. She waved her flashlight like a wand, as if she were a fairy leading them with a beam through a forest to an enchanted lake. The large pool of light on the stadium floor became much noisier as they descended the stairs. The usually mild weather in October guaranteed a good crowd. But tonight there were so many members and guests that more folding chairs had to be added around the three sides of the playing field facing the platform, right to the railings that marked off the rows of permanent seating. Last-minute arrivals had swelled the attendance to fourteen thousand and many were looking for seats. Members clustered together and conferred, speaking into each other's ears and making hand signals that they hadn't heard part or any of what was said. Occasionally a laugh pierced the racket of shouts and buzzing conversation weaving itself into the seamless noise. Tonight there were fewer laughs and shouts than usual and the noise louder, almost covering the accompaniment of chairs scraped over plywood. Some in the crowd were sitting quietly, holding placards in their lap.

When they got to the stadium floor, Mary looked around at the overflow audience. She had to shout over the noise.

"Where do we sit?"

"You're kind of late," the usher shouted back. "I don't see four empty seats together."

"We don't care," Gwen said. "We're going to split up."

"Good luck." The usher left them.

"Are you going to be all right?" Mary said to Madeline. She was worried about Madeline, but secretly liked the idea of sitting alone with Roger.

"Oh, Mom, what could happen to us here?" Madeline said, eager to hunt for seats.

"You never know," Mary said, trying to act the concerned parent.

As she spoke, Gwen and Madeline were standing on tiptoe, looking for empty seats. She was annoyed but knew any show of irritation would seem petty. Attempting to build on a mutuality of interest, she glanced at Roger. He was staring at the throng. Irked again, she spoke to Madeline.

"Where are we going to meet afterwards?"

"We're going up front when it's over. We'll find you later."

"Bye, Dad." Gwen's look warned, don't be like her mom.

Gwen and Madeline disappeared into the crowd. Mary and Roger stared at each other across the illimitable space of their absence.

"It's only you and me now, Roger."

She wondered if she should have said "I" instead but decided that informality was better. She certainly didn't want to sound like a grammatical prig. But "us," with its hint of closeness, would have been the best choice, she realized too late. If this meeting was to be important for the future of their relationship, Roger must see that she could be his friend. And of course, wasn't being alone with him a sign fate was helping her? She moved nearer. Roger kept himself from moving away.

"Yes," was his barely audible reply.

Chapter 22

They pushed through people standing behind the outermost ring of extra chairs arranged around the seating area.

"Please excuse us, excuse us, please," Gwen shouted above the noise, "we have messages for the podium."

"Can't get started without us," Madeline declared.

She banged her knee against the back of a metal folding chair and winced. She closed her eyes, fought the pain, opened them and saw Gwen wriggling past rows of seats. It was one of the few times she envied Gwen for having a slimmer, more flexible body. Hers brought her more looks from boys but sometimes she wanted dexterity as well. Shoving a couple of women aside and gone before they could say a word, she dragged her leg, hobbling after Gwen.

Reaching the space between the extra rings of chairs and the inner seating area, Gwen raced around groups of conferring members and towards the podium. Grimacing with pain, Madeline tried to catch up. They wanted to sit as close as possible to Sarah Edelbacher. They wouldn't presume to go up and speak unless she happened to see them. Madeline had told Gwen that at the meetings she attended she had seen Sarah Edelbacher sitting in the first row before the meeting began. Madeline's limping pace eventually brought her to the front row. The bruised knee was bright pink below the hem of her navy blue skirt. A patch of skin had been scraped by the edge of the chair, leaving a row of cherry red lines like claw marks of an ill-tempered cat. "What's wrong, Maddy? Ooooh, your knee." Proud of her injury, she shifted to take some of the weight off that leg. A small compensation for being slower.

"I'm all right. Let's find seats."

Gwen saw two empty seats at the end of the fifth row and put Madeline's arm over her shoulder and led her towards them. She helped her into the aisle chair and turned to sit in the one next to it.

"Those are reserved for friends of mine."

A woman with a sharp face glared from the third seat. She wore a heavy brown coat buttoned to the collar. Topping her narrow head was a large tuque with a pom-pom that flopped over to her neck. Gwen put her hands on her hips.

"We were attacked outside the stadium and had to fight them off. She's hurt."

So who were "them"? She sounded like that sneaky tramp, making lies stand for excuses. His lies were more colourful but her excuses were better. Wasn't everything for Sarah Edelbacher? That was one way to see it.

"Why didn't you take her to the first aid station?" the woman said in her edgy whine.

"Because she doesn't want to miss anything."

She glanced around for sympathy. Those occupying nearby seats pretended to be interested in the latest issue of the pamphlet passed out at every meeting or kept talking among themselves. She sat down and looked at Madeline's knee. Madeline took the cue and with an amorphous combination of feigned and real pain put her head back, made assorted faces at the dome. The woman kept staring at them as her friends arrived. Both were solidly built, looked as if they worked out with weights. One, thickset and pie-faced, had a voice that scraped like steel wool.

"Those are our seats."

"There was nothing on them," Gwen said.

The woman nodded in the direction of her seated friend.

"She was keeping them for us."

"She did a bad job."

"Are you going to leave?"

"We can stay by right of possession." Gwen heard her mother say that once about something and it seemed appropriate now.

"Suppose we kick your asses off them?"

"Try it. We were attacked outside and had to defend ourselves against those guys and my girlfriend was hurt and she's resting and we're personal friends of Sarah Edelbacher."

"I believe that," the other muscular woman snickered. "Forget it, Val, let's go find seats before it starts."

"Get a good rub-down," Madeline said lazily through half-closed eyes.

"How would you like a slap, smart-ass?" the stocky woman said, leaning towards her.

"Not if you'd like it too much."

"Not enough."

"Thought so."

"Little bitch."

"Shouldn't you be looking for seats?" Gwen said.

The whacks of a mallet boomed and echoed, hammering the crowd noise into smaller and smaller pieces. "Od—der, od—der," Maxine Horner shouted between the whacks. After a dozen poundings on the oak block there were only whispering bits left. "This meeting will come to order, this meeting will come to order." Maxine Horner waited for that instant of flattened silence she created at every meeting. Fashioning it each time with her mallet was a renewed pleasure. To most she appeared to wait a long time before proceeding. But nobody ever said anything.

The women left and Gwen and Madeline looked sideways at each other, grinning slightly. Madeline sat up and Gwen examined her knee. She touched the scraped part with a tentative finger and felt around the bump to find out how large it was. After a consultation of grimaces, they decided the damage was minimal.

"Volleyball tomorrow," Gwen said.

"After the snake dance," Madeline said and wiggled her shoulders.

The woman in the third seat stared at them until the podium got her attention.

"There will be a change in tonight's program," the chairwoman boomed into the microphone as if it didn't exist and she had to shout. "The scheduled lecture on child prostitution in Bangkok had been cancelled, and also the informational talk about adopting children from Romanian orphanages. They have been rescheduled. Our secretary-treasurer and wife of our founder has asked to address this meeting on a matter of great significance to everyone. I have so agreed and will now turn the meeting over to Mrs. Kind."

Already on her feet, Wissie walked briskly towards the lectern with what she would have considered a look of noble disinterest. In her right hand she held several sheets of notepaper. They were a prop. She knew what she was going to say. No one could outdo Wissie at this when it counted. Passing the chairwoman she nodded and put her notes on the lectern. She looked out at the quiet audience and waited for a while. The complete lack of sound was not the fidgety attention that Maxine Horner enforced. Everyone knew this was important. Unified in the intensity of its curiosity, the crowd stared. She held onto the sides of the lectern. Her voice was solemn, as if she must deliver a monumental and grievous message.

"Fellow members, I apologize for coming here tonight and disrupting our gathering. But I had to. You know what EFC means to me and Cobbie. He founded this organization over seven years ago to help children and it's been a wonderful experience for us working with such good people. But sometimes your heart can be broken utterly by those you trust. I'm afraid that's what's happened to me. Somebody I trusted and had the greatest respect for has betrayed us. I can't say this without even now thinking I may be wrong, that it's all a nightmare. But I'm afraid it isn't. The evidence is too powerful."

She paused to look down at the sheets of paper. When she raised her head and spoke, bitterness gradually overpowered her sadness.

"Our president has betrayed us. She is writing a book in which she accuses us of profiting from children, not helping them. I have been given excerpts from this book and they are shocking. Everything we stand for is denounced, including the exposure of perverts and calling for their just punishment. She will be given the opportunity to respond to these accusations. We are fair, even to those who aren't fair to us. But first I will read a couple of these excerpts. You decide if she is worthy to be your president."

After sporadic initial murmurings of disbelief when Sarah Edelbacher was first attacked, the silence in the stadium acquired a compressed intensity. The official greeters and security guards stood in the darkened upper tiers with the ushers. Their flashlights glowed like fireflies. Wissie put on her glasses and held up a sheet of paper. As she read she mimicked Sarah Edelbacher's voice, making it sound sarcastic and mean.

"The whole idea of EFC is a fraud cynically perpetrated by the Kinds to make themselves look good, nothing but pure public relations. The best authorities unanimously agree that sexual perversions have deeper roots than the outworn belief that some men are born bad. This is simplistic at best. People who support organizations like these need to do some reading and reflection, get rid of their prejudices and give up their ignorant hatemongering."

Wissie paused to let the words sink in before picking up another sheet.

"Some members are appalling in their vicious ignorance and thirst for blood. An abused child is an excuse to begin hunting for any man who seems aberrant in behaviour. Any victim will do. One wonders if some of these women are only man-haters in disguise wanting to take revenge for real or dare one say imagined slights. Some meetings resemble lynch mobs looking for the first man, which would automatically exclude the males there. But it is the ordinary members who are the most pathetic. They expect easy answers to their general angers and personal griefs, and there are none to be found in a reasonable view. They are at best naïve, at worst accomplices of the more dogmatic and vengeful."

Wissie stopped, took off her glasses, put the sheet down and looked out over the assembled heads. It didn't sound too bad. Academic enough, and yet it had enough bite to jar almost everybody. A little borrowing could accomplish a lot. None of the members would have read those disgusting articles. Horrible stuff. Now for the fairness routine.

"I have more, but that will give you an idea of what I'm talking about. My sources wish to remain anonymous for their own protection. I do not nor do I want to know who they are. This material was mailed to me and the covering letter said that only by chance did they discover the manuscript and get an opportunity to copy passages. And they assure me they are members in good standing. Several details in the covering letter would seem to support that.

I'm willing to listen to our president and hear her response. I sincerely hope none of this is true. I invite her to the podium. We will listen together."

Wissie's eyes sought out the president in the front row and rested on her. She was satisfied by the stupefied look on her face. She turned away from the lectern and walked in deliberate steps to her chair. Sitting down, she heard the crowd's loud murmuring. As a judge of crowds she was satisfied. Before rising to her feet Sarah Edelbacher watched Wissie Kind take her seat again. Surprised at the sudden weakness in her legs, she couldn't hear the words of supporters coming to her from nearby seats. She had expected something, but nothing so obvious and cheap. She didn't know whether to laugh it off or indignantly deny everything. She knew from the crowd noise that Wissie's mudslinging had worked even with some of the moderates. She knew the radicals had been waiting for an excuse to get rid of her. Walking around to the side of the podium and up the narrow stairs, she hadn't decided yet on the right words. Stepping onto the podium, she could see Wissie out of the corner of her eye. With wobbly legs she approached the lectern. Her audience was in front of her, the one she had addressed so many times and from which she had received so much applause over the years. Everyone was quiet again as she held onto the sides of the lectern to keep from shaking. A couple of voices cried out encouragement, and she saw Gwen and Madeline standing on chairs and waving amid the seated conformity. She bit her lip, holding back tears. She heard some boos, directed at her or them or meant for all three. It was strange, but she felt she was there to account for her whole life. This had little to do with the radicals or even Wissie. She, Sarah Edelbacher, was being called upon to justify her very self. The lies were merely a pretext for this moment, because Wissie was being used as an instrument on this night when a deeper accounting would have to be made that only the one who was about to speak would ever understand. The crowd was a unit once more, Gwen and Madeline having sat down, and silence flowed towards her to engulf her with its question. She wouldn't answer that question but one she had asked herself. She would be speaking to one person. That made it much easier, because if she was satisfied it wouldn't matter what anyone else thought.

More boos, louder than before. "We're not pathetic," cut through the booing. And "You betrayed us." Several voices burst out with denials, as if those members felt they were defending themselves.

"I will not answer lies," Sarah Edelbacher said with a calmness that surprised her.

"You're a liar yourself," came back quickly. The radicals were in action.

"Let her speak," several voices shouted in unison.

"More lies," came loudly from the rear.

These words went unanswered. Silence returned and Sarah Edelbacher waited until she was ready to speak. When the moment arrived, she removed her hands from the lectern and clasped them lightly together in front of her waist. She began in that low, never hurried voice of hers.

"I've been put in the untenable position of having to answer a false accusation without being given time to prove myself innocent. It's almost inevitable after such an accusation that, no matter what I say in defence of myself, I will look completely guilty to some, partially so to others, morally tainted in some way to many and innocent to a few. The damage has been done, even though none of you has seen this imaginary book and I have not been given an opportunity to confront my accusers. I must contend with that because sometimes public life puts you in an unfair position, forcing you to accept bad terms. I hereby tender my resignation as president, and this is the last time I will address you from this podium, not because I am guilty, as I assuredly can prove I am not if given enough time, but simply because the Kinds wish me gone. If I told you why, my reason would seem self-serving, though I don't deal in unfounded accusations. They have beaten me with a pre-emptive strike. I will go, and say only this in my defence, that I joined this organization and accepted the presidency solely because I love children and want to see their lot in the world improved and everything I have done during my tenure has been directed towards that end. If you agree with anything said or implied against me tonight, if you've ever disagreed with me in the past, ask yourself why I would turn on you and this organization and betray my dedication to the welfare of unfortunate children. During these never easy seven years my greatest happiness and many sorrows and not a few troubles and too many quarrels weighing down our constant hopes have been here beside you and the kids with a love that has given me strength and I will never forget."

Among the ranks of moist-eyed moderates well-placed radicals stood up and waved placards prepared before the meeting. One read "Edelbacher Betrayed Us," and another, "Sarah For Perverts," a third, "Shame On You" and a fourth, "Unfit for President." A fifth was more direct: "Get Out." The rest of the radicals stood up and all began to chant "Go, Go." Ragged shouts of "No" and "Never" came from a few moderates. Gwen and Madeline got up on their chairs and began to yell, "Stay, Stay." Moderates picked up their chant and began standing and yelling, until "Stay, Stay" resounded in rushes of exhilarating surf towards the podium. This was the moment Sarah Edelbacher had wanted. Trust and love she never thought she would receive were hers. She floated in an ecstasy of approval. She knew that none of the years had been wasted. This was God's reward for her selflessness, her quiet devotion to the cause of millions of children.

Gwen had lost herself in the chanting, feeling part of a vast affirmation of something beyond understanding that fizzed through her blood. She gladly gave up control, became one spark in a blaze that hurled them like fiery confetti up into this night. She was somewhere in that pulsing sound, conscious only of an opening and closing, the universe of the many becoming one. Two feet above the stadium floor, she was thousands in the air.

The hard thing that jabbed into Gwen's back shoved her forward. She tilted, a hand pulled at a leg of her chair and she toppled onto the floor. She landed between her chair and another in front, hitting her forehead against the steel edge of the back of it as she fell. She had skewed to the left, collapsing on her shins and jamming her right thigh against the chair legs, her feet sliding from under her. Dazed, she looked up and saw the stocky woman raising the placard that jabbed her and chanting but staring down at her, eyes granite. Jarred out of her trance by the bump of Gwen's shoulder as she fell, Madeline jumped down and began to lift her. A whack on the back of Madeline's head made her wince and sag forward.

"She's the one who wanted our seats," Gwen said into her ear. "Don't move. Pretend you're really hurt. I'll try to get her."

She slowly gathered her legs under her as Madeline slumped down. Using her as cover, Gwen braced herself with her hands and feet. She eased out and dove at the woman's legs, knocking her over onto the floor and sending the placard spinning off into the crowd. Completely surprised, she fell backwards heavily onto the aisle flooring. Her head slammed into the plywood and she lost consciousness for a few seconds. When she came to, she saw only friends who had gathered around to revive her. Gwen and Madeline had jumped up and gone.

Radicals began streaming to the front and waving placards on sticks. Usually less than five per cent of the audience, tonight they were more than double that. Knowing this was their opportunity to oust Sarah Edelbacher, they had come out in force. Their leadership had been told at a secret midweek meeting with Wissie at the mansion that she would be initiating a move on Monday night to get rid of the president and would be supporting one of them to replace her. They had been shown passages from the spurious book and were convinced. She had asked them to come up with a replacement, knowing it would be Val Inman, the woman now lying on the stadium floor. Her close associate was Liz Schimmel, her workout friend and among those who were helping revive her. Together they had fashioned the radicals into the smoothest functioning unit in EFC, always adept at publicity and a constant source of stress to Sarah Edelbacher. Wissie knew that using them was the only way to get rid of her. The book by itself wouldn't be enough. They would never be as easy to deal with as Sarah Edelbacher. But the moderates might be dissuaded from rallying around their president if she gave them Val Inman as a credible successor. The reason she had selected Sarah Edelbacher for president was to ensure the other woman wouldn't turn EFC into a political weapon instead of a glorified publicity machine. Cobbie Kind's image as a humanitarian must not be compromised by word or deed of any president.

Wissie was ready to let everything go for her husband's sake. If the president took most of the membership with her when she left or if the radicals used the presidency to assail targets indiscriminately and thereby pulled apart the structure she and her husband had held together so carefully, no matter. He must be safe from trouble. She watched the radicals approaching the podium. The gathering placards swung closer to the president. Wissie raised her eyes to fix on a point above the audience. What happened must be for his ultimate benefit.

The radical leadership had instructed their forces to move towards the podium after Sarah Edelbacher had spoken in her own defence. They were to be ready in case she didn't voluntarily resign or if a show of popular support made her think twice about leaving office. They had been told not to disrupt proceedings unless Wissie Kind left the podium. Maxine Horner had been looking at her for a couple of minutes. Now Wissie nodded at her. Support was much greater than expected. Maxine Horner stood and went to the lectern and spoke into Sarah Edelbacher's ear so she could be heard over the crowd noise.

"Is your decision to leave final?"

"Yes."

"I shall announce that this meeting is open for nominations for a new president."

"I'll get out of your way."

Sarah Edelbacher turned to go and a great groan and outburst of denial went through the stadium. For a moment it was one voice. Even the radicals stopped their clamour and watched that erect figure walking towards the stairs. Her life as leader had been a common property and experience. She was taking a part of everyone with her, the shared experience and time binding them together. Breaking this bond left a loneliness like an abandoned trust. In one way or another she had been a focus for everyone.

Sarah Edelbacher walked as if she had no control over her movements, something setting her in motion and she must obey it. She wasn't aware she was clenching her teeth. At the edge of the podium she looked down the stairs and saw the faces of the girls upturned towards her. They had come to stand with her. She smiled at them and without a break in her stride turned around and walked back to the lectern into a treble halo of cheering for "Sarah." The tidal wave of noise made Maxine Horner swing around, and when she beheld

Sarah Edelbacher returning, she looked at Wissie. Wissie's smile didn't change but she made an almost imperceptible sideways motion with her head. Her movements were slight, but the chairwoman was schooled in reading them. This one meant, don't do anything yet. Striding past, Sarah Edelbacher barely paused to look at Maxine Horner. "I'm not ready to go," she said. The chairwoman left, glancing at Wissie for some indication as to what to do next. Wissie's smile didn't change. The radicals, surprised to see the president again, quickly redoubled their yelling and their waving of placards. They still couldn't be heard over the cheers of the moderates. Sarah Edelbacher waved her arms above her head, making sweeping motions with open palms to get silence. It came, even the radicals waiting now, their placards still.

"I left before I was ready," Sarah Edelbacher said with a grin and bits of nervous laughter drifted around the assembly. "I must tell you why the Kinds want so badly to be rid of me. I have reason to question the moral conduct of Cobbie Kind. If what I have seen and heard are true, he isn't a saviour of children. He is a fraud. We have been used, part of a scheme for his own twisted glorification and for media ratings. Without disclosing as much tonight, I was going to call for a cessation of all our activities until this matter could be cleared up. Wissie Kind's slander has forced my hand, putting me in the position of defending myself with an attack, which somehow never seems altogether morally right. I'm going to tell what I know to the responsible authorities. We'll see who is lying."

One of the demonstrators swung a placard on its long stick and hit the lectern. It was only two feet from the edge of the podium and the podium six feet above the level of the seating area, well within striking distance. Demonstrators began banging their sticks against the edge of the platform in a ragged rhythm. She looked around. She was alone on the platform. She waited for the security guards to restore order but none came. Stiff cardboard placards flung like sharp-edged Frisbees came in a swirling flock towards her. Among them were smaller pieces of cardboard with razor blades wedged into the corners. A corner sliced into her forehead, another caught her in the throat. She felt dizzy with pain, leaned over, stumbled out from behind the lectern and towards the front. Sticks clubbed at her knees and shins and she went down, falling to her full length in slow stages of knees, elbows and shoulders as blows struck her at random until they had pounded her flat and her head rolled lolling out over empty space.

"Bitch."

With both hands Val Inman swung her placard like a sledgehammer. It struck Sarah Edelbacher on the side of the neck. The cardboard folded, cushioning the impact of the stick, but it was swung so hard Sarah Edelbacher's head jerked and the stick snapped in two. Another stick beat her dangling head as others slashed and stabbed. Streaks of blood reddened stick ends and cardboard. Blood dripped from her head. Only people nearby could see what was happening through the melee of swinging placards. Gwen and Madeline had run up onto the podium when they saw her fall. Gwen grabbed her ankles, dragging her towards the protection of the lectern. Madeline grabbed the microphone.

"They're killing her. We need help. Please. Please hurry up."

"That's Madeline," Mary shouted.

Roger was already up and elbowing his way through the crowd, his eyes fixed on the podium. Mary tried to follow but her cries of "My daughter's up there" had little effect on the mass of bodies attempting to get away from the trouble. She shoved them but members shoved back, almost pushing her over into the herd of feet stampeding through the aisle at the side of the regular seating. Roger's size enabled him to get within a few yards of the podium after two minutes of toiling hard with his hands pushing shoulders aside. Only his towering glare kept him from being manhandled in return. He could see the girls bending low over the body. They hadn't been hurt. He made for the stairs. But still dozens of pairs of shoulders had to be eased by or elbowed past. By now Roger Chalmers had handled more women this night than in his whole life.

After she pulled the inert body back onto the podium and behind the lectern, Gwen bent down. The side of the bruised face showed the swollen right eye closed, the dark hair wet where it was matted with blood. The torn flap of lower lip seeped blood onto the flooring. Broken teeth were stained red. A smeared trail led from the edge of the podium.

"Is she dead?" Madeline moaned. "I think she's dead."

"Where are they?" Gwen shouted, straightening up.

Gwen's words were barely audible in the din. As they stood with the body at their feet, cries, screams, curses and overturned chairs seemed irrelevant, too late to matter. Fights that had broken out between radicals and moderates looked like buffoonery. When the lights above the tiers of stadium seating came on, their glare seemed indecent. The added brightness made the crowd less panicky. Security guards shouted through bullhorns as they came down the steps and across the field. A siren approached in waves of increasing wails.

At the front of the podium the security guards tried to break up the fights. Radicals began swinging placards at them. They were subdued, handcuffed and led away by the city police, who arrived immediately after the ambulance. A security guard flourishing his bullhorn and another with a black eye stepped onto the podium and came over to them. The one with the black eye swore softly and felt his chin. They glanced at the body. "What're you doing here?" blustered the one with the bullhorn.

"Where were you?" Gwen shouted at them to keep from crying. Her fists shook at her sides. Madeline sat down with her back against the lectern and sniffled, knees drawn up to her forehead. Gwen thought she heard her father's voice but didn't turn to look. Paramedics scrambled up the stairs with a stretcher and hurried over to Sarah Edelbacher.

"Is she alive?" Gwen asked.

"Barely," one said. "Who is she?"

Gwen sobbed as her breath caught. Madeline put her arms around her knees. With practiced and careful patience Sarah Edelbacher was moved onto the stretcher and taken away. As she was carried across the field and up the stadium stairs to the exit, people along the way strained for a glimpse and some were crying. Her husband, who had been lost among the confusion and fighting, joined her there. The seating area was emptying fast and stairways and aisles were clogged, police officers having to make a path for the president.

The security guards disappeared. The police asked Gwen and Madeline some questions. Roger showed the police a few cards and that satisfied them. Indifferent to the arrival of her father, Gwen wanted to know where Sarah

Edelbacher was being taken and spend the night at Sarah's bedside. Her father said that finding out the name of the hospital was all they could do now. They would phone early in the morning and find out her condition. Mary found them and cried, hugging Madeline. "Mom," she groaned in her mother's straitjacket embrace.

In the car no one said anything for a long time. Gwen finally spoke.

"They'll get away with it."

"They?" Mary said.

"You don't know?"

"Don't know what?"

"Didn't you see anything, Mom?" Madeline said, slumped against the rear seat, speaking to her mother's back.

Mary was suddenly tired of her self-imposed apology for being herself.

"I'm not blind."

After Madeline and her mother got out at their apartment, Gwen fell asleep on the back seat. She dreamt she held the beaten woman in her arms and that her battered body became a ball of golden light and then a white dove that flew up through the open stadium dome into the night towards the stars. She had raised her arms and called it back but it vanished. Gwen was alone in an empty and cold arena with dark rows of seats surrounding her and only those stars of exiled light, the lost eternities, the shattered mirror of infinity flung crystalline sparks across the blue of the final mystery. At the moment she awoke Sarah Edelbacher died.

Chapter 23

In the next few days the Kind media promoted the idea that the death of Sarah Edelbacher was the work of a cabal of perverts together with malcontents in EFC who were afraid of being exposed after Wissie read excerpts from the book and so had murdered the president to cover up their connection with her. Kind newspapers published the excerpts and Val Inman appeared on Kind television declaring EFC would find guilty members and turn them over to the police. At the next meeting she was elected president by acclamation. Hundreds of thousands of Sarah Edelbacher's loyal followers had already quit. The Kind media ceased its coverage of meetings and the television program was cancelled. At the end of the year Wissie resigned as secretary-treasurer, citing the burden of overseeing her husband's charity work as the reason. All funding stopped and the agreement with Civic Stadium was terminated. The police investigation uncovered nothing. Charges brought against radicals taken into custody that night were dropped the next day. Video of the meeting disappeared. The verdict of the inquest was death due to injuries inflicted by a person or persons unknown. Without the Kinds the organization lingered on for two years in banquet halls and in church basements. Acrimonious debates reduced membership to club size. It disintegrated into splinter groups.

Two months after the inquest the Kinds went on a world tour taking them to the most impoverished parts of the globe. Stories about him appeared regularly on his network, and editorials in his newspapers extolled his contribution to the welfare of children. "Old-Fashioned Goodness Still

Thrives" was the headline of one and "Does He Never Rest?" another. In the media he didn't control, nothing appeared that contradicted this picture of him or questioned Wissie's role in the events of that night. A couple of small magazines and some fringe You Tube vloggers called for an investigation of the Cobbie Kind media empire. The criticism alleged political favours in high places. The man himself remained immune.

Without any further incidents at Sylvia's, everybody there believed the crisis was over, and Speaker told them enough to reassure them. Lynch emerged from the basement. But he was careful in skid row and along the waterfront and didn't go near the garage. Warts moved into a basement suite in the east end. Within a month Speaker got Al into one of the apartments Gwen wanted to get for Lynch. He found a place of his own until he left the city. He promised to visit Sylvia and try her apricot-cauliflower bread and potato sandwiches ("the trick is thin, your toast crispy fried potatoes with an egg in between"). But he never did. She put something aside for a while. Before leaving, he wrote a letter to Gwen and Madeline.

Dear Gwen and Madeline:

Somebody owes you an explanation after what's happened. I'll try because I'm mostly ideas, anyway. I don't have your hope for society. A man like that gets away with what he does because most people are looking after their own comfortably small situations and coping with their own troubles. They are consumers being swallowed whole. He controls too much of this consumer-swallowing economy to be touched. Maybe. That word is all I'm good for. And a few thoughts before I leave this city forever.

What makes a monster? I don't know the final answer but I have a theory. He's obviously a genetic freak who takes advantage of poverty and greed. The disposal of baby girls is an old story and maybe has something to do with the male fear of women. But part of this horror is a society that refuses to recognize that there aren't any separate groups, only the one group including everybody. Whenever you break it apart, you destroy something. You begin to see differences of age, sex, race, and character, you give psychopaths and sociopaths room to work. These egocentrics refuse to recognize the ordinary boundaries of behaviour. They exist everywhere, but our society gives them more of an opportunity by locking people into categories. A person is a woman, then a sexual object, then genitals, then how young doesn't matter, it's a question of money. We all understand money. We've signed up for money, to make more to buy more to make more to buy more. Almost everyone does it, and some of us like to show off. And sex, like everything else, is for sale, for a ring or a prenuptial agreement or legal tender or very tender that's money or cash per orgasm. Sex and love are paired. Don't believe it, they're enemies. Sex is a kick in the ass to start multiplying. Love is a very human mystery, a mystery that binds us together beyond anything else. In villages in the Caucasus it is not uncommon for a girl to give an old man a bath in a stream. It's not a scandal, it's part of that region's ethos, of all ages living together as families, no so-called rest homes, no paranoia about dirty old men, no wet dreams about pre-teen nymphomaniacs, no bored cosmopolites playing musical chairs with genitals, no futile search for the ultimate thrill. They live long and happy lives without medicare, drugs, doctors or psychiatrists. Some of them have gone to live in a big city and they haven't lasted. The breakdown begins. It's a world of lonely strangers.

We're nomads riding our bit of dust through the galaxies. Our beginning and ending are irrelevant, our significance a delusion. But our brain, that fine instrument balancing fantasy and truth, searches for a meaning that explains us, in the hope it proves us necessary. That search is the loneliest in the universe. If the planet ever has visitors after we're extinct or a few of us have gone to another solar system, what will they think of our leavings? Artifacts of lust and rust? From the junk we leave they will conclude we liked to pretend. Our racism, sexual roles and identities, nationalism and militarism are based on fantasies about ourselves. We don't like the practical. We accept it but are always yearning for something else. Other animals are much more prone to tolerance, can live together much more peaceably because their brains are wired for survival. If they are well fed and comfortable, they're not hostile unless threatened. They are in their reactions more like machines, at least well-made ones, than we are. We are machines that have never quite worked. We do wonderful things, not only for our comfort but because we are curious. So we do more than any other animal could or would. And don't use half the stuff we create. We are the dissatisfied animal yearning after something we can't ever define. In some ages it's God, in others it's a psychopathic leader who thinks he's God. We want reason for an age, then turn away and exalt emotion. Our tools, science and technology, have always been at the service of our unstable nature. We are a biological experiment, one perhaps of many to come, but only those rare apostles of reason have had the wisdom to see beyond the immediate. In that respect most of us are true animals, but our dissatisfaction makes us do to each other what no other animal would do to its own. Ideas of perfection and beauty torture us with their impossibility, the psychopaths and sociopaths lurking among us ready to use our frustration for their own self-anointed benefit. It is human to be rational and irrational to be a human. Nothing will change this basic psychology, unless it is a process of slow evolution to some more truly reasonable and far-seeing nature. But do we have time? There are still wars. The great ideas and religious insights have been promulgated and people ignore them in their daily doings. Every society depends upon the few intelligent decent people it has, not on political abracadabra or philosophical pontificating that cloaks a grab for the goodies. I knew you were among those very few when I first met you. You are daughters of reason, whose passionate certainty is about a rare and beautiful state beyond mere guile and the fatuously seductive worship of systems. I've always preferred the daughters of reason to the sons of mayhem, the flagpole and glory gang. A lot of time is wasted on the outdated need to have everyone believe males are more necessary than they are. There is an unspoken feeling between the three of us. Only unspoken can it not be misunderstood. The best feelings never get into poetry. Words are commercials trying to sell you something. They lie so you'll buy. There are invisible words. We don't have meanings for them yet, and maybe we never will. We live the best of our life on the air of assumption, a syllable of hope for our species in our long or short stay here.

Thank your father, Gwen, for helping me get Al into that apartment, and especially after I had the gall to use him as a reference.

Goodbye.

Speaker

They read the letter as they sat cross-legged on the floor of Gwen's bedroom.

"He thinks a lot," Gwen said grinning, "and thinks a lot of us, Maddy."

"It's all right, Gwenner. I'm pretty well over him. It's like a cold. I'm at the I've-got-to-get-back-to-school stage. I'll survive."

The Kinds returned from their world tour near the end of April, four months earlier than planned. The Kind newspapers and radio and television stations announced the return and said that he had exhausted himself in good works and needed a rest. The curtailed trip had been a personal as well as a public relations success. He had been supplied with young girls by a male secretary accompanying him and Wissie and had satiated himself in sexual brutality. The victims included a girl in Nairobi so badly beaten she suffered brain damage and another in Bangkok who died after being ruptured by sodomy. As usual, Wissie knew none of this. He would go out on evening excursions, telling her he was paying a surprise visit to a shantytown to distribute gifts. She would warn him about the thieves and murderers rife in the streets of those cities and he would tell her his secretary was armed. Because he would pay well for what he wanted, pimps and madams were always ready with girls. His identity was carefully hidden, the usual sex tourist, a wealthy businessman. When "accidents" happened in the brothels, the locals cleaned up the mess. He wore disguises to keep the remote likelihood of discovery even remoter.

He and Wissie got into their limousine at the airport. As she drove out to the mansion, he leaned back in the seat beside her, eyes closed. The notebook affair was out of the way. Not absolutely cleaned up. But no danger now. Probably in a garbage can. Everybody told. Contributors to worthy causes. Given enough to those. About time they were more than tax deductions. Too many dark ones. Blonde two years ago already. Europe. Pricey. Bum split pink. Rosy apricot cunt. No tight like that. Ease, please. Please Daddy. Pleasure is the measure. Old Hammerhead. He's bringing the goods. Slit little pinkie slitter. Switcheroo. Right up the rear. Flubflub cheekies. Speed up, that suck sound. Pull back, peeling off a hot skin. Sphincter gripping the head. Sensitive, hurts to stop. Can't stop it. Squeeze sploosh. Like a cramp. Sploosh. Is there anything better? Nobody gets them younger. Like to breed all nubbers. Harem beauties kept up the Amazon, bare bums toddling out to greet Daddy as he gets out of a helicopter with a handful of suckers. Dream in this lousy world. Hypocrites. Grandpa copping a feel. Lap job. Getting in and out of her jumper to play giggles. Tummy tickles. All he can touch. Nowhere as good as anywhere. She'll lie there thrusting herself up at you when she's in diapers.

Wissie occasionally glanced at her husband. Poor man had overworked himself again, even on his vacation. Everything went so well. She put herself in that situation and they went after her. Turn the crowd against her. Easy enough after she'd insulted the founder. Starve them. They can't be trusted after that. They'll fight and knock each other off. Sad what happens when people are ungrateful, take advantage of a great man's generosity.

Using the remote control inside the limousine, she opened the wrought-iron gates and the long black car slid up the asphalt driveway. It glided around a lazy curve, stopping in front of the house. Notified by telephone, the maid was waiting on the front steps to welcome them home and help take in their luggage. Wissie noticed she was trying to hide something behind her stolid face.

"What's the matter, Inez?"

"Your son is here, madam."

Hiding her surprise, she looked at her husband. His eyes were enough. He was glaring at the maid. Wissie spoke before he could say anything.

"Where is he?"

"In the library."

"We'll see him in an hour."

"I will tell him, madam."

"Let's get unpacked."

Buoyed by his wife's resilience, Kind recovered. Lifting the trunk lid, he spoke roughly to the maid.

"The valises go in my study. Beside the desk."

"Anything else, sir?"

The maid's response wasn't a question. Wissie would fire her two days later.

They agreed to meet in Wissie's study before going to the library. They hadn't seen or heard from their son in ten years. The last time was their daughter's wedding reception, when he had shown up uninvited, gotten drunk and was thrown out after lunging over to the microphone on the orchestra stand and calling the wedding a farce like every other bad joke Cobbie Kind had foisted upon people. This was the culmination of a series of confrontations with his parents over many years. Since the reception neither they nor his sister Wendy had mentioned him and no attempt was made to find out what happened to him. Among the extended family he was considered the cruelest burden Cobbie Kind had to bear. As with anybody who dared to upset her husband, Wissie had without hesitation consigned her son to the ranks of the damned. She had seen early on that he didn't want to be part of his father's media empire or help with his charity work. She considered him a biological failure, as if she had given birth to an idiot. Her son had betrayed her husband, so must be forgotten. The charities were too important. She wouldn't waste her time thinking about a son so ungrateful as not to emulate a great man as best he could. The good work done meant more than a dozen Kind children who were stillborn failures. As they went to meet him, she felt irritation at having to deal with somebody they had rejected and who wouldn't obligingly remain trashed.

The library was on the second floor at the rear of the house, next to Wissie's study. It was larger than either study, three walls entirely of bookshelves, except for a stone fireplace in the one opposite the door. Above the bookcases in the fourth a row of leaded windows in a criss-cross pattern overlooked the garden. A tan leather armchair stood in each corner, standing lamps beside two chairs and mahogany tables with lamps alongside the others. An antique oriental carpet of cream and vermilion occupied the centre of the parquet floor.

Wissie opened the door and went in ahead of her husband. Cobbie Kind sat in the chair beside the fireplace, crossed his legs at the ankles and put his hands on the armrests. Wissie stood on the carpet. Their son was sitting in a chair in a window corner. He had been reading. She noticed the ponytail and worn-out pair of jeans and sweater with holes in it. He hadn't changed much, still thin and those intent eyes that always troubled her.

"What do you want, Paul?" Her voice was flat, peremptory.

He closed the book he was reading and laid it down on the windowsill. The eyes stared but the voice that replied was almost friendly.

"I came here to congratulate you for the job you did on Sarah Edelbacher. Initially messy but a good cover-up afterwards."

Wissie wasn't fooled by the tone. He had been one of the difficult ones.

"How did you get in?" Cobbie Kind blurted.

"Told the maid enough. We share a weakness for family relations."

"She shouldn't have let you in."

"Same old dad. Picking on the help and the helpless."

"You're a trespasser. I'm phoning the police in five minutes."

"Don't try to blame us for that woman's death," Wissie said, jumping in to keep her husband from becoming more upset. "She brought it on herself by attacking your father after we exposed her book."

"You both know there's no book. But what he knows and you don't is that she had something exposing him as a pedophile."

"She had nothing."

"I gave her a notebook. Cobbie Kind listed with others who pay big for baby girls."

"You're disgusting and disgraceful."

"Ask him about Wendy. He beat her. She was swollen with bruises. Then he used her until she was bleeding. I heard the screams and whimpers from behind a door. I saw afterwards. I've hated him ever since."

Wissie shook her head and wrinkled her nose as if she smelled fly-swarmed droppings. She folded her arms across her chest and put one foot directly in front of the other, her posture for telling somebody off or praising the impressionable.

"I can't believe you'd bring in Wendy. Your father told me what happened while I was in the hospital. She fell down the stairs. He injured himself trying to save her. Even had her blood on his shirt. And you're so quick to turn it into something dirty. Wendy loves her father. You tried your best to ruin her wedding. Ask her what she thinks about that. You always were a troublemaker. I don't know how I had a child like you. To hate your father the way you do. After he's helped so many children. And to accuse him of such things with your sister."

Wissie didn't quite examine her speech for flaws but she was satisfied. Drumming his fingers on the armrests, her son shook his head once in the same sharp way his mother had but without wrinkling his nose. He had taken a long time, wondering if and how he would say it. But finally he knew he could say it all.

"You're so deep into denial you're feet are sticking out of the ground in China. Wendy was too young to have any memory of what happened. Do you know what it's like being on the other side of the door when your baby sister is being beaten and you can't do anything about it and all you're thinking of besides her being hurt is that you're next? And she crying so loudly you're sure she's going to die. You never forget you were so glad you weren't taken into that room and beaten you pretend nothing is wrong when he comes out. Besides what he did to her, he made me a coward. I was five but I've despised myself since. I loathed being nice so he wouldn't do it to me. This bald blubber staggered out breathing spit and collapsed on the sofa while

Wendy cried in the dark in that room. The mouth of the doorway screamed at me. But the worst was the way he took her in, leading her by the hand as she toddled along beside him, his voice so soft, and she holding onto her favourite doll, the one with the yellow curls. She held it by its arm, the legs dragging along the floor. And when he shut the door behind him, he looked at me and smiled. Remember it all, Dad, the way I've had to, remember as one of those fathers who's used his own daughter before she could tell anybody about him. She was the first, wasn't she? You've never regretted it, have you? No, you wouldn't, because to all those like you being a prick is part of having one. You made one mistake, the silent witness. I'm going to write it all down, let people know what you really are. You're going to have to explain. While waiting for someone to find something, or sell you out. Everything's for sale, you know that. You could hire somebody. I'll try to make things difficult for him until I'm finished. After that I won't care. I'll have done what I had to do. Speak for my sister."

Cobbie Kind began laughing and the deep bellowings filled the library. They were empty sounds each exactly alike, monotonous waves of an invisible tide that washed against the walls and echoed back onto the listeners to drown still other waves but drowning together with them too in one loud reverberation of nothing. His eyes bulged, saw nothing around him but something his wife and son could not. His heavy shoulders and chest shook and his head became as pink as a ham. He tried to smile but he was laughing too hard. He put his slabs of hands on the armrests to steady himself. The sounds kept coming in insistent escape from the cavity gaping at their release. A man known to be humourless himself and to ignore the humour of others, Cobbie Kind was transfixed by a joke. He could see it and didn't care if anybody else could. There was no joy in his laughter. It was the sound of a man who can't laugh.

The booming regularity of it bothered Wissie. She had never heard anything like this before from her husband. She glanced over at her son to see how he was reacting. His eyes were intent on his father. Moving slowly towards that heaving torso, the bulbous head bobbing, she put out her hand, tentatively approaching his shoulders bulking under a pigeon grey cardigan, a finger touching it as lightly as she could, but he whirled to face her. Her finger jerked away. His violent movement had bent and almost snapped off an armrest but the laughter stopped. His eyes glared up at her. Silence filled the room like another sound. Smiling, Wissie tried to stare some control back into him. This worked and his face became less taut. With her fingertips she began to stroke his shoulder gently.

"You must not be upset. The suddenness of this has got to you. Everything will be all right. You know that very well. You know that, don't you?"

As he looked up and listened, his lips pushed together into a dark pink welt. He spoke like a spoiled boy.

"I want him gone."

"Yes."

"Now."

"Yes."

Her head swung. She faced her son. He had stood up to leave. She waved him away with her other hand.

"Get out. You're nothing to us."

"He's not my father, you're not my mother. He's the twisted man-child you should've had. I've managed to survive you both. The only thing that hurts is you've turned Wendy against me."

He walked quickly down the stairs and out of the house into the spring air under the soft grey of an April sky that comes around Easter. He breathed in the honeyed air of blossom smells as he ambled along the sloping curve of the driveway to the gate. He broke the electronic beam of light. The gates flapped open slowly like huge skeletal wings and he walked between them.

As he was shaving the next morning, the world suddenly changed for Cobbie Kind. The bathroom mirror vanished and he slumped to the floor unconscious. The crack of his head striking the pedestal sink as he fell and the thump of his body onto the floor brought in Wissie. He regained consciousness in a private ward, the victim of a stroke. It left him speechless and his left side paralyzed for the remaining thirteen months of his life. Attended by nurses, he was pushed around his estate in a wheelchair. He drooled like a baby. Desperate, Wissie hired a wet nurse and he was breastfed.

When he died it was noted in all the media except his own that neither his son nor daughter attended the funeral. Afterwards all Wissie's energy went into designing an enormous burial vault for her husband.

"Guess what?" Madeline shouted into her phone to Gwen after she heard about the stroke. She was so loud her voice was distorted into a screech.

"The baby killer had a stroke. They say he'll never walk or talk again, and he isn't expected to last long. I guess I shouldn't be so glad but if someone's going to get it, there isn't anybody else I'd rather put first in line. Tell me I'm not bloodthirsty."

Gwen nodded to herself.

"Getting him would've taken years. But I was going to do it. I promised my mom and Sarah. I miss Mom so much. I'll never be happy again."

"You will some day, Gwenner."

"It's been too much, Maddy. It's hurt me."

"Know what my mom said when she heard about it? Guilt got him. Rotted his brain. She told me guilt can turn your heart and brain to sludge. If you're slimy, your insides turn to slime. If you're hard, you turn into a stone. You don't get away with anything. I said, what if you're good? She said, you turn into a special kind of softness that's love. And I said, so if you're good, you must be soft in the head. She got mad, said I twisted her words. I told her she could get as soft as she wanted and she'd still be my mom."

"She's her."

"She's her."

"Like my dad."

"Like your dad."

Madeline began whirling around in her bedroom.

"The other night I was dancing on the moon and asked myself, what would I be, what's really me?—the last leaf on a tree."

"Tell me, Maddy."

"Yesterday morning I was sitting at my computer and my mom came to the door.

"'I'm making a special omelette for breakfast. I got pastured eggs from run free or range free chickens, whatever they're called, and grass-fed butter, raw, from organic cows, and Italian Parmesan. No factory stuff. I went through a lot of trouble.'

"'You always do.'

"'That's right, Madeline. This time it's because I'm trying to prevent my daughter from continuing to make a terrible mistake.'

"She left. I sat there and did something I'd put off for the past few weeks. I had a conversation with invisible people. Bald vegan doctors with their stick arms and creaking voices. Vegan You Tubers, the cherry pickers and the ones with crazy eyes. Animal rights organizations that spend lots of money on posters. To all of them I said, You don't know me. Only I know me. I'll march for the animals but not into your prison. I don't want your stupid reasons to explain my cravings, or when I get sick. You want everyone to follow your diet. You don't want to hear excuses from those who try and have to give up. You believe we all have the same body. We don't. You have to believe we do because, if you admit to being even a bit wrong, everything you believe in will collapse. You've got to assume that in saving the animals you're saving us. And as our bodies and minds get weaker on your diet, we aren't able to see that by freeing the animals you're taking our freedom away. You're reducing us to their level because there's something in you that needs to feel compassion, but that feeling has made you self-righteous instead of understanding. You don't march for children who are abused, tortured, raped and murdered by sick men. But I shouldn't be surprised. You don't have time for little girls who can't speak for themselves. You're too busy speaking for the animals.

"In a trance I glided into the kitchen and sat at the table and my mom hurried to get a plate and fork and put most of this giant omelette on my plate and I ate it and was silent.

"'Why are you so quiet, Madeline?'

"'I'm thanking those hens and cows for making me feel better than I have in a year.'

"'What about me?'

"'Want a hug?'

"'Not if it's going to break your arms.'

"I gave her a big hug.

"'You're not like me, Madeline. Not like your father either, thank God.'

"'I'm like me.'"

"Things have been happening here too. My grandma brought a tin of cookies made with real—. I ate half of them. Right in front of my dad and grandma. They didn't say anything, so I said, 'That's the last time I eat these cookies. Too much sugar.'"

"We'll make our own with maple syrup."

"Yeah, I'll feed the rest of these to my dad."

"My mom is going to make another omelette next week, and a cheesecake with real—. You're invited."

"May you reign over the land of beauty."

"May you rule over the land of truth."

"Aren't we something?"

"Aren't we though?"

Chapter 24

The laws of adversity, of demand. A small man overlooked in a careless moment, in the perhaps of a lapse of universal memory. A footsore foot soldier in the army of his peers, carbuncle on the soul. The old streets a mesh of parallel lines, trapdoor for the Untermenschen, lair of the lost, broken places smeared with stink. A rebel quelled within the sight of tall buildings, a limper, wheeze coming from chested dreams he coughs in seasons of damp and sweat. Between his neck and collar a drop of water icy slithers down his spine. Hurrying nowhere. Nothing matters and matters so much.

He hobbled along Alexander Street. The garage was a block away. It was early Sunday morning, the garage would be closed, but Lynch didn't want a chance meeting with Doughnuts and Zimmo. Eight months had passed since Sarah Edelbacher's death and more than three weeks since Cobbie Kind's stroke. The cold winter had been hard for him and a wet spring not much better. Sleeping in a mission bed and eating charity food helped, but liquor took what money he had. A winter cough still bothered him and he was wearing his only clothes, an old stained pair of long johns, the survivor of those plaid shirts the girls had given him, hiking boots and work socks from a charity, suit pants found in a dumpster and a leather coat he had stolen in a pub. The lining was thin and forty-five per cent polyester and he had been looking for something that would have kept him warmer, but he only had a moment in the dimness to see and snatch it off a corner seat when the owner went to the washroom. May was turning warm and he didn't wrap the coat so tightly around himself any more but still jammed his hands into the pockets. The boots had been too small and were tight yet after two months of breaking them in and this slowed him down. This morning he wanted extra speed with each pinched step as the garage got closer on the other side of the street, the office door and the bay doors shut, no van or cars around the pumps or on the lot. He didn't have the money to buy a truce with the garage. The tight boots had kept him from taking a roundabout route to Sylvia's house. He needed a meal and at least one night's sleep there. Hoping he could talk her into letting him stay longer, he didn't pay any attention to the ache in his head. A single thought now. Hurrying in those boots, but nobody yet.

"Hey, Lynch."

The words floated out on the cool air, not a command but an invitation. He stopped and waited, staring at the garage. No one, nothing, not another sound anywhere. The quiet morning surrounded him. From a patch of tall grass at the side of a warehouse across the street strands of a broken cobweb floated past his eyes. He took a step, hesitated, and barged through the silence.

Made in the USA
Monee, IL
19 July 2020